Zera and the Green Man

Sandra Knauf

Greenwoman Publishing

Zera and the Green Man

Sandra Knauf

GREENWOMAN BOOKS

Published by Greenwoman Publishing, LLC
P. O. Box 6587, Colorado Springs, Colorado,
80934-6587, U.S.A.

First published in the United States of America

ISBN: 978-0-9897056-0-8 (paperback)
ISBN: 978-0-9897056-1-5 (ebook)

Cover drawing by Paul Spielman.
Cover photography by CanStockPhoto 11569383
Cover and interior design by Zora Knauf.

For my parents,

William Richard Cato

and

Darline Love Price

Acknowledgements

I have jokingly said, "It takes a village to get me published" and that is not far from the truth. To those who have ~~suffered over~~ read this manuscript through the years and offered support, great or small, I thank you. A special thanks to the following: D'Arcy Fallon, who fanned those first sparks and patiently mentored me for many years; Diane Hoover, Andy Nelson, and Charles ("Cuttlefish") Bowles, who put me through a real writers boot camp (also known as our critique group); Donald Maass, for his invaluable instruction; Andrew Knauf, best friend, sexy husband, and truest patron of the arts (one who pays the bills); my younger daughter Lily, who offered great editing advice and warmed my heart with the comment "I was surprised — it was good!"; Cheri Colburn, beautiful friend and brilliant editor; artist and so-helpful friend Paul Spielman; and, mostly, to my older daughter Zora, who saved this manuscript from limbo.

Zera and the Green Man

There should be no monotony
In studying your botany;
It helps to train
And spur the brain —
Unless you haven't gotany.

— from "Botany" by Berton Braley

Chapter One

Friday, March 21

Squeezing through a thicket of ninth graders outside of Ms. Casey's classroom, all Zera could hear was complaining about the biology test. Mike "Biggie" Lane, at his locker, was blocking the door, and as Zera drew closer she got a whiff of his cologne. *Musk . . . and sweet jasmine. Not bad, but too strong — as usual!* "Nice cologne, Biggie."

Biggie looked pleased. He moved to let Zera into the classroom as girls behind her chattered.

"Did you study?" a girl named Melody asked her friend.

"Not enough."

"That sucks. I can't believe this. Right before break."

If they knew I wasn't nervous about this test, they'd think I was nuts. No one spoke to her in Biology, no one except Abby, her only friend at Manning High School.

The first one in the room, Zera sat down and flipped open her notepad. She touched the leaf-shaped BIO icon on the screen and her thoughts turned to something that should be happy, but wasn't, her fifteenth birthday the next day. Musk and jasmine still clung to her nostrils. *I wish I had a boyfriend. Not like Biggie, but someone . . . someone who'd give me flowers for my birthday.*

Wrapped in her thoughts, she didn't notice the movement on the window sill. *Some kids have parties, I can't even hang out with Abby. All because of a freaking fast-food franchise opening.* Zera frowned, thinking about how her uncle's work, and his control-freak girlfriend, always came first.

The one-minute bell rang and a few seconds later Biggie's voice boomed, "Holy crap! You didn't see that when you came in?"

He's talking to me? Zera looked up to see Biggie thundering across the room.

What? Zera unconsciously ran her fingers through her bangs. She started to say something but was stopped by the sight of Biggie at the windows, a smile plastered on his face. He was staring up, bug-eyed at . . . *giant, six-foot-tall flowers*?

"Look at them! Just look at them!"

Students coming in, making their way to their seats, froze.

A clamor erupted. "Hey!" "Are those for real?" "No way. Gotta be a joke." "I've never seen flowers that big." "What the h . . . ?"

Her classmates' attention focused on one big plastic pot, at the end of a row of nineteen others on the sill. From it sprang a half-dozen zinnias that touched the classroom ceiling. The round, multi-petaled blooms, wider than basketballs, were in electric shades of hot pink, red, yellow, orange, purple, and a blue brighter than the Colorado sky. Green leaves spread out like umbrellas from stems three inches thick.

Zera stood up. The flowers' beauty pulled her toward them like a magnet. They were so big that their white roots had burst the container, and in a dozen places they spilled out like spaghetti. The label that marked the pot with the student's name who planted it clung to a plastic shred, printed with black marker in capital letters: ZERA GREEN.

The room got quiet.

Zera shifted, folded her arms. Her mind groped for an explanation. Abby was now standing beside her. Abby's large brown eyes, accented with way too much black eyeliner, stared transfixed at the blooms. "So pretty," she whispered.

Someone said what everyone had noticed, "It's *Zera's*." All eyes went to her. Abby looked at her questioningly.

It can't be, Zera thought. *It's impossible. Our class planted those seeds yesterday. And we planted spinach . . . and lettuce.* A sense of disconnect came over her, like a thick wall of glass separating her from the others. She moved closer, slowly, to the pot with her name on it. She touched a leaf, but knew without touching. *They're real.* Everything in the room suddenly seemed brighter, more in focus. A chill rippled down her spine.

Behind her, Becky McGowan said, "Wow. Oh, wow!" Chatter and giggles followed.

"I don't get it," Zera said aloud, and a few muffled laughs responded. *I planted spinach. These flowers are full grown, and most seeds don't even sprout this soon. Not for days. How could they sprout, grow, bud and blossom, two or three months' growth, in one night?* The row of pots held the other kids' seeds for their plant projects, watering tubes running to each pot for automatic watering during spring break. Grow-lights hung suspended from the ceiling. Ms. Casey had told them yesterday, "When you get back from break, we should see some seedlings to put in the greenhouse." *Seedlings. Nothing in the other pots but brown soil. That's what should be in my pot. Is this some kind of a joke? Who'd do that? And HOW?* Zinnias, Zera knew, even the big ones, didn't get that big, ever.

The flowers were emitting delicious odors of raspberries, vanilla, something bright and citrus-y, mingled with a note of green, a scent like a summer meadow. But there was something else too — something masculine, and something floral. *A hint of musk — and jasmine?* Zera, despite her anxiety, found her eyes closing. *Wonderful . . . but, wait. Mom and Nonny grew zinnias. They didn't smell like this. They didn't have much of a smell at all.*

"Mmmm, smells pretty in here," Biggie said in a girlie voice. He snorted a laugh.

Zera gave him a look and thought, *It must be strong if he can smell it over his cologne.*

Abby moved closer. "What's going on?"

Before she could answer, a familiar high-pitched voice came from behind them. "Oh my!" The class turned to see Ms. Casey. Their teacher's hands had flown up to her mouth, her eyes were wide.

The second bell rang. No one budged.

Ms. Casey walked over to the sill. A slim finger touched Zera's label. "They're gorgeous. A blue one? I didn't know zinnias came in blue. In fact, I'm certain they do not. Blue flowers are quite rare." She emphasized *quite rare* as her half-smile turned into a smirk. "Zera, what do you know about this?"

Zera swallowed, and as she spoke the words caught in her throat, "I don't . . . know anything."

"Your uncle, he's a biotech scientist, isn't he?"

"Yes."

Ms. Casey narrowed her eyes. She breathed in deeply and the half-smile reappeared. Zera noticed that the blue color of the zinnia matched Ms. Casey's blazer. It occurred to her, *she's smiling because of the perfume.*

The smile disappeared abruptly. "Students," she ordered, "take your seats. When I return, we'll start the test. Zera, come with me."

After Ms. Casey explained the situation to Mrs. Tinsel, the high school's pretty-yet-tough-as-nails principal, Mrs. Tinsel summoned Security on the wall-sized media and communications monitor. "Richard, I need you to review the surveillance video for last night and this morning before school," she said to a nearly life-sized, mustachioed Mr. Brockheimer. "Mr. B," as the kids called him, was the head of Security, and he stared, dead serious, as Mrs. Tinsel continued. "Check the camera that shows the entrance to Ms. Casey's classroom. See if anyone entered the room with a . . . an enormous pot of flowers."

Confusion clouded Mr. B's expression, but he nodded obediently. "Sure. I'll get right back with you." The screen went blank.

Zera, in the chair across from the principal's desk, squirmed while they waited. *Why my planter?* she wondered. *And why would anyone do something this weird anyway?* She recalled how, the day before, when she'd planted the seeds, she'd been thinking about Nonny's garden. She'd been thinking about *zinnias*. Nonny always joked how zinnias should be Zera's favorite flower. After all, Nonny said, they shared the letter "Z." When Zera planted those seeds she was thinking about her fifteenth birthday, about how she missed her parents, about how she wished she could live with Nonny. She was also thinking about the event of two days ago and her horrible embarrassment about that. Her hands moved from the chair arms to clasp tightly in her lap. *Those were spinach seeds. I know what zinnia seeds look like. They're thinner, longer, flatter . . . spinach seeds are round and lumpy.*

Mr. B appeared on the wall to report he'd found nothing upon reviewing the tape.

"Thank you." Mrs. Tinsel pressed the screen for her secretary and asked her to get Zera's uncle, Theodore Green, on the video-phone.

Zera shifted her position on the chair, unclasped her hands and clutched the chair's arms again. *Great, they're bringing him into this.* She avoided the adults' gazes. The Toad was her pudgy, thick-lipped, glasses-wearing, warty-handed uncle, whom she'd been living with since her parents' deaths. He was all that was left of her family, besides herself and Nonny. He worked as a scientist at Biotech Multinational. While they waited, the air in the room seemed to be getting stuffier by the second.

She caught her breath when her uncle appeared on the video screen. The Toad looked even more awkward than usual, sitting at his desk in his cubicle, one hand fidgeting with his black-rimmed glasses. Zera could make out the warts on his hands (although Ms. Casey and Mrs. Tinsel probably wouldn't notice). Seeing him uncomfortable brought a different disquiet. *It's the first time he's ever had a call about me from school.*

Apologizing for the interruption, Mrs. Tinsel explained the situation and began quizzing The Toad about his biotechnology work — had he given his niece some "strange seeds"? Was it possible that she had brought something to school yesterday that she shouldn't have?

As Zera watched her uncle squirm, she thought about how in the city of Piker, Colorado, anything weird or different (meaning her and her family) was unacceptable. *How can he stand it here, growing up where he did?* Again she longed for Ute Springs, where she had the freedom to be herself.

The Toad straightened in his chair. Peering up into his much smaller work monitor, his squinted eyes darted at the images of Zera, Mrs. Tinsel, and Ms. Casey. "Strange seeds?" he said. "Certainly not. And removing anything from the corporation's premises would be a serious violation of policy." He cleared his throat. "Mrs. Tinsel . . ." He fidgeted with his glasses again. "I seriously doubt Zera would ever do such a thing, even if she had the opportunity. Do I need to come down to your office and help clear this up?"

"Thank you, Mr. Green, but no. We just wanted to talk to you. This is a mystery, but we'll get to the bottom of it."

They ended the call, and Zera, pleased that her uncle had stuck up for her, was also a little surprised. The Toad rarely showed such firmness around authority figures.

Ms. Casey shook her head. "I can't figure it out," she said. "Not only the flowers, but a zinnia in *blue*. They don't exist. I know my floriculture."

Mrs. Tinsel smiled at Zera from behind her desk. "It was your plastic pot, Zera. No one else had these giant flowers. You can tell us, let us in on the joke." The principal sighed, as if it were suddenly no big deal. "I can understand students wanting to do something entertaining, a little prank before break to have a little fun." She leaned forward, her voice lowering to almost a whisper, "How did you pull it off?"

Zera leaned back in her chair. "I don't know how it happened," she said for the second time. For a moment she thought of playing Tinsel's game, saying she did it. She would have loved to tell them something, to be done with this, the misery of sitting there with them, the wall-sized monitor, and the closed room that felt like a prison. Anger overtook that emotion. *To heck with them.* She leaned forward, smiled defiantly at Mrs. Tinsel.

The adults exchanged looks. Ms. Casey excused herself to go back to her classroom, asking Mrs. Tinsel's permission to leave Zera in the administration office for the rest of the hour, so as to "not cause any further disruption."

Guilty before proven innocent. Nice. "What about the test?" she asked Ms. Casey.

"I'm sorry, but you'll have to take it after school."

She left and Mrs. Tinsel locked eyes with Zera. "There's no proof you did anything, but I *will* find out what happened. Giant flowers do not just grow overnight. Not in my school."

"Hey, Plant Chick!"

Zera, in line in the cafeteria, looked around and couldn't tell where the female voice came from, but she saw two girls from Biology ahead of her — giggling.

"Zera Green's got a green thumb all right," a boy said behind her. She ignored the comment. A few kids from Biology giving her a hard time was to be expected; six-foot-tall zinnias were growing in a pot labeled with her name.

She turned around to see it was a junior named Jake, rumored to have been expelled from another school for marijuana use. He slid closer to her and asked, "Ever grow any weed?"

"No."

The boy tossed his long blond bangs, smiled sideways. *Is he flirting with me?* The thought was not a good one. *He thinks I'm bad. I've never had a boyfriend, finally a guy notices me, and it's Jake*. She looked back at him. *He's cute . . . but no. Heck no.*

A slight panic set in as he held eye contact. Before he could say anything more she blurted out, "I don't do drugs."

Jake broke the eye contact, whispered something under his breath, and put distance between the two of them.

Oh god, why don't I just wear a sign, "I'm a weirdo AND a jerk?" Zera blushed. She wished the day were over, especially the after-school exam. She'd be in a room with Ms. Casey, alone. *Please, let this all be forgotten before I come back from break.*

Paying for her food, Zera saw Abby wave at her from a table by the windows.

"Well, that's one way to get attention," said Abby as Zera got to the table.

"Put a giant bouquet in the classroom and be sure it has your name on it."

Zera sat down her tray. "Yeah, that's me, criminal mastermind. Only I didn't do it."

"You didn't? How, then . . . ?"

The girls from Biology stared at them from a nearby table.

Zera heard "Plant Chick" again. "I don't know." She climbed over the bench. "Now my new name's 'Plant Chick' and Tinsel's out to get me. This has been the crappiest week ever."

"Sorry," Abby said. "I shouldn't have teased you."

"It's not only what happened today," Zera hesitated, opened her milk carton and took a sip. "It's been the whole week." She glanced around, checked to make sure no one was listening. "I started my period, day before yesterday."

"Your first time? And you didn't tell me?" Abby put down her sandwich. "Are you okay?"

"Yeah, I'm fine. But I had to go to Tiffany. I thought I was going to die of embarrassment."

Abby's black-rimmed eyes narrowed. "She didn't think of talking to you earlier? What an idiot." She looked down at her plate. "It must have been terrible, not having a mom to go to."

"Yeah. I miss her so much."

"I know." Abby gave her an understanding smile.

Zera shifted on the bench, not wanting to think about her mom, but it was impossible. It was painful enough she was gone, but sometimes Zera really needed her. What would her mom say about Jake, if she told her about the rumors, or how would she help her deal with what happened in Biology? Mom always had the right answers. "Tiffany asked me all these weird questions, ran out and bought me a bunch of stuff, and then, that night at dinner, she told my uncle, right there in front of me."

Abby's jaw dropped.

"'Zera's a young woman now.'" Zera imitated Tiffany's high-pitched voice. "She had this stupid smile on her face. The Toad didn't even know what she was talking about, he was staring at her, like 'Huh?'" Zera looked around again, lowered her voice more. "Then she said, 'Zera got her period!' I wanted to die."

Her friend's dark eyes flashed. She bent over, started digging through her backpack, and pulled out a small wrapped package. "It's not much, but maybe this will cheer you up. Since we can't hang out tomorrow."

Zera clapped her hands together as she saw her friend had brought her a birthday gift, to school. *Abby's the best. Maybe this birthday won't completely suck.* She unwrapped the package, opened the small box. It held flower-shaped earrings made of powder-blue glass. "They're so pretty, Abby!"

"You don't mind they're flowers? And blue? I bought them last week, before . . ."

Zera laughed. She imitated Ms. Casey. "'Blue flowers are *quite rare*!' Of course not. I love them."

Zera got up, walked around the table, and gave Abby a hug. "Don't worry. I'll get over the trauma of everything. If I live through tomorrow."

"You will," said Abby, "and we'll celebrate your birthday next week, when we get the whole week off."

Outside the cafeteria, a group of budding aspen trees congregated near the courtyard. As Ms. Casey walked out of the east exit, one of the trees began to sway slightly, all on its own, then gradually faster, its movements suggesting urgency. It bent and swayed, its branches reaching toward the auburn-haired girl holding a pair of blue earrings in the cafeteria window. Then its branches swayed toward Ms. Casey. The other trees followed suit. No one noticed the movements, not the students lunching in the courtyard, not Ms. Casey or the other teachers on the sidewalk, not the janitor emptying trashcans into a dumpster. No humans noticed, but the pigeons did. They were a rowdy crowd, a dirty dozen who flew in for lunchtime every day, striding around jerkily in the newly-greening grass, making coo-cooing pigeon-comments about humans and food. They waited for the inevitable French fry, piece of bread, salad scrap, or pizza crust to fall on the ground.

Spooked by the trees' excited emotions and movement, the pigeons made ape-like warning grunts to each other, shook themselves, and took flight. One of them flew right over Ms. Casey and relieved himself, splattering the teacher's blue blazer.

Chapter Two

Reclining on a pile of pillows on her bed, Zera's thoughts rotated like a carousel — through the events of yesterday, that morning, then back around. For the sixth time that hour she ran her fingers through her auburn hair, which was now streaked with an inch-wide swath of electric-green. Her heart bolted each time she glimpsed herself in the mirror, in dread of Tiffany's reaction, but underneath the dread was determination.

I had to do this, to show I have a right — to something. The carousel started again and her thoughts returned to Biology, fourth period. *Plant Chick.* Mrs. Tinsel never did "get to the bottom of it" and the zinnias remained a mystery. Zera took the test after school, and, as she expected when she checked her grade that night online, she aced it. Ms. Casey had her plant a new pot with spinach seeds, and when she got home her uncle hardly mentioned the event. Still, it bothered her, not knowing what had happened.

She twisted the strand of green hair around her finger.

Sitting up on the bed, Zera scratched the back of her neck where the collar of the hideous dress itched. The synthetic fabric of the watermelon-hued frock irritated the skin around her neck and arms. She lifted the material at the hem, her lips twisting with distaste. The dress had been the final straw. *They don't care that it's my birthday, that I don't want to go.* She thought about how pleased her uncle's girlfriend had been presenting her with the poofy-sleeved gift. "It's from the 1980s, Zera! An Italian designer! This style is so *in* right now." Tiffany had looked so happy that Zera couldn't say what she thought, *I don't want it.* Tiffany Taylor divided her life into four passions: vintage couture shop owner at the Cyber-Mall, Faces of Success cosmetic distributor, desperate bachelorette determined to marry The Toad (she practically lived with them, even though she had her own place), and, in Tiffany's mind, Zera's much-needed female role model. Dark thoughts galloped through Zera's mind, images of Tiffany wearing the famous designer dress and having *no* hair.

Getting the dye was easy. Tiffany had given her a whole drawer full of Faces of Success beauty supplies long ago: gels, sprays, creams, potions, and paints. Of course she'd been disappointed that Zera didn't take much of an interest in them, but that never stopped her from buying more. Dye & Go, a temporary dye, was the only product not in a pink container. It came in a leaf-shaped bottle and was made with plant extracts. Tiffany had added Dye & Go to the rest of the drawer's contents only because it was something Zera's uncle had developed at BioTech Multinational. Zera remembered how Tiffany had held up the bottle with a kind of dismissive air. "It's not Faces of Success or anything," she said, "but maybe it'll come in handy for, I don't know, Halloween?"

Using the dye was as easy as its name suggested, and matching her nail polish to her hair color was not a problem. Zera just opened a plastic case holding 101 bottles, Tiffany's Christmas gift to her last year.

Now I've got to spend my birthday at some big deal event for a bunch of scientist nerds. That morning The Toad had actually wanted to let her take a pass on going. "She doesn't have to be there, Tiffany," he said. "She could celebrate her birthday with her friend Abby, while we're gone."

But Tiffany insisted. "She's your niece, Theodore, one of the last members of the Green family. She should be there, spending her birthday with her family." As usual, when Tiffany cracked the whip The Toad backed down.

Zera slid off the bed and walked over to her white, gold-paint-trimmed, fake Louis-the-whatever-it-was style desk. She opened a drawer and rifled through it. *The only good things that have happened today were the calls.* First, Nonny had called that morning with a birthday greeting. She was joined by Hattie Goodacre, her mom's best friend, and Hattie's son, Ben, who had come to visit Nonny just to call Zera (Hattie didn't have a video-phone). Zera and Ben had grown up together in Ute Springs. Zera noticed Ben's looks were changing; the boyishness was fading and his voice was different too, deeper. He had seemed almost shy talking to her. *He was probably just preoccupied, thinking about what he has going on for spring break*. Then, around noon, Abby called. Seeing them all had made her very happy, for awhile anyway.

Zera picked up a bottle of Fruit Punch flavored Bubblemaniac Bubble Gum. She popped open the top and shook out a tiny capsule, frowning as she noted that the gum was the same color as her frock. She popped the capsule into her mouth. As it contacted the moisture of her saliva it grew twenty-five times its size, as big and squishy as a marshmallow with a sweet-tartness that made her mouth water. The curious sensations made her grin in spite of herself.

Zera looked around her hated bedroom, a pink and white monstrosity of ruffles that Tiffany insisted on decorating when Zera came to live with her uncle. *It'll be three years in April. Would The Toad have even taken me in if Tiffany had not pushed him?* She doubted it, and that was another reason to resent Tiffany. If Tiffany hadn't butted in, she would be living with her grandmother. Zera walked to her window and moved aside a frilly curtain. The street below was frigid, wet . . . ominous. Village Glen, their suburban neighborhood, stretched before her in all its sameness, rolling expanses of lawns, cookie-cutter shrubs dotting the corners of each near-identical townhouse, all the townhouses in predictable earth-tone colors. Normally, she would find a cold, wet spring day like this mysterious and a welcome change from always-sunny, always-dry Colorado weather. Today it just seemed depressing.

The street was empty. She guessed most of the kids were

probably spending their Saturday online at one of the Cyber-Malls, or playing in v-game rooms with friends, or watching movies on wall-screens. "Couldn't have asked for a nicer day," Zera said aloud. With a start, she remembered something. The story of the day she was born, one she'd heard at least once a year, but hadn't heard now for three. Her mother said the day had been cold and rainy when Zera's father drove her to the hospital. While her mom struggled with labor pains every few minutes, Zera's father drove though the wet streets, saying, "It's a beautiful day to have a baby!"

"I said to him, 'No it's not!' but your father was *so happy*." Her mom had laughed every time she told it.

Just like today, Zera thought between chomps of gum, *perfect birthday weather*. The sweet picture of her parents always brought, after a moment of joy, gloom. And the gloom brought another thought. The single thought that haunted her most, the one which smothered everything. She sent it out to her parents once more: *Why did you have to die?* Zera left the window and plopped back down on the bed.

Several minutes later, her spirits revived again. The unanswerable question never stayed for long, not anymore. It came and went, like an awful yet familiar ghost, a ghost who wore clunky boots and tromped in and out of her life like a bully. The bully pushed her around for a while and then left the playground. Zera sat up cross-legged, her head bobbing in time to heavy metal music from her Ear-Tunes, a small set of crystal-studded earrings with attached clear earplugs that played downloaded music from a bracelet-selector. The throbbing beat drowned out her thoughts, including what might lie ahead at her uncle's big event. Zera stuck her tongue in the middle of the huge mass of gum, stretching it thin between her slightly open, puckered lips. Slowly, she began to blow. The bubble got bigger. And bigger. Zera's dark blue eyes widened as she watched the bubble grow huge before her. Then she saw nothing but pink. *Frickin' awesome.* She didn't hear the door open.

"Just what do you think you're doing?" Tiffany screeched.

Zera jolted, but didn't turn toward the door. Despite the fact that Tiffany's voice made the hairs on the back of her neck stand up, even over the sound of heavy metal, Zera willed herself to not react.

"That is so low class, Zera," Tiffany said, "so unbelievably *gauche*."

Zera had looked up "gauche" a long time ago. It was one of Tiffany's favorite words in describing Zera's behavior. It meant "lacking social grace." Zera's lips eased into a smile, the defiance bringing a scary thrill that made her stomach feel ticklish. *You may ruin every birthday, Tiff, but even you have to admit this is one hell of a bubble.*

In her peripheral vision she saw Tiffany, arms crossed, in the doorway.

Zera pursed her lips to try to force a bit more air into her creation and *phisssh* . . . As the bubble deflated, a few bits stuck to her cheeks. The bottom floated down past her chin and stuck to a spot on her neck.

"I cannot believe it!" shrieked Tiffany. "Oh . . . my . . . God. What have you done to your hair?! Zera, turn off those E-Tunes now!"

Zera couldn't help but laugh, a burst that released her tension like the exploded bubble. The laughter stopped when she turned toward Tiffany. Dressed in a strapless gown and flawlessly made up, blonde Barbie-like Tiffany would have been the perfect vision of femininity if not for two things, the sub-zero scowl contorting her face, and her double chin, her only physical flaw. Tiffany's small hands, placed squarely on her hips, showed pink-tipped claws almost digging in as she glared with tilted cat-like eyes. *Menacing. Very menacing.* Zera's skin turned to gooseflesh. She imagined for a second that Tiffany might pounce and pop *her* like a bubble. *How can my uncle be with someone so scary?* she thought, for the umpteenth time.

Zera pressed a button on her bracelet, turning off the music. "It's just a little color," she said, pulling off the deflated gum. "You gave me the dye."

"Not the nails too!" Tiffany's eyes pierced holes into the ten electric-green fingernails.

"You gave me that, too."

"We're leaving in ten minutes for the opening," Tiffany growled the words, her pink-painted mouth snarling. "Get yourself cleaned up, throw away that gum, and get downstairs.

There's no time to fix what you've done to yourself, but I promise, you will answer for this." She took a step toward Zera, lowering her voice. "You're fifteen today, Zera. *Fifteen.* You went through something big this week, a rite of passage. I understand that. But I really thought that you might begin acting a little more mature." Casting a last contemptuous look, Tiffany turned on her high heels and exited the room.

Zera got up, went over to the mirror above the fake Louis dresser, and began picking off the remaining bits of gum. *Mom and Dad would have laughed . . .*

She rolled the accumulated gum into a ball and checked the mirror for any wayward pieces adhering to her lightly freckled, heart-shaped face. *If I could just go back to live with Nonny.* That was the impossible dream; she had barely been allowed to see her grandmother in all this time. Their only contact, for almost three years, had been through the v-phone, v-mail, and twice-a-year visits — a week during summer, and a week during Christmas break. Theodore and Tiffany always had some excuse for not letting her stay longer.

Tonight's going to suck, Zera said to herself, throwing the wad of gum, hard, into her room's flamingo-hued plastic trash can. *All for Tiffany, all for The Toad.*

Chapter Three

Theodore Green, his thick lips pressed together in concentration, stood at the mirror above the fireplace mantle, trying to knot his bowtie. Its black fabric was decorated with a pattern of white twisted-ladder-shaped double-helixes, symbols for DNA, or, as he liked to call them, "the building blocks of life." His actions were jerky and excited; he'd had to listen to Tiffany complain for the last five minutes about Zera's green hair and nail polish, something he didn't find that alarming.

"That niece of yours. I don't get her rebelliousness. You're nice to her, I go out of my way all the time . . . why would she do that?"

"It's just her age," he said. "She's a good kid." Most of the time he shared information about Zera with Tiffany, but he hadn't mentioned the zinnia incident at Manning High School yesterday. He had too many other things to focus on with tonight's events. Tiffany always wanted to help, and usually her help was valuable to him, but this time he felt like he should deal with it on his own.

"Let me do that," said Tiffany. She tied his tie in a flash.

As Theodore buttoned his cuffs, he saw the scattering of ever-present warts on the backs of his hands, one of the reasons, he knew, his niece had given him the nickname. He had discovered that she called him "The Toad" last year when doing laundry. There was a piece of paper in a pocket of her jeans and unfolding it, he saw it was a note to Abby. It was about how "The Toad" had work that weekend and Tiffany told her she couldn't have Abby spend the night. There was a cartoon drawing of "Uncle Toad," a chubby amphibian with Theodore's warts, glasses, lips, and his unruly shock of dark hair. Abby had written, "Bummer!" and drew a smiley face with its tongue out. Theodore didn't hold it against Zera. She was just a kid and she had a lot to deal with. He knew she liked him even though she didn't often show it.

He wished he could get rid of the warts. They were inexplicable; all the miracles of modern medicine hadn't been able to get rid of them. Zera knew Tiffany had been personally trying to find a cure since the two of them met. The chubbiness, well, he'd had a bit of a stress-eating problem since his sister and her husband died, and the weight, fifty pounds of it, had come on slowly but surely. Now he was tipping the scales at 230. *Tiffany sure was helpful in getting me this suit,* Theodore thought. *It looks stylish, hides the bulk. And the glasses aren't bad either.* Although the majority of people with eye problems had corrective surgery these days, Theodore, mainly out of fear, chose to wear glasses instead, and Tiffany handpicked them all, making sure they were distinctive, vintage styles. He also liked old wristwatches, ones with hands that went around a clock face, and he was wearing his favorite gold-toned one today. *Gotta look my best today, he thought. I may be addressing a crowd.*

Deciding she couldn't put it off any longer, Zera came down the stairs into the living room. The first thing she saw was her uncle. *Too bad there's no suit in the world that can make him look like anything but a toad.* Instantly she regretted the thought. To be truthful, it wasn't the weight, or the warts, that made him The Toad — it was the fact that Tiffany had so much influence over his life. His weakness disgusted her.

The Toad turned. "My, Zera, you certainly look, well, nice."

Goofy looking and a bad liar. "Thanks."

"That green streak, though . . . it's a little much, don't you think? You really should have asked first." The Toad's large eyes narrowed behind the glasses.

Zera looked around the room, no sign of Tiffany. "She gave me a whole drawer full of the stuff. I didn't know I wasn't supposed to use any of it."

"Hmmm . . ." The Toad adjusted his glasses and appeared to be deep in thought. He cleared his throat with an "Ahhh-hem."

Here it comes. I wonder what it'll it be this time, no v-phone for a week or I'm going to be grounded from celebrating my birthday tomorrow with Abby, or . . .

"I know it's your birthday and you don't really want to go to this event, but acting out is not the answer," he began. He stared at the green streak. "Is that Dye & Go?"

"Yeah. Made with henna, and those ocean plants. It's the only stuff I found that I'd use. It's temporary."

The Toad's "pseudo-father figure" expression changed. A glimmer of amusement crossed his features. "Well, maybe it won't be so shocking to the people at Biotech, because it's one of our own products. Do me a favor though, Zera. Don't ever pull something like this again. I'm not going to punish you, this time, not on your birthday, but I want you to consider yourself warned. Fair enough?"

No punishment? Cool! Zera's face broke out into a huge smile.

It was then that she spied the three boxes by the front door. The smallest, about a foot tall and wide, had holes in it. It was stamped with large red letters: LIVE MATERIALS and FRAGILE.

"Are those for me?"

"Got your name on them."

She went to them. The address labels were penned in curly, elaborate, old-fashioned script that she'd have recognized anywhere without reading the name. *They're from Nonny! Three presents! She didn't even tell me. Maybe my birthday's not going to be so bad after all.*

"Can I open them?"

Tiffany appeared in the doorway that led to the kitchen. She wore her favorite jacket, a white fur from the 1970s.

Dead animals, thought Zera, *figures.* "You *may* open them later," said Tiffany. "We have to leave. Get your coat."

"But this one says 'Live Materials.'" Zera pointed to the box with the holes. "Maybe it's a pet, something alive." *The opposite of your coat.*

"Don't be ridiculous," Tiffany said. "Your grandmother knows you can't have a pet."

Zera's new bubble, one of brief happiness, burst. Tiffany spoke the truth. In the last three years she had asked for a pet many times, anything to make her feel a little less lonely. Tiffany was clear on the matter. She didn't think The Toad should allow animals in his home. It was unclean, and inconvenient, and he didn't need *another* responsibility. As usual, The Toad didn't go against her advice.

"You know," her uncle said, gesturing at the box, "I'm pretty sure it's a plant. We get shipments like that at the lab all the time. It'll be fine until we get back."

"A plant? Can't I just open it and see?"

"Why in the world would Guinevere send a plant?" Tiffany said, puckering her highly-glossed lips in disapproval. "You don't need any plants."

Zera glared at her.

"You can wait." Tiffany said. "You should get some kind of punishment for your hair-dying stunt." She turned to the Toad. "Did you get the E-SAT washed?" The E-SAT was The Toad's brand new vehicle, a huge Electric Suburban All-Terrain truck that he'd bought with his first-ever work bonus.

"Yep."

Tiffany glanced at Zera, at her hair, and shook her head slightly in one last display of disapproval. "Then let's go."

Chapter Four

They arrived at dusk to find the brand new All-American Burger Depot lit up like a patriotic amusement park. The building mimicked the American flag, a big concrete rectangle painted red, white, and blue with stars and stripes. For the Grand Opening, fiber-optic Christmas lights in the same colors decorated the building and the outside patio.

Zera nearly retched when she spied the twelve-foot-tall plastic bull, glowing atop the restaurant. He wore cowboy duds — jeans, a red gingham shirt, chaps, and a fringed vest — and held a lasso that curled above him to form the six-foot-high neon words "All-American."

She had to ask as her uncle's E-SAT pulled into the parking lot, "What is that thing on top of the building?"

"That, Zera, is All-American Mac."

"Ewww." From inside the vehicle she heard the throbbing beat of a band playing country and western music.

"This is a huge event," said Tiffany.

"Yep," The Toad croaked out the word. "The biggest ever. The franchise CEO's here, BioTech execs and scientists, even the mayor. Tomorrow is the Grand Opening for the public. It'll be an even bigger party then." Theodore braked, suddenly pitching them forward. "Sorry. Hey Tiffany, did you see the Channel 8 news van?"

He'd pulled into a parking spot crookedly and had to back out again. Zera could almost see the nervousness radiating off her uncle.

"I sure did. Channel 11's here too." Tiffany checked her makeup in the lighted mirror on the visor. "You know, they may want to interview you."

The Toad pulled into the parking spot again, this time on the yellow line on the passenger side. "Good enough," he said under his breath. He turned off the ignition and pushed his black-rimmed glasses up on his nose. "I've prepared a short speech. I hope it'll be enough."

Walking toward the building, they saw a group of people across the street with signs. "What's going on over there?" Zera wondered.

About twenty protesters marched on the sidewalk, carrying large signs. Six policemen, in riot gear, stood watch. Zera read, "All-American Does Not Represent ALL Americans; Bioengineering is not good for man or other living things; YOU ARE WHAT YOU EAT. One says, 'The Green G's are coming.' Who are the Green G's? "

"Who cares?" Tiffany said. "They're all a bunch of nuts."

Theodore looked over at the group. "The Green G's are the Green Guerrillas, an environmental activist group."

“Oh, I’ve heard of them,” said Zera.

“The Green Guerrillas . . .” Tiffany hugged her coat around her, shot a look at the protesters. “That’s the organization your old high school friend became involved in, isn’t it?”

The Toad blushed. “Lily Gibbons started it.” His eyes searched the crowd. Zera thought he looked like he was afraid he might see her there and wondered about Lily Gibbons — she’d never heard of her before. After a few seconds The Toad’s furrowed brow relaxed. “I don’t think we have to worry about that group. I doubt they understand the science behind what we’re doing.”

“Maybe,” said Zera, “they understand common sense instead.”

Tiffany turned to Zera, her cat-eyes narrowing. “Listen, missy — this is a big night for Theodore, for all of us, and we expect you to be on your best behavior.” Her hand went up to smooth her blonde tresses. “Otherwise, your uncle might have to make you wait to open those presents from Guinevere.”

“As far as I know,” Zera said, glancing at the red, white, and blue building, “this is still a free country.”

“Ladies,” said The Toad, “I think we need to calm down.”

“I have a right to my opinion,” murmured Zera. She silently dared Tiffany to follow up on her threat. She knew Tiffany could be mean, but it wasn’t her style to do something truly hateful in front of her uncle.

Entering the double doors, the trio was greeted by the

franchise's female mascot, a robotic cow-human.

"All-American Marilyn," The Toad said.

Marilyn, like All-American Mac, stood upright and had a human body shape. The hard foam structure gave her bovine facial features the texture of human flesh. She was decked out in a tight red jumpsuit, blue scarf, and high-heeled pumps. She held two American flags, one in each hoof.

"Let's put our coats away and get our nametags, shall we?" Tiffany said.

Standing in line for their nametags, they watched Marilyn's routine. In an electronically activated voice, she breathily exclaimed, "Try our Beefy Fries. They're All-American!" At the words "All-American," she waved her flags. Next came a shimmy-dance from horn to hoof as she exclaimed, "Our milk-shakes are Moo-Licious!" She ended with a "Mooo! Mooo! Mooo!" while turning her head from side to side, winking.

An older man working at the table winked at Tiffany. "They should have named her Marilyn 'Moo-roe,' don't you think?"

"Oh, how clever!"

Another man who looked to be in his late 20's, but was balding (Zera could see the bare top of his head in the security mirrors overhead) walked up to them. He wore a navy blue suit almost identical to The Toad's. The dark hair that circled his head matched the color of his large, furry eyebrows, brows that reminded Zera of caterpillars. "So, Theo," he said, "what do you think of Marilyn?"

"Hey, Harv. She's all right, I guess. As long as she sells hamburgers."

"And don't forget Beefy Fries." Harv laughed and gave Theodore a friendly clap on the shoulder.

The Toad beamed.

"It's gonna be your night, buddy," said Harv. "Gonna be your night."

Theodore introduced Tiffany and Zera to Harvey Headstrom, one of the newer scientists at BioTech Multinational. Zera noticed that he clapped The Toad on the back again when he said something about meeting the deadline for the project. Zera's attention drifted as they chatted about her uncle's new E-SAT and his lame vanity plate: NU CR8N, New Creation. She caught herself absentmindedly staring at the glowing reflective pattern the light made on Harv's shiny head until Tiffany nudged her. Embarrassed, Zera diverted her gaze. A dark sea of geekdom surrounded her. Most, obviously from BioTech, wore eerily similar dark suits and white shirts. *Although The Toad's DNA bowtie is icky, at least he doesn't look totally cloned. I stand out like a sore thumb — a big, sore, pink thumb.*

A huge monitor for Americo, the pharmaceutical company that created Burger Depot and funded Biotech's work, hung on the wall opposite the nametag table. Americo products flashed across the screen as a spokeswoman's voice said: "Our research has made acne a thing of the past. Our next goal is to rid the world of cancer."

Instead of the usual teenaged fast-food employees, waiters in black and white uniforms stood at attention behind the service counters. Conveyor belts under heat lamps moved forward while 3-D technology on the wall monitors showed pictures of the franchise's offerings, glistening and sizzling. Zera didn't see anyone under the age of twenty and breathed a little easier. *It's embarrassing enough to be seen in public in this dress, much less by kids my age. I'll have to remember to avoid all TV cameras, though.* She fingered her green strand of hair and fidgeted, rocking on her heels as the strains of an old tune she recognized, *Thank God I'm a Country Boy,* drifted through the room. Zera groaned inwardly. *Maybe I should go to the restroom and escape out a window.*

Tiffany noticed Zera squirming and shot her a look that carried an unmistakable warning — *You'd better cool it.*

"Have you seen Mr. Cadger?" Theodore asked Harv.

"Over there," Harv pointed, "talking to the Burger Depot people and the reporters. Chet Wrangler is going to speak first, then Cadger. In fact," Harv said, as he looked at his watch, which held a mini v-phone, "it's about time. You'd better find a seat."

Zera followed Harv's nod and spotted The Toad's boss in the next room, a short man with close-cropped blond hair, in the middle of a crowd. The tables around them were set with linens, silver cutlery, and crystal — details that amused Zera — *pretty fancy for burgers*. In the far back of the room someone had turned off the band equipment and the walls glowed with large projections of ads from Americo. The ads showed medical advancements Americo had helped produce. One was a repeat of what the spokeswoman on the monitor had said about acne and possible cancer cures. Another explained that a bio-engineered smoking cessation pill was well on its way to making cigarette smoking a vice of the past. Zera wondered if Harv wished they would work on curing hair loss instead.

Tiffany tugged on her arm. "Come on." Zera was pulled away in the direction of Bob Cadger. Zera heard her uncle say behind her, "Chairs are filling fast. . . Tiffany . . . ?" Zera looked back to see him follow them in his usual puppy-dog manner, until he was intercepted by another co-worker.

Elbowing her way to the center of the fray, Tiffany interrupted the small man with dandelion-colored hair talking to a man with an electronic notepad. "Good evening, Mr. Cadger."

"Oh, hello," Cadger said, turning from the reporter. A look of recognition flickered across his face. "You're Theodore Green's girlfriend, aren't you? We've met before, at the company picnic, I believe."

"Yes." Tiffany flashed her most winning smile. "I'm Tiffany Taylor." Zera noticed that she brought a slender hand up to her double chin for a moment. Giving him a 1,000 watt smile, Tiffany shook hands with Cadger, then put a hand on Zera's shoulder. "I'm sorry to interrupt, but I just wanted Theodore's niece Zera to meet you. She's the youngest member of the Green dynasty. It's so exciting that the opening is today. You see, it's Zera's birthday. Her fifteenth."

"Well, happy birthday, young lady." Cadger shook Zera's hand. "My goodness, what a lovely dress, you look like quite the princess tonight." Zera stifled a frown. She guessed she was taller than Cadger by at least four inches. She smiled back half-heartedly. His eyes darted to her swatch of green hair, causing her to blush. Still, she stood straight and maintained eye contact. She'd heard a few things about Cadger from her uncle, mostly comments about how his boss didn't know a lot about science, but made a hundred times more than the other employees, the ones who did the "real" work.

"I imagine you're quite proud of your uncle today," Cadger said. "Who knows, if you follow in the Green family's footsteps, maybe one day you, too, will work for BioTech."

Zera's stomach lurched. An urge to run, to claw her way out of the crowd, filled her. She suddenly realized why Tiffany made such a big deal of her being there. *Of course, Mr. Cadger knows all about Green Seed Company, it was once the biggest seed company in the world.* The images of several forebears, all renowned botanists, flashed through her mind. *This is just an opportunity for them to look good by parading around with the poor orphaned niece. Yeah, sure, Mr. Cadger,* she longed to say, *I'm sure I'll work for you one day. When hell freezes over!*

The urge to run subsided. Zera took a deep breath and put on her fakest smile. "As you know, Mr. Cadger, my grandmother,

Guinevere Green, owned the Green Seed Company. She's never approved of what is being done in genetic engineering — and neither do I."

Cadger's eyes registered shock, but his flashing smile diminished only slightly. He turned to the staring reporter, "Oh, the youth of today, such kidders!"

"But I'm not — " Zera began.

"Zera!" Tiffany said. "Mr. Cadger, I am so sorry. I guess since it's her birthday, Zera thinks she can just say whatever rude thing comes into her mind!"

Cadger's smile tightened and he ran one hand over his close-cropped yellow hair. "Believe me, I understand. I have two teenagers of my own." He turned to Zera, eyes focusing on her green hair just long enough to convey disapproval. "Young lady, progress is a good thing, always has been, always will be. In fact, it's the *only* way. You'll find that out one day." He turned to the reporter, effectively cutting them off. "Now, as far as the future of biotechnology . . ."

Tiffany took Zera's arm and began leading her away from the group.

"Wait a minute. Excuse me," a middle-aged woman with poofy red hair moved in front of them; another reporter with an electronic notepad. She smiled at Zera. "I heard you say you didn't 'approve of what is being done in genetic engineering.' I'm just curious, what do you mean by that, exactly?"

Tiffany let go of Zera's sleeve. Caught between Zera having

a reporter's undivided attention and being afraid of what Zera might say, she was momentarily unsure of what to do. Zera's reaction was the opposite. Everything she had heard growing up about genetic engineering and plant life came flooding back. She took a deep breath. "My grandmother always said there are a lot of things that can go wrong with bioengineered crops. She explained to me how genetically-engineered crops can't be contained in their fields. Pollen can get carried away by wind, bees, and other insects, causing the plants to reproduce with wild plants or non-GM crops. This forever changes the wild plants' or non-GMO crops' DNA — DNA that's taken millions of years to evolve. She's always said that it's a tragedy to our food supply waiting to happen."

"And your grandmother, she's . . ."

"Guinevere Green, of Green Seed Company."

"Well. We've certainly all heard of Green Seed Company. Interesting," said the reporter. She moved closer to Zera. "I've researched this topic. Biotech Multinational's literature says they've taken steps to ensure such events, bioengineered plants escaping into the wild for example, won't happen. That they've spent millions in failsafe procedures."

"Failsafe is impossible."

Tiffany went into red alert. "I'm sorry," she said, putting her body between Zera and the reporter. "I hope you're not thinking of quoting a fourteen year old without permission. Everything she just said is *off the record.*" She grabbed Zera's arm and this time did not stop dragging her away until they were a good distance from the crowd.

"Fifteen!" said Zera. "Today's my birthday, remember?"

"We'd better find a seat," Tiffany whispered to Theodore when she found him. "But you're sitting next to Zera, I've had enough of that brat for one day."

The Toad gave Zera a look she knew well, raised eyebrows, wrinkled forehead. His expression clearly asked, "What did you do now?"

As they sat waiting, Zera felt satisfaction about speaking up, rude or not. It surprised her that she'd had the courage. *Nonny would be proud.* Her satisfaction was a little undercut, however, by fear of Tiffany's revenge. Zera didn't feel quite so certain now that Tiffany would let her open her grandmother's gifts when they got home.

On the stage at the front of the room, Bob Cadger's secretary introduced Chet Wrangler, the CEO of All-American Burger Depot. A giant of a man in a tan suit, Stetson cowboy hat, and faux alligator boots, stomped up to the podium. His long, thick mustache and doughy features reminded Zera of a walrus, yet his massiveness, his tree trunk body and legs, brought to her mind the image of a mighty oak.

"He looks almost as strange as I do," Zera said under her breath.

"Shhh." The Toad narrowed his eyes at her from behind his dark-framed glasses.

"Good evening." Wrangler tipped his hat. "I appreciate y'all coming tonight to our little celebration, the Colorado opening of Americo's first All-American Burger Depot."

Applause thundered from the audience.

"I want y'all to know that we couldn't have done this without our partnership with the scientific geniuses at BioTech." Wrangler bestowed a smile as big as Texas upon Cadger, seated to his right.

Cadger nodded in return.

"Tonight," continued Wrangler, "you'll taste two of our newest products. First our dee-licious Beefy Fries, developed from a potato enhanced with the genes from a cow! These babies are going to once-and-for-all change the words 'French fries' to 'American fries.' *All-American* fries!"

The crowd chuckled.

"These beefy fries have been off the charts in every single taste test. They're going to be big, real big." Wrangler spread out his long, meaty arms to illustrate exactly how big. "I just hope they don't get too big, and make hamburgers obsolete — or my little 500,000-head cattle ranch back in Texas is in trouble!"

The crowd laughed again.

During this part of the speech, several people smiled at her uncle, and Zera watched him actually puff up. *Just like a toad*, she thought. She'd heard all about The Toad's masterpiece, Beefy Fries, for months. They were made from something that looked like a regular potato but were far from it; they oozed a little of a blood-like substance when harvested and sliced into fries. The Toad said that was just a minor concern, and soon they'd have a "new and improved" version. Zera thought up another nickname for her uncle, "Lord of the Fries." She envisioned another amphibian, a frog, sitting on a lily pad, his tongue darting out at winged fries mooing and buzzing above his head.

"Our second creation," Chet Wrangler said, "is our Marilyn Milkshake, named after our sweet little mascot, whom I'm sure y'all have met."

The crowd nodded and smiled. A few people chuckled. Someone called out "Moo!"

"These milkshakes are rich and tasty, and they are absolutely cutting edge, having both public satisfaction and health in mind. They are the first milkshakes ever that *induce* weight loss, by way of a secret ingredient added to the recipe." Wrangler winked.

"Ooooh!" murmured the audience.

Wrangler's grin revealed a glitter of white teeth below his mustache. "I welcome you to a new era, an era where good old scientific know-how is paving the way for our food. And this is only the beginning. We've got a lot of projects, just as fantastic, on the back burner."

A man yelled out, "Yeah, the Bunsen burner!" and a few in the crowd tittered.

"But what is so extra-special about All-American," Wrangler

hooked his thumbs into his front jean pockets, and sweetened his voice to molasses, "is that we've created a homey, warm atmosphere where you can enjoy a nice time out with your family. And that's what we care about most at Americo — *family*.

"Anyhow, I won't keep you longer, I know you're all hungry, and itchin' to try this food. You're gonna love it, I guarantee it! So now I'll turn y'all over to a man most of you know and love, Mr. Bob Cadger, President of BioTech Multinational. Thank you!"

An upbeat music number started playing as the crowd clapped, but the word "itchin" made Zera remember her scratchy dress. She rubbed the back of her neck where the ruffled material irritated her skin the most. The audience applauded louder as Cadger changed places with Wrangler at the podium. Cadger now wore a top hat decorated with stars and stripes. Zera heard chuckles of admiration and a couple of comments about Cadger's "sense of humor."

The microphone stand automatically adjusted itself to Cadger's height. Cadger looked up at Wrangler. "Thanks, Chet."

Cadger clapped along with the crowd as Wrangler took a seat. He then took the microphone from its stand, walked up to the edge of the stage and grinned. His audience, glassy-eyed with admiration, stood and clapped. Zera looked around and sighed. *What do they see in this guy?*

"That's a vintage microphone," Tiffany said to Theodore, "I

wonder why he's using an old one, the kind with a cord?"

Theodore shrugged. "Beats me."

"Wow, what an act to follow!" Cadger said. Holding onto the microphone's cord, he dropped it down past the stage, nearly to the floor, then swung it back up in a long arc, catching it in his hand.

The audience went wild. Zera almost gagged. She'd seen a rock star from about fifty years ago do that once on a Home Theater concert and knew Bob Cadger was just copying him.

"Isn't this a great evening!" Cadger motioned for his audience to sit back down, all the while smiling, gee-whiz-boyishly and arrogantly at the same time. The music stopped. "When Americo approached us five years ago, they wanted to see what we could do in the arena of fast food. They knew of our work, our fantastic successes in the field of genetic modification. They knew that in less than six years, we'd grown from a very small company into a *multinational corporation*."

Tiffany said, "And they couldn't have done any of it without you, Theodore."

The Toad grinned and looked around expectantly, as if he were ready to be called to the stage himself.

"I am *proud*," Cadger said. "We are a team of *winners*. I want to thank Mr. Wrangler and Americo, but I especially want to thank *all of you*."

Several minutes later, and without any mention of her uncle, Bob Cadger received a standing ovation — and for a moment, seeing her uncle's disappointment, Zera forgot all about her birthday.

Zera winced as The Toad slurped his chocolate shake from its crystal tumbler; it sounded like sludge being sucked down a drain. When they sat down she saw that his hair, combed neatly when they arrived, had begun reverting to its usual messed-up state. His cowlick had returned and two patches of hair stuck up in opposite directions at the back of his head. No one had spoken a word during the meal. A few people from the lab had visited their table to compliment her uncle on the Beefy Fries, but The Toad only nodded in return, his expression grim.

Harv Headstrom walked up, carrying a plate. Between mouthfuls of fries he said, "Wow, Theo, these are so good! They taste exactly like steak and potatoes!" He licked his lips, raised his caterpillar eyebrows. "It was weird, though, that Cadger didn't single you out for all your work."

Theodore gave Harv a frosty look and no reply as Harv stood in silence for a few awkward seconds. Zera again noticed the reflective quality of his balding head and looked away quickly. Harv mumbled, "I guess I'll see you at the office," and walked away.

Zera picked at her salad. The idea of trying the Beefy Fries or a Marilyn shake made her stomach lurch. At a table near them, she'd overheard one of the scientists say that the "secret ingredient" in the milkshakes was the genetic code from some kind of parasite, attached to a cow's "milk" gene in order to create "weight-loss milk." *I don't even want to know the details..*

Zera looked over at that table again and her fork slipped from her grasp as a sudden brightness filled the room and a dizziness overtook her. *No*, she thought, *that's ketchup, not blood*. For a moment she thought she saw blood on the corner of the scientist's mouth, blood on the fries. For that moment, even the scent of copper had filled her nostrils. She did a double-take and her head cleared; the "blood" turned back to ordinary red ketchup, the smell disappeared. *This place is getting to me*, thought Zera. *I'm going bonkers. Too much information.*

Theodore broke his silence. In a croaky voice, barely above a whisper he said, "He led me on, Tiffany." He glanced around. "Not one word, not one stinking word. And I'm the one who single-handedly created Beefy Fries. Damn it!"

Zera was shocked. She'd never heard her uncle swear.

"You should have known something was up when they didn't let you name them." Tiffany daintily dipped a Beefy Fry into a puddle of ketchup and Zera had to look away before she put it in her mouth. "They've been walking all over you and you've let them."

The Toad didn't respond. Shaking off the blood-ketchup thing, Zera remembered the Beefy Fry naming episode. Months ago The Toad submitted a scientific name for his creation. He'd bragged to Tiffany and Zera how he'd cleverly combined the Latin name *Solanum tuberosum*, for potato, with the one for cattle, *Bos taurus*, into *Bos x tuberosum* and added his own name as inventor — Green, or *greenii,* for the Latin translation, on the end. *Bos x tuberosum greenii* was rejected as a name by corporate headquarters in preference of *Bos x tuberosum sparkii* — in honor of Bob Cadger's dog, Sparky.

"You're right," The Toad said. "I'm one of the greatest minds in this field and I haven't received my due for anything. BioTech's walked all over me."

Zera tried to be invisible, taking small sips from her water and not adding anything to the conversation. She also knew about The Toad's other "products." Although she always pretended she wasn't interested when he talked about them, she listened attentively. She'd heard about Biocorn, the corn spliced with a bacteria that immediately killed any bug that nibbled on it, and about the New World strawberries, strawberries that had their genes combined with those of the great strawberry-worm. The strawberries were designed so that the caterpillars would not recognize them as food. The only flaw was that the strawberries looked a bit like the caterpillars, green with yellow spots and long black hairs — not very appetizing. Zera thought BioTech Multinational's products were disgusting, but also strangely mesmerizing. She couldn't help but feel sorry for her uncle.

The Toad sat up straighter and raised his voice a little. "This is the last straw. Things are going to change."

"It's about time," Tiffany said. "Because he doesn't deserve the money, or the glory. You do." She jerked her blonde head in the direction of Cadger, sitting at the largest table in the middle of the room, surrounded by admirers. Cadger hadn't said a single word to The Toad since they got there.

Tiffany touched the corners of her mouth with a star-spangled napkin then looked at The Toad, her eyes steely with determination. "You're brilliant, Theodore, but you're not a businessman. We need to change that. I know how to get ahead. I grew up poor, the shabbiest dressed kid in Rosemont High, but I worked my way out of it. I know what it takes to get what you want."

Tiffany's words and the alley-cat-hungry look in her eyes sent a shiver up Zera's spine.

Back at the condo, the sight of Nonny's packages thrilled Zera. With all the drama of the evening, including a discussion between The Toad and Tiffany on the way home about what "they" were going to do about Theodore's situation at BioTech, she'd forgotten about her presents.

"I hope I can open them now," she said to her uncle, ignoring Tiffany and what she'd said earlier.

"Sure," The Toad said.

"Suit yourself," Tiffany added, letting Zera know that this was her decision, too. She plopped down on the sofa and kicked off her high heels. "But hurry up. I'm exhausted, it's late. We all need to turn in early tonight."

Zera ignored the remark and went for the boxes. She opened

the one with the holes first.

"It's a Venus flytrap!" Taken from its protective paper nest, she held up the plant in its glass pot with detachable clear glass lid. The flytrap was small, about five inches tall, and a bright green color.

"Pretty interesting, Zera," The Toad had recovered enough from the evening to grin roguishly at her. "That's a carnivorous plant, you know. Eats flesh. Woooo . . . scary . . ." he wiggled his long, warty fingers in the air.

Tiffany rolled her eyes, but Zera's sparkled. "This is so cool!"

"Imagine, sending someone a plant on their birthday," Tiffany said. "That mother of yours is certainly an oddball, Theodore."

Zera opened the other boxes. One held a book entitled *Plant Oddities and Their Care*, and in the largest, heaviest box, was an antique terrarium.

Zera admired the rectangular fourteen-inch-tall iron and glass terrarium. A series of pointed arches stood joined together on each side, three across the front and back and two on each side. The separate base was all metal, patterned in twining vines. A fancy cut-glass knob opened the iron top. Zera sighed. *It's beautiful.*

In the bottom of the box was a light pink envelope from Nonny Green, the flamboyant script addressing it to "My Darling Seed."

Zera smiled. Her name, Zera, meant "seed" in Hebrew. She took out the envelope and opened it. The outside of the card showed a gorgeous spring bouquet of flowers in reds, blues, purples, creams, and chartreuse, nearly exploding from an earthenware vase. Three tiny fairies flew around the blossoms. Zera instantly recognized it as one of her mother's paintings. *Dad had this painting in his music studio. Nonny made it into a card.* Zera's throat tightened. *Nonny, you're the greatest.*

She looked up at her uncle and saw him swallow hard, knowing he recognized his sister's work. "Beautiful card," he said.

Zera opened it.

My Dearest Zera,

Happy 15th birthday! I found this little Venus Flytrap at the Denver Botanical Gardens. She seemed to speak to me, to tell me that she would be the perfect birthday present for you. I know it's not the "real" pet you've been wanting for so long, but I'm sure you'll find her interesting and educational.

All in Ute Springs (including your furry and feathered friends) send their love and birthday wishes. We love you and miss you so much.

Nonny

P.S. The terrarium is a family heirloom from

> 1891 — a gift from Queen Victoria to your great-great-grandmother Rose. A token of appreciation for some herbal advice, I believe.

Zera felt, finally, as if it were truly her birthday, as if her mother, father and grandmother were there with her in a small but real way. She hugged the card to her chest. "Nonny says this terrarium belonged to my great-great-grandmother Rose. It was a gift from Queen Victoria!" Zera's hand caressed the pointed arches, the crystal knob on top. "I love it!"

"Hmmmm," murmured Tiffany. She got up from the sofa and walked over to the terrarium. "I wonder how much it's worth."

"I remember it," The Toad said. "It used to sit in Nonny's, my Nonny's, conservatory." He picked up the Venus flytrap and turned it around in his hand, examining it from all angles. "Nice-looking plant. You know, Zera, plants are fascinating . . . everything that eats, everything that's alive, depends on plants to stay alive, in one way or another."

"Yeah," Zera said as she kept an eye on Tiffany, "we studied that in school. They supply food and oxygen for the planet. But I knew all that anyway."

"It doesn't look that fabulous to me," Tiffany said, "considering it was supposedly a gift from a *queen*. I'll never understand your family's attraction to plants. To me, they're just something you have to take care of — water, feed, dust — and they bring dirt into the house. Silk plants are far superior, and *they've* been around for ages, too." She tossed her mane, as if the fuss they made over the terrarium was a little too much for her to bear.

"I'll take it upstairs for you, Zera," The Toad said. "It's pretty heavy."

Clutching her plant and book close to her, Zera followed him up the stairs to her room.

Zera studied the plant. *It's lovely,* she thought, *so tiny, so perfect. Such a pretty green color, and the reddish traps look so delicate!*

After a quick shower, she changed into pajama bottoms and a badly faded rock group T-shirt that had belonged to her father. Curled up on her bed, she began reading *Plant Oddities and Their Care*. It was weird to have a real book in her hands again; she hadn't been around books very much since she left home. The Toad felt computer libraries were superior to real ones because all you had to do was ask a question, and the answer would almost instantly appear, or the computers would talk and tell you the answers, or take you on a video journey showing you the answer, if you preferred that. Zera loved paper books, their smell, and their weight in her hands. She liked flipping through pages, making discoveries.

In this book, full of delightfully bizarre and attractive illustrations, Zera found that the scientific, or Latin, species name for her Venus flytrap was *Dionea muscipula*. Zera read that the flytrap's ancestors were discovered in the United States in 1760. At that time they were called "Fly Trap Sensitive." The Latin name translated into "Aphrodite's Mouse-trap" but they were commonly called "Venus Flytrap." *So,* Zera mused, *the name comes from both Aphrodite, the Greek goddess of love, and Venus, the Roman goddess of love. How cool!* She thought about how fun it would be to have a collection of plants in her room, how it would make Tiffany's flamingo-colored decor of frills and ruffles more bearable. Inspired by a quote she remembered, tacked to the bulletin board in her father's music studio, "Love is Nature's second sun," she chose to name her flytrap "Sunny."

"Zera, your uncle's going to walk me home now!" Tiffany's voice rang from downstairs. "Lights out time! And be careful that you don't make a mess with that plant. I do *not* want any water on the furniture!"

And a goodnight, happy birthday to you too, Tiff. Zera turned off the light and said goodnight to Sunny, whose pot sat in the terrarium, on her night table. Zera fell asleep thinking about her grandmother.

In the dark, sphagnum moss-filled terrarium, Sunny shut and opened all fifteen of her traps in quick succession. It was her way of paying homage to Zera's fifteenth birthday, and saying goodnight to her new friend.

Chapter Five

Monday, June 2

Water everywhere! Flying, rushing, torrents! Surrounding! Enclosing . . . Struggle. Blackness. Nothing.

Zera fought to wake up. Sobs forced themselves through her constricted throat.

A honeyed voice whispered, “It’s okay. Go back to sleep.”

Zera’s eyes opened and her rigid body slowly relaxed. Her breathing returned to normal. She turned on her nightstand light. The room was empty, her thin cotton blanket knotted around her legs. She untangled it, smoothed it down, turned off the light. Closing her eyes, she imagined she saw two stars twinkling in the distance. Her mother and father. Gone forever. She thought about the river accident, a tragedy she did not witness but always experienced so vividly in her nightmares.

This time, for the first time, she didn’t cry when she woke. Her heart didn’t continue to pound with horror. Turning again to her nightstand, she gazed into the darkness. She saw the outlines of her plants. Sunny, in the terrarium, and five others now surrounding her. Zera’s fingers brushed the gray-green surface of one of them. She plucked a few soft, elongated leaves, held them to her nose. *Lavender. Smells so good. It helps.* Soothed, she drifted back into sleep, the leaves cradled in her palm, her nightmare receding.

"Wake up, Zera. Up and at 'em." The Toad knocked on her bedroom door, croaking, "Time to get ready for school." When Zera didn't respond, he opened it. Zera opened an eye; the room was dark, the windows still electronically tinted dark for night.

She squinted in the direction of his voice. From the hall light she could see the shadow of his head, spikes of bed-head going out in all directions.

"Ughhh," she groaned, pulling the covers over her face.

The Toad flipped the wall switch. "Rise and shine. You missed the alarm. It's late."

The room lit up in harsh forty-watt-times-seven light from the chandelier. With the activation of the light switch, the darkness on the tinted windows faded, revealing sunny skies between the ruffled curtains. Zera groaned again.

When the door clicked shut, she threw off the blanket. She rubbed her eyes, sat up, and stuck her tongue out at the door. She got up, went to the window. The Village Glen lawns were all the exact shade of green, with about a third just slightly different. She could spot the fakes easily, they had a sheen that stood out to her like neon. The latest and greatest fad in home improvement: plastic lawns. People had been ripping out their grass all spring because of climate change; in Colorado's case, drought. *All the better to look pretty, have zero maintenance, and save water. Who cares that they are fake and will never have that fresh grass smell? Or give off oxygen?* She saw a few garage doors open and the cars leave. *To work. To school. Everything so much the same.* Yet, it was a shiny, early June day, and Zera's spirits began to lift, like the trilling of bird song in the tree near her window. She noticed a few nice touches. Just across the street a real rose bush bloomed, and on two small porches, pots of petunias. *Real ones!* Directly across from the condos, a vibrant pot of purple flowers on a porch caught her eye. The blooms were moving, jiggling, almost as if trying to get her attention. *That's weird. What is doing that? A cat, maybe a bird?* She squinted. The pot seemed to glow brighter in hue, and the movement stopped. No animal came out, no bird flew away. Zera shook her head and turned away from the window.

It would be a nice day if it wasn't the last week of ninth grade. I can't take another summer here. A lot had changed since her birthday. She and Abby had fun that spring break week celebrating her birthday — they had a sleepover, hung out, surfed the Internet, listened to music and skateboarded. But after break, Abby got a boyfriend, a 17-year-old named Thor. He was even more extreme than Abby, two years older, with two piercings (tongue and eyebrow), dyed black hair, and all-black clothes like Abby. Almost instantly they were inseparable. Within a few weeks Abby had abandoned Zera almost completely. Now summer was coming. One week with Nonny at some point, the rest awful. Zera wondered what agonizing camp experience Tiffany had lined up for her. Last year was the worst, six weeks of hell at Make-Over Camp, whose motto, “Grooming, hairstyling, diet and fashion — our modern young woman focus!” said it all. Zera groaned, flopped back down on the bed. Maybe Abby would break up with Thor. Or maybe a miracle would happen and a boy would be interested in her. She’d been trying to talk her uncle into letting her try to find some kind of work, volunteerism, anything so the summer wouldn’t stretch before her like a prison sentence.

Rolling on her side she looked at Sunny in the antique terrarium, surrounded by five other plants in small terra-cotta pots. The gloom lifted somewhat. “I forgot to say good morning. How can I stay bummed with you guys around?”

Zera had started collecting plants since her birthday, but Tiffany stopped her when she found out. “We’re not letting things get out of hand,” she said. “You’re not turning this bedroom, that I spent a lot of time and money decorating, into a *jungle*.”

Zera’s hand flew over to the terrarium. She lifted the lid so the condensation inside could clear. In doing so, she accidentally brushed the lavender plant sitting next to it. A cool, fresh smell escaped from the leaves, filling her nostrils. For a moment everything seemed bright again. She remembered the nightmare and a particular soothing voice.

That voice seemed so real.

Zera came to breakfast wearing one of her usual ensembles: cut-off jeans, red high-top sneakers, and a black T-shirt featuring the name and flaming guitar logo of her favorite oldie rock group, Pyro. *Oh great, she's here again.*

Tiffany sat at the glass and chrome table. As usual, she looked Zera over. Predictably, her pouty lips twisted into a disapproving curve as she took in Zera's T-shirt. But today the expression lasted only a second before something unusual happened. It was replaced by a *smile*. "Good morning," she practically sang. Zera was surprised at what Tiffany wore. The top of a ruffled apron was visible over her shirt.

"Uh . . . Good morning." Zera was caught off-guard. She couldn't believe the delicious smell in the air. Tiffany had prepared a real breakfast — eggs, bacon, pancakes were on the table, on her plate! Tiffany never cooked, much less prepared a sit-down meal for the three of them. *Have I entered another dimension?* The Toad sat semi-slouched over his notepad across from Tiffany, reading.

Tiffany sipped a diet drink, Skinny 2000 Death By Chocolate. The Toad was partaking in the feast, only having smaller portions than he would have had some months ago. Lately for breakfast he'd been having a StrongMan protein drink or power bar.

"Isn't it a gorgeous day?" Tiffany smoothed down the collar of her seashell-pink blouse.

"Yeah, I guess so." Zera sat down.

"I made you breakfast." Tiffany giggled.

Tiffany looked positively pleasant as she sipped from her pink straw. *She giggled, how weird!* Zera remembered how The Toad was nice to her the night before, asking her if she wanted anything special for take-out because he was taking Tiffany out to dinner. *Something big is up.* Zera's eyes went to Tiffany's left hand. *No ring, thank God.*

As Zera peered down at the scrambled eggs, the memory of Make-Over Camp sprang up in her mind. With it came a shiver of dread that she fought to smother. *Maybe Tiffany has found something even more disgusting for this summer, maybe that's why she's acting like this.* She picked up her fork. "This looks great," she said. She was afraid to ask the reason for the special meal.

Tiffany just continued to look like *Alice in Wonderland's* Cheshire Cat. *Super weird.*

"Good morning, Zera." The Toad looked up from his notepad over the top of his black-rimmed glasses. Zera groaned inwardly. He wore his pseudo-dad expression — serious, yet friendly.

It was harder to even think of him as "The Toad" lately. He had changed a lot since the opening at All-American Burger Depot. As they'd talked about during the ride home that night, The Toad and Tiffany began to focus on making big changes in Theodore's life. Zera noted that while he kept his vintage spectacles and watches, almost everything else about his appearance had changed. His fanatical working out had paid off. In just two months he'd dropped over thirty pounds and seemed determined, almost self-assured. *Although his dorkiness hasn't disappeared, and he still slouches over his notepad, he's different; a buffer, better dressed, more formidable Toad.*

"Good morning, Toa . . . Uncle Theodore."

"Got to get to the office early today." Her uncle pushed up his glasses with one finger before tapping it on the old silver timepiece around his wrist. "I'm on a tight schedule." He put the notepad into his briefcase.

Tiffany's brow furrowed as she looked him over. "I know just the shirt you should wear."

"This one's not okay?"

"Well, we do want to make the best impression possible, don't we?" Tiffany exuded cat-like confidence. "Trust me, I know what will be perfect. And you should wear the gray jacket, not that blue one."

The Toad adjusted the glasses again. "If you think so."

"Are you meeting someone important?" Zera asked.

"Actually, we both are," Tiffany said. "But it's not a subject you should be concerned with. What I mean is, you should concentrate on enjoying your breakfast."

So that's why she's acting so nice. The Toad has something going on. Maybe he's finally getting that promotion. She breathed a sigh of relief that Makeover Camp wasn't in the cards, at least not today, but didn't like how they were keeping awkward secrets.

Chapter Six

Theodore jogged alone in the running room at Biotech Multinational's gym. His legs, stronger from the weeks of intense exercise, pumped beneath him, his chest rose and fell in full, measured breaths, light perspiration beaded on his forehead below his dark shock of hair. He easily kept up with the moving floor of fake stone as the four walls surrounding him showed a landscape leafy and dappled in light.

Theodore passed the same grove of trees once every mile, and kept his eye on the glinting river far off in the distance. The river always sounded the same. It didn't roar, like the rapids on the Arkansas River, it was steady and melodic. Even so, it always reminded him of the Arkansas River, and his sister Sally's death. Sally and Ewan, killed in a flash flood that wouldn't have happened if the lands around the river had been preserved, instead of being stripped of trees and vegetation for mining. Of course their deaths also might have been avoided if the two were not such adrenaline junkies — always wanting to go out and do things like ride rapids, climb the highest peaks in Colorado, fly a single-engine plane, or spend weekends skiing black-diamond slopes. He'd teased Sally for being a "hippie," living in Ute Springs, being an artist and working on save-something causes all the time; that is, when she wasn't pushing her limits physically. They'd always argued good-naturedly; he on the side of progress, she questioning his definition of "progress," and yet she always let him know she adored her little brother.

He used to think about his sister's death every day, but since the evening at Burger Depot, life had changed. That night he'd made a decision that he would not be pulled down by his grief (which was not easy, given Zera's resemblance to Sally) or by feeling sorry for himself because his career wasn't going the way he planned. On that night, he formed a purpose. He would take *action.* And now, finally, it was paying off. He'd lost a lot of flab, and he kept a positive attitude most days. Today as he jogged, he whistled and thought over his itinerary. *I'll do my early morning workout, check in at the office, pick up my stuff, and then just walk out those doors.*

An attractive woman in a skimpy jogging outfit appeared behind him on the left wall. She ran up, passed him, then turned and smiled, a smile both encouraging and flirtatious. "You're doing *great.* Keep it up!"

Theodore smiled back at the holographic image, even though a second later he felt silly. His wristwatch buzzed — 7:50 A.M.

"I'm done," he said. The machine-room obeyed the comment. In tandem, the woman disappeared, and the walls and road slowed to a stop. A door, invisible in the moving landscape, became visible again and Theodore opened it into the rest of the gym.

After showering and changing, he returned to his cubicle. His desk now held only his computer, a framed Glamour-Girl holograph of Tiffany, and a school holograph of Zera. Theodore picked up Tiffany's picture. *I hope this works,* he thought, gazing at the image, *because I can't come back here. I've got to leave without saying anything.* He looked at Zera's picture. *I hope this is going to work out for you, too, kid.*

From over his cubicle wall, Theodore spied the top of Harv Headstrom's shiny head. He watched it bob down the corridor, approaching his office. *Probably making his third trip to the coffee bar this morning, or his third trip to the bathroom. I hope he doesn't stop to say hi.*

Harv peered over the five-foot-six-inch-tall cubicle wall, his caterpillar eyebrows hovering over bright brown eyes. "Hey Theo, how's it going?"

Theodore put the picture down and for the first time in a long time he smiled at Harv. "It's going *great*."

Harv's caterpillars reared up. "Yeah?"

Theodore nodded.

"Well, cool, it's about time!" Harv went around to the door of Theodore's office. "Wow, you really cleaned off your desk, I don't think I've ever seen it not buried."

"Uh . . . it was due," Theodore said flatly. He didn't want to encourage Harv to stick around.

"I was just heading down for a cup of joe, thought I'd say hi.

See you at the meeting before lunch."

Oh, no you won't, Theodore thought. Instead he said, "Later, Harv."

Burger Depot had turned out to be a huge hit, just as expected. Americo had opened five new restaurants since the grand opening, with ten more scheduled by the end of next year. And still, Theodore had received no recognition from Bob Cadger. He'd tried to talk to him, and had his appointment "rescheduled" numerous times. After a while, Theodore gave up.

He opened his briefcase. *So long Biotech Multinational,* he said to himself as he began to play over in his mind last night's dinner at *Chez Escargot.*

He and Tiffany had shared a candlelight dinner in the darkened, richly-decorated dining room just hours after Theodore got the news. Tiffany was surprised at the invitation to dinner and on their arrival at the restaurant purred, "What's the occasion, Theodore? I'm on pins and needles! Tell me!"

"You'll find out soon enough."

He waited until after dessert. Behind his glasses, Theodore's eyes shone as he pulled out from his breast pocket two airline tickets to Los Angeles. He laid them on the table and announced, "Tiffany, it's happened."

Tiffany picked up the tickets, then looked at Theodore. A hint of confusion, then disappointment, flickered in her eyes, as if she were expecting something else. "What . . . what's happened?"

"Somebody finally recognizes my worth. My potential." Theodore brought out his ever-present pocket computer. "I've received an offer from Void Chemical. You've heard me talk about them. We've been in contact almost since the time of the Burger Depot opening. They're bigger than Biotech. Way bigger." He started punching in numbers. "Tiffany, they want me as president of their Biotechnology Division, and — this is my starting salary." He handed the pad across the table. Tiffany's slender hand trembled as she took it. She peeked at the display. It read: *$ 900,000.00*.

"Oh–my–God!" She squealed and bounced up several inches in her chair. A few diners looked over and Tiffany flashed them a lottery winner's smile.

"Tomorrow I'm leaving Biotech and I'm not even giving them notice. I'm never going back. And that's just the beginning." Theodore's voice lowered, "We can get out of here. I'll finally have the chance to be all I'm destined to be."

"Theodore, I am so hap . . ." She stopped, looked at him wide-eyed. "You said 'we' . . . Does that mean . . ."

"Yep, no more slaving over equations and hypotheses while the powers that be take all the credit, and the money. Langston Void, the top CEO at Void Chemical Corporation, wants to meet me tomorrow, wants me to personally bring him the signed contract. I told him about you, how you encouraged me, and he invited you, too. He wants to meet you."

"You said 'we'll' before, Teddy . . . ," a hopeful eagerness brightened Tiffany's face. "Does this mean, well, that you might want to . . ." she looked around the room, "take our relationship to the next level?"

Theodore turned pale. He took a gulp of wine. He cared about Tiffany, but had no desire to even think about the "M" word. Before Sally and Ewan died, he and Tiffany had been on exactly two dates. Then she showed up the day after his sister's death. She'd read about it in the papers, wanted to comfort him. Before he knew it, she was a big part of his and Zera's lives. She'd been hinting at marriage for months, but he didn't know if he would ever be ready for that. His mother had been married three times; he just didn't believe in that institution. Yet he needed Tiffany's help with Zera, an area where he was clueless and she was confident, and he needed her enthusiasm. Tiffany's ambition and drive were contagious. More than anything, Theodore wanted to succeed, to be someone important, and Tiffany understood this like no one else.

"We both know I couldn't have done this without you, Tiff, and I do want you to come out with me to L.A. You've always said you'd like to maybe live out there someday, and I thought you could help me find a place to live. There's just so much going on, and if I get this job there will be a lot to figure out."

Tiffany flashed her eyes up at Theodore's. "I didn't mean to sound like I was pressuring you, but we've been together for a long time now. I just don't want you to forget that. That we're a *team.*" The last line hung in the air like a tease — and a threat.

"That I know." Theodore took another gulp of wine.

"Now," Tiffany said, "what are we going to do about Zera?"

In the cubicle, as Theodore put the holographic photos in his briefcase, he thought more about Tiffany's question. *What to do with Zera?* Once again his excitement over a new future, a future that finally involved serious money and status, dimmed. It was strange. He was elated yesterday, he thought it was the best day of his entire life, but the more he thought about it . . .

Zera has only a few more years until she's out of high school. It should be okay. Mom should be able to handle it, and if she can't she'll tell me. And Zera will be happier too.

Chapter Seven

During fourth period, Biology, Zera concentrated on doodling. She'd already filled up half her electronic biology book's memory with sketches of plants, and now, with her writing pen, she created a leafy, swirling vine that climbed up one side of the screen before twining around the word "Green." Flowers of all sizes sprung from the vine: sunflowers, carnations, lilies, and snapdragons. Zera penned in expressive faces — sweet, scowling, serious, funny — from cooing, smooth-faced baby flower buds to large, blowsy, wrinkled granny blossoms with drooping heads and withering petals. She tapped a button, and then touched her pen to flower after flower, coloring one pink, another lemon yellow, and another burnt orange.

Plants, she thought, as the teacher droned on, reviewing what would be on their final exam, *they supply almost everything.* Zera glanced at Ms. Casey, who drew a sprouting bean on the hologram board. Split in two, the bean had a hair-like root snaking downward in soil and a tiny stem and oval leaf reaching upward into the air. Zera looked around; most of the kids were as bored as she was. Biggie was repeatedly poking the tip of his pen into the bottom of one of his shoes, and Becky McGowan, sitting in the next aisle, just stared glassy-eyed at the teacher, her mouth half open. Abby was texting under her desk, probably Thor; she hadn't even looked at Zera since they got to class.

Zera thought about how Ms. Casey's lecture could be a lot more exciting; it was, after all, the birth of a plant, something of a miracle. Since the arrival of Sunny on her birthday, Zera had become obsessed with plants. They'd been a regular part of her life before coming to live with The Toad, but she had never really "seen" them or tried to understand them until she had her own. In the weeks since her birthday, Zera had absorbed dozens of books on houseplants, cacti, trees, bulbs, shrubs, herbs, wildflowers, grasses, and garden flowers. It seemed natural to her to seek out books, instead of reading them on the computer, and it took her a while to discover why she had that preference. She finally figured out it — it was because the books themselves were made out of plants; from the paper, to the ink, to the varnish on the covers.

Most of her free time was spent reading, learning about plants' uses, their art, and their history. She'd read fascinating accounts of plant explorers searching exotic countries, horrifying tales of women herbal healers in medieval Europe burned as witches, and modern discoveries in the field of plant intelligence. An old book she'd recently read, entitled *The Secret Life of Plants*, showed that plants had been found to react physically to the emotions and thoughts of *people*. She also read that Luther Burbank, the most famous plant breeder in the history of the

United States, had talked about the effect of human thought on plants over a hundred years ago, a half-century before the book came out. The topic thrilled and intrigued Zera. She planned on looking for more books that summer.

Coloring the flowers on her electronic book's notepad, her thoughts turned to Nonny. *Nonny would like this drawing. She'd probably think I was following in Mom's footsteps as an artist.* Though Nonny had sold the 150-year-old Green Seed Company when Zera was just a baby, and had never spoken much about it, Zera was now curious. *I'd like to ask her why she sold it. I never cared before, but now that I know something about plants . . .* A familiar longing filled her. Zera bore down harder on her pen, working on the leaves, filling them with color. *Three-and-a-half years since I've gotten to spend any real time with her. Why do Theodore and Tiffany have to be such jerks?*

"Ms. Casey," the intercom blared. "Please send Zera Green down to the office."

Zera looked up at her teacher and hurriedly capped her pens. She didn't see that all the flowers she'd drawn were now animated, engaged in soundless conversation, mouths working, eyes blinking, buds and petals nodding.

Ms. Casey checked the clock. "Since it's only a few minutes until lunch, you'll want to take your things with you."

Zera's heart thudded. Without looking at the notebook she turned it off. Nothing unusual had happened to her since March with the zinnia incident, which, as she expected, was soon forgotten. Even the kids forgot to call her Plant Chick after the break. *Did I do something wrong? Should I ask why? No, it might be embarrassing, or, worse, I might sound like a whiner.* She tried to look calm, as if it were no big deal, as she gathered her supplies. Her classmates stared, a few grinned. Biggie said, "Uh-oh" under his breath. Ms. Casey didn't hear it, but a couple of kids chuckled.

The trip down the long, brightly-lit hallways seemed to take forever. Zera saw no one, but could feel the mechanical stares of the digital surveillance cameras at each corner, red indicator lights glowing. Her sneakers made an empty slap-slap echo on the polished surface of the linoleum and the lemony smell of floor wax filled her nostrils. Her stomach felt queasy, partly from nerves, partly from the smell, as she shuffled past posters advertising the contents of the vending machines that stood like sentinels near the cafeteria. She glanced at a poster reading CAFE-COLA KEEPS YOU ALERT. It showed a bug-eyed boy sitting in the library with a history book, a geology book, a math book, *and* a can of Cafe-Cola, all opened in front of him. The HI-PROTEIN SQUIGGLES ARE A GREAT AFTER-SCHOOL SNACK poster showed a group of teenagers on the school steps. They laughed, heads thrown back, as if sharing a terrific joke, their hands plunged into bags of the bright-colored, chemically-flavored and vitamin-fortified, gummy-worm treats.

Eyeing another camera, Zera was gripped by self-consciousness. She shifted the notebook around and wiped her damp palms on the hips of her jeans, thinking of Tiffany's warning that her rock and roll T-shirts were "inappropriate for school." A comment which was inevitably followed with a smug, "I'm surprised they let you wear them." Without thinking, Zera brought her notebook to her chest, covering the flaming guitar logo on her Pyro T-shirt. When she realized what she had done her arms came down and her jaw clenched. *No. I love my T-shirts.* She had a whole trunk-full that belonged to her musician father; really old ones, featuring a variety of rock bands from The Beatles to the White Stripes. *They can't be calling me in to change my shirt, kids wear stuff like this all the time.* The only other thing she could think of was that something had happened to The Toad, or to Nonny. That last possibility, too horrible to consider, made her catch her breath.

Zera found the receptionist's desk empty and no one else in the office but Jake, the boy she'd embarrassed in the cafeteria during spring break. He was sitting in a chair next to the door, obviously waiting for his turn in the principal's office. He looked up at her, ran his fingers through his blond bangs. "Hi."

He doesn't hate me? The guilt over what she'd said to him in March had stuck with her. She blurted, "I'm sorry about that comment. About drugs."

To her surprise, he smiled. "It's cool. I shouldn't have said that to you. I say stupid stuff sometimes, that's why I'm here now." He locked eyes with her. "I just thought, well, those shirts you wear are pretty awesome."

"They belonged to my dad," Zera said, cringing inside as soon as the words left her mouth. *That's not awkward.*

"Yeah, I heard about that. Sorry." He hadn't looked away.

Zera couldn't help but notice how blue his eyes were. "Um, Tinsel told me to tell you to come on in when you showed up," he said. "She's going to 'deal with me' later." The grin broke out again. "Good luck."

"Uh, okay. Thanks."

Zera went to the principal's office door. *Yep, I am smooth.* She swallowed, and knocked.

"Come in," a welcoming voice called.

Zera cautiously opened the door to the sight of Principal Tinsel, sitting behind her desk, bestowing upon her the best Miss America smile ever. She waved Zera in. The too-big smile and friendly wave caused Zera to purposely bring up her notebook again to hide her shirt's logo.

She entered on rubbery legs, trying to have an expression more pleasant than worried.

"It's so good to see you again, Zera," Mrs. Tinsel said.

Zera was startled to see The Toad and Tiffany sitting in chairs across from Mrs. Tinsel's desk. Theodore nodded hello and Tiffany looked like she had that morning, only happier, if that were possible — the Cheshire Cat who had now swallowed the canary. Zera slowly let out the breath she'd held since entering the room, hoping no one noticed. *Okaaaay*, she thought. *The not-so-dynamic duo is here. No one looks upset. Whatever it is, it can't be too bad.*

"Hello," Zera took a couple of steps toward Mrs. Tinsel's desk. "Hi," she said to her uncle and Tiffany.

"Your uncle is here to take you out of school a few days early," the administrator announced. "I hear you're going to your grandmother's this summer."

What? Zera's heart thumped with joy and her stomach now felt like it was filled with fluttering butterflies. Thrilled butterflies, *free* butterflies. All she could do was stare at Mrs. Tinsel. "Nonny's?" She turned to The Toad and Tiffany. "Really?"

They nodded.

"We've made all the arrangements." Tiffany said. She rose gracefully from her seat. The Toad attempted to follow suit, but caught his jacket pocket on the arm of the wooden chair, pulling the entire chair forward with a screech. Everyone pretended not to notice as he un-snagged himself. "You just need to collect your things from your locker and turn in your books," said Tiffany, taking over for Mrs. Tinsel. "I even packed your suitcase for you."

The principal stood. "You had only one more final, tomorrow in Biology. Your work in that class has been the best we've seen here at Manning, so we don't really feel we're stretching the rules by letting you leave with an 'A.' Good luck with your new job, Mr. Green."

Zera looked at them both questioningly. Tiffany seemed in

competition to try to outshine Mrs. Tinsel's smile wattage while The Toad stood there, looking, if anything, a little uncomfortable.

"Thanks," he said, shaking Mrs. Tinsel's hand.

Fine. No explanation for the kid. Now I see what was going on this morning. The two of them were making big plans.

Jake nodded and smiled at her when she left. A few minutes later, just as the bell rang for lunch, Zera shuffled out of Manning High School behind The Toad and Tiffany.

"So, this job, it's a really good one?" she asked The Toad on the way to the parking lot.

"Yes, it is. But it's not finalized yet."

"When will you know?"

"Tomorrow."

"Is it in Colorado?"

"L.A."

"Los Angeles? Wow. So we'd be moving there? Or . . ." She didn't want to say it, ask if there was a possibility she might stay in Colorado with her grandmother.

Tiffany cut in. "Let's not talk about it right now. We're in a hurry."

Ignoring Tiffany, Zera asked, "And Nonny knows I'm coming? How long am I staying?"

"Your Uncle Theodore called her last night. We don't know exactly how long you may be with your grandmother this summer, but we'll let you know as soon as we know."

As soon as "we" know. Tiffany was always talking like they were married.

Heading toward Tiffany's car, Zera thought, *I don't know what's going on, but I couldn't care less right now. Getting back home is good and I'm going to see Nonny!*

Tiffany, sashaying directly in front of her, wore the pink shirt she had on at breakfast, accompanied with a tight black skirt, black leather flats, and a faux leopard-skin purse. A pink silk scarf covered most of her hair, and, to complete the weird 1950s-era movie star look, she put on a pair of cat-eyed sunglasses.

"Did you bring my plants?" Zera asked The Toad as they neared the convertible.

"Of course he did." Tiffany turned around to face Zera. "It would have been very inconvenient for us to find someone to take care of them as we'll both be out of town. We've had to do a lot this morning, Zera. I had to make at least a dozen calls just to get my work responsibilities in order!" She turned to The Toad. "I just thought of something else we'll have to figure out. Moving your things." She laughed. "Though you'll certainly be able to afford to replace most everything."

"Can I see them?" asked Zera.

Tiffany tossed her keys to The Toad. He caught them for a moment in one large warty hand, before fumbling and dropping them.

"It's the round one, right?" he asked, picking them up.

"Yes, Teddy."

He unlocked the trunk. It was filled with suitcases; two black ones that belonged to her uncle, her red plaid suitcase, and several large leopard-print ones, Tiffany's. Stuck in a corner was a cardboard box filled with plants. Sunny sat secure in her terrarium, in the middle of them all, cushioned by a thick towel.

Zera peeked into the terrarium and saw that one of Sunny's beautiful traps was brown. It looked burnt. She gritted her teeth at the sight. "What happened to her?"

Theodore leaned over to look, his expression puzzled. "Goodness. How did that . . .? Oh no." He turned to her, looking a bit pale. "It was me, Zera. After packing, but before loading the car, we were having lunch and I put very tiny piece of burg-fry in one of the traps. It must have been too much protein, and it burned it. I'm sorry."

Zera felt her face go hot with anger. It was bad enough that Tiffany had no doubt rummaged through her drawers, throwing her things into a suitcase, and probably making faces of disgust as she went through her clothes. *Now this. The Toad poisoned Sunny.* She glared at her uncle but almost instantly regretted it. He looked almost sick himself. The anger subsided. *She'll recover.*

The realization that she was going to see Nonny surfaced again. *I need to focus on how happy I am to be getting out of here.* The Toad must have been the one who had carefully packed the plants, and he'd done a good job of that. They were all cushioned, secure. She let her anger go and it sailed away like a dandelion seed on a breeze.

"Accidents happen, I guess," she said. "Could I have them in the back with me?"

"There's no way you're setting that cardboard box on *my* upholstery." Tiffany strolled over to the trunk and, with a bit more force than necessary, slammed it shut.

With Tiffany in the driver's seat, the trio headed west.

Chapter Eight

In the back of Tiffany's metallic gold convertible, which Zera had dubbed the Barbie-Mobile, Zera watched the suburban scenery speed by as rock music pounded through her silver hoop ear-tunes. She'd found the hoops in her jewelry case, in a bag on the back seat, along with a lunch sack holding a vitamin bar and a can of diet soda, Tiffany's idea of a sack lunch.

Zera glanced at Tiffany and her uncle. Tiffany had been chattering nonstop since the ride began. Zera tried to listen in earlier, but with the car's top down, it was impossible. She decided to listen to music instead.

Half an hour out, she texted Abby. Abby was the only thing that she'd miss in Piker (although Jake and his smile, and eyes, had flashed in her mind more than once since leaving the school). She hoped Abby would be a little disappointed that she'd left so unexpectedly. A few minutes later she received a reply: "Sad for me but SOOOO HAPPY 4 U!!! Hope u get 2 stay! Sorry haven't been around as much lately. Miss u already!" A panorama of grasslands replaced tract homes as they flew across cattle ranching country. Herds of cows, heads bent down to the grass, tails swishing, seemed oblivious to all but their world of sky and grass and biting flies. Zera wondered if any of them were destined to end up at American Burger Depot.

As the heavy metal beat of Metallica drummed in her ears, the landscape changed again. The car now climbed toward the towering peaks of the Rocky Mountains, the road winding through boulder-strewn meadows and forests of white-barked aspen trees mingling with fragrant pines. In some areas it was beautiful. In others, where they'd had wildfires over the last few years, blackened sticks of trees covered hundreds, sometimes thousands, of acres. The sight of that devastation made Zera shudder, especially when she thought of how Nonny said it was mostly due to global warming and that it would get worse. As she spotted the white tip of Pikes Peak, the tallest mountain in the Chipita Range west of Ute Springs, her mood changed again. A wave of happy anticipation coursed through her. *Home. It's been so long. Will it all be the same?*

Two hours after leaving Piker they arrived. Driving under the street-spanning "Welcome to Ute Springs" banner, Zera remembered that the small town had been named for its mineral springs. They were called "healing waters" by the Ute and other nearby Native American tribes who sought them out eons before white settlers arrived. Back then, the site had been a sacred place. Now it was a popular tourist town, though remnants of its mystical past clung to it. Many artists and musicians, including Zera's own parents, had made Ute Springs their home, and most of them said they could "feel the energy" in their surroundings.

As they drove into town via Ute Avenue, Zera took in the

familiar landmarks: brick and clapboard buildings lining the streets and hilly side roads, the town clock, cast iron streetlights that looked a hundred years old but were actually installed during the previous summer. Townspeople worked in flower-filled yards, walked down the sidewalks, visited with neighbors. She found herself smiling, and couldn't stop. There was Nell's Coffee House, on the corner of Ute and Pawnee. A huge coffee cup, made out of wood and tin with a swirl of carved steam, hung above the door. Across the street, on the roof of Doc Dennin's Western Wear, reared a full-size fiberglass palomino horse, golden with white mane and tail. The horse's mouth was open, as if snickering with the same glee that bubbled within her. She saw Sadie Hawkins' art gallery, the Carnival Arcade, the Hemp Shop, the Happy Goat Cheese Store, and the Hopi Age Bookstore. On Canyon Avenue was the burnt-orange tiled roof of her old brick elementary school. *It's all still the same!* Zera glanced up at The Toad and Tiffany, to make sure they weren't looking at her in the rear-view mirror. Years of memories flooded her mind, memories of her mother and father, her grandmother, her *home*.

They were driving slowly when she heard Tiffany's comment. "Here we are, Hippie Town."

"You know," quipped The Toad, "in New York City they like to carry Gucci bags, but in Ute Springs, they carry bags of goat cheese."

Tiffany laughed and Zera couldn't help cracking a grin in

spite of herself.

"It's been a while," said Tiffany.

"Yes, it has." Her uncle's expression was now somber. "Now, when I come into town, it always makes me think of . . . Sally and Ewan's memorial service."

"I remember it well," said Tiffany. "Guinevere nowhere to be found, off on one of her 'spiritual quests.' It's lucky you were there for Zera."

Zera stared hatefully at the back of Tiffany's blonde, ponytailed head. *Lucky?* she thought. *The only luck I've had since that day is right now, getting the chance to get away from you.*

The Toad made a left turn and the Barbie-Mobile crept up seven blocks of steep gravel road, past a candy box assortment of Victorian homes in various stages of grandness or dilapidation, to Nonny's home. Zera's home.

Hidden from the street by a wild tangle of chokecherry shrubs and evergreens, the property came into view as the car turned into the driveway. The landmark of the grounds was Cache Mountain, a nine hundred-foot-tall colossus in back of the two acres. The mountain gave the space a protected, nest-like feeling. A sense of well-being swept over Zera as the car edged into the driveway.

Details of her home always faded with absence, and it stirred her to see it again. Besides the main house, there were six other buildings on the property. Zera searched for the small, robin's-egg blue cottage with its attached greenhouse/solar energy collector. It had sat at the far north end of the property, barely visible from the driveway. This house, nestled amid apple, sour cherry, and plum trees, was Nonny's home, or at least it had been, when she wasn't "adventuring." But the house had been standing empty for a few years now. After Zera's parents died, Nonny had moved out of the cottage and into the main house so she could better take care of the dogs and chickens.

A trio of tiny buildings sat on the other side of the driveway. Once they'd been two-room vacation cottages, rented out to tourists, but by the time Nonny bought the property they'd been empty for years. One became a chicken house. At its door hung a sign Zera made when she was six, "Fresh Eggs," written in childish white letters on a green background and sprinkled with glitter. Her mom had praised her artistry. "It's perfect, honey, a *masterpiece*." Zera's mother had treated every piece of her artwork as if it were a Picasso or an O'Keeffe.

Next to the chicken coop was her mother's art studio, the lavender cottage. In front was a fountain, a seven-foot-tall metal flower. Below the petals four fairies had been welded to a rotating rim. As the sun-powered fountain ran, the fairies appeared to fly beneath the flower, just out of reach of the glittering "rain." Purple lilac shrubs grew on both sides of the doorway and were still in bloom.

The last cottage, painted pink and green, was Zera's childhood playhouse. On its small brick porch sat a life-size bronze figure of three-year-old Zera, chubby hands holding a bouquet of wildflowers.

Off in the distance sat a low-slung barn which was never used for livestock by their family, but had been used for parties and concerts. Another barn, this one taller and built of stone, stood near it: her father's music studio. Zera remembered playing outside as classical, jazz, or rock-and-roll music drifted from the building. Memories came in waves, crashing through her.

Tiffany stopped the convertible in front of the stucco main house. Two stories tall, it was painted barn red with a stained wood balcony extending across the front. The lower floor, dominated by a huge wrap-around porch, was furnished with comfortable wicker furniture and enclosed by rose-covered trellises. Hundreds of fat, pinkish-white buds swelled among the green leaves. Zera's mouth dropped open. *The roses, how could I have forgotten them? That perfume.* Without thinking, she took in a deep breath, as if she could smell them now, before they even opened.

Tiffany stopped the car and the front door of the home opened. Out flew Alice, Zera's Dalmatian.

"Alice, stop!" yelled Nonny, following Alice, but the command was useless. Alice leapt into the back seat and on top of Zera. Whining, the dog covered Zera's face with canine kisses. Alice increased her whining in volume when Zera cried out in pleasure.

Tiffany leapt out of the car and threw open the back door. "Oh, that dog. That dog!" she screamed. "She's probably scratching the upholstery! Out of my car! Now!"

"I can't get up," Zera said, laughing. "She won't let me."

Tiffany grabbed Alice's collar and Alice growled. Tiffany let go.

"Theodore, do something! *My upholstery!*"

Zera said, "I'll get her." She eased out the door, one hand on the dog's collar. Alice, pressed against her as if attached with glue, left the back seat happily.

"Good girl, Alice."

The dog whined in reply and stuck her nose firmly into Zera's palm.

Nonny, wearing a sunshine-yellow skirt and denim shirt, surveyed the scene from the porch, then, as fast as her turquoise-topped cane allowed, hop-hobbled down the stairs to her granddaughter. Cato, Nonny's elderly black Labrador retriever, accompanied her with a matching stiff-legged walk. Within seconds they were at Zera's side. Cato trembled with excitement at the sight of Zera, even while staying protectively next to Nonny.

"Hi, Cato!" Zera said. Nonny's hair, now completely white, shone in the sun. Although Zera had seen her a half-dozen times since she'd been living with The Toad, and through v-phone and v-mail many times, she still hadn't gotten used to the dramatic change of Nonny's now pure white hair and deeply-lined skin.

Nonny took Zera's heart-shaped face in her hands. She kissed both cheeks and then her forehead. "Zera Katherine . . . my angel. How I have missed you! Look at this, you're now taller than I am. And your hair has grown so long." Nonny brushed a strand from Zera's face.

"Nonny," said Zera. The word was muffled in a bear hug and Nonny's scent, a rich mixture of honey, sandalwood, and rose.

Nonny turned her attention to her son. The Toad gave his mother an awkward hug. As she squeezed him tight with one arm, she placed a generous smack of a kiss on his cheek. "It's so good to see you, Ted. You too, Tiffany. Goodness," she said, two fingers gently probing one of his biceps, "your arm is as big and hard as a tree branch. Have you been working out?"

The Toad looked embarrassed. "Yeah, actually I have."

Nonny raised her eyebrows. "It's certainly paying off." She took Zera's hand and began to lead her up the stairs. "Let's go in, honey." Over her shoulder she said to Theodore and Tiffany. "You two come on in. And, Tiffany, I'm so sorry. I do hope Alice hasn't left any nasty claw marks on your upholstery. Ted, maybe you should check the back seat, sometimes when Alice gets excited she tinkles just a bit . . ."

"Hummph." Tiffany straightened her black skirt. "Dogs!"

Nonny led Zera and Tiffany to the kitchen and offered them lemonade.

"No thanks," said Tiffany, as she eyed with distaste the big kitchen's glass-fronted cabinets crammed with dishes and the slightly-beat-up refrigerator. “We’ve only got a few minutes. We’ve got a plane to catch in Piker.”

“I have a couple of questions, Tiffany,” said Nonny. “Sit.”

Chapter Nine

After searching the back seat for traces of dog pee, Theodore unloaded Zera's belongings. *What if I don't see her again for a long time?* He'd grown used to having Zera in his life. Yes, she could be a brat, yes, she didn't like Tiffany, but he knew that underneath the acting up she was a good kid. Pangs of regret surged through him. *I see a lot of myself in her. The way she loves botany. The way I used to.* He picked up her suitcase, the box of plants. *Got to stay on task. I need to focus on what's happening today — with my career, with my future. This could be the biggest day in my life.*

He joined the women in the kitchen. "Your car's fine, Tiffany. No damage done."

Tiffany looked up from the table. "Good."

Nonny poured her son a glass of lemonade and motioned for him to sit next to her. Theodore sat down, took a big drink.

"Well, Ted," said Nonny, "I am just absolutely thrilled to have this child back, no matter what the circumstances. But I am a bit confused about your change of heart."

Theodore wiped lemonade off his mouth with the back of his hand. "I've been thinking of letting Zera come for a visit, a longer visit, for some time, Mom. We've certainly spoken about it before." Theodore looked around the room, avoiding her eyes. "It's just that circumstances haven't permitted it. Work . . . you know."

Nonny smiled pleasantly. "What you know is that I can smell b.s. a mile away."

Theodore squirmed inwardly and cast his eyes down. Not a good idea. The sight of his mother's prosthesis, visible below her skirt, made him queasy. The artificial but surprisingly lifelike limb ended in a sandaled foot, the color of the "skin" slightly different from her tanned flesh. He'd seen her only a half dozen times in the last few years, and each time he'd been jarred by the sight. It left him light-headed.

He took a deep breath and tried to focus. The whole atmosphere of Ute Springs, the place where he had grown up, had him off-kilter. As he walked in the door, the sense of time standing still had nearly overwhelmed him. Nothing had changed; furniture in the same places, same pictures on the wall. It even smelled the same. June in Ute Springs. He still felt like a boy, like a kid who had to prove himself, who might never be good enough. "To tell you the truth, like I told you last night, Mother, I thought we'd try it out — letting her stay here for the summer. But, as I mentioned over the phone, we, I, I think she should find some kind of summer employment, just a few hours a day, something to reinforce a sense of responsibility."

The speech sounded phony even to him, but that was okay. He could tell by the glint in his mother's eyes that she was fighting back saying plenty about what she thought of his behavior these past three years. But since she was so thrilled to have her granddaughter back, he knew she wouldn't ask too many questions. It would work; Zera staying here, for at least a little while.

An idea came to him. When he mentioned summer employment, a memory of when he'd been the closest to a joyful life, came to him. He blurted out the idea. "Maybe she could find a part-time job at that amusement park up the pass?"

"The North Pole? Yes, I remember when you worked there as a teenager." Nonny paused for a long moment, as if she too were thinking about those days. Her brow furrowed and she sighed. "So that's it? The same story you told me last night?"

"That's the story," Theodore and Tiffany said in unison. They flashed each other a startled look. Tiffany nodded at Theodore in a not-so-discreet way toward the direction of her car outside.

"And you don't know how long she'll be staying?" asked Nonny.

"Not yet. I have a meeting in L.A. late this afternoon, and then we'll have a better idea."

"We'll?" said Nonny.

Theodore checked his vintage silver wristwatch. "Mom, I can't stay. I'll call you as soon as I know. You have my phone number, and I've written down where I can be reached, if there are any, um, emergencies or anything."

Theodore stood and fumbled through his wallet, looking for the number. As he did he brushed the ragged corner of an old paper photograph, hidden behind some credit cards. He saw the photo in his mind for a moment, and he thought of *her*, the girl he loved when he was a young man, living in this house. *It doesn't seem like so long ago* . . . It took an effort to redirect his mind to the business at hand, rifle through the rest of the wallet, and find the slip of paper.

He handed it to Nonny. Tiffany got up and headed for the door.

"Ted, there's something I have to tell you before you go," Nonny grabbed her cane and made her way up. "I made plans some time ago to spend most of this summer in the Amazon, visiting the Kayapo Indians in Brazil. I'm scheduled to leave in three weeks."

Theodore didn't move. Zera stared at her grandmother. *She has not changed,* Theodore thought. *I thought she was taking it easy, taking care of herself . . . and she's traveling again?* "The Amazon? But what about your . . . leg?"

"Can't let a thing like that stop me. Don't worry, I get around fine. It'll be fine, the Kayapos are very . . ."

Theodore interrupted her, "I'll call you as soon as I know."

Chapter Ten

Zera and her grandmother watched the Barbie-Mobile's gold rear-end disappear from the driveway, leaving a trail of dust.

Zera put her cupped hands to her mouth. "Good-bye!" she yelled.

Nonny laughed. "Those two." She slipped her arm around Zera's shoulders, "Phony baloney all the way through. I guess I'll have to get the story from you, if you know it."

Zera shrugged. "I don't know a thing, except it seems like he might be getting a great new job. I think it's an interview. This has all been a surprise to me too." *As is learning that you're leaving in three weeks*, she added to herself, her heart sinking, *Just when I get back. Then what?*

"We won't worry ourselves about it. Not now at least." Turning to go back inside, Nonny Green spied the box of plants sitting on the porch next to Zera's suitcases. "What a lovely collection of plants! And your *Dionea muscipula* has really grown." She peered closer and made a face. "She looks marvelous, except for that one burned trap. What on earth happened?"

Zera and her grandmother sat close together on the front porch's big wicker swing and talked all afternoon. They cried a little, remembering Sally and Ewan and how they missed them, yet, at the same time, always felt their presence. They laughed, remembering the good times.

Zera's head rested on Nonny's shoulder. Her eyes went to the heavy silver bracelet encircling Nonny's left wrist. It was engraved with thick leaves, interspersed with strange symbols that Nonny once told her were some kind of Celtic tree alphabet. Nonny said she didn't know what the symbols meant, that the bracelet was a family heirloom. Just seeing it brought another good feeling; she'd never seen Nonny without it. The closeness of the moment made her think about something she'd wanted to ask Nonny for a long time.

"When you lost your leg in Tibet," she began, in a voice barely above a whisper. "Theodore and Tiffany said you fell off a mountain." She looked up into her grandmother's dark blue eyes. "I never asked you about it, and you've never really told me what happened either . . ."

Nonny smiled, rubbed Zera's hand. "Never be reluctant to ask me anything, or tell me anything. Life's too short."

Nonny told Zera that yes, she'd been in Tibet, after finishing a three-month stay at a Buddhist monastery.

"I was trekking across the Himalayas, on my way to India. A young guide named Hani accompanied me." Nonny looked off into the distance, as if searching for that time again. "We were going across a narrow mountain passage when my donkey — Daisy, I'd named her — was spooked by a snake, a Himalayan pit viper. Daisy lost her footing and we both went down an eighty-foot ravine."

"Oh, no." Zera didn't realize she was squeezing her grandmother's hand. "Sorry."

Nonny's gaze focused on the mountains. Zera, too, observed the silent giants and felt that they were listening, and waiting for Nonny to continue. The day had turned dark and cloudy and the smell of an afternoon thundershower hung in the air. Nonny's far-away look disappeared with a nod of her head. "Daisy didn't make it, the poor dear, but I was luckier. Hani was so incredibly brave! He risked his life getting me up the side of that cliff. I had a concussion, four broken ribs, and a shattered left leg."

Zera sucked in her breath at the picture of Nonny, crumpled and broken. Nonny continued, "Somehow he got me to the closest village, and there I stayed, first fighting off a terrible infection in my leg. Ultimately, there was just too much damage. They got me to a hospital and the leg had to go. Then began the long process of healing."

"That's why they couldn't find you for so long after Mom and Dad died."

"At first they couldn't send word about what happened to me because all my identification and money, in my backpack, had been lost during the fall. But the hospital was in the city. I was there, recuperating, when I heard about your mom and Ewan."

"It must have been horrible! Stuck there."

Nonny was silent and Zera knew something was off. "Darling, I wasn't exactly stuck there," said Nonny. "My leg was gone, but I'd been in the hospital a month when Sally and Ewan died. I thought Tiffany probably told you; I could have gotten home for the funeral."

"What?" Zera couldn't believe what Nonny was saying.

"I couldn't face it."

"I don't understand."

"It was too much. I'd just lost a limb, then a daughter and a son-in-law. I felt like I had nothing left. Coming home was not going to bring them back." She hugged Zera. "I can't imagine what you think of me."

I needed you, thought Zera. *I needed you so much! You still had us. Me and your son!* She said, instead, "It was hard for me."

"I know, dear, I know. I am so sorry. It's no wonder Tiffany steamrolled the custody thing, influencing Ted not to even consider me as a guardian because of my artificial leg." Her brow furrowed.

"Tiffany wants to marry Uncle Theodore, but I don't think he feels the same," mumbled Zera. Her mind was reeling from the disclosure; everything seemed wrong. *How could she stay away?*

"It doesn't hurt?" She gestured to her grandmother's leg.

"Not usually. Sometimes I still get 'ghost' pains, but not often. It's strange because it still feels like it's there, sometimes it still itches. Those odd amputee things you hear are true, I can attest to them. But there are benefits too." She winked. "Now I can go as a peg-legged pirate on Halloween, something I've *always* had a secret longing to do."

Zera didn't feel like laughing, but she gave her grandmother a smile.

A rumble of thunder sounded in the distance and within seconds a flash of lightning ripped through the sky at the base of the mountains. Cato, lying a few feet from the porch swing seemed oblivious (the poor guy was mostly deaf), but Alice started to whine. Drops began pelting the metal porch roof.

"Let's go in," said Nonny.

After a dinner of pasta salad, Zera confessed to Nonny something was bothering her. "It's about Theodore. I feel kind of bad about it now. He is your son and my uncle . . ." Zera stalled, carrying their dishes to the sink. Her heart beat a little faster as she hoped Nonny wouldn't think she was awful. "When he got fat, I nicknamed him." She blurted it out, "I nicknamed him 'The Toad.'"

"Hmmm." Nonny hobbled over to Zera and patted her hand. "A sometimes inappropriate sense of humor runs in this family. He's kept us apart for three years, and that's hard to forgive. Most people spend their lives fighting their inner dragons; it's sometimes not easy to tell what lies in their hearts. And we've all been grieving, and grieving is different for every person and can be a long process. I'm just thankful you found ways to keep that sense of humor through all this! Even if it is a little mean." She looked away for a moment. "You know, I always told him all he had to do to get rid of those warts for good was rub a raw potato on them and bury it under a tree during a full moon. But he never believed that. I noticed he still has them."

Zera didn't say anything. She'd heard Tiffany mention "Nonny's Weird Wart Cure" once, when her uncle was thinking of following those very instructions. It had caused an argument, ending with Tiffany vowing to never take him seriously as a scientist if he considered it. To Zera, the wart cure sounded strange, but she'd read a lot in books lately about things that seemed impossible; it pushed her to keep an open mind.

"Maybe I called him that because Tiffany hated my name. She said Zera sounded like a gypsy or something. When Uncle Theodore told her it meant 'seed' in Hebrew she thought that was even weirder." Zera shut the utensil drawer a little too hard.

Nonny shook her head and frowned. "I remember you v-mailing me about that. That she even suggested you change it, a little while after you moved in?"

"She kept hinting, telling me I could 'reinvent' myself if I wanted to, have a 'new start,' a name I picked out if I wanted. I was thirteen years old! Uncle Theodore got so mad. Then she dropped it."

Finished with the dishes, the two walked over to the window to watch the rain, which had slowed to a soft shower. "Tiffany's also mentioned how 'bizarre' it was that Dad took Mom's last name when they married. She said she couldn't understand why any man would take his wife's surname. She always acts like the Green family is made up of the world's biggest weirdos."

"It's a pity Tiffany doesn't have a better imagination. Maybe we are kooky. So what? I once heard a story about a woman who lived alone most of her life on a small island off the coast of Scotland. She spent her life studying plants and made several important discoveries. One day a journalist, interviewing her, said he'd heard her called a crack-pot by one of the townspeople. Well, this lady looked the journalist right in the eye and said, 'Perhaps you've got to be a little cracked to let the light come through.'"

Nonny laughed. "We should put that on a family crest. I just wish you could have known Ted when he was younger. Before his father died. You know Ted's father was much older than I, don't you?"

Zera nodded.

"He was twenty years older, Zera. It was so hard on Ted, losing his father when he was only eight years old. Sally was seventeen, and she had a hard time too, but Ted was devastated." Nonny's eyes softened and a darkness swept over her features for a moment. "Well, did you think up one for Tiffany? A nickname?"

"No," Zera said, still a bit embarrassed. *None I can say out loud, anyway.*

After the rain stopped, Zera went back outside alone. No more than five steps away from the porch, Nonny's Siamese cat, Merlin, surprised her by leaping out of a lilac bush. He circled around her ankles, purring.

"Merlin, how you've grown! Where have you been?" She picked up the cat and nuzzled him. *Mmm. Hay. Definitely the barn.* Merlin closed his blue eyes and purred louder.

Zera put him back on the ground and began to walk down the long gravel driveway, checking out the gardens on both sides. Dusk was her favorite time of day, when all the colors looked intense, and tonight the air smelled fresh and sweet from the rain. Zera breathed in deeply, savoring that sweetness. Looking around, she noticed a tingling sensation going through her, the unmistakable feeling of *déjà vu*. For a moment everything looked as it had before, years before. *How can it be possible that everything looks the same; the vegetable garden, even the window boxes on the cottages? It's like I've been in this exact moment; even the air smells the same.*

As she neared the chicken house the odd feeling grew, and she also had the distinct sensation that someone was watching her. Her eyes went immediately to the vine-covered side of the cottage. *That was weird, the light seemed to shift. It looked like a . . . that's silly, for a moment I thought I saw a face.* She checked above her, expecting to find dark clouds that had changed the light. No, everything was the same. She shook off the impression. As she got nearer, it was obvious; nothing *could* be there but the vines. *All the excitement, and I'm getting tired, I guess.*

Zera entered the coop and recognized two hens, Flora, the golden Silkie, whose barbless feathers were fluffy, almost like fur, and Athena, the auburn Rhode Island Red. "Hi, ladies," Zera said. The hens sat calmly on their nests, following Zera's every move with tiny, bright eyes. Nonny had said they still had about a dozen bantam, or miniature, hens in all, but most were still out in the garden, scratching for bugs or taking a few more dainty pecks off weeds and vegetable leaves before bedtime.

With a jolt, Zera recognized a plant in its hanger near the window. A fuchsia, with dark green leaves and hot pink and white drooping flowers, bloomed as one had years ago in the very same spot. *Where did Nonny find one just the same?* She remembered something about the plant from one of her books. Over a hundred years ago, back in the Victorian Era, the plant was nicknamed "lady's eardrops." *It fits. They look like old-fashioned dangling earrings. But I'm sure it's not the same plant that Mom bought. It would have grown too large.* She touched one of the velvety flowers and it swayed.

Thinking of her mom and how they'd taken care of the chickens together brought an emptiness that Nonny could never fill, no matter how great it was to see her again. Zera directed her attention back toward the chickens. *It's funny that they didn't cackle when I came in. Normally, their feathers would be ruffled when someone unfamiliar entered their territory. But they're acting as if they remember me too, just like Merlin did, as if I'd never left.*

Zera turned to leave. Behind her the blossoms on the fuchsia vibrated and swayed, all on their own, excited by an unknown energy.

Shutting the door to the chicken house, Zera headed to the barn. Out of sight, on the vine-covered side of the chicken house, something stirred. A green countenance, a male face made of leaves, an entity both human and vegetable, watched Zera. The face of leaves wore an expression of kindness and gentleness, ancient wisdom and ancient songs, songs older to the world than the human race. The Green Man smiled.

Zera stopped, turned around. *Was that . . . a face? No, silly. You're just jumpy, imagining things, because it feels so unreal to be home!* But she definitely heard something, *felt* something. A faint murmur in the leaves and grass, a tender rustling of leaves in the breeze, and the distinct feeling of being watched. She looked all around her, strained to listen. *A voice, voices even. I can almost hear them. Almost.* That particular sensation of being watched by a loving gaze was one she knew. She'd experienced the sensation many times as a child, often while playing outside. And each time she would look up to find her dad, or mom, or both, watching from a window, or elsewhere.

She turned around expectantly, and searched the windows of the house. Blind eyes reflected light, but there was no one there. She turned to the vine-covered coop, blinked. *It's just leaves, you weirdo. Wow, it's not like me to be spooked by chickens, a fuchsia.* She took a deep breath, rubbed her goose bump-covered arms. *It's getting late, the temperature's dropping. I'm freaking out from being back home; I'm imagining all these things. It's because I'm wishing Mom and Dad were here, too.*

Shaking it off, Zera made her way to the barn, walked around, peeked in the windows, and then headed back.

Relaxing again on the porch swing before bedtime, watching a nearly full moon rise in the east above the house, Zera asked her grandmother how everything managed to stay the same.

"Honey, your mother and father had a lot of friends in this small town, people who truly loved them, and who love us. While we were away, those friends saw to it that everything was taken care of. They continue to help me out a lot. And Hattie Goodacre has been a godsend."

"Mom always loved Hattie," said Zera, imagining the tall, exuberant woman. "She was her best friend."

"Hattie keeps this property up, now, as far as the plants. She comes for half a day on Saturday, usually with Ben, if he doesn't have school work."

Zera nodded.

"And of course you remember Cosmic Dan?" said Nonny. "Well, anytime I need house repairs, he's there. You would not believe the love that surrounded me when I returned home and the support I've had these three years. Incredible."

It was nearly midnight when Zera and Nonny went to bed.

Zera kissed her grandmother goodnight and climbed the stairs to her bedroom. It, too, was exactly as she left it. One side of the room had a reading and study area with a computer. On the floor in front of the bookshelves her father built was a multi-colored braided rug, and upon it sat an antique desk and chair. A table and two chairs upholstered in a chenille fabric of colorful peacocks on a white background stood near the windows.

In the other half of the room was a brass bed covered with a floral quilt, an oak dresser with an oval mirror, and shelves filled with musical instruments, dolls, and toys. The walls were papered in a pattern of large cabbage roses in pinks, reds, yellows and whites, their twining leaves and stems in three shades of green.

It's been so long, thought Zera. She looked at the cloth and china dolls lining one shelf. *I was still a kid. But just who am I now?*

She put on a white cotton nightgown and climbed into bed. As she lay there under the covers, she looked up at a ceiling that twinkled with glow-in-the-dark painted constellations — yet another memory of her mother.

She started thinking about what Nonny had said, about going off to South America in a few weeks. *She didn't know I was coming until yesterday*, Zera reminded herself. Then she thought of Nonny saying that she actually could have come to the funeral but didn't. "Everyone's different, has different needs," her grandmother had said. Still, the hurt of it all seeped in. She heard

Tiffany's voice, in the car, *"Guinevere was nowhere to be found, off on yet another one of her 'spiritual quests.' It's lucky you were there for Zera."*

Nonny had always been a big part of her life, but now Zera remembered that Nonny had been gone a lot. *Most of the time,* Zera admitted. Zera also remembered her mother saying that when she and Ted were kids, their mother had been gone a lot, though she hadn't given any details. *Did I finally make it back just to be left again? Couldn't Nonny change her plans this once?* She was home, but felt lonelier than ever.

As she began to drift to sleep, soft words echoed in Zera's ears.

"Welcome back . . . you're home now."

The voice was soft, sweet and feminine, both familiar and comforting. Zera was so close to sleep that she only half heard it, like a whisper in a dream. It came from the corner, from the top of her suitcase — where Zera had placed her box of plants.

Chapter Eleven

"I thought they'd have a chauffeur waiting for us when we got off the plane," Tiffany complained, "with a sign saying, 'Void Corporation for Mr. Theodore Green.'" Her eyes searched the crowd. "I don't get this. I suppose we should go get our luggage."

Theodore's gut clenched. She was anxious, and so was he, but here she was, as usual, Tiffany worrying about Tiffany. She'd even changed clothes in the plane while making several passengers wait to use the bathroom. *You'd think she was the one getting a new career.*

Theodore shrugged. "We just got off the plane a minute ago. There are hundreds of people here, let's just . . ."

"Mr. Green and Ms. Taylor, I presume?"

A tall man with dark hair and green eyes moved toward them and all the females in the vicinity turned his way. Thanks to Tiffany's ongoing fashion lessons (lessons Theodore didn't have an interest in but nevertheless learned from), Theodore noticed that the man wore a very expensive Italian designer suit. He stopped in front of them. Tiffany's eyes were glued to this man. She looked flustered and one hand flew up to her chin for a moment. Although Theodore didn't usually notice what other men looked like, he knew one thing from the female five-alarm reaction around him — this one was very handsome.

Before Theodore could answer, Tiffany threw back her shoulders and beamed, "Yes! We are Mr. Green and Ms. Taylor, I mean."

The man extended a muscular hand. "I'm Langston Void."

"Pleased to meet you, sir," said Theodore, shaking it. "This is my girlfriend, Tiffany Taylor."

Void took Tiffany's hand and brought it to his lips, bestowing a kiss. "Ms. Taylor."

Theodore adjusted his glasses. *That's a little weird.* He could tell Tiffany didn't mind. Her makeup did little to hide the genuine flush now staining her cheeks.

"I'm so pleased to meet you!" she gushed. "Theodore told me all about you. Please call me Tiffany."

"What a lovely name. Just like the jewelry store."

"That's where it came from." A girly giggle burbled out of her.

Void appeared not to notice. "Please, both of you, call me Langston," he said warmly. "Let's pick up your luggage. Our limousine is waiting. I'll be escorting you to your room at The Grand, where you two can freshen up before dinner at The Posh."

As they followed him outside, Tiffany grabbed Theodore's hand and squeezed it. "Don't you think he looks like a famous movie star, Theodore?" she whispered. "Can you believe it — a limo, The Grand, The Posh? This is like *a dream*."

Sure isn't Biotech International, thought Theodore. He was quite pleased that the CEO of Void Chemical Corporation had come out personally to meet him.

Thirty minutes later they arrived at their suite on the top floor of The Grand. Gilded and silk-upholstered furniture, crystal chandeliers, and marble fireplaces decorated the suite, and on the balcony was a fountain — with not one, not two, but three peeing cherubs. A satin-bow wrapped box of chocolates sat on the coffee table, compliments of Void Chemical Corporation.

Tiffany ran through the rooms, exclaiming over the toiletries, "They're full size!" the fake flowers, "Gorgeous! And they smell like those samples you get in magazines!" the fully-stocked wet bar, "They even have Skinny 2000 — can you believe it?" and the box of chocolates in their white satin box, "Modiva! The most expensive chocolates in the world!"

Minutes later, as they stood on the balcony looking at the city skyline, Tiffany sighed deeply, her lips pulled down in a kittenish sulk. "Teddy, I'm worried. I don't know if my clothes are going to be, well, good enough for dinner at The Posh."

Theodore fumbled in the breast pocket of his jacket and pulled out a small gold-colored envelope. "Langston gave me this in the limo when I handed him the signed contract. There's a boutique downstairs, maybe you'd like to check it out."

The sparkle returned to Tiffany's eyes as she opened the

small envelope. It held a Titanium American Excess card, printed with the company name and the name of Theodore Francis Green.

"Just put whatever you need on my bill. Heck, buy a new dress. But watch it when you go out," Theodore cautioned, "the limit is only one hundred. One hundred *thousand.*"

Tiffany threw her arms around Theodore's neck, and kissed him on the cheek. "Who would have ever imagined. Tiffany Taylor, the poor kid from Rosemont High, in the best hotel in L.A., about to go to the best restaurant in L.A! This is the happiest day of my life!"

"You look *amazing,*" Langston said.

Tiffany's giggle returned as Langston complimented her on her new outfit, a hot pink, strapless, sequined gown with matching shoes and bag. Theodore, standing beside her in the tuxedo that had been waiting for him in his room, had never felt more dressed up. Round, gold-framed eyeglasses and a matching gold watch were his stylish, though quirky, Tiffany-chosen accessories. Langston, also in a tux, looked like the leading man in an old Hollywood musical. Theodore half-expected him to break out in song or dance as he introduced his group to the "guests of honor" at the celebration dinner: his stunning, blonde date, Crystal, a Monica's Secret underwear model; Troy Sylvan, the head of Void's Research and Development department, described by Langston as "my right-hand man"; and Troy's gorgeous, red-haired date, Zirconia, whom Theodore was sure he'd seen on television, though he couldn't remember quite where. Out of the four of them, only Troy, a short, few-pounds-overweight man with sharp facial features, a black goatee, and longish blond hair pulled into a ponytail, stood out as a non-beautiful person.

"That's a fabulous dress, Tiffany," Crystal said.

Tiffany smiled winningly. "Thank you."

Always a little uncomfortable in social situations, Theodore was glad the initial attention was mostly on Tiffany and not him. *It's a good thing she came along*, he thought. *I may have the job, but I sure don't want to get started off on the wrong foot.*

The headwaiter appeared. "Your table is ready," he announced. He seated them all at a marble-topped, candlelit table near a window overlooking the lights of the Hollywood Hills. "Your waiter will be here shortly."

"Looks like the best seat in the house," Theodore said.

"It is." Langston carefully took his napkin and unfolded it, placing it on his lap. "I hope you don't mind that I've taken the liberty of ordering for us all. We'll be having the Star Gala, a dinner The Posh prepares only for its most special guests, all in celebration of our new president of VCCs Biotechnology Division."

"Wow," said Theodore.

"It sounds wonderful," Tiffany said. Under the table, she reached for one of Theodore's hands and gave it a little squeeze, her code for, "You could have said something a little better than 'Wow.'" The hand-squeeze made Theodore think about how he'd had his warts burned off again just two weeks ago and was already getting bumps.

The waiter came out with three kinds of caviar and creamed turtle eggs on crunchy toast to accompany plates of oysters and shrimp. He clapped his hands three times, and a fountain in the form of a two-foot-high mermaid rose from the center of the table. Applause broke out as champagne streamed from her conch shell and the waiter filled glasses for them all.

"To Theodore," said Troy.

They all clinked classes in a toast.

"I think these turtles just might be on the endangered species list," Langston stage-whispered, before popping a piece of egg and toast into his mouth with gusto. Everyone chuckled.

Troy, a bit of egg lodged on his black goatee, laughed the loudest; a merry, high-pitched laugh that, along with the goatee, made Theodore think of that goatish Greek god, Pan. "You're too much," Troy said to Void.

The cream o' truffle soup was followed by lobster tails in puddles of sherry cream sauce sprinkled with herbs and thin broiled slices of rabbit and ostrich. The main course featured thinly sliced, rare veal surrounded by steamed vegetables of green and orange carved into the shapes of huge gemstones. Star-shaped potatoes had the restaurant's name written on them in letters of melted butter.

"My, I think we've tasted about five types of animals!" said Crystal.

"Six," said Langston.

For the next course, Bradley brought a tray of imported cheeses and then rolled out a silver cart carrying a miniature tree, covered with dark cherry-red fruits the size and shape of small pears.

"Oh my," said Tiffany. "Is this Theodore's tree?"

"Sure is," Langston said. "It's a pherry tree."

A thrill went through Theodore.

"Mmm, pherries. My favorite!" exclaimed Crystal. "I buy them all the time at the market."

Behind his gold-framed glasses, Theodore eyed the tree. "Wow," he said, regretting the word as soon as he said it. "I mean, I remember doing the work for this cross-breeding during grad school. The patent sale paid for a new car. That was almost a decade ago. I knew pherries were available in California, but they're not in Colorado yet."

"They've been in L.A. for six months," said Crystal. "They have a hard time keeping them in stock; they're always sold out!"

"Such an interesting name," said Troy. "Pherries. Like the little flying fairies." His thin lips curved upward. "Did the fairies help you out on this one, Theodore?"

"Not that I know of," said Theodore, grinning. "I'm a man of science."

"I'll drink to that." Langston raised his glass. "To science."

"To science!" The crystal rang musically as the group clinked their glasses once more.

They hand-picked their pherries and declared them perfect.

For dessert, a flaming rum dish, Chocolate Revelry, was prepared at the table. Everyone agreed the luscious combination of chocolate, cake, whipped cream, and two kinds of rum, was divine. Finally they shared a rare blend of coffee, grown on a special mountaintop in Hawaii and fertilized by only the guano of rare, endangered, tropical birds.

Tiffany oohed and ahhed at each presentation, while Theodore felt like a fish out of water. He had never had this much attention, ever. He used his best table manners, just as Tiffany had coached him, making only one false step, when he accidentally splashed champagne from his glass during a toast. Langston had thought it funny and splashed a little out of his, too. Troy followed, roaring with laughter. The women raised their eyebrows over the childishness, but laughed too.

On the subject of biotechnology, Theodore found both men hanging on his every word. Langston said, several times, "Theodore, we've been looking for someone like you for a *long* time," and Troy nodded in agreement. While the swirl of the women's conversation — on shopping, restaurants, and celebrity gossip — played in the background, Langston and Troy sat enthralled, listening to Theodore's theories on the future of gene-splicing.

"You will not believe it Friday, when you visit the laboratory," Troy said to Theodore over coffee. "We are working on projects that are going to make what's been done in the biotech arena look like child's play."

His date, Zirconia, who had stopped talking to Tiffany about shopping long enough to pay attention, nodded, and her long red curls bounced like Slinkies. "But I heard it's top secret, so you can't talk about it here," she said, placing a crimson-tipped finger to her crimson lips.

Looks like she's had a little too much champagne, thought Theodore. "I can't wait to see it," he told Troy.

Troy dabbed his goatee with a napkin. "Langston, now that Theodore is president of VCC's Biotech Division, we'll let him in on *all* the secrets."

"If we're going to the lab Friday, I guess tomorrow I'll get set up in my office?" Theodore asked.

"Oh no," Langston said. "No reason to rush. We're going to have a little fun first."

"Excellent!" exclaimed Tiffany, who was obviously feeling the effects of the champagne as well.

Void gave Tiffany a green-eyed wink. "It's enough to make even me giddy at times."

Back at the hotel, Tiffany told Theodore about a conversation she'd had with Crystal during a trip to "the little girl's room."

"She was really nice, Theodore. She asked how long we'd

known each other, and she said we'd all get to be great friends!" Tiffany kicked off her shoes, went over to the sofa. "They really like you."

The way she said "they really like you" grated on Theodore's nerves. He was happy the night was a success, but Tiffany always had this surprised attitude when things went well for him.

"And guess what I found out?" Tiffany asked. "It's quite the shocker."

"Hmm?" Theodore, taking off his tuxedo jacket and hanging it over a chair, went to get a glass of water at the bar.

"I made a comment about Langston, how I had a lot of experience in cosmetics and studying facial structures, and that I'd noticed that Langston was just so incredibly attractive."

Pouring a glass of water, Theodore yawned. *Doesn't sound like a shocker to me.*

"I told her that Langston reminded me of an actor, but I couldn't quite put my finger on it and she said, now Theodore, get this: 'A little Nicky Wayne, the nose and the chin, and a little Robert Ransom, the eyes and the lips.' Theodore, he's had a lot of plastic surgery!"

The information didn't compute with Theodore. "Was he in some kind of accident or something?"

Tiffany laughed. "No, silly. Crystal said before the surgery he was all money and brains, no looks at all! Well, he had an okay body, but his face was just . . . yuck. Crystal worked at

VCC before she became a model and said that his dad used to make fun of him all the time, when Langston worked as a scientist. So after he died, Langston had all this surgery."

Theodore felt a little ill. Sure, plastic surgery was something every celebrity out there was doing, not to mention scads of wealthy and even not-so-wealthy people, but Langston, changing most of his facial features? *Beyond strange*. He felt like he'd spent several hours with someone who was partially a . . . a hoax. "That's really weird."

"Oh, Theodore, you're just hopelessly old-fashioned."

"Maybe. But I just wasn't raised to be comfortable with those kinds of things. You said Crystal worked at Void Corporation?"

"For a while. She was Langston's dad's secretary. But after he died, she got into modeling and then started dating Langston. That was a couple of years ago."

Theodore shook his head. "I can't get over it. Plastic surgery."

"He's just trying to improve himself. Crystal said he had a pretty tough life. That his parents split up when he was a baby and he never saw his mother again. His father was pretty mean. Crystal said she's also had work done, and so has Zirconia."

"That doesn't surprise me."

"Everyone does it here. I wouldn't mind doing something about, you know, this double chin."

"Tiffany, your chin is fine. Please don't get sucked into that mentality. And not everyone does it here. Troy Sylvan doesn't."

"Crystal said he's the odd man out. That she's always fixing him up with models, but he never seems to date any of them for long."

"Hmm." *The term La-La Land entered Theodore's mind, and not for not the first time that day.* "That doesn't mean a lot. One thing's for sure, we're not in Kansas, I mean Colorado, anymore, Tiff."

"That's for sure. It's *so* much better here." Tiffany picked up her shoes and took them to the closet. "I'm beat, and I feel a little sick from all that food. I'm going to have to spend a few hours down in the hotel gym tomorrow."

"We'd better get up early, then. Langston says he has a big day planned."

Chapter Twelve

Tuesday, June 3

"UR UR UR UR Urrrrrr!"

"URRR Ur Ur Urrrrrr!"

First one bantam rooster crowed, then the other, as if they were challenging each other in a raspy barnyard duel. The racket came in through the open window.

What the heck . . . Zera turned over in her bed, pulled the quilt up to her chin. *Crowing?* She opened her eyes and for a moment couldn't remember where she was. Then a sensation, bittersweet, swept over her. Bitter because of the lost time, sweet because for the first time in what seemed like forever she didn't feel disappointed upon waking up and realizing where she was.

The room glowed with the dawn. A chilly breeze pushed through the open window and tousled the curtains. Zera got out of bed, pulling the quilt off and wrapping it around her as she made her way over to the window to close it.

She stopped at the view. The lower mountains surrounding Ute Springs glowed dark purple, blue, and green. Several miles in the distance, Pikes Peak loomed, its snow-white top shining. *All this in an Easter egg sky of pink and turquoise . . .*

Her gaze traveled to the box of plants sitting on top of her suitcase. *Something about them . . . another dream.* She couldn't remember what the dream was about, but she recalled a soothing voice, the comfort of feeling looked after and safe. She was glad they were there with her. *I need to find perfect places for all of you today.*

Zera dressed and hurried downstairs. In the living room, Cato and Alice wagged their tails in greeting from their sleeping spots on the furniture.

Through the large pocket doors leading into the kitchen, Zera saw Nonny.

"Good mornin', Sunshine. You're up with the dawn, just like I knew you'd be."

Zera grinned back as a ritual, nearly forgotten, came back to her in perfect clarity. "Mornin', Grandma Moon," she answered. For as long as she could remember, they had greeted each other by those names in the morning — Sunshine and Grandma Moon.

Nonny nodded toward the dogs. "Still spoiled rotten, as you can see."

"As they should be," Zera said.

Nonny took a sip from her coffee mug. "I told Hattie we'd come by and see her today. She called yesterday evening while you were outside and invited us to lunch. Is that all right with you?"

"Sounds great, Nonny."

After a morning of chores, tending to the animals, and unpacking her clothes, Zera moved her plants.

Nonny suggested "giving them a summer vacation too," so Zera brought all but Sunny to the porch. Knowing that they, like people, could be sunburned, she chose a lightly-shaded spot until they got used to being outdoors. The Venus flytrap, whose natural home was in a bog or swamp, stayed upstairs in her room near the window on the table.

Nonny insisted they walk to Hattie's.

"Are you sure?" Zera said uneasily, thinking about the steepness of the streets and her grandmother's handicap. "Uncle Theodore said you had a special-equipped car."

"I do, and the car works fine. So do I. My dear, if people can run the Boston Marathon on one leg, I sure as heck can handle a few blocks."

Through no fault of Nonny's, it took them over an hour to get to the bottom of the hill. A half-dozen neighbors spotted them during the seven-block descent, and they all wanted to welcome Zera back and chat for a few minutes.

It seemed to Zera as if the early June morning was beautiful just for her; the temperature pleasantly warm, the sky dotted with white clouds suspended like fat cotton cushions. Zera delighted in them, so close overhead. Her heart, for a change, felt as free and buoyant as they looked. Never had the sky seemed this bright in Piker.

As they walked down Ute Boulevard, the door of Nell's Coffee House opened. *It's Cosmic Dan!* Dan was lanky but moved elegantly. He always wore jeans, usually with a cotton, button-up shirt and cowboy boots. He wore his hair naturally, in a medium-sized Afro, and his exotic features, combined with the fact that he was a virtuoso electric guitarist, reminded not only Zera, but everyone who met him, of the rock legend Jimi Hendrix.

Everyone in town knew Dan's story. He happened through Ute Springs long ago, on his way to college in California, but he fell in love with the town and stayed. Dan abided by a personal philosophy of "love, live, and learn as much as you can." He'd sampled twenty professions so far in his life, a new one almost every year, and he'd done it all for fun. He'd been everything from bank teller to ice cream truck driver to city councilperson. Cosmic Dan had also been one of Zera's father's closest friends.

"Well hello!" said Nonny. "Look who I have here."

Cosmic Dan appeared uneasy as he took in Zera. "I knew you were in town, you know how word travels." His voice sounded strange. He cleared his throat, rubbed the back of his neck above his aqua cowboy shirt. "My goodness, girl, if you don't look just like your mother."

Zera beamed. Her grandmother had said exactly the same thing at least three times yesterday. It gave her more pleasure than sadness; she'd always thought her mom was so pretty, and she rarely thought of herself in that way. She went over to Dan and gave him a hug. "Nonny told me about all your help. Thanks."

Dan looked a little embarrassed. He rubbed his chin. "It was nothing, and I mean nothing."

The two smiled at each other in silence and Zera couldn't help but notice, with a little sadness, that Dan's afro now had some gray hairs.

"How's your Uncle Theodore doing?" Dan asked.

"Fine. He's in Los Angeles, at a job interview."

"I see. Where're you two headed?"

"To Hattie's."

Dan laughed. "Oh yeah, Hattie mentioned that last night. I saw her at the grocery store. Ben was with her and she teased him about all the questions he'd been asking about you."

"Like what?"

"Not sure, exactly. If I know Ben, he was probably nosing around, seeing if you have a boyfriend."

"Oh." Zera didn't know what to say. Or what to feel, either.

Thankfully, Nonny interrupted. "I hate to rush off, but I told Hattie we'd be there for lunch, and we're already late, over a half-hour."

"You'd better get to Hat's then," said Dan. "She's probably about to come looking for you."

At the end of Ute Avenue they made a right turn up Pawnee Road and began to climb a steep sidewalk riddled with cracks. Nonny Green moved more slowly now, and Zera saw that she was tiring. Zera tried not to worry but had to ask, "Are you all right?"

"It's only another block," said Nonny, working her silver cane. "Don't worry, I'm a tough old bird."

Zera's lungs, unaccustomed to the higher altitude, were laboring to fill themselves by the time they reached the wood and stone house at the top of the hill. Parked in front was Hattie's beat-up old red Toyota truck, Ladybug. Covering the back of Ladybug was a multitude of bumper stickers. One said, TREE HUGGING DIRT WORSHIPPER, another, Lord, help me be the kind of person my dog thinks I am. These were joined by: Love Your Mother (Earth), **Who Owns YOU?**, *Follow Your Bliss*, and **Skateboarding is Not a Crime!**

They climbed the porch's greenstone steps, and Zera saw Ben's skateboard near the door. The sight of it made her a little nervous. She'd seen Ben only briefly in her visits back to visit Ute Springs, and when Dan said Ben had been "nosing around" asking if she had a boyfriend . . .

Before she had a chance to finish that thought or knock on the door, the door opened. A tall woman with a full, but not heavy, figure and waist-length, tawny tresses streaked with gray stood before them. Hattie was one-quarter Ute and it showed in her wide nose, dark eyes and generous mouth. She wore a floral print dress, wood jewelry and flip-flops, her finger and toenails painted a glittering cobalt. The expression on Hattie's face turned from thrilled to concerned as she looked at Zera, then Nonny. She glanced out at the street in front of her house.

"Guinevere, do *not* tell me you walked here!" Zera was surprised at her upset tone. "What were you thinking?"

"I'm fine, Hattie. Just fine."

After an exchange of greetings and hugs, Zera and her grandmother followed Hattie's musky-spice perfume of patchouli through the house and out the back to the enclosed garden.

The soothing sound of Aspen Creek, running along the back of the property, filled Hattie's garden. Following an elliptical stone path, they passed a compost pile and rabbit hutch before entering into the depths of a half-wild fantasy garden. Metal sculptures and stone statues stood tall among potted blooming tropical plants and vines. Carved faces of beasts peered down from a ten-foot-tall totem pole. In one corner was a tiny pond, surrounded by tall grasses, with a hammock under a cottonwood tree; at another, next to the back fence, stood a picnic table covered with a tablecloth. As they drew nearer, Zera saw their lunch: stuffed pita bread sandwiches, fruit salad, a pitcher of lemonade, and a chocolate cake decorated with real scarlet nasturtiums.

"Mmmm." Zera murmured. Her stomach growled, loud enough for Hattie to hear.

Hattie chuckled. "Worked up an appetite, eh?"

That was a little embarrassing. "Yeah."

"You've certainly outdone yourself," Nonny said.

"Guinevere," Hattie said, placing a hand on Zera's

grandmother's shoulder and continuing to emanate an aura of concern, "you know I can't cook. I didn't make any of it myself, except the lemonade. Jean down at the bakery made the groovy cake. Didn't even charge me for it. Everyone in town is thrilled you're back, Zera."

"Where's Ben?" asked Nonny.

"At his father's. He said he wanted to see Zera, but then he took off. I think he got nervous waiting around. He's a little shy about seeing her. Ah, adolescence." Hattie winked at Nonny.

"Boys," said Nonny. "They try to act tough, but . . ."

Zera felt a blush creeping into her cheeks. She had never thought of Ben in that way, aside from that brief moment in fifth grade when he almost kissed her on Valentine's Day. When she didn't let him, he acted like it had been a joke, that he didn't really like her in that way. Though she knew he did. She could tell by the card he had given her. It wasn't a funny card, or a card featuring some superhero that the other kids traded, but one with a pretty illustration of a heart surrounded by flowers and birds, bought at the drugstore. It was awkward for awhile, but they were still kids, still friends, and so they got over it. When she thought of Ben, memories of summer days flooded back: riding bikes together, building forts from sticks and mud down by the creek, chasing lizards, and eating wild raspberries.

They sat down to eat, using Hattie's mismatched floral dishes, blue glass goblets, and worn silver-plated cutlery. *Everything even tastes better here*, Zera thought, as she relished her first bite of sandwich. She didn't know what she enjoyed more — the company, the food, the garden, or the waterfall sound of the creek.

While enjoying the cake, Hattie said, "Zera honey, your grandmother shared some v-mails about Tiffany. She sounds like a real pain in the butt."

"I think it bugs her that I'm not one of the popular kids at school," Zera said. "We don't have much in common."

"You're not mainstream, honey," Hattie said, "and, believe me, that's good. Don't ever feel bad about being true to yourself. It's kind of sad; Tiffany must be very insecure, or she wouldn't push so hard."

"True," said Nonny, "but I can't help but to be furious every time I think about how she suggested that Zera change her name."

"It would never happen, so don't be furious, Guinevere," said Hattie, "it's not good for you." Hattie raised her glass to Zera. "Here's to having you back." As she took a sip of lemonade, Zera noticed how Hattie's fingernail polish matched the glass. *How cool. No one Hattie's age in Piker would wear blue fingernail polish.*

She wondered what her uncle was doing today, if he had even thought about her. She had thought of him several times. *Might as well face it, he's only into himself, just like Tiffany. I don't want to go back. Ever.*

Hattie offered them another piece of cake. "This is so weird.

I just remembered that Sally mentioned something about Tiffany changing *her* name."

Zera's eyes widened. "Really?"

"This was a few weeks before the accident, when Ted and Tiffany had just started dating. Sally said Ted told her that Tiffany changed her name when she got out of high school. That she was poor or something, wanted to change her image."

"I never heard that," said Nonny. "Do you remember what it was?"

"No," Hattie looked up at the treetops, "I can't think of it. Maybe she didn't tell me." She looked at Zera and her eyes shone mischievously. "Maybe it was something really weird, like Zera!"

"Maybe it was Hattie," Zera teased back.

The conversation turned to the amazement they felt at Zera's spur-of-the-moment return.

"Maybe the two of them will elope in L.A." Hattie speculated.

"Now, that would be interesting," Nonny said, "but I don't get the vibe that Ted really loves her."

"Things can develop," Hattie said.

"I suppose anything's possible," said Nonny, "though I think I would have noticed something when they were over yesterday." She sighed and took another bite of cake.

Zera poured herself more lemonade. No matter what Hattie said, she did not think it possible that her uncle and Tiffany would ever get married. She'd seen true love with her parents; there was no comparison.

Nonny changed the subject. "Ted insists that Zera find work this summer. He suggested the North Pole, which is peculiar since he hated working there as a teenager. Too much fun and frivolity for his serious nature, I suppose."

"I remember that," Hattie said, swiping a stray piece of chocolate icing off her plate with a finger and licking it. She winked at Zera. "Didn't he get fired by Santa?"

"Yes. Ted told the children it was all fake, just to be spiteful. It was the summer after Ted's graduation, right after that girl he was dating broke up with him."

"Oh, I remember her, the cute little granola."

"Granola?" Zera said. "What's that?"

"Oh, that's what Guinevere used to call hippie girls way back when. Remember, Guinevere?"

"Yes. Back in the Stone Age. I was one of the very first, with my leopard-skin headband."

Hattie grinned. "They wore only natural-fiber clothes, no makeup. Ate only health food, you know, like granola and yogurt when they first came out . . . it was a word we heard when we were young. Boy, the fact that we thought those foods odd really dates us both, doesn't it?"

Nonny nodded, an eyebrow raised in agreement.

"Uncle Theodore went out with someone like that?" Zera asked. "Sounds like the opposite of Tiffany."

"Your mother adored her," said Nonny.

"Sally used to mention her once in a while," Hattie said. "Her name was . . . dang, I can't remember it! Get in your late forties and things get fuzzy. I know it was a sweet, old-fashioned name."

"Whatever happened to her?" Zera was curious to hear about a part of her uncle she never knew about.

"Don't know. She left for college and then her parents moved away to another state. Everyone kind of lost touch. It'd be interesting to find out."

"Yes, it would," said Nonny, "but it'd break her heart to find out what Ted's up to, creating Beefy Fries and who-knows-what other abominations." She took a sip of lemonade. "Lily Gibbons. That's her name."

Zera thought she recognized the name but couldn't remember where.

"Lily. A beautiful name. What a memory, Guinevere. Hey, not to change the subject, but I've got an idea. Why don't you let Zera work for me this summer?" She turned to Zera, "What about it? How'd you like to be a part-time gardener? It's hard work, but fun. And you'll learn a lot."

Zera's eyes sparkled. "I'd love it! I've been studying gardening and plants since my birthday."

Nonny and Hattie exchanged a glance.

"Another gardener in the family," Hattie said. "It's in the blood. You know, Zera, it's been rumored that the Greens have the gift of being able to talk with plants."

"I talk to mine all the time."

"But do they talk back?" Hattie kidded.

Zera laughed, an odd laugh that the women didn't notice. She thought about what she'd heard — or, she reminded herself, *thought* she'd heard, now more than once, that they *were* talking to her. *Best not to bring that up, or they might think I've got psychological damage from being around Tiffany.*

Hattie took Zera on a garden tour. At the water garden, Zera spied a submerged pot of horsetail. The hollow-tubed plants looked exactly like a clump of two-foot-tall, bright green, pointed straws. She admired how thin black and gray joints divided the stalks into horizontal sections. "Those are really cool. The name is *Equisetum* something, isn't it?"

"Yes, *Equisetum,"* Hattie said. "You do know your stuff. It's Latin for horse. *Equisetum hymale*."

"*Equisetum hymale.*" Zera let the words roll over her tongue as she knelt down for a closer look. "What a cute frog." She put her hand under the water stream coming from the spitting amphibian statue. The water felt cool, and Hattie's fancy butterfly goldfish, fat-bodied and unwieldy, comically wriggled up to the surface to see who was visiting.

"I love horsetail," Hattie said. "But it took me awhile to figure out why they called them that. They're not hairy at all, not the ones I've seen anyway. Then someone told me that many of the species get whorls of tiny stalks growing out from the joints of the main stem, and that those look bushy, like little horse tails."

"I saw pictures of those in a book," Zera said, teasing the gulping-mouthed goldfish with her fingertips. *They are quite the little beggars.* "Aren't they one of the oldest plants on Earth, around even before the dinosaurs?"

"Yes. They were here over a hundred million years before conifers — even, you know, cone-bearing plants, like pine trees. Horsetails are the granddaddies, about four hundred million years old, the ancestors of grasses and rushes." Leaning over, Hattie touched a stalk. "They're so primitive they don't even produce flowers. And they used to grow as huge as trees!"

Zera tried to imagine what that would be like, living among giant ferns, horsetails and dinosaurs. She drew in her breath. "Who is *that*?"

She stared up at a ceramic plaque, partly hidden among grapevines near the pond. It showed the green face of a man. A face made of leaves. *I know this face.* Her mind flashed on her plants, and a familiar voice echoed in her mind, *"It's okay. You're home." That voice . . . yesterday in the garden . . .* Those moments perched on the border of her consciousness like unseen birds. A vague joy surged through her, a budding sense of power that she didn't understand, a power that held a tinge of fear.

"That's the Green Man. Haven't you heard of him?"

"I don't think so. But he looks familiar."

"Oh, Zera, the Green Man is awesome! He's an ancient

symbol of man's oneness with the earth." Hattie went to the sculpture, and moved aside vines so Zera could see it better. "In Europe, carvings of the Green Man are in the architecture of many old churches, some nearly a thousand years old. No one can tell when he first came, or from where; it's like he's been a part of mankind forever. He's ancient, mysterious, sacred — and very cool."

Zera could not take her eyes away. Distracted, she dropped her hand into the pond and the goldfish brushed against her fingertips fondly. Unseen by Zera and Hattie, a water lily bud pushed up from below the water's surface and opened fully into flower.

"He's just so . . ."

The gate creaked open. The spell broken, Zera and Hattie looked over.

". . . interesting," Zera finished.

"What's interesting?" Ben walked through the gate and went right over to the pond. He stood next to Zera, almost close enough to touch. A thrill went through her as she looked up at him. Dark eyes and hair, tan . . . he looked so much taller than when she saw him at Christmas. *He's changed so much! He's so . . . cute.* The thought embarrassed her. She had to force herself to tone down the big, stupid smile she knew was on her face.

"Hey there," Hattie stood up. "Zera and I were just talking about the Green Man. How groovy he is."

Ben grimaced at his mother, and then grinned at Zera, a grin that caused Zera to look away.

Ben's attention suddenly focused on the tree next to them. "Green Man? Ugh. Any cake left?"

Hattie insisted on driving Zera and Nonny home in Ladybug. Hattie had arranged with Nonny that Zera would work three mornings a week, plenty for someone her age who needed to make up for lost time with her grandmother. Going up the driveway, Zera's heart raced as she thought how Hattie told her Ben would be helping out this summer too. Ben had been really sweet at Hattie's, teasing Zera about life in "the big city," and answering her questions about all the kids she'd known in Ute Springs. *He is so cute*, Zera thought for the umpteenth time. She thought about his jokes, his smile, about how tall he'd grown.

As Hattie stopped the truck, an intoxicating scent enveloped them. All three knew the source of the scent, even before it came into view.

"I've never seen anything like it," Nonny said. "They were just buds this morning. Some not even near opening."

Zera, pulled out of her daydream, jumped out of the truck, and ran to the porch.

Nonny and Hattie followed her and they stood in the driveway, staring in awed silence. Nonny shook her head in disbelief.

Every rosebud covering the front porch had opened in the few hours that they'd been away. The trellis, the porch columns, even the stair railing, were all draped in voluptuous, creamy white roses. The air was filled with a lemon-rose perfume.

Finally, Hattie spoke. "I'm a firm believer that plants are intelligent, and, who's to say, maybe they even have a will." She looked at Zera and her expression was serious. "They're welcoming you home, honey."

Chapter Thirteen

Friday, June 6

For three days Langston Void, Troy Sylvan, and the models concentrated on razzle-dazzling Theodore and Tiffany — L.A. style. Crystal and Zirconia whisked their "new best friend" to designer boutiques, fancy department stores, and exclusive spas where they indulged in massages, herbal wraps, and a barrage of beauty treatments. Company credit cards flashed through the city like a plastic wildfire. Theodore and Tiffany wined and dined at exclusive restaurants, spotting movie stars, and other members of the rich and famous set. Tiffany was especially thrilled that some of these celebrities knew Langston.

Langston wowed Theodore, taking him to box-seats at a Dodgers game, out for an afternoon cruising on Void Chemical Corporation's eighty-foot yacht, and on a morning flight across the country "just for kicks," on a company jet. Theodore found that it wasn't that hard to get over the thought of Langston's extensive plastic surgery. The first day they spent together it was awkward; he caught himself staring a few times. But after he got used to Langston, he didn't think about it much. Besides, the guy had had a hard childhood; it wasn't that surprising he'd done something extreme. He learned from Langston that his mother abandoned him when he was just a baby. He had been reared by a succession of nannies, none of whom stayed more than a year or two. His father had only one consuming interest, Void Chemical Corporation. Now the family business had become Langston's main interest in life as well. Theodore felt a kinship with Langston, having had one parent absent for most of his childhood, and another absent for all of it. He thought he may have discovered an employer and role model who could become something even more, a friend.

On Friday at 7:30 A. M. Theodore stepped into the sunlight outside The Grand. He felt terrific; squeaky-clean, doused with expensive cologne, and handsome in the new Italian suit and shoes that Tiffany had bought for him. He even had a new hairstyle, a suave, slicked-back look created by Crystal's personal hairdresser. André had made a personal visit to their suite that morning so Theodore would look his best on this important first day.

Theodore stepped onto the sidewalk of a street lined with palm trees and humming with morning traffic. Smiling to himself, he gripped the handle of a vintage crocodile-skin briefcase in his left hand while, with his right, he took a pair of sunglasses from a jacket pocket. A slightly built, uniformed man with graying hair opened the door of the white company limousine. "Good morning, Mr. Green."

"Oh. Good morning to you . . ." Theodore couldn't

remember Langston's driver's name, even though he'd been chauffeuring them around for three days. Langston was letting Theodore "borrow" him on his first day of work; Theodore would lease or buy his own car, maybe a Porsche, that evening. He stood there, glasses in hand, groping for the man's name — he thought he'd heard it, was sure he'd heard it, but all he could remember was Langston calling him "Driver." Theodore put on his sunglasses and climbed in. "Uh . . . thanks."

Minutes later, the eighty-two-floor concrete and glass skyscraper towered before him. Theodore craned his neck, looking up at the logo of Void Chemical Corporation, a giant planet Earth with "VCC" emblazoned across it in white, lightning bolt-style letters. Pride filled him. *I have arrived,* he thought, a smirk twisting his wide lips as a joke occurred to him. *Both career-wise — and in this limo.*

After a ride in a "CEO Only" elevator to the top floor, he was greeted by Langston's secretary Brigette. Brigette looked so much like the buxom and beautiful Crystal that Theodore did a double take, but Brigette was a little heavier and her hair was black. "Good morning, Mr. Green," she said, rising from her desk. "Mr. Void told me you were on your way. I'll escort you to his office."

Theodore followed her down the hall to the massive double doors of Langston's office, emblazoned with inlaid gold letters, a "V" on one, and a "C" on the other. They stepped across the threshold into a wood- and mirror-paneled room.

Langston's ebony desk stretched out in front of them, twice as large as any desk Theodore had ever seen. Framed holograms covered it, most of them shots of Langston with famous Hollywood stars and just-as-famous political figures. On the wood-paneled wall behind the desk was a small painting of Langston's father, a corpulent man with thinning hair, wide lips, and a slightly buck-toothed smile. Langston, of course, looked absolutely nothing like him.

"Hey, Theodore," Langston said, getting to his feet.

"Morning, Langston."

Brigette departed, and Langston walked over to a wall where a huge, holographic cubist painting hung. Even with all the geometric forms and wild colors, Theodore could see the painting was a rendering of Crystal in a skimpy bikini. Langston pressed a dark strip on the wall's edge and the six mirrored panels slid apart and into the wall, revealing a bar stocked with refreshments — bottled juices, frappuccinos, cappuccinos, lattés, energy drinks, sodas, and sparkling mineral waters. Bowls of non-caloric candy sparkled in crystal bowls, and a shelf of tiny glass bottles of rainbow-hued pills lined the top of the cabinet. These mood pills were used to enhance or create pleasant emotional states, temporarily making the mind a little sharper, calmer, happier . . . whatever you were in the mood for.

"Cool," Theodore said.

"See anything you'd like?"

"How about one of those StrongMan drinks?"

"A man after my own heart." Langston grabbed two glasses. "This reminds me, wait until you see our private gym. It was featured in *Billionaires Quarterly*, and is the envy of corporate execs all along the West Coast."

He filled the glasses and handed one to Theodore. "But I digress. Today's the day." His green eyes narrowed as he motioned for Theodore to choose one of the leather chairs in front of his desk. "Before we head to the lab, I've got a lot more papers for you to sign. The acceptance contract you brought back with you from Piker was only a general agreement. These go into more of the specifics."

"Sure." Theodore sat down, placing his briefcase on the chair next to him. The men each took a healthy swig of their StrongMan brew. The paperwork lay on Langston's desk, topped with a shiny gold pen. Langston pushed the stack of papers over to Theodore, who, after putting on his reading glasses, began studying them. Langston watched patiently, taking sips of his drink. "No hurry on this, Theodore," he said warmly. "I want you to take your time. Be sure this is what you want."

There was a lot there, contracts on everything from regular drug testing to personality testing, to the relinquishing of all his creative work to VCC, even everything that he worked on in graduate school and was not owned by Biotech Multinational. Panic surged through Theodore. *This is heavy duty. Heavy duty as in ironclad.* But this time the wordplay wasn't as funny. *I should get a lawyer*. He looked up to see Langston turned in his chair, staring at the portrait of his father. *The man without a father. It'll be okay,* Theodore told himself. *I trust him.* He cleared his throat and when Langston turned, he nodded. "Everything seems to be in order." Theodore picked up the pen and began signing documents.

When he was finished, Langston's celebrity-handsome mouth broke into a broad smile, a smile of large, flawless, very white teeth and healthy pink gums. The men stood. Langston shook Theodore's hand. "Let me welcome you officially to VCC. Now let's go see the lab."

Chapter Fourteen

After a brief stop to check out Theodore's new office (a half-size version of Langston's with a just-as-awesome refreshment bar), the two men took the executive elevator to the roof. A helicopter waited, motor running, blades rotating slowly and powerfully. The men clutched their briefcases, bent down, and ran. Langston's hair and clothes whipped about, but Theodore's usually unkempt hair stayed put, thanks to the massive amount of styling gel applied that morning by André.

They got into the helicopter and shut the door to — silence.

"Isn't it great?" said Langston, running his fingers through his hair. "Totally sound-proof."

"First rate," said Theodore, trying to admire the leather seats and the roomy interior, while at the same time thinking how he was about to get lifted up into the sky — in a helicopter. *That'll sure put my new deodorant to the test.*

A tanned and muscular man with a blond crew cut sat at the front of the chopper, behind the controls. As he turned to face his passengers, Theodore noticed the name Cooper Davies embroidered atop the planet Earth/VCC logo patch on his pocket.

Langston introduced the square-jawed pilot, adding, "Coop's

an ex-Marine. But now he's in VCC's branch of service."

Coop shook Theodore's hand. "It's an honor, sir." Theodore made an effort not to wince. *Now I know what a grip of steel is. This guy is ripped.*

Moments later they were sky borne, whirling through L.A. smog and looking down onto an endless landscape of concrete and cars.

After a buzz over the city, the chopper headed toward the desert. As they traveled east, the vegetation became sparse and the temperature so hot that waves of heat visibly radiated from the land below. Forty-five minutes later the Void Research Facility building came into view. Langston pointed to it, a spot of green on the horizon amid a beige landscape of mesquite, clumps of pale grass, and dry, cracked earth.

The chopper hovered like a dragonfly over a low, sand-colored building about the size of a football field. The grounds, which covered twice that much land, consisted of an asphalt parking lot enclosed by a twenty-foot-high electric fence topped with razor wire. Guard towers stood at each corner of the property and Theodore's skin crawled when he saw the glint of laser guns flashing from their windows. The thought came to him that the complex would be identical to a maximum security prison if not for one detail: the entire rooftop of the building was a sparkling jewel of glass and greenery. Sixty-six pyramid-topped greenhouses, connected together, six deep and eleven long, covering the entire surface.

"You've got some pretty heavy security," Theodore said.

Langston shrugged. "Got to. The building alone cost over $150 million, and the projects we're working on are literally priceless."

"It's nothing like BioTech Multinational."

Langston's mouth tightened. "Make no mistake, Theodore; you're in the big leagues now."

The helicopter circled to the rear of the building and hovered above a landing pad, also painted with the VCC-Earth logo. Coop set the chopper dead center and cut the motor.

A door to the building opened and Troy Sylvan stepped outside. Theodore hadn't seen him since dinner at The Posh, though he'd heard a lot of good things about him from Langston these last three days.

Troy jogged over to the chopper. "How was the ride, Theodore?" he asked. Grinning, he pumped Theodore's hand.

"Great."

"Everything running smoothly?" Langston asked Troy.

"You know it." Troy turned to Theodore. "Congrats! Finally, you're one of the team. Wait till you see what we've got going here," He stroked his black goatee excitedly. "You're gonna flip."

They entered the building, and Troy directed them down the hall to the clean room/dressing room where they donned white laboratory coats, plastic shoes, safety glasses, latex gloves, and what looked like blue shower caps. Before entering the laboratory, Langston paused to look at himself in a full-length mirror, above which hung the sign, "ARE YOU CLEAN?"

Langston slipped up his safety glasses with the thumb and forefinger of one gloved hand and surveyed his not-quite-so-debonair self. "The only thing I hate about this place is the *attire.*" To the two men he said, "Ready? Then let's go."

Langston pressed a black button on the wall opposite the entrance. A set of elevator-like doors slid open, and the three stepped into an immense, brightly-lit laboratory buzzing with activity. A hundred pairs of eyes turned toward the door and all talking stopped. Theodore's pulse raced. *They know that the boss — no, the BOSSES —* are *here. Just last week I was in their position; now I'm the one to be noticed.*

Theodore scanned the room to find row upon row of tables, each holding thousands of round glass Petri dishes and plant specimens. Dozens of lab technicians were involved in various tasks: transplanting tiny plants to the dishes, transferring larger plants to pots, working under microscopes with tiny syringes, injecting plants with bacterium laced with the DNA of other species, typing notes on electronic notepads.

"This is where the newest and most promising ideas in the fields of agriculture and cosmetics are tested," explained Troy. In a low voice he added, "The ones that aren't top secret, anyhow."

Troy keeps mentioning "top secret." They must have something really big going on. Probably a new fruit or vegetable combined with a mammal, like the burg-fry. Excitement stirred within him; he couldn't wait to find out.

A printout banner taped to one wall read "MATERNITY WARD."

Theodore pointed. "Clever."

"Not very professional," Langston frowned, "but apropos, don't you think?"

Troy led them to a table where a small, mousy woman rapidly transplanted large seedlings into plastic pots filled with soil and fertilizer pellets. She seemed surprised and a little self-conscious to see Langston, but she continued her task. Theodore watched, transfixed. Tiny leaf buds swelled and began to open as she moved them into the bigger pots. Roots and stems grew before his eyes. *This is incredible, much more than I expected.*

"Here," Troy said, "we are working on designing a superfast-growing oak tree. Waiting one hundred years or more for a mature oak is unacceptable. And soon it's going to be a thing of the past. What we're doing here will eventually provide raw building materials — oak for floors, furniture, cabinets — in a fraction of time. Not one hundred years, but ten. Teresa is potting up our solution, a combination of mice growth genes inserted into the DNA of the oak. These seedlings are two hours old."

Theodore's eyes widened behind the safety glasses. "So it's a success?"

"Well, let's put it this way, we're still working on getting a few of the squeaks out."

The men guffawed and the lab technician, up to her elbows in plants, smiled politely. Theodore thought she looked like she'd heard that joke many times before.

They walked to the next row of tables, full of microscopes, as a technician arrived at his station. The young man, who looked to be in his late teens, appeared startled when Theodore caught his eye. He quickly pulled his cap down over his of hair, wisps of which were going everywhere, turned, and took off at a fast clip down the aisle. Although he left quickly, Theodore could swear the young man's hair was turning from blond to blue, the same color as the plastic cap. He was moving away so fast, but his skin seemed to be lightening too, becoming paler. *Weird.*

Langston noticed. "What's with that guy?" he asked Troy.

So he saw it too.

"That's Dubson," said Troy in a low voice, giving Langston a knowing look.

"Oh," said Langston.

Theodore moved closer to the men. "Did I just see what I thought I saw?"

Troy sighed, frowned. "We weren't going to tell you about Dubson until later. That kid is from our Youth Volunteer Scientist Program, a program where young people who get into a scrape with the law can work off their debt to society, so to speak, by putting in time at the lab, taking part in a few harmless experiments. It's all legal, I assure you. He signed a waiver." Langston looked around, and his voice dropped. "We've developed a cream that's applied to the skin. The cuttlefish gene spliced to some stem cells. The cream is applied before the cells die, and is absorbed into the skin. The results are fantastic. Short term, but incredibly promising."

"You're doing *human* experiments?" Theodore's voice rose, and several lab techs looked over. This was unheard of. His mind raced. *Cuttlefish.* They were related to octopi, known for their amazing camouflage techniques, their ability to change the pigmentation of their skin to their surroundings. Is *that* what he saw? And this guy was running around the lab? He felt color rising to his cheeks, a flash of something that was akin to anger. This was too much! He had a million questions.

Langston saw his irritation. He took him by the arm and led him away from the tables. "Theodore, it's inevitable that man will take the genetic engineering work to the next level. That is what we ourselves are genetically designed to do, to find out how far our minds, our research, can take us. VCC is just the first one to do it. Dubson was happy to volunteer. He thought it was marvelous to see if he could have this camouflage ability. Can you imagine? It's like the closest thing to *human invisibility*. The applications are incalculable and the military is very interested, as you can imagine. And this program, with these volunteers — it's a great way to keep that bottom line down."

Contradicting thoughts battled in Theodore's mind: *This*

isn't right — they are using these kids — fought hard against — *Human invisibility? That is the coolest thing ever!* Langston was staring, trying to read him. Theodore swallowed hard. *I'll sort it out later.* "This is some cutting edge work, that's for sure," Theodore said in a husky voice. An inkling of the possibility of what might be in the top-secret lab teased his mind. *I'm in,* thought Theodore, *I signed the papers. Either it'll be me or someone else as president of the Biotech Division. I've always wanted this.*

Langston smiled. "There will be plenty of time to talk about this later. We should get on with the tour." Troy led the way to a part of the lab where technicians sat at benches hunched over Petri dishes. He explained that the fingernail-size sections of choco-cane, a previously engineered combination of sugar cane and the cacao tree, had been placed in a nutrient mixture. To this mixture the lab technicians added, by syringe, a solution of a disease bacterium.

Troy explained that the bacterium had a gene, the milk-producing gene of a cow, spliced into its DNA. "We're going for a milk chocolate plant. Can you imagine the money we'll make?" he said. "Instant chocolate!"

Although his mind was still fixated on the cuttlefish and Dubson, Theodore watched the technicians perform a process he knew well. This was how all genetic engineering work began. The bacterium invaded the plant, entered the plant cell's nucleus, and inserted some of its own DNA, while at the same time smuggling in the foreign DNA — in this case, a cow's. Then the scientists would wait until the slips of plants grew roots. They'd pot the plants, move them to the greenhouse, and from there, wait until the newly created life-forms matured. Soon they would find out whether the experiments succeeded or failed. Most failed. Theodore knew that science hadn't advanced to the point where they could predict exactly where in the genome the new DNA would land, so the procedure had to be performed thousands upon thousands of times. If the gene landed in the right place, the company hit the jackpot; there would be new products to patent in the world market. If the gene landed in the wrong place, the combination might not show up, might show up weakly, or the plant could be a freak. There were a lot of throw-aways in genetic engineering; one of the problems was collateral damage to genes near the target area (making for even more mutations), but a single success more than made up for it in the sales department.

He took a deep breath. "Very impressive."

Next to a wall, they visited a thin man whose face showed a lot of razor-stubble. He stood in front of a "gene gun," a steel- and safety-glass enclosed contraption about the size of a small microwave oven, covered with dials and hoses. Troy explained that this project involved inserting a disease bacterium containing the gene of a walrus into the nutrient mixture holding a tomato cutting. Troy introduced this man as Max Albright.

"Max was one of our brightest interns," Troy said, "and now

he's one of our most devoted scientists. He developed this little idea himself, the walato. It's a tomato/walrus combination that will allow, we hope, the popular temperate-climate fruit to be grown in the Arctic, year-round."

"Exciting," Theodore said. He meant it, it *was* exciting, but he couldn't get his mind off Dubson.

"We're determined to find a success soon," said the exhausted-looking Albright, his eyes glassy and bloodshot. "This is the three-thousandth and fifty-sixth batch." Hand trembling slightly, Albright turned the dial and pressed the button. A tiny red light flashed and the contraption made a tiny "POP."

"Trying to get it in the right spot on the genome is like a blind man trying to hit the bull's eye in game of darts," Troy said. He told Albright to keep up the good work.

"Thanks, sir."

"Now, at long last, it's time to see the really cool stuff," whispered Troy. *Really cool stuff?* Theodore wondered. *What in God's name could that be?* Already it seemed that VCC was way ahead, *dangerously ahead,* of the game in their research already.

Returning to the clean room/dressing room, Troy secured the door behind them. He searched the dressing areas and bathroom to make sure they were alone and then called Security from a wall v-phone.

"You'll need to come over and unlock the door," he said to the guard on the monitor. "We're going downstairs."

The guard nodded. "Yes, sir."

"We'll call you in about twenty minutes."

Langston went to the sign next to the mirror that read "ARE YOU CLEAN?" and swung it aside. Theodore saw a secret key pad and scanning device hidden underneath. Langston took off one glove, punched in a series of numbers and letters, and laid his palm atop the scanning device. A high, whining tone emitted from the scanner and the mirror below slid into the wall, revealing a long, dim, downward-sloping corridor. He extended his arm. "After you, gentlemen."

Everything's so cool, and so cloak-and-dagger — now a secret passageway? Light-headedness came over Theodore. He wasn't sure if it was elation or dread, but his palms were sweating. For some reason, *Alice in Wonderland,* Alice falling down the rabbit hole in particular, entered his mind. *This is what free falling feels like. All I can do now is wait for the landing.*

The trio entered the passage and the mirror-door slid closed behind them as lights along the passageway brightened. Theodore looked up and noticed a tiny camera hovering above them, driven by silent, helicopter-like blades. It was so small that at first he thought it was some kind of insect. *Holy cow.* He could feel the adrenalin coursing through him. *This IS the big leagues.* The camera followed them as they descended. Down they went, at a gentle slope, for about sixty feet. At the end of the corridor, this time uncovered and in the wall next to a set of double doors, Theodore saw a second scanning device.

"It's your turn," Langston said to Theodore. "It's easy. Just punch in the secret code, Demeter 911, and then place your palm on the scanner. It's been set up already to recognize your hand."

"But how, how did you get this set up so quickly?"

"We've had a few days together. I've had your prints since that first dinner together."

Theodore shook his head. "Again, so very impressive, Langston." *I've never seen anything like this.* "Demeter? Isn't that the Greek goddess of agriculture, fruits of the harvest?"

Langston laughed. "And of course 911's the number you call for emergencies. Troy's got an incredible sense of humor, don't you think?"

Very funny. Theodore entered in the code and laid his now-sweating palm against the scanner.

The door opened.

Bright, white light caused the men to squint as they entered the room. The first impression was of an outdoor plant nursery. Rows and rows of overhead fluorescent lights made the place as bright as natural sunlight. Theodore took in the green leafy plant life. There were trees — and humidity. His skin absorbed the warmth, the mugginess. Then he noticed a sickeningly sweet floral smell, tinged with the scent of bleach.

Theodore's eyes adjusted, and details emerged. Closest to him, a row of vines on a long trellis held strange fruits. Small and round with filmy coverings, blue, green, brown, hazel, with black centers and white rims. They hung in clusters, like grapes. But these grapes stared blankly. For a second it didn't compute.

It was as if his mind couldn't accept what he saw. *They're eyes,* Theodore thought. *Eyes!* Dozens of eyeballs in a cluster, hundreds of clusters along the row.

His heart thudded, his mouth dropped open in stupefaction. He couldn't speak. His throat felt closed up, strangled.

Forcing himself to shift his gaze, Theodore saw most of the other plants were trees, growing in large containers in neat rows. A row of gnarled, twisted trees bore huge, garish red flowers, unlike any he had ever seen. Some of them held mature fruits. Theodore's head swam. These fruits, recognizable even though encased in milky membranes, were *hearts*. Hearts with thick veins — live, beating hearts. *Human hearts.* Over the sound of the fans stirring the moist, sickeningly perfumed air, Theodore heard the slow but unmistakable beatings — thump-thump, thump-thump, thump-thump — as they pulsated with life. His own heart seemed to stop as he noticed the medical equipment attached to the trees, white, whirring machines with digital printouts and graphs and little red lights. *Like a hospital.*

Theodore gaped at another row of trees. They were also gnarled and ugly — and covered with pairs of lungs! Breathing in, breathing out. One word echoed in Theodore's head. *Alive.* There was more medical equipment, and then, across the room. *My God, livers?* Theodore's stomach churned at the site — big, dark, and sloppy wet-looking *human organs.*

Theodore's gaze fled, only to land on a long three-foot-high tank-like structure filled with soil. White trellises rose from the structure with white, ghostly vines scrambling to the top, vines with super-thick hairy stems and huge, pale leaves. The stems needed to be thick in order to bear the weight of the large fruit. They weren't thick enough. Around each big bowling ball-sized fruit globe was a net of mesh tied onto the trellis support. Through the mesh, Theodore could see the hair of the fruit poking out. Long hair. Human hair. No faces, just *hair*.

"Welcome to Fort Knox," said Langston.

"Now *this* is cutting edge, baby!" exclaimed Troy.

Theodore's knees buckled and everything went dark.

He awakened to the overwhelming sensations of his nostrils on fire and his sinuses filled with an icy wind. His eyes flew open and he gasped. Above him hovered a very overweight woman with pretty brown eyes. Eyes that looked familiar. She peered down at him where he lay on a couch.

"The smelling salts worked. How are you feeling, Mr. Green?" While the words were kind, her tone had a definite undercurrent of disdain.

Where am I? Do I know this woman? The nurse wore white scrubs and had her dark hair pulled back severely with a trio of bobby pins on each side. The slightly wrinkled and softer flesh of her face revealed she had to be at least forty. For a second she looked familiar but no, he didn't know her. Everything seemed scrambled and he struggled to remember. *Where am I?* He saw Langston and Troy sitting in chairs at a nearby table. They looked at him with concern, tinted with a trace of amusement.

"You're in the break room, near the lab," said the nurse matter-of-factly. "You've been out for a couple of minutes."

It all came back to him. *A nurse, of course there's a nurse. It's like a hospital.* The blood drained from his face.

The nurse said, "If you feel sick, I'll help you to the bathroom. It's right around the corner."

"I'm okay," Theodore said, sitting up.

The nurse looked back at him with an expression of barely-concealed annoyance, as if the idea of a grown man fainting, let alone vomiting, over some emotional disturbance disgusted her. Theodore cleared his throat, turned to the men at the table. "I . . . I knew you were running some computer programs, checking out the theories, the data I've been sending you from work I did in college. I was just fooling around, coming up with wild ideas. I had no idea that you were implementing this work."

"I think you're done here now," Langston said to the nurse. Troy walked to the door and held it open. The nurse quickly packed the contents of her medical bag and left.

Langston stood. "There's been a small team on these projects for years. We started checking out your theories way before you sent them to us as, well, your computer system did not prove much of a challenge to hack into. Everything you hypothesized has been an incredible success," said Langston. "Everything has worked! Every single man/plant combination you came up with, the protein mixtures, anti-rejection formulas.

Everything worked just like it was meant to work. This is success beyond all expectations."

Theodore, still reeling in disbelief, reached for his glasses on the table next to him and put them on. "You hacked into my files? This is all illegal on so many levels, Langston. How could you do this? It's one thing to examine an idea and quite another to make it a reality." He rubbed the back of his head, where he had a bump from the fall. "Those balls of hair. Good God, that must have been my melon-hair idea. I never meant for these things to be created!"

"Every bald man, and woman, is going to be beating a path to our door," Langston said, his voice flat. "Now you know why we had to have you. You are a genius. An Einstein, an Edison, a Luther Burbank times ten! But those men didn't have the backing of a powerful multi-national corporation, or the money Void Chemical Corporation has to grease the wheels with the politics of it all. When word of what we have done gets out, mankind is not going to worry about the legality. We're going to save lives, Theodore! The money will be astronomical! With us, all your dreams will be realized."

"We also had to have you, once we started testing these theories," Troy said, "or you would have sued us."

"Yeah, I would have." Theodore stood up. He felt wobbly, but his anger steadied him. The disgust crashed through him in waves. *Maybe I still can.* Langston repulsed him. *I trusted him and all he wanted to do was steal from me.*

"But you would have had a hard time winning," Troy said. "With the holdings VCC has, we would have kept you in court forever. You would have had a hard time proving *anything*."

Langston shot a menacing glance at Troy, and then turned to Theodore. "That would never happen, Theodore. We're friends now. We care about the same things."

With friends like you . . .

Langston walked over to the cooler and pulled out two bottles of StrongMan Rejuvenator. He opened them and brought one over to Theodore. "You've signed the contracts. We don't want to turn this into something negative, put the false word out that you've been leaking this technology for years. We're one of the major corporations in the world already, Theodore. Soon, we're going to be *the* major corporation. *Your* work is our crowning achievement. Do you know what all this means? It's The Golden Rule. You know, 'Those with the gold, rule.' We will have it *all*." He paused, taking a drink from the bottle. "Though, I will make a confession. To me, the power, the money, pales in comparison to the actual work. This is the most exciting step mankind has ever made. Bigger than going to the moon, bigger than the atomic bomb." His green eyes flashed. "For the very first time we are gaining absolute power over nature. And we're getting closer to immortality, Theodore, thanks to your brilliant mind. Do you understand what I'm telling you?"

"No." Theodore didn't. *It's too much.*

"It means we are there. We can do anything we want!" Langston's voice turned soft, soothing. "I know it's a bit much to take all at once. We should go now, take you back to L.A. and let you get some rest. After all, we've had a lot of time to get used to the idea of what we're doing. You've only had today. I certainly understand."

"Yeah, it's some heavy stuff, Theodore," added Troy. "You need time to soak it all in."

Chapter Fifteen

Friday, June 6

Sitting on the edge of a flower bed, Hattie picked up a four-pack of garnet-hued snapdragons. She turned over the container, gave the sides a squeeze, tapped the bottom, and scrunched one plastic cell. A single plant, along with its root ball and soil, plopped into her hand.

"Now what you do, Zera, is try not to disturb the roots. In most cases, even though they may look all twined together, they'll be fine. When they go into the ground they'll spread and grow." She showed Zera the plant, gently cradled in her hand, her glitter-orange fingernail polish contrasting against the natural colors. Hattie placed the snapdragon in one of the holes she'd dug, gently backfilled the dirt, and then plopped out another "snap" as she called them. "Some folks take out all of the plants at once and leave them lying on the ground while they dig the holes," Hattie's brow wrinkled in disapproval, "but always try to imagine yourself as the plant; your roots have been protected and often damp since germination. Would you want your roots lying there exposed to the wind and sun?"

"No." Zera winced, imagining that it would probably feel like an exposed nerve. She remembered when she'd once chipped a tooth and how sensitive it was. Even a cold drink hurt.

"Here you go, baby," cooed Hattie to the young plant. "You're going to like it here." She planted the others and sprinkled them with warm water from her watering can.

Hattie, Zera and Ben had arrived that morning at Elsie Mayfield's garden. Elsie was one of Hattie's wealthy clients in the nearby ski resort town of Pinyon. Ben was working in the front, weeding a huge rock garden and pruning rose bushes that wouldn't be ready to bloom for at least two more weeks.

When Zera saw the roses, she couldn't help but think about the ones at Nonny's. They had bloomed so beautifully that day, but by the next morning, all the blooms were brown and withered, as if someone had sprayed them with herbicide. The sight had left her confused and upset. Hattie came by to see them but could think of no explanation, except maybe it could be a fast-acting and deadly virus that she'd never seen before. Zera had seen Nonny staring at the dead blossoms a few times. Once she looked at Zera like she wanted to say something, but stopped herself. Uncle Theodore still hadn't called. He had sent them a short text saying they got to L.A. okay, and that was it. Zera didn't want to think about it. The possibility of leaving Ute Springs in three short weeks and moving to Los Angeles was even worse than the ghost with clunky boots.

Other than the phantom of leaving her home haunting her thoughts, things were going well. It was Zera's second morning out as a part-time professional gardener-in-training. Ben worked with his mom, too, so they had spent half the day together yesterday as well. That second night home, Zera realized she had a crush on Ben. It felt strange; Ben was a childhood friend — they had played together as toddlers! But she couldn't deny her feelings; every time she saw him her heart would beat faster and the palms of her hands would get moist with sweat. She was pretty sure he liked her, too — she caught him looking at her all the time.

Zera found she could concentrate on the plants as she toiled beside Hattie. It wasn't so easy when Ben was around. As they planted snapdragons and weeded, Zera thought about how much she enjoyed digging in the dirt. She loved the soft soil, the rich, earthy smell of it. Being outside in the open air, surrounded by living creatures (green and otherwise) was her idea of bliss.

"Dang, it's hot out here." Hattie untied the scarf from around her neck and dabbed her brow. A few long strands of her tawny, gray-streaked hair had come out of her ponytail and she pushed them from her face. "It's about time to break for lunch."

Ben came around the corner and joined them in finishing the planting. When Zera caught him looking at her again, both of their hands in the soil, side by side, the tension in the air became almost palpable. She avoided looking at him directly; she was sure that her feelings would show.

As the three of them hand-watered the rest of the snaps, Elise Mayfield opened the back door of the immense house and strolled out on the verandah. "Hello, Hattie! Everything looks wonderful!" The small, older woman had short blonde hair and wore elegant clothing: black pants, a white silk blouse, pearl necklace, black mules. Elsie picked her way down the steps. "I was wondering if you had a moment, Hattie, before you leave." She lowered her voice to a smoky almost-whisper. "I want to show you what is going on in the vegetable garden."

The mysterious way she said this piqued Zera's curiosity.

"Sure." Hattie introduced Zera, and while Ben stayed to load the truck with their tools, Hattie and Zera followed Elsie around the side of the house to her vegetable garden. The narrow patch ran the length of her six-car garage and was filled with rows of lettuce, chard, radishes, kohlrabi, chives, beans, carrots, and a patch of mint. Newly planted tomatoes in black plastic containers were interspersed among the herbs and veggies.

Zera saw immediately why Elsie Mayfield was alarmed. *Those poor little lettuces. The outer leaves look like Swiss cheese.*

"I've discovered that we have a terrible slug problem." Elsie said. "I need you to apply some slug killer."

"This *is* terrible," Hattie said, "but I think what you have here is a duck deficiency problem."

"A what?"

"If you had a pet duck patrolling the grounds, they'd gobble up those slugs in no time."

"Oh, really!" Elsie Mayfield reacted as if Hattie had just said the most ridiculous thing imaginable.

Zera stifled a smile.

"Don't you have *something* we could use?" Elsie frowned at the lettuces. "If you don't have anything in your truck, I'm sure I could find something in the potting shed. I think I saw something in there a while back labeled 'slug bait.'"

"Now, you know I don't believe in using poisons," Hattie said good-naturedly.

"Well," said Elsie, "I don't believe in using *ducks*."

Zera scratched one dirt-stained knee and looked down at the vegetables. *Awkward!*

Hattie explained to Elsie a couple of other, non-toxic, slug control solutions — beer in saucers to attract the slugs (who would climb in and drown), or boards for the slugs to crawl under during the day (so they could be easily gathered and destroyed). Elsie fidgeted with her string of pearls.

"We can deal with the problem without poison," Hattie said, "but it'll take a little time, a little work. Now, do you want to do something good for the ecosystem, or have instant gratification?"

"Instant gratification," Elsie said without a moment's hesitation. She smiled sweetly at Zera. In spite of herself, Zera smiled back. She couldn't help but find Elsie's swagger impressive. Elsie continued, "I know what I want. I want those slugs dead. And I don't have time to mess around with beer and boards and such. I'll have Juan try to find the slug bait."

"Don't have him do it. I'll look, Elsie." said Hattie.

After Elsie left, Hattie mumbled to Zera that it was a lost

cause, at least for now. "I think I've got a length of old, damaged garden hose in Ladybug we can use." Hattie went to the truck, returning with the hose she'd saved. She showed Zera how to cut it into six-inch lengths and then Hattie put the bait into the pieces, and placed them just outside the garden area.

"At least if we do it this way there'll be a little better chance of not harming beneficial insects. If you just put this stuff on the ground it's going to get into the soil, and into the food, even if it's in minute particles. This way, you can just throw away the lengths of hose when they're filled with dead slugs." Her expression clouded even more. "Damnit, they'll still be in the landfill, but . . . I wish she'd listen."

"At least you tried," Zera said.

"I always will."

Elsie seemed quite pleased that things were done her way.

The three left and headed off to lunch.

At a tiny park across from a convenience store, Hattie parked Ladybug. They washed up at the store's restroom, bought drinks and a few food items, then trekked back across the street, grabbing their sack lunches from the truck and finding a picnic table.

Eating her peanut butter and jelly sandwich and playfully protesting as Ben "stole" from her container of strawberries, Zera listened to Hattie talk about Elsie's "groovy" salmon-pink and lemon-yellow *Primula denticulata*, or drumstick primroses, which were in full bloom. Then Hattie informed them she'd purchased a mobile v-phone the afternoon before.

"Ha," said Ben to Zera. "She swore she'd never get one."

"I know I did," Hattie said, "but with Grandma Wren getting up in age — she's ninety now, you know — I worry about her. I want her to be able to call me if she needs me, and it's impossible to find regular cell phones anymore. Besides, some of my clients have almost insisted on it." She mimicked a hoity-toity voice: "'Hattie, you can *see* what plant we're referring to if we *need* your *advice*, and you're not *here*' — as if nothing could wait a day or two. It's solar-powered. I've had it for a week and still haven't used it. I tried last night, and it didn't work; I'd forgotten to keep it sun-charged!"

Zera and Ben laughed. "What'll be next, Mom?" teased Ben. "A home theatre, with three walls covered with LCD flat screens? Maybe a computer in Ladybug?"

"Never!" said Hattie.

"What's the big deal now?" said Ben. "After all, you do have a *mobile-v*."

As they finished their food, Ben told Zera that he'd caught two garter snakes while at Elsie's.

"In the rock garden?" asked Hattie. She picked up a potato chip and popped it into her mouth as her silver bracelets jingled. When Ben nodded, she said, between chews, "Thought so. They like it there." She took a long chug of water and explained to Zera, "Elsie's terrified of snakes, and we told her we'd remove any we found. I don't like doing it because they're a valuable part of the ecosystem, but she said that if we didn't, her boyfriend would kill them."

"That's awful," Zera said. "They're completely harmless!"

"Well, that's the way it is," Hattie said. "Did you put them in a bucket?"

"Yeah," said Ben, "They're in the shade so they'll be okay. They were freaked out after I caught them and kept trying to slither out. After I put some weeds over them they calmed down."

"We take them to our garden," Hattie told Zera. "Would you like to see them?"

"Sure," Zera said. She imagined Ben capturing the snakes and a lightness filled her chest. She had never even touched one.

They finished their lunches, and while Hattie went to her truck to make her first mobile-v call ever, to a nursery to check on a flower order, Zera followed Ben to the back of the truck. Ben pulled out a large weed-collecting bucket that was now covered with a work shirt and a bungee cord. He hauled it to a shady spot underneath a tree and partially uncovered it.

Zera got down on her knees and peered in. She reached in and gently pushed the weeds aside, and Ben crouched down next to her. She could detect the scent of Ben's shampoo and a slight sweatiness, a combination that made her pulse race. It mixed in with the smells of the wilting plant material, fragrant and green. The weeds felt cool and moist as they brushed her skin.

She spied them. Two snakes, around a foot long, were lying next to one another on the bottom of the white bucket. They were black with thin, almost luminous yellow stripes running down the length of their backs.

"Oh, look at them," Zera murmured. She leaned in, keeping the shirt over the top of the bucket as much as possible. She smiled at Ben. "They're so pretty. They're ribbon snakes, *Western* ribbon snakes." To the snakes she said, "Poor things, taken from your home. Don't worry, Ben and Hattie will take good care of you."

"Ribbon snakes?" said Ben. "Are you sure?"

Zera nodded. "Yeah. Garters are mottled, more irregular." Zera blinked. She wasn't sure how she knew this, but she was certain. She'd never studied snakes before and yet, *she just knew*.

The snakes, who would normally seek shelter when exposed, stayed still and calm. She touched one with her finger and it stretched out its body. Without thinking, she stroked its back with her finger, and it did not move. It felt cool, smooth. Its eyes closed drowsily. The second snake looked on, lying still. Zera watched them, mesmerized. She'd never touched a snake before, yet it seemed natural to do so and natural for them to respond without alarm. *So beautiful.*

Ben started to put his hand into the bucket and then pulled away, eyes huge. He quickly got to his feet. "Mom!" he yelled in the direction of Ladybug. "Come quick!"

He gaped at Zera. The snakes had slithered up her hands.

Each had wrapped itself tightly around a wrist, twice, ending with its tail in its mouth. These double circles were stretched taut but motionless. The snakes' eyes were open and staring up at Zera. Zera sat still and tranquil, seemingly oblivious. Her lips were parted with a slight smile, and a faraway look shone in her eyes, as if nothing out of the ordinary was happening.

Chapter Sixteen

Hattie came running. She saw the snakes, in their inexplicable tail-in-mouth positions around Zera's wrists, for only a second before Ben reached down and grabbed them both, flinging them across the grass. Hattie gasped, an orange-nailed hand flying to her mouth.

Ben choked out the words, "What the hell *was* that?" He looked at Hattie, then at the parking lot and the park, as if expecting answers somewhere else. "Those snakes couldn't have . . ."

Zera had not changed her tranquil expression, or her position on the grass.

"Are you okay?" Hattie squatted down, touched Zera's shoulder. "Zera?" She raised her voice. "Zera!"

"You . . . you don't think she's been bitten?" Ben asked, his face pale. He grabbed Zera by both shoulders and shook her.

Zera shuddered. The calm expression disappeared. She looked up at them as if she had come out of a trance. "I, I heard them," she said, her voice shaking. "They said they're in danger, we're all in danger."

Zera blinked. She couldn't believe her own words. Her eyes filled with tears. *What is happening to me?*

"They *spoke*?" said Hattie. She shook her head, rubbed her goose bump-covered arms. "I can't believe what I just saw."

Zera had stated the truth, as insane as it seemed. She *did* hear the snakes, and that *is* exactly what they had said. They didn't move their mouths, they didn't literally speak, but she clearly heard them. *All are in danger.*

"What danger?" Ben asked, looking around again. "There has to be something to this; it's got to be some kind of a joke." He looked at Zera as if she were a different person than the one he'd been flirting with all morning.

"You didn't hear them?" Zera asked.

"No. This is messed up. I need a minute." Ben set off towards the park.

A part of Zera desperately hoped that Hattie, with her impressive store of horticultural and animal knowledge, would have an answer to all this. That somehow a grownup would step in and make everything okay. *Maybe she'll say, I don't know, sometimes snakes can coil around you . . . and speak?* Her heart thumped. *That's not going to happen.*

Hattie bent down and put an arm around Zera.

Zera took a deep breath, wiped her eyes on her T-shirt and tried to collect herself. *Ben had seen it. Hattie had too.* She took another deep breath. *It'll be okay. I'll figure this out.* She got to her feet.

"We're going back to Ute Springs," said Hattie. She yelled at Ben's disappearing figure, "Ben, get back here!"

Heading down Golden Eagle pass, six miles out of Pinyon, Hattie took a turn onto a dirt road instead of continuing on to Highway 24, the road to Ute Springs.

Completely lost in her thoughts, Zera hardly noticed that Ben was sitting very close beside her, looking at her with concern, yet still completely freaked out. Zera's mind was filled with the words. The snakes' words. She had heard them so plainly, *We're in danger. All are in danger.* She couldn't believe that Ben hadn't heard; the voices were so clear, so urgent. The possibility that she was losing her mind seemed the most obvious, but they'd seen the snakes too, seen them coil around her. There was something about it, something she couldn't figure out that seemed familiar. And how did she know they were ribbon snakes, *Western ribbon snakes*, to be exact, not garter snakes like she'd been told? She had no knowledge of snakes, she had never studied them. Yet she even knew the name of the genus, *Thamnophis.* It was the same genus as garter snakes, but they were a different species, they were *proximus. How could I possibly know all that?* She shuddered.

"It'll be okay, honey," Hattie said. She patted Zera's leg, and her silver bracelets jingled. "I've decided to stop by Grandma Wren's first. She may be able to help." She gave Zera a reassuring glance, yet Zera read worry in Hattie's dark eyes.

As they climbed upward along the dirt road, the serpentine Falcon Pass, the scenery changed. They found themselves surrounded by stands of ponderosa pine, aspen, and scrub oak. Then the road dipped downward, back into boulder-strewn meadows, and after two more miles they slowed to a large gate just off-road. Horses grazed among the tall grass and wildflowers behind a fence.

The red truck pulled into a gravel driveway. By that time the sense of shock had eased. Zera watched as Ben jumped out to open the heavy steel gate. The truck rattled up a steep driveway to a shabby double-wide trailer. Its exterior was faded white and turquoise, with smeary orange rust patches along the roof. Next to it sat a tire-less 1950s Ford truck that was propped up by concrete blocks. The truck had once been red but was now bleached to a dull orange-pink.

The trio climbed the trailer's rickety wood stairs and Hattie knocked.

To the tune of high-pitched barking, the door opened.

Grandmother Wren was tiny, under five feet. Her face, wizened with age, reminded Zera of a doll her dad had given her when he'd been researching early American music in Appalachia. It was an apple-head doll, its head made from a carved, then dried, apple that had become dark and wrinkled. Grandma Wren's hair looked like the doll's too, snow white, like cotton batting. Only her eyes were not doll-like; they were the black-brown of strong coffee — clear and alert — so like Hattie's and Ben's. A dingy white sweater covered her floral-patterned dress, and she wore cloth house slippers.

"Grandmother," Hattie said.

"Hattie, Ben! Come in." Grandma Wren pushed the door open wide.

Inside, Grandma Wren put her arms around Ben, and Ben hugged her tenderly. Zera thought it was sweet, and she was hopeful that maybe Ben was a little calmer by now.

"I had a dream about you three nights ago," Grandma Wren said to Hattie. Her voice was sandpapery, yet the words were gently spoken. "And I had a dream about you, too, Zera Green," she said.

Grandma Wren eyed Zera. Zera stared back, marveling how she'd said those words so matter-of-factly.

"We need your help, Grandmother. Something's happened," said Hattie.

"I know. I've been waiting."

They were stunned by her comment.

The tiny living room, strewn with books and newspapers, smelled of musty dog, cooking oil, and relics of the past. A poodle, hairless except for its head, feet, and the tip of its tail, went from barking at Grandma Wren's feet to hopping back onto the couch. Its tail wagged as it watched Zera.

Grandma Wren took Zera's hands in her own. Under their boney, leathery surface, Zera felt warmth and strength.

The woman studied Zera's face. "When the Creator first made the world and all the living things in it, all the plants and animals could communicate. They still do, it's just that most people don't hear them anymore. You do."

Looking into Grandma Wren's eyes, Zera felt calm for the first time since the snakes had wrapped themselves around her wrists. She had always suspected something about herself, something she felt within her very core but could not name — a sense that she could understand things about nature, about the feelings and intentions of living things, plants and animals. But she'd never had any proof that it was anything more than an overactive imagination. And, then, after her parents had died . . . *Those feelings disappeared. I had almost forgotten them.* She looked away, avoiding Grandma Wren's gaze. *It couldn't be real.* But her instincts told her it was. An excitement surged within her. She wasn't insane. The snakes *had* spoken to her. Zera's head swam with thoughts. *What does it all mean? Why would they speak to me? How could I have this connection to Nature?*

She looked into Grandma Wren's dark eyes and blurted, "But I'm not even Ute!"

Grandma Wren cackled, revealing a strangely beautiful jack-o'-lantern smile. Still holding onto Zera's hands she said, "My dear, knowledge and wisdom do not belong to only one group of people. *They belong to all humankind.* Please, sit down," she said, still chuckling at Zera's declaration. "Have a glass of water."

Zera and Ben went to the couch, and the hairless poodle moved so they could sit down. Then it climbed over Zera and nestled between them.

Zera noticed the room contained an assortment of taxidermied animals: a huge beaver attached to a piece of giant driftwood on the wall above the television set, a big-mouth bass on the adjacent wall, a diamondback rattlesnake on a side table (rearing up, fangs bared), and a small gray squirrel atop a bookcase with a walnut in its paws.

Hattie, who was about to sit down in a chair next to them, whispered, "It was Benjamin's late great-uncle Clyde's hobby. We all think they're weird, but Grandma Wren feels that they serve as reminders of what we should *not* do to nature."

"Oh." *Yeah, pretty creepy.*

"That's Cookie," said Grandma Wren, nodding at the dog from her rocking chair. "I don't know why she lost her hair, but she's been like that for months. I keep a sweater on her when it gets cold."

As Zera petted the dog's cool, oddly naked flesh, Cookie wagged her tail, and then rested her head on Zera's leg. *She needs sunshine*, thought Zera. The information came to her as if it was simply common sense, even though she was as ignorant of dog skin conditions as she was of snakes. "Does she get outside much?"

Grandma Wren's face crinkled. "She hasn't been outside, not for any long period, since her pen was damaged last fall. I don't like her out there, because of the cougars. I just haven't been able to keep up with things . . ." Her eyes brightened.

"That's what is wrong with her!"

Zera nodded.

Hattie cut in. "You know about the snakes, Grandmother? How could you? I wouldn't have believed it if I hadn't seen it myself. It was like the old stories, but I *saw* it happen."

Hattie told the story of the snakes while Grandma Wren sat there, rocking gently. Ben wore an expression of disbelief and something that looked like just-under-the-surface anger. He fidgeted and avoided eye contact with Zera. *I'm having a hard enough time,* thought Zera. *I can't even imagine what he thinks about it all.*

When Hattie finished, Grandma Wren said, "Zera, I am ninety years old. I grew up here in the mountains, listening to my grandmother tell the stories about the Ute. Our stories. That was long ago, before our storytelling tradition was nearly abandoned. I remembered them all, though, and passed them on to whoever would listen. Hattie's heard them."

Hattie nodded.

Grandma Wren continued. "Three nights ago the guardian visited me in a dream. In it, the world was turned upside down. Plants no longer knew who they were; people no longer knew who they were. Too many no longer see that they are a part of the natural world. Man and woman, for so long, have forgotten their first roles as protectors." She looked up at Hattie. "The guardian told me you would bring Zera. She is going to help change things."

Zera's stomach lurched. Out of the corner of her eye she saw Ben shake his head.

"Who, or what's, the guardian?" asked Hattie.

"The guardian is the link from the spirit world to our world." Grandma Wren leaned forward in her chair. "He takes many forms. Last night he appeared as Dancing Crow, a medicine man my family knew when I was a child. I'd forgotten about him, he's been gone for over eighty years."

Zera spoke up. "What were the snakes doing, Grandma Wren?"

"They told you about the danger. But they were also telling you about life." Her thin, leathery arm gestured toward the pitcher on the coffee table. "Please, have some water."

Hattie poured herself and Zera a glass. Zera, surprised at her incredible thirst, downed half the water in one long drink, took a breath, and then finished the rest.

"The snake's bodies made the ancient sign," Grandma Wren said. "The sign of the Great Round. Are the snakes, having tail in mouth, consuming themselves or are they creating themselves?" Her brown-black eyes bored into Zera's as she answered her own question. "It is both. They were showing you the cycle, the continuity." Her gnarled hands slowly formed a circle in the air before her. "The relationship of eternity to time. Consumption and creation. Snakes, because they shed their skin and become new again, are also the sign of rebirth, renewal. The guardian did not show me what you are called upon to do. What danger is upon us. For this we have to go to Tava."

"Tava?" asked Zera.

"Our people called it Tava, which means Sun. That was its name for 10,000 years. When the white settlers came, they named it after the explorer Zebulon Pike. Our people still go there to find answers. It is a sacred place for vision quests."

Zera had loved Pikes Peak of all her life. It was the highest mountain near them, towering gigantic and majestic, snowcapped through most of the year. Zera had hiked to its 14,000 foot summit several times with her parents; the last time had been the summer they died.

"We must go to the mountain," said Grandma Wren. "Tonight, as the sun sets."

Chapter Seventeen

After finding a sweater for Cookie and checking on her food and water, Grandma Wren changed into pants and a flannel shirt and gathered coats for the mountaintop excursion. She found a pair of trousers for Hattie that Hattie's father, Joe, had left behind on a hunting trip last fall. She brought out a large beaded buckskin bag from the back of the trailer and asked Hattie to put it in the truck.

Ben said, "I don't believe any of this," to his mother as they were getting in the truck.

Hattie shrugged, "That's your right, Ben."

Ben, the last to get in the truck, slammed the door.

His anger brought sadness to Zera. Her thoughts went from the disturbing — *Maybe not only am I crazy, but Hattie and Grandma Wren are too* — to a somehow worse thought, *He probably doesn't like me at all, now.*

On the silent drive to Ute Springs, Zera retraced the afternoon's events. Her heart thudded again as she pictured the snakes, their words echoing the warning, *We're in danger. All are in danger.* She struggled to understand. She didn't know what Grandma Wren meant by plants and people no longer knowing who they were. It was too vague. She had tried to ask more questions at the trailer, but Grandma Wren only said, "We will learn more tonight."

The truck rumbled down the two-lane highway as trees raced by and a cloud-decorated sky projected colored patterns on the windshield. Zera found herself drifting into a waking dream, an intermingling of two worlds — one real, one fantastical. Other words filled her mind; sweet whispered words she'd heard as she lay half-asleep in her bed, both here and in Piker. *Go back to sleep, darling. Welcome back. You're home now.* She *had* heard them. It wasn't her imagination. They were real. What was unreal is that she was somehow supposed to help "change things." *I can't even change things in my own life, so how can I change things for anything else?*

Zera, squeezed next to Ben, "accidentally" nudged him and Ben's eyes met hers, but for only a second, before they both turned back to the landscape. It was clear; he didn't have anything to say to her. She felt no thrill when he looked at her that time. Grandma Wren, wedged comfortably on her other side, between herself and Hattie, napped while they drove.

Nonny raised herself from a wicker chair on the porch and, cane in hand, limped down the stairs to the driveway, her face set in a scowl.

"Where have you been?" she asked as Ben opened the truck door and Zera climbed out. "Is everything all right?" At the sight of Grandma Wren, the lines on her face deepened. "I don't mean to overreact, but I've been waiting for over two hours. No one seemed to know Hattie's mobile-v number. I was worried!"

"Everything's fine, Guinevere," Hattie said. She walked around the truck and placed a hand on Nonny's shoulder. "I'm sorry we made you worry. I should have called you. It's just that something has happened, and we've all been kind of . . . distracted."

Nonny Green's expression changed from guarded relief to concern again.

"Nothing physical," said Hattie. "It's just, well, we'll explain."

A half-hour later, sitting on the wicker porch swing, Nonny had heard everything. Zera revealed even more — the times she thought she heard voices that seemed to come from plants, the feeling that someone was watching her outside the chicken coop her first day home, the weird certainty about the ribbon snakes and their Latin name. Hattie added the part about Grandma Wren's dog. Grandma Wren told Nonny about her visit from the guardian and explained why they must go to Tava.

Throughout the accounts, Nonny listened patiently, her mouth tight and her brow furrowed. When Zera shared her experiences, Nonny's hands trembled slightly and she absent-mindedly rubbed the leaf-and-symbol-covered bracelet on her left wrist.

Nonny rose from her swing with the help of her turquoise-tipped cane, and stood at the porch railing. Pikes Peak towered before them, its summit visible through a trio of clouds. Just off the porch, the dead roses hung on the trellis among the still-green leaves.

"Zera, there is something I have to tell you." Nonny propped her cane against the railing. She looked from Zera, who sat on the rug near Ben, to Ben and then to Hattie and Grandma Wren, who sat together in a wicker loveseat.

"When I was a child, my mother and grandmother told me all the fairy stories native to our ancestral homeland in the British Isles. I grew up learning about pixies, elves, goblins, giants, fairies, mermaids, and all the rest. It was almost like a family history, the way they told those stories." She nodded at Grandma Wren. "Like your people's stories, Nellie, the stories of the Native Americans, ours had been passed down for generations. Tales of another world that co-existed with ours, and tales of its supernatural inhabitants. Tales that were a source of delight as well as instruction."

"I loved those stories," Zera said. "Mom read me fairy stories all the time."

"You remember some of them," corrected Nonny. "The ones known in modern culture, but you didn't hear the others, the ones we'd passed down in our family. There were many more."

Zera got up to stand next to her grandmother.

"You see," said Nonny, "by the time I was a young girl growing up, our family had been in America for over a century.

Throughout those years our stories had remained alive, in spite of the fact that many in this country thought they were superstitious beliefs, and to keep them alive was foolish, deviant, even. To speak of certain beings as if they actually existed was dangerous. An aunt of mine in the 1930s had rumors spread about her, that she was a witch, for suggesting that magic existed. People in her town sent nasty, anonymous letters, and her home was set on fire one night, although they got it out before it burned down. She had to pack up and leave."

"I never knew that!" said Zera.

Nonny's face clouded. "I once told a teacher, when I was in the first grade, that I came from the fairies. She said, 'That is a lie, young lady,' and she gave me a sound spanking."

Hattie stiffened. "Good grief!"

Nonny's appearance brightened. "I have to admit I've always had the quality of being a bit full of myself, even then, so that probably didn't help in my dealings with authority, but nevertheless."

"You think you came from fairies?" Zera said, both interest and reluctance in her voice. She glanced over at Ben, whose forehead was wrinkled in disbelief. He was staring off at a few of the chickens scratching for bugs under a purple-leaved plum tree.

Nonny laughed. The tightness in her mouth relaxed and her eyes danced. "Who knows? My mother always told me that we did, that's where our artistic abilities, our imaginations, and our gifts with plants, came from; that's how she explained it anyway. Is it imagination, or is it a link into our own world that others aren't willing, or perhaps able, to see? I look at it as being part of the unknowable, and that gives it even more meaning, and yes, magic, to me."

Grandma Wren reached over and put a hand on Hattie's arm. "You know what I believe."

"Yes, I do," Hattie replied, patting her grandmother's hand.

"You see," Nonny said, "as with Grandma Wren's culture, celebrating our history took its toll. There were no original fairy stories in America, unless you count the rags-to-riches stories about entrepreneurs, movie stars, athletes. Oh, those were *very* important. Still are." Nonny sighed. "Those are the stories that hold the magic here."

"By the time it was my turn to pass our stories down to Sally and Ted, they no longer seemed important. I wanted to do what would be best for them." Her expression turned grim. "It was only recently that I began to realize I had perhaps made a terrible mistake."

Zera's face was bright with wonder as much as Ben's, still staring off in the distance, was dark with skepticism. Nonny's voice lowered. "Some of the stories that were particularly important to our family, Zera, were ones involving someone we called the Green Man."

Zera's eyes grew huge. Nonny got her cane and went back to the swing. Zera followed her. "I've seen him, Nonny."

Nonny stopped the swing's rocking with her cane. "You have?"

"She saw him in my garden," Hattie said. "My ceramic wall art, the face by the water garden." She paused. "Guinevere, Zera had quite a reaction to it."

Ben stood up, his face flushed, eyes wild. "This is all too much. Fairies? Mom, really? You expect me just to believe all this?"

"Ben," said Hattie, "we're talking about what we've experienced. Believe me, we know it's strange!"

"Strange? That's an understatement! I can't listen to this anymore. I'm going home."

"If that's what you want."

Ben took off down the hill and Zera's heart sank.

Grandma Wren caught Zera's eye. "He'll come around."

"Don't be so sure of it," Hattie said. "This is a lot for anyone to handle. Even me, and I've always been open to the . . . not-so-easily understood. Ben has a lot of his father's traits — he's into the practical, factual."

"He's half of you too, Hattie," said Grandma Wren.

A breeze came up, shaking the leaves on the rose canes. The dead roses made crinkling sounds, like autumn leaves. *Whether anyone likes it, something's going on,* Zera thought. A big part of her wanted to believe the snakes were her imagination, but she knew better. She pushed thoughts about Ben out of her mind. "Nonny, tell me about the Green Man."

Nonny looked at the three females as if she, too, were questioning her sanity, then her blue eyes became darker, serious. "I'll tell you right now, the Green Man's spirit is very *real.* I don't understand any of this, really, I'm as astonished as everyone else here, but it seems he's come back to us. When I was a girl you hardly ever heard about him outside of our home, except for the tales of Robin Hood."

Zera's forehead crinkled. "What? The Green Man is Robin Hood?"

"Well, yes, and no," Nonny said. "The Green Man is complex, he represents many things. Primarily he symbolizes the unity of the human and plant worlds." She laid her hand on her granddaughter's. "To this day they perform some of the ceremonies in the British Isles. In one of them, a type of May Day celebration, he's called Jack in the Green. He's also called the King of May, the Garland, *Le Feuillu*, or the leaf man, in France, and *Blattmaske* and *Der gruner Mensch* in Germany. In ancient Egypt he was *Osiris*."

The foreign words tumbled in Zera's head. *Why haven't I heard of any of this?* She stared at her grandmother; she couldn't remember the last time she had seen Nonny's eyes so clear and bright, her cheeks so flushed. She looked twenty years younger.

"Robin Hood is just one of his personas, a bold green knight that robs from the rich and gives to the poor." Nonny's voice rose in excitement, "In that guise he's not so much a figure of wisdom as he is of heroic justice and daring. There's never been a legend in American culture that's similar, except for Paul Bunyan, a giant who chops down stands of forests with his mighty ax and changes the courses of rivers. Rather anti-nature if you think about it. But now we are seeing images of the Green Man again, in garden stores, in poetry, in art. He's returned. And he's not just a cartoon on a can of vegetables."

"I know who you're talking about!" Zera laughed. "*He* comes from the Green Man?"

Hattie nodded. "The legend survives, even in the lamest forms." She looked out towards the direction of the barn. "I bet the snakes' warning has something to do with global warming."

"That would make sense," said Nonny, her expression darkening for a moment. "We have made such a terrible mess of the planet."

"Tell me more about the Green Man," said Zera.

"Your mother did not know about this, though she always sensed it. That's one of the reasons why she kept her maiden name, I'm sure of it. Why she gave you your particular name, and, of course, all of this came out in her art!" Nonny idly rubbed the leaf-and-symbol bracelet on her left wrist. "Our family name comes from our ties to the Green Man. We had always been important participants in the old country ceremonies, since, I'm sure, before recorded history. And our family has always been involved in honoring the connections between man and the green world in some way. I don't know the details, those have been lost, but the story, that we're connected to the Green Man . . . my mother told me this when I was about your age."

"Wait," Zera said. "The name Green comes from your side of the family? It didn't come from Grandpa?"

"No, darling, we used my family name, which was fine with your grandfather. I'll explain it one day, but suffice it to say, he was a man ahead of his times." Nonny smiled. "Ours is the only name I know of that has been passed down through both the maternal and paternal lines for generations."

"The Navajo have a maternal lineage tradition," Hattie said. "Guinevere, I'm stunned. I had no idea. Sally never said a thing!"

Nonny shook her snow-white head. "Sally didn't know. Over the years I began to fear that our history would die out with me, as I am the last of the Greens of our lineage, the last I know of anyway. All my cousins are gone, Sally's gone, and Ted, well, Ted has chosen a path that seems to diverge from our values. I thought that this may be the natural order, to let old beliefs die. But as we see, now, that is perhaps not the way it is meant to be." Nonny's mouth tightened. "Still, all this scares the life out of me, Zera. Signs? Snakes? Hearing and seeing these things? I don't feel brave about this at all, not one bit. In my very bones, I tremble."

They sat silent, mulling it all over.

Grandma Wren stood. Her aged face was twisted with anguish.

She addressed Hattie, dark eyes flashing. "You and Zera seem surprised at all of this. Why? Haven't you felt the truths all along, that there is much more to this world than what you see?"

Hattie and Zera exchanged glances. *What do I really feel to be true, now, in my mind and heart?* Zera asked herself.

"Nellie," Nonny said to Grandma Wren, "these two, and Ben, have been raised in a world where any kind of magic comes mostly from TV screens, electrical outlets, and batteries. *Give them time*."

"Grandma," Hattie said, standing up and looking out toward Pikes Peak, "it's getting late. We should get to Tava."

"Yes." Grandma Wren rose from the loveseat.

"I'm going too," said Nonny.

Hattie and Grandma Wren exchanged glances. "You should stay here. Zera will be fine with us," said Grandma Wren.

Hattie's face clouded. "I don't think it's a good idea, either. Your leg, Guinevere, and the oxygen up there. We'll be going to a place where there's some rugged terrain, once we get to the top of the mountain."

"I'll be fine. And I want to be with my granddaughter."

"The altitude . . . it can put a lot of stress . . ." Hattie began.

Nonny interrupted. "I *will* go." She shot them a look that said the issue was settled.

Zera and her grandmother went inside to change into winter clothing as it would be near-freezing at the 14,000 foot summit. Back in the living room, they found Grandma Wren and Hattie had put on sweaters from the truck. Hattie had taken down her ponytail and brushed out her waist-length hair.

I wish Ben were going, but he thinks I'm a nut job. Maybe I am. Maybe we all are.

Nonny approached Grandma Wren. "I don't think we can drive up there. If I recall, they close the highway at dusk. I was thinking," she paused, "Cosmic Dan's the conductor at the Cog Railway this summer. He'd take us up there. And he'd wait for us, I'm sure."

"I didn't know he was working there," said Hattie, suddenly cheerful.

"Yep," said Nonny. "I told him that it surely was the very last job in this town he hadn't held."

A sly smile spread across Hattie's face. "That man is something else."

Though the Pikes Peak Cog Railway Depot was only five blocks away, because of their hurry, the grandmothers, and the fact that they'd be returning after dark, they took Ladybug. Hattie and Grandma Wren piled into the cab, but Nonny waited, watching as Zera climbed into the truck's bed.

"Here, darling," Nonny said, handing a wool jacket to Zera. "You know I've been waiting for your return to take your mother and father's ashes up to the Peak?"

"Yes, you told me at Christmas. We're not taking them now, are we?"

"No. I'd planned on the two of us going up there soon, though, that's how I found out Dan was working there." She looked worried. "I never imagined any of this."

Zera nodded. "I know."

Nonny's eyes crinkled and Zera saw they were glistening.

Zera's gut clenched. She knew Nonny was worried, more than she was letting on. She was too.

Chapter Eighteen

Zera walked ahead of the others to the white stone building housing the Pikes Peak Cog Railway Depot. A sign in front listed the departure times. Zera took a deep breath and studied it while the others caught up. "The last one leaves at 5 P.M.," she told them.

"What time is it now?" asked Hattie. Hattie laughed when she found out not one of them had taken a v-phone with them. She glanced westward at the sun. "It's going to be close."

Zera opened the door to a bustling scene. Groups of teenagers moved around, chatting and joking, clutching their backpacks, sipping on drinks. Tourists milled about, taking turns peering out the giant picture windows at the foothills scenery and the shiny cog railway cars.

Zera overheard snatches of conversation she could identify by nationality but couldn't understand: French from a tall blonde woman, addressing her two young children; German from a middle-aged man speaking with his wife; and a group of young enthusiastic tourists conversing in Japanese while toying with their holographic cameras. A clock on the wall read 4:48 P.M.

Hattie said, "Real close. And it looks like they might be sold out."

The group paused when they caught the southern drawl conversation of a family of seven near the window — a middle-aged couple, three boys, a grandmother, and a woman Zera guessed to be an aunt. The man was trying to persuade "Mama" to join them on the trip. "Mama, we've already bought the tickets. For cryin' out loud, it's safe!" He jerked at the collar on his shirt.

Mama, heavy-set and wearing a colorful windbreaker, didn't budge. "Y'all go along without me. The airplane ride was bad enough. I ain't doin' it again, goin' up in the sky up the side of that mountain."

The aunt, a skinny, young version of "Mama," heaved a sigh. "I can't leave you here by yourself. If you stay, I guess I'll have no choice but to stay too."

"We'll be right back," Hattie said to Nonny and Grandma Wren. She grabbed Zera's arm and they headed for the ticket booth.

"Hey, Denise," Hattie said. "Do you have any more seats on the five o'clock?"

"Hattie — what are you doing here?"

Zera recognized the woman with the mop of curly red hair as an old friend of her mom's. Denise's gaze met Zera's and she blinked hard. "Oh my goodness! I heard you were back!" Denise tilted her mop of curls to see outside of her booth. "You brought Guinevere with you, and Grandma Wren, too?" She leaned out of the window, waved a thin, freckle-covered hand, "Hi, ladies!"

The grandmothers waved back.

Denise said, "We're booked solid, Hattie. Tourist season's back with a vengeance. I don't know if we could get you in, unless, of course," she nodded over in the direction of the Texans, "they don't persuade Mama to go. That's been going on for fifteen minutes."

Hattie and Zera looked over at the group. Mama stood in the same spot, arms folded over her chest.

"She's not going anywhere," Hattie said. "She was traumatized on the flight here and now she's making her stand. I know how it is."

"You? A fear of heights?" Denise's grin was huge.

"Hey, don't laugh! It's kind of unbelievable, I know. You always hear how Native Americans don't have that fear, how they love to work on skyscrapers and walk around on the edge of cliffs and all that jazz." Hattie's lips pulled down into a mock grimace. "Well, apparently I didn't inherit that particular gene. Heights scare the pee out of me."

Zera couldn't help but snicker. Hattie always found a way to make things comical.

A whistle blew, followed by a deep, melodic voice that Zera instantly recognized. "All aboard!"

All eyes went to a dark, attractive man standing by the door that led outside to the railway cars.

Denise nodded toward Cosmic Dan. "Hattie, Zera, you guys just go on up, you know your money's no good here anyway.

I'm sure Dan will find a spot for you." She turned to Zera. "It's so good to see you, honey."

"You too. Thanks, Denise."

As they walked over to Grandma Wren and Nonny, Dan greeted the now-excited-to-be-boarding passengers. He was dressed casually, in jeans and a tan polo shirt with the insignia of the railway emblazoned over one breast. A tan cap was pulled over his hair. *He trimmed his hair. A lot.* His afro was very short compared to the first time she saw him.

"Yes, ma'am, we'll be spending about forty minutes at the top of the Peak . . . No ma'am, there's no mountain lions up that high . . . Trip takes about three hours total . . . Yes, sir, it is a glorious day to go up . . . Oh, you're from Texas, that's great, we get a lot of visitors from Texas, and we're thankful for every one."

When all had boarded, they approached Dan.

"Hey, Dan," said Hattie.

"Hi, Hattie, ladies." Dan grinned. "Here to join us?"

"Well, we're going to try, if you have room. I noticed there were a couple of folks who decided not to go," she tilted her head in the direction of Mama and the now put-upon-looking aunt, sitting on a bench.

"Looks like we'll have just enough seats, then. I keep two empty, just in case. And you don't need tickets."

Hattie lowered her voice, "Dan?"

"Yes?"

"I don't have a lot of time to explain right now. I'm sure the passengers would like to get on with their tour. Um, we'll need to spend a little more time on the mountain than the allotted forty minutes . . . ," her voice lowered and Dan leaned closer to her, his expression becoming as serious as Hattie's. "Dan, Grandma Wren needs to talk to the spirits."

Cosmic Dan's face registered only slight surprise. He glanced at Grandma Wren, Zera and her grandmother. Hattie's comment was weird, but Zera imagined he heard a lot stranger things than that in Ute Springs. His reply validated that. "Not a problem, Hat."

They climbed aboard and found two empty seats at the front marked "reserved," and the other two surrendered by the Texans.

"See, I told you it was fine," Dan said, adjusting his cap. "We always have seats reserved for 'VIPs.'" He winked at Zera.

As they took their seats, "Mama" and her daughter climbed the outside steps to the car.

"Oh, no, they're going after all," said Hattie.

Grandma Wren nudged her daughter with her buckskin bag, a bag that had drawn quite a few interested looks from the passengers. "Zera and I will go alone."

Mama and her daughter stood at the front, looking for seats.

"I think we should go *together*. All of us." Nonny's grip on her cane tightened.

"It will be fine, Guinevere," insisted Grandma Wren.

"But Nellie," Nonny raised her voice.

"Please," Zera said to her grandmother. "If Grandma Wren says it's okay. It's okay. I can handle it."

Dan bent over Nonny. "Tell you what. I'll make another trip up here, after this one, and I'll bring you and Hattie up."

"But wouldn't that be against company policy, or something?" Hattie said.

"It's no problem. Owner owes me a favor anyway." Dan clapped his hands together. "But now I've got to get the show on the road."

Nonny wasn't happy about it, but she left with Hattie. Anxiety washed over Zera as she watched her grandmother carefully take the steps down off the train. Now she was going to be by herself, alone on a mountain, with Grandma Wren, a ninety-year-old woman. She'd computed the schedule; Dan would leave them alone up there for almost two hours.

After everyone was settled in, the train began to move. Dan stood in the aisle and began his talk on the history of the century-old depot and railway.

"In the next hour and fifteen minutes we'll be going up. Way up. We're already over a mile high in elevation, at Ute Springs, and by the time we get to the top of Pikes Peak we'll be another mile up." Dan held the cordless microphone loosely as he spoke. "This train, made in Switzerland, is a cog railway, meaning that the railway's heavy serrated rail in the center of the track furnishes traction for the cog wheel. This type of engineering was necessary because the grade we're going up is seldom less than 12½ percent."

On the words "engineering" and "grade" there were rumbles of interest from a few passengers. Zera, still preoccupied with the fact that Nonny and Hattie wouldn't be coming, tried to listen but was having a hard time concentrating.

"But don't you worry. This train is safe, safe as can be," Dan continued. "And if something were to happen we do have an additional safety measure. If this train should somehow detach from the track and plunge down the side of Pikes Peak," he made a dramatic plummeting motion with his hand, his appearance now serious, "we have some large springs at the bottom that will cushion the fall." He paused for effect, "Ute Springs."

Laughter, some nervous like Zera's, echoed through the car.

The first few miles of track followed a stream through a steep canyon filled with fir, pine trees and gigantic boulders. Grandma Wren was so small, Zera had no problem seeing out of the window next to her. As they passed a deep ravine, Grandma Wren commented on the wild vegetation growing amid high rock walls. She rattled off a lot of names, some in the Ute tongue, and Zera was again startled to discover she somehow knew them all.

Dan pointed out historical and geological places of interest as the train moved up over 8,000 feet. Now groves of quaking aspen carpeted the valleys between the mountains. The passengers were surprised to see deep wagon wheel ruts from a trail almost parallel to the tracks, a trail made over a century ago by the area's first tourists. Zera's anxiety ebbed as she settled back in her wood seat, lulled by the beauty outside the windows, while the train click-click-clicked up the incline.

The cog went around the mountain, then slowly began the ascent up the Peak. Cosmic Dan told the passengers that the line had to be cut open every spring through snow drifts that were sometimes twenty-five feet deep. Between 9,000 and 11,000 feet, he pointed out different species of trees: Engelmann spruce, subalpine fir, aspen, and lodgepole and limber pine.

At 11,500 feet, the trees, which had steadily grown more squat and shrub-like, disappeared. Chunks of rocks and fields of monster-size gravel were strewn as far as Zera could see. Dan cracked a joke about how Texans boasted that everything was bigger in their state, but this is what was called "gravel" in Colorado. They were above timberline.

Climbing further, along the spine of the summit ridge, an irregular staircase of granite shards outlined a grassy saddle of Alpine tundra. Dwarf herbs and grasses, a carpet of green, hugging ground that wasn't covered with snow. Tiny, flowering alpine plants grew abundantly in the rocks and in crevices between boulders.

Grandma Wren whispered, "A wondrous creation."

Zera pointed out three lapis lazuli-hued reservoirs in the distance. "They're so bright blue; like something you'd see in a pop-up storybook."

Dan started describing one of the few mammalian inhabitants, the yellow-bellied marmot.

"I see 'em!" squealed a boy of about six, his finger jabbing toward the window at a group of housecat-sized creatures with russet-colored fur, ambling across an alpine meadow.

"Marmots are related to groundhogs and their nickname is whistle-pigs," explained Dan. "As you can see, they're social creatures. They travel in groups of six or more. One of them will always be on top of a rock, looking out for danger. If any is sensed, the marmot makes a high-pitched squeal of alarm. They're about twenty pounds in weight and they hibernate for eight or nine months of the year. When they're hibernating their body temperatures go down between 43 and 57 degrees. They've just come out of their rocky burrows for the short summer and are feeding now."

Dan also described the Rocky Mountain big-horned sheep, and Zera spotted a small herd, in their tawny-white coats, gamboling nimbly among the snow and boulders. Several paused to look at the train, their great curved horns glowing in the lowering sun.

Reaching the summit, the train righted itself at a small plateau of granite that stretched out for the size of a city block. It stopped outside a modern station house built next to the stone 1890s version, a building now used as a gift shop and café.

Zera and Grandma Wren disembarked with the other

passengers and stretched their legs. The air was frigid and thin. Tourists chattered as they made their way toward the sturdy iron railings of the overlook areas, pulling out holographic cameras and v-phones; and zipping up their jackets.

Then, total silence. Everyone stood in awe of the astonishing view. Looking down, a giddy delight somersaulted through Zera's stomach. The world stretched out before them in a dizzying 360-degree panorama. *The sky is clear and we really can see forever.* On two sides were many mountains, dark blue-green and purple. Ute Springs lay directly below them, as did Garden of the Gods, a natural wonder of dramatic red sandstone formations, hundreds of feet high, nestled in the valley right outside Ute Springs. She could even see the edge of Piker, over sixty miles to the north. The Great Plains stretched eastward all the way to Kansas. The Sangre de Cristo mountain range, to the south, headed into New Mexico, over a hundred miles away. To the west she could see thirty to forty miles where she knew Cripple Creek and Victor, the historic silver- and gold-mining towns, were tucked into the slope of Pikes Peak, then, mile after mile of mountains forming the Collegiate Peaks and the Continental Divide.

Zera had released her hair from its ponytail so it could provide some warmth for her neck and ears in the wintry air. The mom and dad from the Texan family seemed particularly uncomfortable, hugging themselves and rubbing their arms. The boys ran to a huge snowbank and began packing snowballs into pink hands. "Mama" seemed to have overcome all her fears and was standing at the fence, grinning from ear-to-ear at the astonishing view.

Zera and Grandma Wren stayed at the overlook for ten minutes or so. Grandma Wren had told her on the train that they would wait until everyone had started down the mountain before embarking on their vision quest.

Cosmic Dan walked up. "Enjoying the view, ladies?"

"It's beautiful," Zera said. Grandma Wren nodded.

"I just came over to tell you I'm going to take the others down, but I'll bring the train back up with Nonny and Hattie in a little over two hours. We'll meet in the café. I told the staff to leave it open for you."

"Thank you, Dan," Grandma Wren said.

"My pleasure."

Dan walked away and Grandma Wren said, "Let's go." Refusing Zera's help, she picked up the large beaded buckskin bag and hoisted it over her shoulder.

Zera followed Grandma Wren as she hiked across the parking lot to the back of the old stone station house/café, a place for Pikes Peak visitors to buy coffee, doughnuts, and tourist knickknacks. As they neared the building, Zera smelled the rich, yeasty smell of doughnuts in the crisp air. At any other time she would have wanted to stop for one.

"There it is," Grandma Wren said, pointing to a steep, timeworn trail in the gravel leading down from the building.

"We're going to that group of rocks."

Zera looked to where she pointed, about a hundred yards down the slope. She was glad Nonny wasn't here; it would have been almost impossible for her to get down that trail.

Grandma Wren began descending slowly. The loose fist-sized gravel made for slippery going but Grandma Wren, sure-footed in hiking boots and calm, made her way down slowly. Zera followed, not doing as well. *My flat-bottomed sneakers aren't the best on this surface*. As soon as the thought registered in her mind she slipped, landing on her left leg and hand, sliding down the loose gravel five feet, nearly bumping into Grandma Wren.

"Goodness! Are you all right, Zera?" Grandma Wren had moved off the path.

Zera got to her feet, more embarrassed than hurt. "Yeah." Her hand was scraped up, bleeding, but just a little. Still, it felt hot and stinging.

Grandma Wren continued on, and Zera shook her hand, wiped the dust from her pants. She waited until Grandma Wren got a good ten feet from her before she started out again.

At the bottom, the ground leveled for a short distance. They made their way across a grassy area to a group of boulders that looked like gigantic balls of whitish-gray clay stacked, then squished together, one on top of the other. The boulders made a large semi-circle that hid them from the view of the lookout point at the top of the peak, almost directly above. A dozen feet away was the edge of a cliff. It dropped off to the next semi-flat spot, many hundreds of feet below.

"This is the place," Grandma Wren said, pointing. "See, there is Ute Springs, home of the Creator's breath, and there are the bones of Mother Earth."

"Creator's breath? Mother Earth?" Zera stared quizzically.

"Creator's Breath is what we call the mineral springs, used by our people since the beginning of their time as healing waters. The bones of Mother Earth were given a different name by the settlers . . ."

"The Garden of the Gods," Zera finished. "They do look like bones from here."

Grandma Wren opened her bag and took out a wool blanket. She unfolded the two-by-three-foot rectangle and laid it upon the ground in front of the boulders. The large central motif of the blanket was a white star, woven on a black background. Two borders framed the star, an outside border of white, followed by one of alternating red and black triangles.

"Sit down, please," Grandma Wren said.

Zera began to oblige, but just then an eerie sound, a cry otherworldly and alarming, pierced the air. She sprang up. "What's that?"

"It's the marmots. There."

The noise stopped as Zera's eyes followed Grandma Wren's outstretched finger. Peering through a gap in the boulders, she saw a pile of rocks in a nook about twenty feet away. On top of a footstool-sized rock stood a very large marmot. He and seven others had apparently been enjoying a late afternoon outing before being so rudely interrupted. The others, like their look-out, stared at the old woman and girl, who stared right back at them. For a moment no one moved.

"We surprised them," whispered Zera.

"They are not too frightened. It is odd that they're up this far. There's no food for them here."

Grandma Wren eyed the creatures. They stared at one another, in wordless communication, and Zera could read Grandma Wren's body language as clearly as the marmots could: "Go, *now*." They began to lumber downhill. Zera sat down.

The wind blew and the cold air felt harsh on Zera's hands and cheeks. She put her hands into the pockets of her jacket, finding a pair of gloves in one and a purple crocheted wool hat in the other. She put on the gloves, wincing a little when she put on the left one. She noticed when she crossed her legs that her left leg was sore, too.

From above came the whistle blow of the train and Cosmic Dan's voice calling, "All aboard, all aboard!"

From what Zera could hear, most of the tourists had, by that time, sought shelter and warmth in the café. She heard them coming out, exclaiming about the cold, their voices traveling clearly through the thin air. After a few minutes of activity, Zera heard the sound of the engine whirring and the cog mechanism click-click-click-clicking like a large clock as the train began its descent down the mountain.

The sky grew dim. Zera heard the workers from the café begin to depart right after the train did — calling out their goodbyes and starting their cars. Within a few short minutes Zera knew they would be completely alone on the mountaintop. She wished she had brought something to drink as now her mouth was dry.

Grandma Wren squatted at the edge of the cliff, her back to Zera, her head bowed in contemplation.

The wind gusted, and it seemed to be the only sound left on the mountain. Even the marmots had gone home to their rocky burrows. Zera watched the bright blue sky turn pink and lavender tie-dye. She gazed at the splendor of the sunset while shivering lightly.

Grandma Wren got up, took off her hat and sweater, then her boots and baggy sweat pants. Zera caught her breath. Grandma Wren stood, facing the multi-hued sunset in brilliant red *long underwear.* With her white, streaming hair and dark lined face, she looked thin, ancient, and powerful. Even with her thinness, she did not shiver. Zera choked back an urge to giggle. She couldn't help it; nerves combined with everything being so serious and somber created an anxiety in her that threatened to bubble out in crazy laughter. *If the kids in Piker could see me now, sitting on top of a mountain, watching skinny ninety-year-old Grandma Wren in her red underwear!* Zera cleared her throat. *Stop it,* she scolded herself. *Don't you dare laugh.*

As if reading her thoughts, Grandma Wren looked back and said, "This is the only clothing I could find that represents the favored color, the color one should wear when addressing the Creator."

Grandma Wren's seriousness killed Zera's urge to laugh. Her cheeks grew hot in embarrassment and she looked down at her red sneakers.

Grandma Wren pulled a thick, long bundle from her bag, along with a lighter. Crouching and cupping her hand over the cloth-wrapped stick, she lit it. The dried sage flamed for a moment, then died out and began to smoke. She came to Zera and slowly waved the white smoke around her, then herself, chanting as she did so.

"Hey-a-a-hey! Hey-a-a-hey! Hey-a-a-hey! Hey-a-a-hey! Hey-a-a-hey! Hey-a-a-hey!"

She placed the still-smoldering bundle on the gravel and turned around again. She knelt directly across from Zera on the blanket, facing the open vista. She sat motionless for at least a minute, and Zera viewed her tiny outline with admiration and respect.

Grandma Wren raised her hands to the sky. "Creator," she said in her gravelly voice, "I ask permission to receive the vision foretold. We sit at the four points of the earth: north, south, east, west. We are open: mind, body, and spirit.

"Creator, behold us and hear our feeble voice. You lived before all, older than old, older than prayer. All belongs to you

— the two-leggeds, the four-leggeds, the wings of the air, and all green things that live. Day in and day out, forever, you are the life of all."

She paused. Zera stared at the back of the tiny, red-clothed woman, her white hair blowing against a kaleidoscope coloring the sky. *I will remember this moment if I live to be a hundred years old.*

Grandma Wren continued, "I send my small and weak voice, Creator, Grandfather, forgetting nothing that you have made; the stars of the universe and the grasses of the earth.

"You have shown us the goodness and the beauty and the strangeness of the greening earth, the only Mother — and there we see the spirit shapes of things.

"You have sent this young woman, Zera, a sign of the snake. Symbol of eternity, of life, rebirth. We ask you in our ignorance and humility what we should do. We have come to receive vision."

They sat for some time, breathing in the sweet, smoldering sage, watching the sky.

Grandma Wren began to quietly chant again. "Hey-a-a-hey. Hey-a-a-hey. Hey-a-a-hey."

Zera closed her eyes, listening to Grandma Wren's voice. Then, silence. She opened her eyes. Grandma Wren was gone.

"Grandma Wren?" Zera looked around. *Where did she go? She was on this blanket. Right here!* A panic swept through her.

"Grandma Wren?" she called louder. She waited. Nothing.

Only the darkening sunset. The sage bundle lay in the gravel, no longer smoldering.

Zera scrambled to her feet, heart pounding like a tribal drum. *Where was she?* She ran to the edge of the cliff, looked all around. *There was nowhere else for her to go.* "Grandma Wren!" she yelled out to the darkening sky.

The air temperature changed. The wind now blew warm. The sky began to change, growing brighter, lighter, bluer, as the sunset disappeared. With it, Zera's fear evaporated. An excitement and expectation in every molecule within her grew as thoughts of Grandma Wren melted away. It was day again. Clouds rolled in, just beneath the cliff. Soft, round clouds, first hundreds, then thousands, stretching out below her like an ocean. Zera's mouth was open, watching.

Through the clouds crept a thread of green, and Zera's heartbeat again quickened. The thread became a tangle of vines, growing larger, stronger. Leaves emerged from the rope-like vines, and the vines took form as they twisted, writhed, turned. They were forming into the shape of a *man*. Zera could not take her eyes away, she could not think. She could only stare, transfixed. Within seconds, a giant stood before her on the clouds, the Green Man.

Zera's heart thudded. She wanted to run but found she could not move. The Green Man, fifty feet tall, was all *leaves*. Giant rolled leaves made up his enormous fingers, his fingernails, his colossal legs, his massive chest, his long, twining hair. Only his verdant face, peering through the leaves, was smooth, the texture of human skin. He walked across the clouds, and as he did the clouds thundered and the rock beneath Zera shook.

Zera's forehead and palms beaded sweat. A gasp escaped her, yet she could not take her eyes away, not even for a second. The green titan looked at her with a fierceness that undercut the kind undertone in his deep voice.

"Everything is sacred and divine," he said.

"You are in the land I live in always. Though I may appear to sleep in the winter, I am very much alive, growing, changing. The same is with all that live!

"We are all one. Star-stuff!" He smiled at Zera, a smile that was both friendly and menacing, and his arms and hands outstretched to embrace the cosmos.

"We are all related. We possess each other in our natures and in our bodies.

"We are all part of the tree of life. We are kept in place by our spinal column."

The figure began to change. The Green Man's legs grew together, turned darker, brown, bark-rough. Soon, they had fused into one thick trunk.

"We are anchored by the roots of our feet and legs,"

Roots curved downward from the base of the trunk, stretching along and down through the clouds.

". . . we stretch toward and welcome the heavens in the branches of our arms." He raised his massive arms. They turned into two thick branches that brought forth more branches, smaller and smaller, up and up and out. Buds popped out along each stem in profusion and became full, fat and pointed, before gracefully unfolding into leaves.

The tree stood thick, full, covered. The Green Man's face appeared high now, in the center of the branches, defined amid the leafy crown. His eyes glowed.

"In our heads are the flowering and fruiting of our thoughts and emotions."

The tree exploded into bloom with thousands of alabaster flowers. Their perfume filled the air, filled Zera's lungs. Just as quickly, the white flower petals fell and the fruits, first tiny and green, grew large. The green faded and the full fruits blushed into luscious globes of gold. The Green Man's face became longer, softer, fair, the lips as full and ripe as the fruit that adorned it.

The Green Man had become a Green Woman.

She whispered. Her voice was melodic, honeyed. "Yes, I am *all*. Male *and* female. One cannot exist without the other. Man and woman are borne of the earth. We are all one. We are all plants. All flesh is grass. It is our life-giver."

Tears sprang to Zera's eyes. She recognized the voice. *It's the voice from my dreams.*

The fruits began to fall from the woman-tree, noiselessly onto the clouds. On their way down they turned fetid; worm holes and bruises appeared on their surfaces as they reached the white clouds and landed. They grew moldy and shrunken. A thick decay smell clotted in Zera's nose. The rotten fruit disappeared. At the same time, the leaves of the tree turned gold, blazing briefly and brilliantly in the blue sky, before falling from the tree in a shower. The leaves, like the fruit, turned brown then shrank, crinkled, vanished through the clouds.

"We are all that lives and all that has lived before," said the Green Woman, whose face now formed in the bare branches.

Zera thought of her mother and father and was not afraid.

"I am the thought of all plants." The skeleton-branched tree turned green, the limbs becoming round and fleshy, as it metamorphosed into human form. A towering woman of green stood before her, clothed in leaves. She was voluptuous, mighty.

She began to move, walking atop the clouds, looking down where the fruit once lay, and shaking her majestic leaf-crowned head. The clouds thundered under her footfalls as they had with the Green Man's.

Her voice grew cold, as did her gaze, and fear crept into Zera's heart.

"Man's greed has far surpassed his wisdom. The plants call to me in despair. They know not what they should be. They know not what they are."

Her face twisted into a horrible mask of anger. "The timeless wisdom of nature, of life, has been defiled, again and again. Man has been given the whole world; yet it is not enough. The answers are there, simple to see, yet his eyes remain willfully closed."

Her voice grew louder, until it boomed. "If the work that man has started does not stop, the world shall grieve as it has never grieved before! That is the message. That is our warning . . ." her voice and countenance softened once again as she paused, ". . . and our plea. Zera of the Greens — you *must* do *whatever* it takes to help set these wrongs right."

Her blazing eyes met Zera's. Zera forgot to breathe. The Green Woman's lips did not move, yet Zera heard unspoken words whispered to her, as vividly and as surely as she had heard the snakes. The gentle voice she had heard in her room, both at Piker and here, was now tinged with anger and hysteria. "You *will* help us, Zera of the Greens. If you do not take action, the natural world will have no choice but to fight against all humanity. And humanity will lose."

Zera's heart raced as an icy wind returned. The Green Woman faded and disappeared. The sea of clouds parted and sped away. The azure sky darkened and a nearly full moon cast the rocks around her in an eerie, white glow.

Thunder rumbled down the mountain. Zera could see the lightning, blinding white zig-zags that brought rocks and trees far below into high relief.

The fury of the weather gripped Zera as the Green Woman's words rang in her ears. *You will help us, Zera of the Greens.*

How can I do that? she thought. *I'm alone in this world.* The thought clutched her in icy fingers of panic. *How can they ask this of me? I'm just visiting my nonny . . . I'm too young.* Tears came again into her eyes and she couldn't stop herself from screaming out into the cold night. "What do you expect me to do? I don't even know what this is about!"

No answer, no response came. She was alone.

The moment the words left her she knew with total clarity — *The Toad.*

Chapter Nineteen

This all has something to do with Uncle Theodore — but how? Zera sat in the freezing darkness, her heart racing. She tugged her jacket around her, staring first up at the moonlit sky, then down at the storm raging below her on the mountain. She closed her eyes and breathed deeply. As her lungs filled with cold, crisp air, she thought of her parents. She looked up to see two bright stars. *I know I'm not really alone, somehow they're with me. I've got to hold on to that. And to figure out what all this means.*

Grandma Wren's voice startled her. "Now we know."

"Where were you?" Zera said to the small figure on the blanket. Grandma Wren was plainly visible as the pale boulders and gravel around them reflected the moon's glow.

The old woman unfolded her limbs and stood. "I was here, all along,"

Zera shook her head. In light of what she had just seen, how could she say what was real anymore?

Grandma Wren moved to the edge of the cliff, peered down. "It's a bad storm. I hope the train makes it back okay."

Her words were calm. *How can she be calm? After what just happened?* Zera got to her feet, nearly stumbling. The burning feeling had returned to her palm, and her leg was stiff with soreness. She gathered up the blanket and shook off the dirt. Grandma Wren held out her hands for it, but instead of putting it into the bag, she folded it in half and wrapped it around her small shoulders. She took a flashlight from her bag and handed it to Zera. "Take this. I find myself very tired now."

Zera insisted on carrying Grandma Wren's bag, and this time she let her.

"Here's the path, to the right a little," Zera said, lighting the area. Once their eyes adjusted, moonlight helped illuminate the path as well. Grandma Wren led them, inching up the incline while Zera kept the light on the ground ahead. The dark climb, more difficult than the descent, seemed to take a long time.

The second time she slipped Zera said, "Damn it!" Grandma Wren ignored the outburst.

At the top, they paused to catch their breath. *It feels good to be standing upright,* Zera thought, stretching. They got to the top just in time. The clouds had rolled in again, covering the moon, and the night grew blacker, the wind bitter. Thankfully, the outside lights of the café were on. Zera moved closer to Grandma Wren as they crept along the rear of the stone building, then around the side. As they neared the front door, snow began spitting from the skies.

Grandma Wren's voice was raspy. "I do hope they remembered to leave the door unlocked."

Me too. Being stranded outside now would be awful.

Grandma Wren was the first to reach the door. She went in,

flipped the light switch and turned to Zera. "Ah, warmth!"

The stone exterior had given no hint of the coziness inside. A gas fire in the large stone fireplace glowed, casting its reflection on the golden pine planks of the floor and dining tables. Thick cotton curtains of green and white checkerboard hung from the windows. Along the top of the walls a stenciled border of pine trees circled the room like a miniature painted forest.

"Nice and toasty," said Grandma Wren, taking off the snow-dusted blanket.

"I smell coffee." Zera made her way toward the long, chrome, '50s-style dining counter. "A whole pot. That should warm us up." She lifted the clear glass dome off a plate stacked with doughnuts. "They left us a plate of goodies, too." Her stomach growled loud enough for Grandma Wren to hear.

Shaky with hunger, Zera knew Grandma Wren must be starving too. *We haven't eaten since noon.* She found she was not eager to talk over what they had just seen, not yet. She got cups from the cabinet and found plates and napkins.

The door opened. Hattie and Nonny, in snow-covered jackets, entered the room.

"Sorry we're late!" Hattie pulled down her hood, shook out her long hair. "We were waylaid at the station with electrical problems. There's a big storm down the mountain. Dan's outside now, making an adjustment to the engine before we can go back down. He said it'd take about twenty minutes. So, how did it go?"

"You're late?" said Zera. "What do you mean? We just got here."

"Zera," said Nonny, "it's been four and a half hours."

Zera looked at Grandma Wren, who showed no surprise.

They sat at one of the round pine tables watching Grandma Wren eat an extraordinary amount of food for someone her age: the tuna and cheese sandwich Hattie had brought for her, potato salad from the refrigerator, a candy-sprinkled doughnut, and two cartons of milk. When Hattie commented on her appetite, Grandma Wren said she'd been fasting since she had the dream, in preparation for the vision quest. Disapproval darkened Hattie's features but she did not comment.

Zera had just finished her sandwich when Hattie, across from her, said, "So do you want to talk about it before we get on the train? What happened?"

Zera took a deep breath. "I saw the Green Man and the Green Woman. They were giants. Like . . . gods." She searched the expectant faces sitting around her. Something was holding her back from telling everything as she saw it. And how could she possibly explain something she didn't understand? "The Green Woman, she was beautiful." Zera looked at Grandma Wren next to her and suddenly felt panicked. She blurted, "They said that 'wisdom has been defiled,' that 'man's work must be stopped.' That plants don't know what they are any more, that the world is in trouble. I don't even know what it all means!"

Hattie shifted in her chair. "Whoa. You saw this too?" she asked Grandma Wren. "A Green Man, and a Green Woman?"

"I saw the Creator," Grandma Wren said. "Sinawaf."

"What?" Hattie's eyes went wide.

"One God, Hattie, many faces," Nonny said.

"We saw what we needed to see," said Grandma Wren. "We must do as we are asked. I remember how our people, when suffering from depression, as they call it now, when they felt empty they would go out alone, into the woods. With arms extended they would press their backs to a pine tree in order to draw from its power and revive their spirit. Now we take pills, made with synthetics. Our connection with nature has been ignored for too long. Without its health, we will never have real health again."

Zera locked eyes with Grandma Wren. The next thing she had to say was even more confusing. "I know one thing. That this all has something to do with Uncle Theodore."

Nonny stared at Zera. "Is that what you saw during the vision? Is that what the Green Man, or Woman, said?"

"No, but afterwards, I felt it. That this all has something to do with him. It's hard to explain."

Nonny nodded and a deep sigh followed. "I had the same feeling, that Ted was somehow connected to all this. The biotech industry, genetic engineering; I knew it had to have something to do with his work. Oh, when all that business started, I knew it was going to be bad, tinkering with the essence of life! Theodore must be involved in something horrible."

"How horrible?" Hattie asked what Zera had been wondering since the revelation had came to her.

"Horrible enough for gods to come out of the sky and speak," said Grandma Wren.

They sat in silence, pondering that. Hattie stood up and picked up the dirty dishes to take to the kitchen area, gesturing to Zera to stay seated when she tried to get up to help. "I had this thought that all this was somehow about global warming," said Hattie. "Although that's here, too. All this plant trouble began when chemical companies started splicing genes of different phyla together," Hattie said.

A chill ran through Zera. This was all too much. She thought of the white roses on the porch, how they had opened, how beautiful they were, and how they had all died the next day. A feeling of dread, that things could be worse, *much worse*, filled her. *The natural world will fight against all humanity. And humanity will lose.*

"What is a phyla?" Grandma Wren asked.

"It's the plural for phylum. Phylum is a scientific word for divisions of living things. For example, in the Animal Kingdom, all organisms with backbones, the vertebrates, are in one phylum, most of what we call insects are in another. Plants are in a separate Kingdom." Hattie walked across the room and deposited the dishes in the sink, then grabbed a towel to wipe the table.

"Divisions?" Grandma Wren said. "That is strange. Our people always knew we were all connected, not divided into groups. The wind and mountains are as much our relatives as the animals and plants."

"It's about levels of being related genetically," Zera said.

The puzzled expression did not leave Grandma Wren's face.

"Remember, Grandma," said Hattie, "how I told you they'd crossed a bacteria with the corn plant, creating insect-killing corn? Or when I ranted about the Beefy Fries? Mother Nature has always had certain boundaries that could not be crossed, like the impossibility, in most cases, of inter-breeding species. Working with nature, man has been able to develop plants and animals through selective breeding, and we've been able to clone plants naturally, but there have always been limits. Now they've crossed a potato with a cow, for God's sake! And that's not the worst of it." She scowled.

"What could be worse?" Grandma Wren asked, her eyebrows raised.

Zera answered. "Genetically-engineered crops can't be contained in their fields. Pollen can travel on the wind for miles; butterflies and thousands of other insects carry it too — animals carry it, we even carry it on our shoes, clothes, vehicles, in our hair. When pollen escapes and reproduces with wild plants, or non-genetically engineered plants, their offspring are then genetically modified. Nonny told me about this a long time ago."

"And what did Theodore think about that?" asked Hattie. "about the contamination?"

"He said they were working on solutions to limit the problems."

"To *limit* them?" Hattie spat out the words.

Nonny interrupted, "The danger is, once our wild plants are contaminated, many, many millions of years of evolution is disrupted. We cannot even guess at the potential for disaster. You can't just look at the plants either. You have to look at every single organism that is even remotely connected to them — every human, every animal, every insect, every bacteria — each eco-system. Everything's affected."

Hattie had a disturbed, far-away look in her eyes. "The bugs that sip the nectar and eat the leaves, the birds that eat the bugs, the people who eat the meat which was fed on the biotech grain that the bees and birds have also fed on."

Zera finished Hattie's thought, "Everything's linked."

"Yes," said Hattie. "We have no idea what we're messing with. They didn't even have the word 'gene' until the 1920s! Some have compared genetic engineering to the splitting of the atom."

Zera couldn't believe what she had heard. *The splitting of the atom?* "The atomic bomb?"

Hattie's face twisted. "Yes, Zera, the ultimate weapon of mass destruction. Nonny, I know Ted's your son and you love him, but there's something demented about it. It's like

Frankenstein, creating, bringing to life, something that was not meant to be."

Nonny looked out toward the black windows of the cafe. "I can't help but think it's my fault somehow."

A sadness enveloped Zera as Nonny took a paper napkin from the table dispenser and dabbed her eyes. Then annoyance at her uncle reared its ugly head. *Thanks a lot, Toad. It looks like you've really done it this time.*

"I wasn't there for him after his father died," Nonny said. "I went off on my own to deal with my grief. I traveled, selfishly lost myself in other cultures. I ran away, left him, a frightened eight-year-old, with Sally, who was just seventeen. And I didn't come back for months. When I did return, it was only briefly, then I'd take off again, absorbed in my own little world, my 'spiritual seeking,' when I had something more important at home the whole time. I was a terrible mother."

I didn't know that, thought Zera. *I knew she traveled, but I didn't know she left them for that long. I didn't know she left Theodore when he was little . . .* She looked at Nonny with new eyes; it was plain to see her grandmother was tormented, yet, now she felt sorry for her uncle. She knew how she felt when her parents died. So lost and alone, terrified.

Hattie walked over and gently touched Nonny's shoulder. "We've all made mistakes." She sighed. "I'm so sorry about the tirade. I'm just rattled, by everything. I can't stop thinking about a quote I read once from the late Japanese master gardener,

Masanobu Fukuoka. He said, 'If we throw nature out the window, she comes back in the door with a pitchfork.'"

Zera saw Hattie shudder, and one reverberated through her own body.

"In the end, we can love and teach our children, but they have to find their own path," Grandma Wren said, her voice steady and sure as she measured the words. "As for your feelings, Guinevere, there is still time to heal your relationship with your son."

"I apologized to them both years ago," said Nonny, "Sally and I were okay. I knew Ted hadn't forgiven me, but I thought I had forgiven myself. Maybe we never do." She turned to Zera. "Right now it looks like we have a bigger problem. Do you know what he was working on?"

"No, I just know that on the way here he and Tiffany were happier than I'd ever seen them." She thought for a moment. "Tiffany was excited the morning we left. They were going to meet someone important. She didn't say who, though."

"When they arrived, Tiffany was positively jittery, she was so anxious to leave," Nonny frowned as she looked out the windows again into the black sky, still sputtering snow. "Ted acted suspiciously. Something was up then, and we need to find out what."

"How do we do that?" asked Zera.

"I'm not sure. We'll sleep on it, I guess. I hate to say this, just when we've been reunited," a look of dread played across

Nonny's features, "but the first thing we're going to have to do is track down Ted. I'll call him, try to find out what's going on. And we have to figure out how you play into this. I worried all evening, leaving you up here tonight with Grandma Wren. I shouldn't have done that. I know one thing, I will not put you in harm's way again."

"Guinevere," Grandma Wren said, "Zera has been chosen."

Nonny's expression of dread turned into one of horror. "She is a child, Nellie. That's not possible."

Another chill rippled through Zera. She hadn't told them that the Green Woman had spoken directly to her, telling her that she must help. But Grandma Wren *knew*. *Chosen? For what? And why me, when there are billions of others on this planet?* The look on Nonny's face made her decide she would not say anything more.

Grandma Wren said softly to Zera, "Trust that you will know what to do when it is time."

Nonny heard. "She will *not* be chosen! I will not stand for this!" She glared at Grandma Wren.

The door blew open, thudding against the wall. Everyone jumped. Hattie yelped.

Cosmic Dan, wearing a hooded parka and covered in snow, stomped into the room. "Hi, ladies." Seeing their startled expressions, he joked, "Gee, I didn't know I was *that* ugly."

Nervous laughter escaped from Zera and Hattie. Grandma Wren and Nonny showed no signs of humor.

Chapter Twenty

For Theodore, the return trip to Void Corporate Headquarters in the helicopter and the limousine ride back to The Grand was a depressing blur. He went through the motions, saying goodbye to everyone, smiling, shaking hands, saying he felt great.

He walked into his penthouse suite and headed for the wet bar. Hands shaking, he picked up a cut crystal decanter full of scotch. He poured himself a tumbler, overfilling it slightly and spilling it onto the marble counter.

"Damn." Theodore found napkins under the bar. He threw a few on top of the spill and shrugged. He brought the amber liquid to his lips, inhaled the harsh aroma, and found he couldn't drink. *No*, he thought. *I've got to keep my wits about me. Got to sort this out.* He emptied the alcohol in the bar sink, and poured himself a glass of water, downing it in several long gulps.

He refilled the glass and ran his bumpy fingers through his now disheveled dark hair. *What do I do? There has to be a way out. How do I take care of this?* He felt sick, his mind full of images — beating hearts, breathing lungs, round pelts of hair, eyeballs. *God, those eyes.* His stomach lurched, like it might heave the water. He leaned forward, head down, both hands against the sink. He swallowed hard and took a deep breath.

Langston and Troy looking at me, as if it were all so fine. So wonderful. They used me, just like BioTech did.

Theodore walked to an overstuffed chair, put the glass of water on a table, and flopped down. The chair faced the terrace. He sat there staring at the big city view, the buildings, the sky, the clouds.

He looked at his hands. The warts were back. *Ugly*. They'd never look normal, and it was his fault. They'd always be repulsive, because *he* was repulsive. *No wonder Mom left.* In the back of his mind he heard her voice. *Just rub a potato on them, Ted, then bury it under a tree . . . What if I should have trusted Mom all along?* He set his jaw, put his hands in his lap. He didn't want to give in to her and her over-the-top beliefs. *Mumbo-jumbo here. Genetic monsters there. What's the diff?*

He licked his still-dry lips, picked up the glass of water and took a gulp. *Can't go back to Piker, either. Sent in my resignation three days ago. Signed a contract with Void.* The thought of that made him feel sick again and he put down the water. He couldn't figure it out. Void seemed to have it all, everything. He could too, if he just went along with it. But the thought of signing that contract brought an image he knew he would never be able to shake — one of him selling his soul.

Theodore jolted from his half-sleep stupor when "Theodore, I'm back," rang out like a cheap musical alarm.

Theodore turned in the chair to see Tiffany, two shopping

bags in each hand. She wore a huge smile and yet another new outfit, a sleeveless polka-dot dress with platform shoes and pink tights. *More pink*, thought Theodore dully.

Tiffany's bright expression faded. "Theodore, what's wrong?"

Theodore lied. "I'm not feeling well."

Tiffany sat the bags on the coffee table. She eyeballed Theodore, then touched his cool forehead. He got a whiff of her floral perfume and it reminded him of the lab. Nausea flooded through him. He pulled away.

"You don't have a fever . . ." Tiffany said. "Did something happen today?"

"Yeah, something happened."

"Well, what was it?" She sat on the sofa across from him, leaning toward him. "Is it something with the company? Langston? What? How long have you been sitting there?"

"I don't know." His voice sounded haggard even to himself, *changed*. "I saw some things today. I was affected by them."

Tiffany's cat eyes narrowed. "What things?"

"I can't tell you. It has to do with the lab work. It's top secret."

"Oh, no. It's not drugs is it? They haven't engineered some kind of illegal drug or something?"

"No, it's not drugs. Just let me be. There are some things I need to sort out."

"Damn it, Theodore," Tiffany stood, placed her thin hands

on her boyish hips, "I'm your girlfriend, have been for a very long time." Just as abruptly, she changed her tone. Softly she said, "You've got to tell me what's going on. We've got a date to go out with Langston and Crystal tonight, to celebrate."

The sparkly word "celebrate" turned to ashes in Theodore's mind. "Tiffany, I saw some things that disturbed me, my own work." He ran his hands through his hair again, his eyes glancing toward the window, avoiding Tiffany's intense stare. "Maybe it should have been okay, but it wasn't. I'm just not sure about anything anymore. I'm not sure . . . that I want all this."

Tiffany stood looking down at Theodore, her small hands, now bedecked in several new, sparkly rings, were clenched at her side. Her expression had changed from concern to anger.

"What do you mean you're not sure?" her voice became as low as his, and guttural, the growl of a tigress. "You can't quit now, you signed the papers today, didn't you? You're the new president of the Biotech Division, right?"

"Yes." Theodore saw Tiffany make an effort to unclench her hands. One of them went to her jaw line and she massaged it. The thought came to Theodore, *it's as if she's trying to rub out the imperfection of it, and the imperfection of this conversation.* A bitter smile came to his lips. *If only it were that easy.*

"You've worked hard for this," Tiffany said. "This is everything we've wanted — you've wanted." She took a deep breath. "Do you know what I think? I think you're afraid of success. Look at your mother, having all that money, that successful seed company handed down through generations, and then going through some sort of 'spiritual awakening' she called it, and giving it all away. The business, all those stocks. You've had to work hard to get where you are. Why would you think of jeopardizing it?"

"It's my life. It's my decision. Just like it was my mom's decision to live hers the way she wanted."

Tiffany bent down, put a hand on Theodore's shoulder. "I'm sorry." Her voice softened even more. "I'm just *confused.* It's hard to understand this complete change. I think you're just unsettled. So much has happened in the last few days. Try to let it go, Theodore. It's *okay* to be a success. *Allow* yourself to be a success."

She looked into his face. "Say it with me Theodore, it's *okay* to be a success."

Theodore stiffened, jerked his shoulder back. "For crissakes, Tiffany. This isn't a support-group meeting."

Tiffany pulled her hand away. "If it weren't for me . . . well, I don't think you're in any condition to discuss anything right now." She jerked her head toward the wet bar. "You've been drinking, haven't you? This whole place reeks like booze."

Getting up, Theodore gave her a long, hard look. She seemed different to him now, desperate and silly. Almost pathetic. "Tiffany, you're clueless." He walked into the bedroom, closed the door behind him and locked it. As an afterthought he yelled, "Call and tell them we're not coming tonight. At least I'm not.

You can do what you want."

Theodore took a shower and changed into a pair of jeans, the only ones he owned, and an undershirt. He could hear Tiffany crying in the other room. Exhausted, Theodore curled up on the bed. Within minutes he had fallen asleep.

From the phone came a soft voice, "Telephone call, Mr. Green. Telephone call . . ."

Theodore, drenched in sweat and breathing hard, opened his eyes but couldn't see anything in the pitch black room. It took five rounds of "Telephone call, Mr. Green" before he figured out where he was. The nightmare was horrible. He reached out one trembling hand and picked up the phone.

"Hello?"

"Hello, Ted. It's your mother."

The glowing phone monitor showed Guinevere, squinting at her son in the darkness. Theodore sat up. Grabbing the collar of his T-shirt, he pulled it up to wipe his damp face. He groped for the switch on the nightstand's lamp, picked up his glasses and put them on.

"Mom?"

"Sorry to wake you."

Theodore made an effort to look and sound calm. "It's okay." He tried to smile. "Mom, I've made a terrible mistake. I understand now." The screen went black.

He pressed the button on the monitor but it stayed dark.

"Mom?" No dial tone, nothing.

Staring into the dead phone monitor, Theodore didn't see the two men wearing business suits enter the bedroom. He looked up when he felt their presence and saw Cooper Davies, the helicopter pilot, and a second, very large African American man who wore his hair in chest-long dreadlocks.

"What the hell are you doing here?" Theodore said as they approached the bed. "Is Langston here?"

"Hey, Theo," said the dreadlocked man.

"Do I know you?" before the words were out of his mouth, Theodore saw the frightening smile on Coop's face, and the rag in his hand.

Theodore jumped up, tried to maneuver past them, but the two men grabbed him. Cooper placed the sweet-scented rag over his face, and for a moment Theodore felt an odd excitement from the drug, right before he went to sleep for the third time that day.

Chapter Twenty-one

"We were cut off," Nonny told Zera.

"Did you see him?" Zera was getting clean water for the dogs' bowl in the kitchen. She glanced at Nonny, sitting at the kitchen table, v-phone in her hand.

"For a second," Nonny said. "It was dark when he picked up the phone. He turned on the light, put on his glasses . . ."

Nonny dialed Theodore's v-phone number.

Zera set the bowl on the floor, thinking about the train ride back down the mountain. No one explained much to Dan, and he'd seemed fine with that. Then, on the ride down, traveling through the storm with its booming thunder and blazing lightning, talking became impossible. Zera knew they were all working on the puzzle of what had happened. She wondered what the future held for her uncle, for herself, for them all.

When they arrived in Ute Springs, the world had calmed again; everything was wet and shining under a bright moon. Hope seemed to fill the rain-cleaned air, and Zera, too, at least for a while. Maybe everything would work out. Ben was waiting for them at the station, soaked from having ridden his skateboard there in the rain, and Zera's heart had leapt at the sight of him. They'd all gone to Nonny's and had a cup of cocoa on the porch before Hattie said they had to leave. Like Cosmic Dan, Ben hadn't asked many questions, and they hadn't offered information. They'd all agreed to get together again first thing the next morning.

Zera sat beside Nonny at the table, watching the blank screen of the phone and the words: "*Ringing. . . . Ringing. . . .*"

An attractive woman's face appeared. "I'm sorry," she said. "The number you have just reached has been disconnected or is no longer in service."

"Now that was his cell phone. I don't know what's going on! I'm going to check directory assistance." Shaking her head, Nonny pressed a button to redial the hotel. Zera saw that her expression had gone from confusion to worry. "What's wrong?"

"I finally got through by calling the hotel. He looked happy to see me," Nonny said. "He told me he had made a terrible mistake. He said that he *understood.* Then . . . we were cut off."

"He said he'd made a terrible mistake?" repeated Zera.

An Indian woman wearing a yellow sari showed up on the monitor. "What city, please?" she asked with a British accent.

"I would like to find out the address for the number 310-555-1293." Nonny watched as the woman typed into a computer. "It's The Grand Hotel in Los Angeles? May I have the lobby number? Thank you."

Anger flared in Zera. *This is weird. Could he be playing some kind of a game? Why would he say he made a terrible mistake, and then not try to call back?* It didn't add up.

Nonny spoke to the hotel operator. "My name is Guinevere Green. My son, Theodore Green, is staying at your hotel." Nonny frowned at the woman on the screen. "Our phone conversation was cut off a little while ago and the operator says the line is disconnected. You can check? Yes, I'll hold. Thank you."

She drummed her fingers on the table.

"The line seems fine, Mrs. Green. We could find no problem."

"Is my son there?"

"I'm sorry, Mrs. Green, he seems to be out for the evening. I'll tell him you called."

"I see . . . I'll try again later." The screen went blue again, then black. Nonny sighed deeply, rose from her chair, and repeated what Zera had overheard. "'Ted's left for the evening.' This is so odd."

Zera stood and pushed her chair under the table. "What are you going to do?"

"The room's registered to Void Chemical Corporation. Well, at least we know that — it's something to go on." Nonny ran her fingers through her white hair. "It's been a long day. Oh, I wish I weren't so old."

"Nonny, you're not old," Zera said. "I know people younger than you who seem *ages* older."

"Thanks, darling," Nonny tried to smile. "Well, that's just

like him, to give me a glimmer of hope." The half-hearted attempt at a smile disappeared and Zera couldn't help thinking that Nonny did look old then. "I doubt I'm even thinking rationally. I'll call Hattie in the morning. But right now we need to get some sleep. What do you think?"

Zera's irritation toward her uncle melted into tenderness for her grandmother, but one thing, something that she still hadn't addressed, was bothering her. "I think you're right, Nonny," said Zera. "A good night's sleep will do wonders. I have to ask you something, though."

"What's that, sweetie?"

"Are you still going to South America in two weeks?"

Nonny turned away from Zera, to grab her cane next to the chair. "I haven't given it any thought, with all this happening all at once. I don't see how I could, but, well, I've had this date set for ages." When Nonny turned toward her again, Zera thought she looked pale. "We'll talk about it tomorrow, okay?"

"Sure." Zera hoped the disappointment didn't show. She gave Nonny a hug and went upstairs.

Zera kicked off her shoes and had just sat down on her bed when she heard a tap-tap-tap at the windowpane.

"It's me, Ben."

She went to the open window and pushed aside the curtain, to find Ben on a ladder. "What are you doing?"

"I had to talk to you."

The window was at her knee level, so Zera knelt down. They were face-to-face.

"What about?"

"I just wanted to say, I'm glad you're home." He looked down at the floor. "I don't understand what's going on but I hope everything works out and you'll be here all summer." He brought his eyes up to look into hers. "At *least*."

At least. In spite of it all, all the freaky stuff that had been going on all day long — he wanted her to stay! Zera's heart leapt.

"I like you, Zera. A lot."

A rush of happiness made her forget everything. She couldn't help herself, she leaned over, touched his dark hair. He leaned towards her. She pressed her lips into his. The kiss was everything she always knew it would be. It was warm and sweet and made her light-headed. Everything seemed intensified, the colors in the room, the cool air, the smell of his hair.

Ben looked into her eyes. "Let's go out for awhile."

This brought Zera back to reality. "Ben, I can't sneak out. We're trying to get in touch with Uncle Theodore. We need to find out what all of this is about."

Ben looked shocked. "Okay, I get it. It's fine."

"It's just that this is more . . ."

"Important?"

Ben didn't wait for a response. He disappeared down the ladder.

"Ben!"

Anger coursed through Zera. *He's not getting by with leaving like that.* She crawled out the window after him.

A half hour later, sitting on the grass near the barn, Zera had told Ben about everything that happened on the mountain.

"I know this sounds crazy . . . but I'm not crazy," said Zera. "It really happened."

"Zera, I saw those snakes too. Yeah, it sounds crazy, but I believe you. Heck, I've known you all my life. But you don't have to go through with it — with whatever's happening."

"That's just it. I'm getting the feeling that I do. That there's no choice. Like I'm going down this path I have no control over."

"Zera, Grandma Wren's the one who's crazy. You've seen her house. My mom's a little off too. I know that. I love her and all, but . . . but sometimes I wish she was more like everyone else's parents. I know you've had those feelings too; remember how we used to talk about it when we were kids? How we wanted to move out of Ute Springs one day, see the world?"

Those memories came back to Zera. How she'd been a little embarrassed a few times by her parents, their artist ways, which always focused on feelings and imagination instead of the solid ground of reality, and how she'd found Ben a good person to complain to. She'd forgotten that she'd said she wanted to move away from Ute Springs. She'd probably been about twelve years old. *For the last three years all I've thought about is coming back.* "Things change, Ben. I'm older. I've been away. And when you . . . when you lose your parents you realize you loved every single thing that was different about them. Especially all those things that drove you nuts. It leaves a great big hole in your heart."

Ben took her hand.

Ben's hand was warm and a little rough. It felt good. She met his eyes and a thrill went through her. The moment didn't last; she had to tell him something, something that she did not want to say. "Ben, I have to find out what's going on with my uncle."

Ben dropped her hand. "Come on. It was hard on me when you left; things changed a lot. Maybe you just *thought* you saw something. Who knows, maybe Grandma Wren's smoke-thing that she took for chanting and waved around the air was filled with some drug or something."

Zera jumped up. "You just said you believed me. Ben, things changed a hell of a lot more for *me* when I left! You have no idea. And you really think your grandma *drugged* me?"

She took off into the darkness and Ben didn't follow her.

Zera had a hard time falling asleep. Thoughts about Ben, how they'd kissed a few more times outside, how he'd held her, and then, how he'd made her so angry, traded places with worry about Uncle Theodore. After tossing and turning and getting up three times, she took out her v-phone, did her own search for the number of The Grand Hotel in Los Angeles.

The woman on the phone said that Theodore Green had checked out.

Chapter Twenty-two

Saturday, June 7

Theodore came to on tangerine shag carpet in the back of a 1970s-era Volkswagen van. He lay on his side, his wrists bound together tightly with multiple plastic zip ties. Daybreak shone through the dirt-streaked windows, illuminating everything in a grimy pink glow. The scent of a biofuel, one he wasn't familiar with, hung in the air. Tilting his head all the way back, he could see the front of the van. Coop, recognizable by his blond crew cut, drove.

The other man, the dark-skinned giant with dreadlocks trailing halfway down his chest, sat cross-legged on the opposite side of the floor. Absorbed in smoking a cigarette and blowing the smoke out of a partially-opened window, he didn't notice Theodore had awakened.

Peering down the other way, toward the back, Theodore saw a few cardboard boxes scattered near the door. The shag carpet underneath him smelled like a mixture of dirt, peat, and manure. After Theodore nervously calculated the number of germs that thrived there, he more nervously calculated that the man sitting near him looked to be about six-foot-six and more than two-hundred-fifty pounds. The big guy was not wearing a business suit like the night before. He had on jeans and a black T-shirt with an outer space shot of planet Earth. Theodore couldn't hear any traffic and guessed they were outside the city.

He felt a sharp digging in his back accompanied by a muffled grunting. Slowly, as not to attract attention from his closest captor, Theodore maneuvered his body to see behind him. It was Tiffany, wild-eyed and wilder-haired. She looked terrified, but also angry, and a large piece of silver tape covered her mouth. Noticing Theodore's untaped mouth, her expression changed to fury. "Mmmph! Mummmph!"

Theodore's initial feeling of sympathy for Tiffany vanished. *She's angry? At me?* He turned back over on his side.

"Hey, look who's up," came a deep, mellow voice from the dreadlocked man. "It's the royal couple! How's it going, Theo?" The man laughed, a heavy, menacing laugh that turned Theodore's skin to goose flesh.

"Who are you?" Theodore demanded feebly. "You're not with Void, are you?"

"Man, you brainy types, so many of you so lacking in common sense. Look at this shirt, Theo," he said, tossing back his dreadlocks, and stretching out his thick-as-tree-trunks arms. "Does it look like I'm with Void?"

Theodore squinted at the words above the blue and white globe. Without his glasses, he could barely make them out. *Save Mother Earth.*

From the front of the van, Coop chuckled. "Bear, Void has

an Earth logo too."

Theodore stammered, "I just thought, seeing Coop . . . no . . . I guess not."

"Don't worry, Theodore," Coop said. He flashed Theodore a look of contempt from his deep-set icy blue eyes. "You'll find out soon enough what it's all about. We're almost there."

Bear shook his head, and then blew a thick cloud of smoke in Theodore's direction. When Theodore predictably coughed, Bear's massive body shook with laughter. Theodore watched as Bear retrieved a coffee cup from the front seat and put out his cigarette.

Coop swerved to make a right turn onto a bumpy dirt road. Theodore and Tiffany rolled into each other and Bear laughed again.

"You two can sit up," he said, and Theodore and Tiffany struggled to pull themselves up.

They traveled for what seemed like forever. Theodore's body hurt. His wrists were sore. He had to pee. Tiffany glared at all of them. She wore pink silk pajamas and white bunny slippers. A gold sleeping mask dangled around her neck. Theodore thought for a few seconds about asking to stop to go to the bathroom but decided against it, especially when Bear continued to stare at him, chuckling richly each time Theodore winced.

They turned onto a second dirt road. Theodore glimpsed flashes of green fields through the windows. *Where can we be?*

Nowhere near the beach or the desert. Somewhere in farm country. Maybe we're not even in California.

At the next turn, they pulled into the driveway of a ramshackle two-story farmhouse. Only ghosts of white paint remained on the house's silver-gray wood exterior. Boards covered all the windows and the porch leaned inward. A tire hung by a thread of frayed rope from a giant oak tree, a sad relic of carefree summer days. The tree had a big hollow space on one side and only a few leaves on its mostly-dead branches. A chill ran through Theodore. The tree reminded him of his nightmare, the one he'd been having when his mother called. A tree even bigger than this one, and voices — voices of anger and accusation. The thought of that tree brought regret. He wished he could have told his mother more. What if he never saw her again? *These people are kidnappers; they might be murderers too.*

Coop drove the van around to the back. There was an outbuilding of the same silver-gray, a few gnarled fruit trees, two old, rusty posts with an old clothesline drooping nearly to the ground between them, and a bent and rusted iron fence standing sentry around a weed patch that looked as if it might have once been a vegetable garden.

Bear opened the van door and grabbed Theodore by the shirt, hauling him out. Theodore trembled.

"Please don't kill us," he begged.

Bear's face contorted. "We're not killers. You guys are the

killers. You're killing everything that's good, man."

Coop came around from the other side of the van. "Now it's time for you to meet the brains of *our* operation."

"What about Tiffany?" Theodore asked nervously.

"She can stay here for a few," he said, slamming the van's door shut. "She'll be fine."

A muffled yell came from Tiffany's taped mouth.

Theodore's heart pounded but he had to say it. "Why don't you at least take the tape off her mouth? No one can hear her out here."

Bear and Coop looked at each other and laughed. "No way," said Coop. "We'd be able to hear her. She'd be yelling her head off, like she did before we put the tape on."

They shoved Theodore through the back door, back porch, then kitchen, and into a dirty, cobwebby living room. The only furnishings were a ratty, burgundy velvet sofa, two beaten-up wooden chairs, and two crates, used as tables, which held ashtrays and reading materials.

A woman with short, honey-colored hair stood at the window looking out. Her frame was small, but far from boyish. When she turned around Theodore's heart leapt. He instantly recognized the pixie-ish face, the broad forehead, large, lovely dark brown eyes, and small, nicely curved mouth. She wore old jeans tucked into a pair of black cowboy boots, and a close-fitting yellow shirt. He was face-to-face with Lily Gibbons, his high-school sweetheart.

Panic over his situation was replaced by an avalanche of thoughts. *Her hair isn't long any more* was the first muddled one. Followed by, *twelve years, and she's even more beautiful. How can she be involved in this? The Green Guerrillas?*

Lily eyed Theodore with scorn. "So, President Theodore has arrived. Bear, sit the scumbag over there!"

Bear didn't mind obliging, shoving Theodore into one of the wobbly chairs. Theodore felt his bladder jar painfully.

Lily moved closer to him. He had not been able to take his eyes off her. She bent down to stare at him up close. She smelled of strawberries.

The word "Lily" involuntarily escaped from his dry lips, but she acted as if she didn't hear it.

"Why did you have to go bad, Ted?" She grimaced. "Oh, you don't mind if I still call you Ted, do you, for old time's sake?" She looked down and noticed his hands. "Still got the warts? You know it's stress that causes them, don't you? You've had them forever." Theodore self-consciously moved his bound hands to between his legs.

"Well, it hardly matters now. You cause more stress than you get. I'm sure your mother can attest to that. Poor woman." Lily gestured to the two men. "Ted, meet Cornelius Washington Carver Curtis, we call him Bear, and my husband, Drew Bly, also known as Cooper Davies. Two geniuses, Bear in the field of biology, Drew in the engineering sciences. And you *do* remember me, don't you?"

She's married? He had never forgotten her. He'd searched her name on the Internet many times. That's how he learned about a group called the Green Guerrillas, a peaceful (he had thought) environmental group that staged protests and tried to make positive changes in the world, the group he'd seen at Burger Depot. He'd heard Lily was the founder, but that's all he knew about her life after high school. In his frequent daydreams he imagined she'd be living where she said she would, on an organic farm, married, with a few kids. They'd be adopted, of course, since Lily was very concerned about over-population, and the little tykes would represent a rainbow of nationalities. This scowling, wedded-to-"Drew" woman could not be further from that fantasy. Throat tightening, he wondered if he could even answer. He forgot about his full bladder. He forgot about everything. His heart raced wildly, and fear made up only a tiny part of the agitation.

"Yes, I remember," he said in a whisper.

"To think, we were once . . ." Lily grimaced, then smirked. "Well, Ted, you're now the proud abductee of the Green Guerrillas. We've been watching you for a long time, your moves at BioTech over the years. *Beefy Fries*. Gee, what a *clever* idea." She shook slightly with a hollow, bitter laugh. "Pretty gross if you ask me. 'What will that guy come up with next?' I thought at the time. Now I see those were the days of innocence. Now you're with the greediest, most unconscionable evil-doers in the biotech industry, Void Chemical Corporation. We know what they've been doing in Research and Development. What you are doing is insane!"

Theodore found his voice. "Lily, I don't know what's going on, why you are doing this, why you have kidnapped me and Tiffany. But I'm a scientist, not an evil-doer. Most of us want to help the world. I know we've made some mistakes, it's inevitable . . ." His thoughts were jarred back to yesterday, the human/plant monstrosities. If he knew anything, he knew that what was happening in that laboratory was wrong. He took a deep breath, tried to calm himself. "I didn't know what they were doing until yesterday. I swear. They were my ideas, but I never expected, never wanted those things to be created. Lily, I was going to get *out*."

Lily's lips twisted in amusement, as if she were witnessing a kindergartner tell a big fib. "Sure you were, Ted, just when those doors opened to everything you dreamed of, which was being a big shot. I would expect a coward like you to say that." She pulled out a v-phone from a backpack on the floor and pressed two buttons. "Hello? Yeah, we've got him. See you tonight."

Her finger rested on the disconnect button. "Now Ted," she said, bending over to peer straight into his eyes, "you are going to call Langston Void and give an Academy Award-winning performance. You're going to tell him that you won't be in today, that you and Tiffany had to fly to Colorado last night and you're not sure when you'll be back. That your niece is in the hospital and had to have an emergency appendectomy. That you got the message yesterday morning but couldn't miss the contract signing, etc., etc. That's why you were kind of out-of-it. From *worry*."

Theodore's mouth hung open stupidly as he tried to register everything she'd just said. *Appendectomy? Fly out to Colorado? How did she know he'd been "out of it"?*

"Wait," he stammered, " — is Zera all right?"

"Ted, Ted, Ted. You just don't get it, do you?" Lily put her hands on her hips and leaned forward again until her pixie face, distorted by sarcasm, nearly touched his. "Let me explain this very slowly: We . . . are . . . the . . . good . . . guys. No, of course we didn't hurt Zera. But, we have a few tricks, so that if Void tries to inquire at the hospital, or at your mother's home, the calls will be routed to us."

"We've been studying this situation for a long time. We know about everything. We've been keeping tabs on a lot of people, watching their every move. It's all in place. You just have to follow through. And you will."

"We need to talk about this," said Theodore. No matter how tough Lily acted he could not believe she had lost all reason. "I haven't seen you in a long time. Is this worth risking imprisonment? You need to let us go, now."

Lily stopped, pulled up the other chair, and placed it backwards right in front of him. She straddled it, her arms resting on the chair back. "This may surprise you, but I've changed. A lot. No more silly idealism. Imagine, I used to actually believe that people would do the right thing, given the chance. That conscience and goodness would prevail over greed." She threw her head back and laughed. "I spent years building an organic farm, building a life, following my dream. Only, in the bitter end, did I finally learn how impossible it was to get big business to put decency over a bottom line. Or to even play fair."

She got up and walked over to Bear and Drew who stood glowering at Theodore. "You should have seen our farm, the one I started with these brave, gifted scientists after college. We just wanted to improve our little planet instead of exploit it, and we were beginning to make a difference.

"Bear, here," Lily continued, "worked wonders in soil and plant productivity through organic methods. He can communicate with plants, just like his namesake, George Washington Carver. You would not believe the discoveries he made! Drew developed some phenomenal solar greenhouse prototypes, pollution control designs, solar farm machinery, new fuels. We were working so hard together to start a new revolution. A green revolution."

Her eyes glazed with tears. She turned away and wiped them. When she turned back they were dry and hard. She scowled. "We were simpletons. You see, when we started to get big, VCC was there to knock us down. There started to be little 'accidents,' overspray of herbicide onto our fields, so our crops were tainted with chemicals, and could no longer be certified organic. Greenhouses vandalized, computers broken into and files stolen and hacked. Then, a couple of years ago, a fire in Bear's laboratory. Bear's wife, Olivia, died in that fire." At these words, Lily's eyes were wild with fury and remembered grief. "We were done," she snapped her fingers. "It was over. Just like that.

"They paid off just enough powers-that-be so that when I tried to do something about it, I ran into brick walls of corruption. What a ninny I was, Ted. But no more. Remember how I used to be a pacifist? Well, that's changed, thanks to people like you." She practically spat at him, her face a mask of rage. "If you don't do exactly as I say, I'm going to let Drew and Bear take you apart, piece by piece. And I'm going to allow myself to enjoy it."

Bear moved in on Theodore. He bent down over him, dreadlocks brushing against Theodore's face. Theodore looked down and saw a tattoo on one powerful fist — a planet Earth with the word "*Mom*" printed over it.

"I'd love to take you down, Theo," whispered Bear.

"Please, no violence," Theodore said, his heart pounding. "I'll cooperate."

Lily looked at her v-phone. "It's almost eight-thirty. Void will be getting to the office soon. We'll wait for the call letting us know he's there." She walked to a crate-table and picked up a piece of paper. "I have a script here that you're going to follow word-for-word. You're going to memorize it, and you have ten minutes to do so." She motioned to Bear. "Better cut his hands loose."

Theodore weighed his options — he was isolated and outnumbered by angry, grief-stricken captors. He didn't see that he had any options but to cooperate. "What about Tiffany?"

"Hmmm, what about Tiffany," Lily murmured. "Let's see," her voice rose almost to a yell, "You tell Void she's with you, you idiot!"

"No," Theodore said, "I mean, what are you going to do with her? She's been in that van all night. She needs food, water, to go to the bathroom."

"Oh, does wittle Theodore have a heart after all?" Lily mocked. "Don't worry, we'll take care of your girlfriend. Drew'll bring her in. *After* you make your phone call."

From outside came a blood-curdling scream. Tiffany.

Chapter Twenty-three

Despite Nonny's worry over Uncle Theodore, Zera heard her snoring, sound asleep just minutes after they went to bed.

Following the call to The Grand Hotel in Los Angeles, Zera was even more awake. Lying in bed, the words rang in her mind. *Mr. Green has checked out.* Zera stared up at the ceiling in her dark bedroom, the glow-in-the-dark constellation seeming so child-like now. She considered waking up Nonny, but decided against it.

She tossed and turned, waiting for the long, terrible night to be over so she could finally . . .

Standing on a small hill, Zera viewed the meadow below, a blanket of tall, moving grass splashed with vibrant wildflowers. Butterflies floated from flower to flower, suckling nectar. Bees gathered pollen. Birdsong and sweet scents drifted through the air. Peace filled her.

She saw him. A boy with dark, wild-looking hair, about her age, running, whooping with joy as he cut a zig-zaggy line through the vegetation. Zera laughed out loud as he stopped and twirled, skinny arms outstretched, dancing round and round. Her laugh turned into a giggle as he dramatically flopped down, disappearing into the tall, swaying grass not twenty feet away. She walked toward him.

He didn't look up. She wondered why he hadn't heard her. She thought of calling to him, but before she could, the meadow around him shrank. Low grass and patches of dirt replaced the tall grass and flowers. He lay in a patch of dirt. His eyes were closed and his expression blissful. He hadn't noticed the dramatic change that had taken place around him. *That's weird about the meadow; but what's weirder is I know that kid from somewhere.*

A small spot in the ground in front of the boy silently erupted. The earth vibrated. The boy opened his eyes. He sat upright and looked around, his expression startled, but not afraid.

He and Zera, who now stood behind him, watched, mouths open in astonishment, as a tree silently and quickly grew from delicate twig to mighty tower. *I know that tree, too. It's the one from Tava. The Green Man and Woman tree. What's it doing here?* They stared at the tree, now grown into a noble giant. A dozen or so birds flew to its branches. They sang in sweet, soothing tunes. The boy smiled, shrugged his shoulders, and lay down again as if what happened was not that remarkable after all. He gazed up into the glowing leafy branches. Zera, too, felt as if there were nothing to be worried about. She wished she were lying under the tree, enjoying the enchantment of the green shadow- and light-filled canopy. She would ask if she could join him.

"Hello," she said.

He didn't turn toward her, didn't move. She tried again, stepping forward. "Hello, hi!" Again, no response.

The day was sunny and calm, and as Zera wondered why the boy couldn't hear her the tree's branches began to sway in the windless air. Zera felt the change. Something ominous. The sun was suddenly too bright. The breeze turned into a harsh, chilling wind. The birds screeched and flew away. Zera shivered. The boy, who had raised himself up on his elbows, looked frightened too. The branches moved on their own with increasing animation. Worry turned to dread. *No,* Zera thought, *no.* She looked from the tree to the boy. He now was changing as the tree had changed. It had changed from a twig to a full-grown tree in seconds; she watched the boy transform, in seconds, to an adult.

Zera stepped backward in surprise and caught her breath — the boy was Uncle Theodore.

The massive branches above her uncle swayed, and began to whip around furiously. She heard the cries from the leafy branches, watched as he stared up at them, his eyes wide in horror.

"Why?" came the wails, the wails of *thousands*. "Why did you do this to us?" Theodore covered his ears with his now-warty hands, his eyes glued to the tree's canopy.

"My God, it's the stomatas!" he cried, trying to stand. His legs seemed unable to support him. *He's going to fall*, thought

Zera, forgetting her fears and stepping forward again. *They, those voices, are going to make him fall.* She reached out and grabbed for his arm but her hand went right through him. *What's happening to me?* she thought. Her uncle tottered but didn't fall. He steadied himself, stood upright, put his hands over his ears again, and before Zera could act, he ran. The meadow grew up again around him again as he fled. Jeers and shouts rang out as he took off: "You don't care about us. You only care about yourself." "You're sick." "Leave this place!"

It came to her, the meaning of stomata. She'd learned in biology they were tiny openings on the undersides of leaves, pores that regulated moisture. They closed when it was dry, opened up in wetness. *Mouth-shaped organs. That's where those voices came from.*

Zera stood, immobile, stunned. Not only at what had happened, but because she now felt what the leaves, what the plants, felt; their sadness and hurt, their anger at her uncle's . . . *betrayal. Yes,* she thought, *that's what they feel.* At the same time, Theodore's fear and horror coursed through her as she watched him run away.

"Uncle Theodore!" she screamed, forgetting he couldn't hear her. She raced down the hillside after him. She tore through the grass, following the path he made, yelling at the tall, frightened man with the wild hair and furiously pumping arms fifty feet in front of her.

And then, he was gone.

Zera stopped, spun around, searched for him in all directions. The wind had ceased. So had the screeching birds, the angry voices of the plants. The path her uncle had blazed through the grass had disappeared. All was calm again. It was as if he had never been there. She looked behind her. The tree was gone, too. *Where has he gone? He needs my help.*

A multitude of wildflowers: black-eyed Susans, coneflowers, Indian paintbrush, oxeye daisies, bee balm, yarrow, wild roses, and others, sent out happy tidings to Zera. She could hear them as she walked among them, the grass beneath her releasing its fragrance. Sunshine. Chlorophyll. The plants murmured in distinct voices, and Zera knew them as individuals; she could tell exactly whose voice belonged to whom.

"*You* wouldn't hurt us," said a scarlet bee balm in a high female voice.

"You understand," whispered a daisy.

"You know we can help each other," said a masculine Indian paintbrush.

"Yes, help each other. To live together," sang a clump of white yarrow in unison.

"We love you," a purple coneflower declared.

She looked at them and realized, she did understand, more and more. *But what about her uncle?*

Nothing but love radiated from the flowers, yet Zera's body felt heavy with worry as she walked along. She found a worn, winding path through the meadow and followed it, still hoping to find him. She wanted more than anything, after seeing him as a boy, to help him.

The path took her to the edge of the meadow where she found a brook.

"We're all one, Zera," it gurgled. "The saying is all wrong, you know. *Water is thicker than blood.* Water is the real blood, of *all* life." It laughed a merry laugh of clear liquid life dancing over round rocks.

For a moment Zera forgot about her uncle. *What a happy brook,* she thought, *so pleasant, and wise!* She gazed at its glittering energy, the sun reflecting off it in a thousand lights. *I can see the brook's spirit!* She saw her own wavy reflection within it — dark auburn hair, her now-smiling heart-shaped face. Their spirits, she knew with absolute certainty, were one.

"Come in," the brook said.

With no hesitation, Zera sat down on its mossy bank, took off her red sneakers, and crammed her socks into them. She slid her feet into the water. *Cold. Delightful.* She grinned at the twinkling water and her submerged feet. She wiggled her toes a few moments before standing and picking up her shoes. She splashed along the edge of the brook, her uncle completely forgotten.

The brook curved around a bend, and she realized she was thirsty. She squatted, cupped her hands, and scooped a measure of sparkling water. As she lifted it to her lips, she hesitated; she remembered something her parents told her long ago, that no natural water sources were pollution-free. Not anymore. Water from a stream could make you very ill.

"It's okay," said the brook. "I'm not contaminated. Please, drink from me."

She heard my thoughts.

The water was icy on her lips and in her mouth. She closed her eyes and splashed some on her face. When she opened them a moment later, she felt the presence of something behind her.

Above the bank rose another tree. She turned and felt a shock. It was hideously burned, blasted by lightning. Yet, its life force remained so strong a multitude of shoots had sprung up from its roots. These new, tender branches were in full leaf, flourishing, trying to bring life to the tree. *How could it still be alive?*

Again, she did not see a face but heard words. In a tired, masculine voice, the tree told her, "If the injured parts are removed, perhaps I may live fully again. Oh, but it is draining my energy."

Sadness filled her. Zera wished for a handsaw, something to help the tree. *Maybe I could bring it water,* she thought, but the ground around her did not feel dry. Everything but the dead parts of the tree looked fresh and healthy. She could not think of anything she could do to help the tree.

An assembly of small, singsong voices broke into her thoughts. "See us."

Around the tree, star-shaped sky-blue flowers bloomed in a

sea of airy foliage. Zera brightened. "I know you. You're called love-in-a-mist, *nigella*. You're pretty."

They murmured like a breeze, "Yes, you know us."

She climbed up the bank and sat under the tree. She peered into the faces of the flowers, into their tiny, light-green, star-shaped interiors. She saw the faces of the Green Man, the Green Woman.

"Hello," she said, as if it were the most natural thing to do.

"Lie next to us, rest, and we will talk to you," they said.

She gladly complied. In whispers they told her of the wonders to be found in the Green World. She learned how countless gifts — foods, clothes, medicines, and everything else imaginable — were created from their existence. They told her that plants wanted it to be that way, that they willingly and easily gave themselves to those who loved them. To those who respected their lives.

"To many humans — because we are not human, because we do not have a human heart or the human five senses — we are seen as nothing," chorused the male and female voices. "Most humans do not see us as we are. We see without eyes. Better than humans see with them. We are alive. We do everything you do. We breathe, we digest, we reproduce. We carry nutrients through our bodies through veins much like yours. And we move. Much more slowly than you, but yes, we move."

They told her they did not have mouths yet could speak to those who would listen, but they could not be heard with human ears. They could be heard only through the human heart.

"Anyone can hear us, if they love us enough," the flowers said. "You love us. You will help us. You are special, Zera. Your family has always been there for us."

They whispered of a world ready to be explored by anyone who would simply watch, and love. They whispered the names of scientists, artists, poets, and philosophers. The names floated gently in Zera's mind, like the soft floating umbrellas of dandelion seeds: Johann Wolfgang von Goethe, Henry David Thoreau, George Washington Carver, Luther Burbank, Emily Dickinson, Rachel Carson, Georgia O'Keeffe. They spoke of others with the name of Green.

Zera wanted, more than anything, to be one of those who knew, who loved, and who helped make things better.

"We are one," the female faces spoke. "Together, we can turn Earth back into a beautiful garden."

"Remember, Zera, our treasures cannot be revealed to those who are not in sympathy with us," said the male faces. "You will help us by doing three things: Watch. Love. And accept your power."

Muffled words echoed outside her head, "Wake up, Zera. Wake up."

With great effort, Zera lifted her eyelids. The day's first sunlight streamed through the blowsy curtains. It shone on the edge of her bed and on the cabbage rose wallpaper around her.

She was in bed. The dream images flickered in her mind, still vivid. *Poor Uncle Theodore.* She remembered all of it. Through the open window a gentle breeze caressed her face and bare arms.

"Get up, Zera."

Her eyes closed again, tightly. *I can't get up. I'm tired. Please, let me sleep. Let me rest. What a dream, what a nightmare!* Pikes Peak, or *Tava*, as Grandma Wren called it, came back to her with all the events of last night. It *was* all real. Today was the day, she would have to do something; she would have to face her destiny as Grandma Wren had said. Her feet felt cold under the covers, when they should have been warm. She touched her hair and it felt hot, as if she'd been in the sun. She shivered from the strangeness of it.

"Zera. Get up. Come over here," said the soft but persistent voice.

Zera's eyes sprang open. *That's not Nonny. I'm awake, now — aren't I?* Her head a jumble of words and images, Zera sat up. No one was in the attic bedroom.

The voice again said, "Zera," and her gaze followed it to the table near the chairs. There, glowing from the sun's rays, was her antique glass terrarium. The birthday present from Nonny that housed her most prized plant, Sunny the Venus flytrap. The voice came from behind the thick glass, from the *plant.*

Zera got out of bed and inched toward the terrarium. The lingering doubt that it couldn't possibly be Sunny vanished. The plant waved her tiny traps about, opening and closing them, while the faint words, "Zera, yes, here," echoed in the air.

She recoiled, but her eyes were glued to the terrarium. "Sunny?" *I must be dreaming still. I have to be.* Zera rubbed her eyes, looked around the room. On a chair next to the bed were the clothes she wore to Tava last night.

"Open the top," Sunny said, her largest trap forming a primitive mouth that spoke to her.

Oh, man, this is real. Zera got down on her knees and swung open the lid. Moisture escaped the terrarium and a boggy, peat moss smell drifted up.

"Ah, that's better," said the flytrap. "It gets hot in the mornings. And now you can hear me better."

Zera, eyes wide, peered down into the terrarium. The beautiful plant, light green with watermelon-pink traps, stretched amid the moss, was talking.

"Hello to you, too," Sunny said. "Isn't it wonderful? We're communicating in sound-words. The first step. I'm so pleased."

"I'm not asleep?"

The flytrap emitted a tinkling laugh. "No, you're not!"

Everything that had occurred the night before, from Tava to the dream/nightmare returned. Theodore was in trouble. They were *all* in trouble. Confusion gripped Zera; everything she had ever known about the physical world was being turned upside down. There was so much she didn't know, what was happening, what was expected of her, what they were up against. Yet, with all her heart, she knew what to do even as she resisted it. The words echoed in her mind: *Watch, and love. Accept your power.*

Gazing at the Venus flytrap, Zera's anxiety lessened. *It is wonderful, if you think about it, being able to communicate. It's as if I could suddenly hold a conversation with Alice.* The graceful figure before her swayed slightly, exhibiting a joyful enthusiasm. Zera remembered how tiny Sunny had been at her birthday, only about five inches tall with fifteen traps. Since then, she had doubled in size. The traps themselves were actually modified leaves, two oval, flat, fringed lobes hinged together like clam shells atop slender stalks. Zera had taken good care of Sunny, carefully monitoring her water, sunlight, and food. The attention showed. She'd grown radiant and strong.

As these thoughts of admiration went out to her plant friend, Sunny said, "Thank you."

Zera's mouth dropped open. "But I didn't say anything."

"You didn't have to, I received it nonetheless. You'll get the hang of it. We can hear you without sound-words, just as you can hear us. As you did in your dream. But, you know, it really wasn't a dream at all."

Zera stared at the plant, thought of her cold feet (*icy cold, from the brook*) and her warm hair when she woke up. Her forehead wrinkled, and the laugh came again. "Don't worry, you'll get it. What I mean is sound-words get in the way, mostly. The important thing is awareness. Let me try this time. See what you can hear, without your ears."

A few moments passed. Zera frowned. "I'm not getting anything,"

"Clear your mind. Relax. It's easy. It's the easiest thing imaginable."

Zera closed her eyes and slowly, consciously, relaxed. First her face, then neck, then shoulders. She remembered how her mom practiced yoga with Hattie. Zera had taken a few mother-daughter classes. The yogi-instructor would tell them, at the end of the session, as they lay quietly on their backs, palms toward the ceiling, to "quiet your mind, listen to your breathing." Zera relaxed her body now, her hands, her wrists, her arms. She breathed consciously. As soon as she had taken half a dozen deep, calming breaths, she stopped. Her eyes flew open. She blurted, "It's something about California?"

"Quiet," admonished Sunny, her traps tilted up toward Zera. "When you interrupt, it interferes. *Keep listening.*"

"Okay," Zera said. She closed her eyes again, determined to relax fully, to get it right. It took a full minute before she exclaimed, "I got it all! You sent that I must go to Theodore, to the laboratory, in 'the place called California.' "

"Yes!" Sunny raised her leaves high, triumphant.

Zera smiled, even though the prospect of going to California, to a laboratory, frightened her. She thought she'd try communicating something now without sound to Sunny. *What will I do there?* she asked.

Do what you just did now. Listen. It will come to you, when it's time.

I should get Nonny. Zera started to rise from her kneeling position.

No, Zera, you are going alone.

At the mention of going alone, Zera tensed. She couldn't receive or send any more messages.

"Calm yourself, Zera," Sunny said aloud. "You can do this."

"I'm trying to, but it's all so confusing. How do you know all this? How do you know about Theodore?"

"Our thoughts and feelings, like yours, travel through the atmosphere, like waves of heat, light, or sound. We also have something that's very like your Internet; we can communicate through the mycelium, a fungal network of tiny, threadlike cells that extend throughout the Earth's soil for billions of miles! Very quickly we find out about things that happen far away. But now, that travel is difficult. Many barriers stand in our way — not just physical, but chemical. So many poisons cause our transmissions to slow, many times to fail."

Through their connection, Zera could feel Sunny's sadness. It was exactly the way she'd felt in the dream with the other plants.

"We're also good at traveling, moving physically, and there is one way we love to travel the most," Sunny said. "Riding the sky."

"Riding the sky?"

"Yes, Zera. Seeds are great travelers, you know, but there are some who are the best travelers of all. You even breathe them in, exhale them. They ride into and out of your body as well as on the winds. Pollen grains and spores. And that is how you shall travel to your uncle."

"What?" Zera's eyes widened. "I don't understand. How could I?"

"You must accept that anything is possible. You must do three things: watch, love, and most importantly, *accept your power*. You are a *Green* — your people have been connected to us for centuries. To embrace this is to follow your destiny.

"Listen to me carefully. You will travel on a spore to California. And you will also remain here. For this to happen, you must accept the green power. When you reach Theodore, he will see you in your size again. There is nothing to fear. No harm will come to you. See the sphagnum peat moss below me, see the spore case?"

Zera's head swam. "You are going too fast. Stay here? Go? Accept the power?"

"There is so little time, Zera. You must *act*. Now! Yes. You can access the powers of Nature, indeed, of the Cosmos, available to you if you accept this cause. If you help us. If you help yourself!"

Zera thought of the dead roses on the trellis. The wildfires all over Colorado. Other natural disasters. Her dead parents. Nature could *hurt. Nature could kill.*

"I don't want these *powers.*"

"Zera, you have to trust. Trust me!"

An uneasiness filled Zera. As she looked at Sunny, she thought of what the Green Man and Green Woman said, and she realized something. *I don't trust them, but I trust Sunny.* She remembered the terror on her uncle's adult face, the joy on his face as a boy. He believed then; she could see it. Watch and love. Accept your power. *I have to do this. I have to help Uncle Theodore.*

"I'll do it."

"I am so thankful! It is an oath, Zera. You know that? You cannot go back."

Her heart thudded again, but she said it, "Yes, I know." She looked down. "I am not going in a nightgown, though." She hurriedly got dressed.

"Come down here," said Sunny. "Look inside."

Zera got down on her knees, gripping the sides of the table. She peered through the side of the terrarium, at the moss Sunny grew in. "How can I see a spore? They're microscopic." She blinked and removed her hands from the table. Her palms had left wet marks. *Oh great, sweaty palms. I'm freaking out.* She thought about her uncle, about Nonny. *I can't be afraid. I have to do this. Theodore is in trouble. We're all in trouble. I have to try.* She breathed deeply, willed herself to relax. She thought of Nonny, Hattie, and Grandma Wren. She thought of her mother and father. Fear threatened to overwhelm her. *No!* she scolded herself. *Breathe. Let it go. Think how Hattie and mom would love this, how they'd think it was the coolest adventure ever!* She focused on the moss beneath the flytrap. *Breathe deeply. Relax.* Over and over, like a mantra, she began to repeat the words in her mind — *Watch and love, accept your power. Watch and love, accept. . .*

Yes! thought Sunny. *Look.*

The glass changed, became a magnifier. Everything became clear. She saw the spore case, urn-shaped and bright orange, almost neon orange. It was nestled at the bottom of lime-green and brown moss strands that now towered above it like a gigantic, caterpillar-hairy jungle. The urn's surface was slightly pitted, like an orange.

Yes, you're doing it! Sunny said. The words gave Zera courage. *I can do this.*

Of course you can, you are a Green. Now relaxed, Zera could hear her friend perfectly. *That is the spore case, Zera, and inside are millions of spores. You are sitting atop one of them. You are unconscious of it at the moment, but you are there, with them. Can you see it?*

Zera moved her face closer to the terrarium. Her nose barely touched the glass, and she felt the coolness of it. Under her nose the glass became foggy, but at eye level it was clear. Zera marveled at the urn's perfect shape. *It's so tiny, so vividly orange*. A seamless rim ran around the top, a lid. She could see how the urn bulged, how full it was. It was so thin and fine, yet she could tell it was hard, almost impenetrable. *So strong, so light. So pretty. I am inside that case,* she thought.

Zera surrendered and found herself inside the spore case. She saw everything clearly; the chamber was orange and vast, like the interior of an immense room. In the next instant she became conscious of sitting cross-legged atop a single spore.

She looked down at her body, her hands. *I am seeing myself,* she thought, *but am I really here?* She wore her cut-off jeans, sneakers, a T-shirt. *I AM here. How is this happening?* Something strong within her told her not to ask, just to *be*. She was here *and* outside the terrarium. She didn't know how, but she knew this to be true. Somehow she understood, at the deepest, most primal level of existence, how something could be, and could not be, at the very same moment. How form, size, mass, energy — all she had ever known of the physical world — both existed as she thought it did, and didn't. And it was all right. She did not feel frightened anymore; on the contrary, she felt more at peace than she could ever remember.

She looked at the spore. It was triangular, smooth and round-edged. She saw that, where she sat, a deep scar-like shape crossed the spore's surface in the form of three skinny letter-Cs, each meeting with the others, touching on two ends, with the three curves forming another triangular pattern in the center. Surrounding her as far as she could see were other spores, like hers, yet different, each a perfect individual, like snowflakes. She remembered how her mother had told her there were no duplicates in the universe — how each blade of grass, each seed, each tree, each human, was a one-of-a-kind miracle. Zera saw that now.

Explosively the lid-like top of the urn shed itself. Zera, attached to her spore and along with the millions upon millions of others, shot up into the air.

A thrill like none she had ever experienced swept through her.

A breeze blew through the room and carried them all away through the open bedroom window. She did not see herself lying unconscious on the floor.

Chapter Twenty-four

Only in her most joyful dreams had Zera experienced what she was now doing — flying! Up and over the Colorado Rocky Mountains she soared on the tiny, triangular ship. She rode the wind past trees, houses, streams, and rivers. Up, then down, then up, up, up again, weightless and free.

She rode high, where house-sized droplets of water made up moist clouds that bounced around her. Then she plummeted, drying and twirling as she neared the earth in puffs of sparkling dust. Slow as a ladybug, fast as a lynx, up, then down again. She zoomed past forest needles and leaves; tasted and smelled their greenness, their life. On she went, west.

After scaling and descending the Rockies, she soared through the dry Colorado Plateau. For a while, among the eons-old features of erosion — arches, canyons, cliffs, mesas and buttes — she drifted. Colors sped by, altered by sun and shadow. She flew over and through trees, shrubs, flowers, grass, and she glimpsed animals: mule deer, rabbits, snakes, foxes.

For a few moments, caught on the back of a hawk, she rose skyward. She tasted the bird's life, its hawk-energy, radiating from where the spore-ship rested, a single satiny barb on a single white feather. The bird cried out, and its call rang joyfully, vibrating through Zera. The hawk spotted a rabbit and circled, targeted. They dove together before she fell free and was picked up by the gusting wind.

Through the aquamarine sky, over the land tapestry, she sailed. Through an array of geologic splendors; past ranches, small towns, and cities. She danced in the cool mist above the Colorado River. The Wahsatch mountain range loomed before her, and up she flew up over these mountains, too. She thought of little but the glorious beauty surrounding her. Time was lost to wonder.

Soon a scorched land of cacti lay before her. More miles disappeared over desert sand. Zera was awed by the barren magnificence, the light and heat. She skimmed over a city that went for miles, with monstrously large buildings and thousands of swimming pools glowing like neon turquoise. Water that did not belong in this landscape sparkled below her. *Las Vegas*. She felt its energy, its vanity, its emptiness. She reached Death Valley, and saw little stirring below, yet she knew that it, too, held life. She continued quickly, up and over the third range of mountains that day, the jagged, dramatic peaks of the Sierra Nevadas.

Beyond the range, the land was fruitful and rich. Now came noisy, smoky cities, a cacophony of cars and people, then wet, quiet farmlands, then drier forests and meadows. Zera thought of patchwork quilts. This one was made with colorful scraps both living and man-made.

By late afternoon, Zera drifted lower, over trees in the countryside. The wind became languid, heavy, moving ever-slowly with its special cargo. It floated Zera to the treetops, down to the sweet-smelling grass, then up again, as if it were playing, trying to make its fondness known. Zera laughed at the belly-tickling sensation, like riding on a slow roller coaster.

The clouds gathered and the sky dimmed. As they drew close to an old farmhouse whose silver-gray wood showed only white traces of paint, Zera felt a heaviness and a charge in the air. It began to rain and the ship carrying her flew between the drops.

Next to the farmhouse stood a gigantic oak tree. Zera knew the oak was dying, its journey in this life nearing the end. The few branches that were not dead were dry and losing leaves. It smelled more of earth, not of the life of leaves. The breeze gently deposited her into its dark cavity — and she was jolted by a blinding, deafening crash.

Chapter Twenty-five

After managing to scrape the tape off her mouth in the van, Tiffany screamed at full lung capacity until Drew and Bear raced outside. Now, ten hours later, she sat bolt upright, tightly wound as a spring, on one end of the shabby velvet sofa.

Theodore slouched at the other end. He wore his glasses, retrieved from the van that morning so he could memorize the scripted phone call to Void. The call had gone off without a hitch.

Tiffany's confinement had not. She had terrorized everyone, all day long. She screamed, kicked, hurled herself at her captors, tried to bite, tried to head-butt Lily, and even managed to fling a glass ashtray (with her hands bound) at the window in the front room. The window didn't break. The captors tried reasoning with her, threatening her, and even tying her to a chair for a few hours, but when they noticed she was crying, they untied her. Theodore watched Tiffany now as she fumed at the other end of the couch, a pink rectangle of chafed skin outlining her mouth. She was a mess, with tangled hair, smeared eye makeup, and wrinkled pink pajamas. Like Theodore's, her wrists were still bound with the plastic zip-tie, but she had struggled so hard, chafing her wrists in the process, that Drew had to pad under them with foam rubber.

Tiffany angrily tossed her hair back from her face, but a strand stuck to a sticky spot by her mouth. She brought up her bound hands and ripped it free with a pinkie, all the while glaring at Theodore. “Imagine, your old girlfriend, kidnapping us both,” she snarled in a voice hoarse from screaming. “What do you really have to do with this, Theodore?”

Theodore said nothing. He’d spent hours trying to talk to Tiffany, to get her to see what he was certain about: while the Green Guerillas made a good show of being menacing, they wouldn’t hurt them. But Tiffany wouldn’t listen. She was determined that Theodore’s calmness betrayed some kind of guilt.

“You didn’t even object when they put the tape back on my mouth!”

“They told you repeatedly to stop screaming. I practically begged you to stop. Just what did you expect me to do?” Theodore held up his own bound hands for emphasis.

“Nothing. Like you’ve done all day,” Tiffany rasped, twisting her wrists in agitation. “We could get out of these things, if you wanted to. We could try to escape.”

He had tried to wriggle free for hours, and she knew it. Theodore didn’t bother responding.

Tiffany got up and walked to the kitchen door. She pressed her ear against it, eyes squinted. After a minute, she stalked over to the window, muttering, “Can’t hear a thing but that radio. All

I've heard all day are snatches of conversation, something about 'equipment,' 'live via satellite,' something about a helicopter." She faced Theodore. "What do you think it all means? And why are they letting us know their names? Their identities? They've *got* to be planning to kill us. And you're just going to *sit* there."

"They're not going to kill us," Theodore whispered. "I told you this before, when Drew took me to the bathroom after lunch, he said they weren't going to hurt either of us. I believe him."

"Go ahead, believe it, Theodore, whatever. They've put tape over my mouth, twice. We're still tied up, have been all day."

"They put tape over your mouth when you wouldn't stop yelling."

Tiffany peered outside, through a large gap between the boards covering a window. "It's raining. Perfect. Even if by some miracle we do escape, we'll have to deal with that."

Theodore had heard a few things during the day too, and he sensed that while the Green Guerillas might not be dangerous, the mission they were undertaking surely was. He had been told in private he'd be going with them and to not, under any circumstances, tell Tiffany. In spite of what Drew said, he wondered if this would be his last day alive and discovered that he wasn't too upset by the thought. The nightmare of the night before played in his head continuously — the tree, the accusations, the hatred, the jeers — those horrible plant voices. In comparison to the nightmare and what he'd seen in the laboratory, the kidnapping seemed almost tame.

Tiffany moved from the window into one of the chairs opposite Theodore. “There’s something I’m going to tell you now,” she said, “because even if we get out of this I don’t want anything more to do with you. Ever. It’s over.”

Theodore remained mute. He’d heard worse threats that day from her.

“I happen to know you’ve thought about that crazy woman. I’ve seen that photo album from your high school years that you keep hidden in the garage.” Seeing his surprise, she nodded. “Yes, Theodore, underneath those boxes of science books. I found it a long time ago.”

She searched my house? Figures.

Tiffany glared at Theodore, large cat-eyes narrowing. “The two of you at the science fair, at that stupid Christmas amusement park. It was disgusting, both of you all pimply and in love. I kept tabs on that box to see if you revisited those precious memories. And you did. Many times.”

When she got no reaction, her voice rose. “The way you acted yesterday cinched it. The way you treated me. Yeah, I’m a twit all right!”

Lily pounded on the kitchen wall to get their attention. “Keep it down in there!”

In defiance, Tiffany let out an angered scream. She then turned her attention back to Theodore. “I’m convinced you knew something was going on,” she said, growling out the words and refusing to let up. “You were just too weird yesterday, too completely *changed*. This kidnapping crap is all a ploy, just to make you look innocent." She got up and started pacing, a pink and blonde tigress in bunny slippers.

"Right," Theodore whispered, "all of this is a huge ploy, so I can be with my girlfriend from fifteen years ago. She's *married*, Tiffany."

Tiffany stopped. "Married? That's funny." She threw her head back and laughed. "Poor Theodore. You know, we had a chance. Langston and Crystal, all those wonderful people we met at Void, treating us like real family, bending over backwards to be our friends, to help us become successful. I had several conversations with Crystal, about what I might be able to do in L.A. for a career if we . . ." She stopped in front of Theodore. For a moment her face softened and her eyes grew teary. Then, they blazed.

"A bunch of slimeball criminals! Eco-terrorists, that's who you're associated with! All this time, did you live some kind of double life? Oh, I wish I'd never met you!"

An explosion of white light filled the living room, followed instantaneously by a deafening boom.

Tiffany jumped and screamed. "What was that?" She cowered near Theodore.

Theodore hurried to the window. "Lightning. The tree's split apart. It's smoking!"

The kitchen door flew open. Lily, Drew, and Bear ran into the room.

"Did you see where it struck?" asked Drew.

"Yes, the oak." Theodore stared out the window at the charred, smoking tree. As the smoke began to disappear in the pouring rain, he made out a figure standing inside the hollow trunk. It was unmistakable, he would recognize her anywhere. His hair stood up on his neck. He whirled toward his captors, his eyes glazed with fear. "Zera's out there!"

Zera stood in the middle of the blackened tree, drenched from the pouring rain. The tree felt warm beneath her feet, not hot, although the smell of scorched oak and dissipating smoke was strong. She coughed once and when she closed her eyes she still saw the white outline of the tree. Her ears rang. She remembered drifting into the tree and then a blinding white light and BOOM. *Must have been* . . . her thinking was still scrambled . . . *lightning?*

She looked down at the soaked clothes hanging on her now full-sized body — cut-off jeans, a vintage AC/DC T-shirt, and her favorite red sneakers. She remembered the day's flight, a journey that lasted no time and forever. And now everything changed again, literally in a flash.

Did the tree give up its life to somehow reconstruct me, in full size? Or am I really even here? She felt the rain on her face, tasted it when she licked her lips. She felt the heaviness of her clothes, her hair. She held out her hands, watched the rain pelt them. She smelled the rain's damp sweetness mixed with the smoke. *I feel real enough.*

She spoke silently to the tree. *Thank you.*

It was then she saw them; two hooded men were running toward her, shouting.

Chapter Twenty-six

Looking out the kitchen window, Nonny Green sipped her second cup of coffee. The sun was halfway up the trunk of the blue spruce; it had to be well after 9:00 A. M.

"I wonder when she's going to get up." Nonny directed her remark through the pocket doors of the kitchen to the dogs in the living room. Alice and Cato looked up, cocked their heads. Alice jumped off a chair, trotted up to Nonny's chair, and laid her head on Nonny's lap.

"She used to get up with the chickens." Nonny stroked Alice's soft, spotted head. "She must be exhausted from yesterday, poor darling."

Nonny tried Theodore's v-phone again and this time she got through to his answering tape. She watched a video of Theodore, looking so professional and serious, telling her, "I am not available at the moment, but I will return your call as soon as possible."

"Please call me, Ted, I need to talk to you," Nonny said to the image. She could see her own worried reflection over her son's on the monitor.

She finished her coffee and stood up with the help of her cane. She checked the living room's mantle clock. "Nine forty-five." Clunking over to the staircase, she called, "Zera, honey, it's time to get up."

No answer.

"Zera. Sweetie," she called a bit louder, "it's almost ten. Hattie and Grandma Wren will be here soon."

Still nothing. Nonny looked at the dogs. Alice was back in her lounging position on the couch next to Cato.

"Alice. Go get Zera." Nonny slapped her thigh.

Alice pricked up her ears but did not budge.

"How about you, Cato, old boy?" tried Nonny. "Where's Zera? Go get her." She waved one arm toward the stairs.

The old black lab slowly got down off the sofa, stretching his back legs on the cushion with arthritic lethargy as he made his way down. He ambled stiff-legged in the opposite direction, to a kitchen counter, on which sat the dog biscuit jar.

"You dogs are worthless. You'd let a one-legged old lady climb the stairs, wouldn't you? Phooey on you, then."

Nonny began ascending the steps, holding onto the handrail with one hand and her cane with the other, calling for Zera. When she made it halfway up, Alice bounded up the stairs. Standing on the landing she watched Nonny continue her climb.

"*Now* you take some interest."

"Zera!" Nonny called, and then caught her breath. At the top of the steps, Nonny felt a crushing pain in her heart. She pressed her free hand against her chest. "Oh, please, don't let it happen now," she whispered. She stood there for a moment, trying to will the pain to stop, but it increased. She lurched to the door of Zera's room and opened it, then collapsed on the floor. She didn't see Zera lying on the floor near the terrarium. She didn't hear the rumble of Hattie's truck in the driveway.

Nonny's heart had stopped.

Hattie entered the house with Ben and Grandma Wren. "Guinevere! Zera! Are you here?" The dogs were barking wildly, Alice upstairs at the landing, Cato downstairs. Alice ran halfway down the stairs, barking frantically, then back up.

Panic gripped Hattie as she raced up the stairs. Ben followed her.

"Oh, no!" Hattie's hand flew up to her mouth to stifle a scream. Nonny, lying in the doorway, Zera on the bedroom floor near her terrarium. Hattie bent down over Nonny while Ben rushed to Zera. Zera was breathing, although unconscious, but Guinevere had no heartbeat. Hattie began CPR and yelled at the top of her lungs, "Grandma, call 911!"

Chapter Twenty-seven

From the kitchen table, Zera saw Drew and Bear on the back porch, taking off their black rain parkas. It had stopped raining.

"Find anything?" Lily asked as Drew opened the door, her voice rising above the rock and roll music playing on the radio.

Drew's eyes darted from Lily to Zera and back again. "I was sure it was some kind of elaborate trap," he said, "that somehow Void had figured out our plan and sent the girl to trick us. We've looked for an hour. There's nothing out there, no trace of anyone or anything. And we would have known; those cameras I set up would have shown *something*."

"Camera five showed something all right," said Bear, standing behind Drew. He nodded at the large color monitor on the counter top. The screen was split into eighths, each section showing views of the road, the house, or property. "A girl appearing out of nowhere in a hollowed-out dead tree, just after it was struck by lightning. But Drew's right. There's nothing out there, nothing showing *how* she could have gotten there."

He reached in his jeans pocket, pulled out some acorns, and plunked them on the table. "There were a lot of these around the base of the tree. An almost-dead tree. Doesn't make sense."

Lily picked one up and shrugged. "Maybe the winds blew

them in? You guys need to sit down and hear this. Zera's been telling some pretty fantastic stories."

Zera stared at the men. Drew with his serious, square jaw and piercing blue eyes looked intimidating, as did Bear with his mighty heft. But from the moment they ran to her, to help lift her from the tree, she knew they were friends, not foes. Still, when they brought her in and she saw her uncle, his wrists bound, his panicked eyes searching hers, asking over and over if she was okay, she was furious. She started yelling at them all, but her uncle calmed her. He said it was okay; that he had done something terrible that these people were trying to fix. He said Zera could trust them, that they wouldn't be harmed. Zera believed him and felt no fear.

Despite what Drew said, the two men sensed the same absence of threat from her. *Drew's fighting it. He won't let himself trust me.* She couldn't explain it, how she could *feel* their thoughts. Lily and Bear's positive energy toward her, Drew's skepticism. The realization that she was tapping into something she didn't understand didn't frighten her, it only brought more confusion.

Is this ability a gift . . . from accepting power from the Green Man and Woman? There's been so much that's happened these last twenty-four hours, how can I even guess? At the tree, the men had only asked if she was okay before they rushed inside with her, left her with Lily, and went out again. Lily had briefly searched her. Then she got her a towel to dry off.

"Fantastic stories, you say?" Drew ran his fingers through his blond hair. "Maybe I ought to rig up a lie detector."

Zera smiled at Drew, who tried not to return the smile and failed.

A physical energy, an excitement, stirred around Zera. As with the snakes, she heard the words clearly in her mind: *Pick one of us up.*

Zera glanced at the others. Their expressions said they hadn't heard.

PICK ONE OF US UP. The tone *demanded.* Zera's heart pounded faster in realization. The words came from the acorns!

She plucked one up and held it in her palm. The cap of the acorn popped off and rolled off her palm onto the table.

Drew took her wrist, saying, "What's this?"

Zera closed her hand around the acorn. It cracked lengthwise and she felt a squirming. The acorn was sprouting. A thin white root slinked downward, out the bottom of Zera's closed fist, as a stem pushed several inches from the top. Drew dropped his hand. Before their eyes, the stem produced five buds that grew and unfurled into leaves. She felt the life force slow. She opened her fist.

Drew said, "I felt it. I felt the energy."

Bear picked up an acorn. "This can't be." He crushed it with his fingers. He examined the contents.

Drew leaned in. "Is it robotic? Something man-made?"

"Looks like an acorn," said Bear.

Zera handed Bear the seedling and he examined it, tore a leaf, smelled it, tasted it. "It's real, man."

Without a word, Zera picked up from the table the tiny fragments of the other acorn, put them in her hand and closed it. She produced another seedling.

The Green Guerillas' mouths dropped open.

"That's one hell of a trick," said Drew.

"I think we need to hear those stories," said Bear.

The two men pulled up chairs and sat down.

Zera took a deep breath and started at the beginning, from the time when she first thought she heard the voice in her bedroom. She told them about the snakes and the spirit quest with Grandma Wren, Nonny, and Hattie. She told about the dream, and of that day's journey across the Western United States. Drew's mouth opened at times, as if to say something, but then it would close, as if he'd decided against it. Bear listened raptly, a huge smile spreading across his strong features. Several times he laughed out loud, a velvety belly-laugh. Once was while Zera told about the Green family history and what Nonny had said about fairies.

"George Washington Carver said it was so," Bear said, his eyebrows raised. "He mentioned the Greens. And he knew about the fairies, too." While Zera was recounting the dream, Lily's brown eyes shone teary-eyed at the part about Theodore, until Drew noticed. Then her expression hardened. She muttered, "Serves him right."

Zera couldn't get over the fact that this was *the* Lily, Theodore's high school sweetheart; the one Hattie had talked about. She acted tough, like the guys, but Zera knew it was just an act. Zera could *feel* she was a friend. Zera found it amazing that her uncle ever dated someone so cool.

"It's inexplicable," Drew said after Zera finished. "If I hadn't seen you with my own eyes, standing in the middle of that tree . . . if I hadn't seen what the camera caught . . . I'm a man of science, but there's a physical realm out there that science has not even touched. Still . . ." He rubbed his crew cut.

I can sense exactly what he's feeling, Zera thought with a start. *He doesn't believe it but he's not going to let me know how he feels. And he's keeping an eye on me.*

"It's fantastic," Lily agreed, "but I believe her. I've felt the presence she speaks of many times."

"Her story is true," said Bear. "I know it to the core of my being. My great-grandfather knew George Washington Carver, worked with him in the 1920s. Carver wrote of the Greens in his diary. My great-grandfather inherited that diary, and I read about them, and about Carver's close relationship with them."

"Your great-grandfather knew George Washington Carver?" Zera said.

"Sure did." Bear grinned proudly. "I was named after him."

Zera drew in her breath. It was one of the names said by the Green Man and Woman. She knew a little about Carver from her plant books. He was genius in the field of botany, known as the

Wizard of Tuskegee and the Black Leonardo. She recalled reading that people like Thomas Edison and Henry Ford offered him a huge salary to work for them, but he turned them down. He said he wanted to keep his discoveries free for all people. He said that God provided the plants to help people, and God didn't charge a fee, so why should he.

"Carver told my great-grandfather that flowers spoke to him, as did hundreds of other living things in the woods," said Bear. "He was always talking with God and the plants. You can read it in his autobiography. My grandfather wrote that Carver said the Greens reminded him of the fairies. Said they had the connection. He called them 'Helpers of Nature.'"

A pounding came from the door leading into the living room.

Lily sighed. "I'd almost forgotten."

"Wow, she was quiet for a long time," Drew said. "Did you tape her mouth again?"

"Yes." Lily said, lowering her voice. "She wouldn't stop screaming again after Zera was found. Tiffany was positive that Mr. Langston Void was right outside the door waiting to rescue her. 'Langston, Langston, I'm in HERE,' she kept yelling. I had to."

To the closed door Lily trilled, "Be with you in a moment, Tiff."

"So, Theodore doesn't know anything about all this?" Bear asked Zera.

"No," Lily answered for her. "He saw Zera for a minute but I didn't want him in here with us. Then, as soon as she finished the story, you guys came back."

Zera added, "He seems different now, really sad."

"He was so upset when he saw you outside," Lily said, "until he saw you were all right. He's still in there, pacing."

Zera frowned and looked down at the kitchen table. Her uncle had bent to look at her face. He'd appeared terrified, but when he saw she was okay, he started apologizing. He went away mumbling, "It's all my fault." Zera could feel his despair. She thought of Nonny, and was filled with worry. *What is happening in Ute Springs? I've been gone all day. Hattie and Ben, everyone's probably frantic, worrying about me.*

She said to Lily, "If what I saw in the dream is what's happening to him, he's going through a lot."

"Too bad we don't have time to tell him what *you've* been through," Lily said, slightly sarcastically. "I'd be interested in his reaction."

"I know everyone's got some good inside them," Drew said, "but it's almost hard to believe with him. Those creations . . ." He winced.

"What creations?" Zera sat up straighter. Her eyes searched Bear's.

Bear nodded toward Lily, as if saying, "She's the boss."

"Go ahead, Bear, she should know," Lily said.

Bear cleared his throat. "This isn't easy. I guess I'll just say it. Zera, Void Chemical Corporation, with your uncle's help, has developed human/plant combinations. Eyes that grow like clusters of grapes on vines, trees that produce human hearts, and a lot more." He hung his head. "It's sick, man, *really* sick. That's why your uncle and Tiffany are here. We . . ." He looked down, shame-faced. "We took them last night. We had to make them come with us. To help stop all this."

The room seemed to spin as Zera's mind tried to reconcile the thought of these people admitting they were *kidnappers* with the monstrous images Bear described. *Heart trees? Eyes?* "Oh, God," she whispered, "So that's what it's all about, what the Green Woman spoke of."

"I'm sorry, Zera," Drew said. "Void Corporation is worldwide, and they're into a lot of bad stuff, but they couldn't have done this without Theodore. It's seems your uncle's gone to the dark side, the side of greed and arrogance." He shook his head, looked down at his military-style watch. "It's almost six. We've got to get going. What should we do with Zera?" he asked Lily. "Leave her here with Tiffany?"

"Man, I wouldn't wish that on anybody," Bear said.

"I have to go with you," Zera said to Lily.

Lily, her forehead wrinkled, looked at Bear, then Drew. "I know it sounds crazy . . . but I think she should."

"I agree," said Bear, without hesitation.

"Are you two out of your minds?" Drew slammed his hand down on the table. "I'm against it. We could lose *everything*. This is going to up the risk considerably! We could lose our freedom. We could go to *prison*."

Lily stood. "As you've said yourself many times, Drew, there are worse things to lose than your freedom. I feel strongly about this, that it's the right thing to do. Still, I won't let her go if you say no. We're a team."

They stood looking at each other. Zera sensed the turmoil in Drew, the fear of making a mistake, then the letting go of that fear. She felt something else — *This is a person who loves taking chances*. "What the hell," he said, his mouth set. "We're probably headed for jail anyway."

Zera watched the Green Guerillas from the doorway. Lily removed the tape from Tiffany's mouth and said, "We're leaving."

Theodore stood up from the sofa, but when Tiffany stood, Lily told her, "No. *You're* staying."

"What do you mean?"

"Theodore's going. You're staying. We're going to feed you again, take you to the bathroom, but then we're leaving you here for a while."

"But," Tiffany's face contorted with anger, "you can't leave me here!"

"I'm afraid so."

"How long will you be gone?" Tiffany whined. "What'll I do?"

"I'm sure you'll think of something." Lily gestured at a

small stack of environmentally-themed magazines and books on a crate. "Maybe you can read something. If everything goes smoothly, we'll come back for you tonight. So I advise you to hope for a good outcome on our part."

"Oh!" Tiffany scowled. "I can't believe you would do this to another woman. What kind of a monster are you?"

"Tiffany," Lily began, " — or maybe should I say Agnes? As in Agnes Roach from Washington High School?"

Tiffany's face flushed. "What?"

"We've researched *everything*. We know about your identity change after high school. It's none of my concern personally; I just want you to know that I know. Now I've explained the situation and you need to deal with it. It's that simple. By the way, we're both human and have two x chromosomes, but that is where the similarity seems to end."

"What about her?" asked Tiffany, nodding toward Zera.

"She's coming with us too."

"Oh, I get it; even *she's* in on it. One big, happy family." Tiffany flashed a look of contempt at Zera, and Zera looked away, embarrassed for Tiffany, or Agnes. *Agnes Roach.* Zera stared at her shoes. Before the last few days, it would have been easy to laugh. Now, compassion blossomed in her. That explained why Tiffany acted so crazy about names, and about acceptance. More than that, Zera *felt* something strange coming from Tiffany. She could feel her fear, and that she, too, had a lot of sadness. *Sadness?*

"Well," Tiffany continued, with a defiant toss of her hair, "I don't know what kind of demented game this is, but you're not going to get away with it." She glared at each of them. "None of you. That I *do* know."

She plopped back down on the sofa with an "I am going to win" smile. *It's all fake*, thought Zera. *She's the unhappiest one here.*

Without a word to Tiffany, Theodore left the room. Zera noticed that as he brushed by Lily, they had a reaction to each other, undetected by the others. Lily drew away, avoiding eye contact, and Theodore looked flustered. *I felt it*, thought Zera. *A charge filled the space between them.*

She didn't have time to ponder it. Bear put a hand on Theodore's shoulder and directed him out the back door, then into the van. Zera followed. A few minutes later, after tending to Tiffany's needs and securing the house, Lily and Drew joined them.

As they headed down the bumpy gravel road, Bear sat cross-legged in the back of the van with Zera and Theodore. Shaking his mane of dreadlocked hair, he said, "Theo, in spite of everything, I feel for you, man. A woman like that. Unbelievable."

From the driver's seat, Drew needled, "You know the saying, 'Behind every *good* man . . .'"

"I care about her," said Theodore. "She's a good person."

Zera thought about Agnes Roach. She imagined a different Tiffany, young and vulnerable. She admired her uncle for sticking up for her.

Theodore gazed out the dirty van window. He'd asked Zera if she was okay when he saw her again, and she felt his concern, but then his eyes went vacant, as if he were somewhere else.

Lily, from the front passenger seat, turned to Bear and said, "You need to get a blindfold on him."

An hour later Zera watched out the dirty window as the van crawled down a quiet street in a decayed section of Los Angeles. To her surprise, she had fallen asleep and had awakened to find her uncle, his blindfold now off, with Bear sitting beside him.

Bear asked Zera, "Did you have a nice nap?"

Zera nodded.

Before falling asleep, she had been worrying about all of them. Not only about herself and her uncle, but about Tiffany, and her grandmother — how Nonny was taking her disappearance back home. She knew the Green Guerillas were going to be in trouble with the police, big trouble, no matter what happened next. She strongly sensed that they knew they would be caught and would have to answer for the crimes they had committed, were committing, and those they were surely about to commit.

The van turned down a trash-strewn alley and about midway along stopped behind a small brown house.

Once inside, Zera, Theodore, and the Green Guerrillas shared a dinner of organic peanut butter and jelly sandwiches with almond milk, eaten in nervous silence. Zera looked around the dining room, noting that there were no pictures on the walls, no rug on the wood floor, just the bare necessities — an old table, a few chairs, a beat-up plaid couch. *It's just a place to meet, refuel, and then carry out whatever it is they do.*

Watching Theodore eat, Zera sensed something about her uncle she couldn't quite pinpoint. He was obviously miserable, every pore of his being screamed that, but he also seemed changed; exactly how, she wasn't sure. The only things he'd said to her were "Are you all right?" and "I'm sorry." He hadn't asked a single question about how she got there. He looked older, and yet he was dressed casually, in jeans and a white T-shirt, a combination she'd rarely seen him in. She thought about the boy in the dream, about how Theodore had once been happy. She wondered if any trace of that boy still existed.

After dinner, Lily stood up and announced to Bear and Drew, "I'm going to change. We've got fifteen minutes."

Drew nudged Theodore. "You're changing too. Let's go."

Theodore shrugged, stood up.

"Wait," said Bear. "Something's been bothering me. Give me one minute." Bear went to the adjoining kitchen, pulled out an old, wrinkled potato from a bin near the refrigerator and cut it into fourths. He gave the pieces to Theodore. "Here, man, rub these pieces on your hands. I'll bury them." Bear winked at

Drew. "Sorry, I guess it's the doctoring instinct. Just can't stand seeing him suffer. Plus, it's a full moon tonight. Perfect timing." Expressionless, Theodore did as he was told. Bear went out the back door with the potatoes and a big metal spoon he had taken from a drawer.

Drew just shook his head and muttered, "Hocus frickin' pocus."

Drew led Theodore out of the dining room, down a hall, and into another room. Through the closed door, Zera heard him bark orders. "Clean up. Put on the suit. Be quick about it."

Everyone met in the living room. Zera did a double take when Lily walked in. She now wore a prim gray skirt and jacket with a white shirt and black shoes. Her hair was covered with a shoulder-length brown wig in a conservative hairstyle. Small pearl earrings replaced the dangling leaf ones, and she held a briefcase. She wore red lipstick. She looked like a completely different person. Her outfit matched Theodore's; they looked like high-level office managers.

Theodore stared into Lily's eyes.

"So, do you recognize me this time?" Lily asked.

"You, you were the nurse at the lab?"

"Yep, that was me — in a fat suit. We were figuring out a way to break into the lab on our own — before you came along and made it easier for us."

"Then you should know something about my reaction . . . to those experiments."

Lily turned away.

Zera felt the growing apprehension they all shared. Strangely enough, she felt no fear and no butterflies.

Lights from a vehicle entering the driveway flashed into the darkening room.

"It's show time," said Bear.

Theodore's startled expression at the sight of the Void Corporation limousine did not go unnoticed. He hesitated in approaching it.

Bear gave him a nudge. "Man up and move it, Theo."

Lily opened the limo's door and in the light they saw the driver, slightly built, graying, dark eyes. When he got out of the car and came around, Zera noticed he was not much bigger than she was.

The driver greeted them all, and then locked eyes with Theodore. "Hello, Mr. Green."

"You're . . . you're Langston's driver," Theodore said.

"I'm Jerry. But all you know me by is 'Driver.'"

Remembering how he struggled, and failed, to remember his name just a day earlier, Theodore couldn't look him in the eyes.

"Is Void taken care of?" Lily asked Jerry.

Jerry nodded. Noticing Zera, it was his turn to be startled. "What's she doing here?"

"I'll tell you all about it tomorrow morning, over breakfast, when this is over."

Jerry nodded again, accepting Lily's statement without another word. Drew just shook his head.

Lily was the last to get in. Theodore and Bear sat on one side; Lily, Drew, and Zera faced them. Through the dark-tinted windows Zera watched the house recede from view.

Lily switched on a light. She looked over at Theodore, and her eyes narrowed. "This is the plan, Ted. Listen up. We're going to VCC headquarters, and then taking the helicopter to the Research and Development Facility." She gave him a moment to take that in. She continued, slowly, as if she were talking to someone who might have problems following instructions. "You and I, once we get to company headquarters, are going to go through the front doors, to the guard station. You will tell the guards at the front desk how I, *Jenny Muldoon*, was your assistant at Biotech, and you just hired me today. You'll tell them we're going upstairs to your office to get some paperwork. You'll have to sign in, etc., but don't worry; those guards are not going to dare question anything you do. You're the new *president*."

"We'll hang out in your office for a few minutes while the tapes are being set up. Zera, you'll go with Bear and Drew. When we're finished, we'll meet you at the helicopter."

"Do you think it's a good idea for Zera to come?" Theodore said. "Isn't this going to be dangerous? Do you really want to risk harming a child?"

"I'm not a child, Uncle Theodore," Zera said. "It's okay. I'm supposed to go."

"What?" Theodore rubbed the back of one hand. "I don't even know what you're doing here, how you got here . . . that tree." His voice took on a faraway quality, and he looked out the window again. The scenery had changed as they neared downtown. Strip malls, lights, heavy traffic.

"Don't worry," Zera said. "There's no time to explain now, but," she lowered her voice, "I saw your dream."

Theodore jolted. He met Zera's gaze and for the first time that afternoon he was fully there, he didn't seem to be straddling two worlds, the world of living-in-the-now overshadowed by the world of his private nightmares.

"I saw it," said Zera. "The meadow with the tree, the plants. I saw you when you were *young*."

Theodore's eyes widened behind his glasses, and she felt his disbelief, worry, a tiny bit of gratitude that someone may have witnessed his suffering and may actually know the terror he'd been through. "But . . . but, that's impossible, Zera."

"It's not," Zera's voice remained low. "I was there too." She looked around at the others, who were absorbed in their conversation. "I know I'm supposed to be here. Nonny told me some amazing things about our family, the Green family. We're supposed to be protectors of the Green World, Uncle Theodore."

"What?" There was something deeper than disbelief coming from her uncle. Zera could feel the word "protector" turn over in his mind. A glimmer of something akin to remembrance.

Drew was listening in. “Some protector,” he spat the words. “God help us *all*.”

Lily tapped Theodore on the knee as he stared at Zera. “All I have to say to you is, don’t mess this up. Don’t try *anything*. Because if you do, your little Tiffany may be out in that farmhouse for a long time.”

“Now,” said Lily, “We’re going to go over it again. What’s my name?”

Chapter Twenty-eight

The limo glided to a stop at Void Corporation Headquarters' front entrance. Jerry got out, strode around the car, and opened the door for Theodore and Lily.

"You'll be going in through the back entrance," Lily said to Zera. "I'll see you soon." After smoothing her skirt and grabbing her briefcase, Lily whispered to Theodore, "Remember, *Jenny Muldoon*. Your former assistant at BioTech."

The lobby was dim as most of the lights in the building had gone off after five. At the front desk sat two men in uniform. They made for an odd couple; one large and flabby, with bulldog jowls, the other smaller and pale, with sharp features and wavy hair. As Theodore and Lily approached, the smaller guard stood.

"Hello, Mr. Green," said the large one. "We missed you today."

"Yes . . ." Theodore eyed the man's name badge, ". . . Fred, I had business in Colorado I needed to attend to." He signed the check-in sheet, pressing down hard so his hand wouldn't shake. His heart lurched as he thought, *if ever there was a time to try to turn the tables, it's now.* He thought about what would be the worst that could happen. *She's not armed, and Zera has no fear of Bear and Coop, um, Drew. I don't think they'd harm her.*

I'd be a hero, to some. . . hated by others . . .

He handed the pen to Lily and her eyes bored into his. *No, I can't consider it. I won't risk anything happening to Zera, and . . .* the next thought turned his heart to lead. *There's no winning outcome, not for me. All I wanted was to make good, and . . . everything's gone wrong.* Theodore cleared his throat. "This is my former assistant from Biotech Multinational, Penny Muldoon. We're very lucky she's decided to join the Void team."

Lily beamed at the guards and held out a hand to Fred. "I'm happy to meet you." She turned to the wavy-haired guard, whose nametag read Howard Blake. Howard extended a skinny hand. "Pleased to meet you, ma'am," he said in a vague southern accent. As they shook hands, Theodore thought he saw Howard wink at Lily. *My god, could the guards be in on this too?* A weird relief that he didn't try anything filled him, even as he felt like a coward.

"Yep," Theodore said. "Plane just got in, and we, um, wanted to do the paperwork tonight."

"No problem, sir," said Fred, obviously unconcerned with Theodore's story. Theodore and Lily walked to the elevator and Howard called after them. "We'll see you soon."

"Let's hope not," Lily said under her breath.

She turned, smiled, gave a little wave. "Thank you!"

In the "CEO Only" elevator Theodore looked at Lily. They were alone for the first time. His heart skipped a few beats, but he couldn't help himself, he couldn't take his eyes off her. She was gorgeous. Lily avoided his gaze and seemed preoccupied with the elevator buttons. She'd told him in the limo that the elevator would be bugged, and warned him not to say anything.

Up they went swiftly, eighty-two floors to the top. Weak-kneed with emotion, Theodore was unable to think about anything but whether Lily felt anything but disgust for him. He thought back to when they'd dated, how they'd spent almost every minute of their free time together their senior year of high school, sharing lunch every day, going out every Friday and Saturday night, taking long, romantic hikes in the mountains until nightfall . . .

The digital voice of the elevator announced with a soft, feminine tone, "Executive floor."

They entered the lobby. A woman sat at the desk — a familiar buxom blonde. Theodore gasped. "Crystal?"

The woman looked up and smiled. She smiled differently than Crystal, not as wide. Another Crystal-look-alike, like Langston's secretary Brigette, this one with short blonde hair and gray eyes. Theodore breathed a sigh of relief.

"You're Mr. Green aren't you? I recognize you from Brigette's video directory. I'm Meg; I came in this evening for a couple of hours to finish some work for Brigette. Mr. Void worked late; he just left a little while ago." She stood and offered a pretty hand. "I was just getting ready to leave myself."

Theodore shook her hand, quickly and nervously,

introducing "Jenny Muldoon," and cringing as he remembered that he'd called her Penny downstairs.

"Unless you need anything; then, of course I would be happy to stay," Meg offered.

"Oh, no," said Theodore. "We're quite fine . . . I'll see you around." He led Lily down the hallway.

"Nice going," muttered Lily. "At least you got my name right this time."

They walked past Langston's office, with its gigantic double doors inlaid with the large, gold letters — "V" on one, "C" on the other. The next office, his, showed a brand-new metal sign. A gold planet Earth with three lines written across it in script: *Theodore F. Green, President, Biotechnology Division.* Without thinking, his hand went up to touch the lettering.

"You finally got what you wanted," Lily said.

Theodore jerked his hand back. For an instant he felt courageous. He met Lily's eyes and said boldly, "No, actually I never did."

She looked away. "Let's go in, shall we?"

They entered an office, smaller, but nearly identical to Void's.

"Nice," Lily said. Her sarcastic tone told Theodore that she'd obviously made a quick recovery from Theodore's surprise statement. His heart sank. Lily opened her briefcase and took out a notebook. It held a hidden scanning device. She pressed several buttons and looked at the display.

"Great job, Drew," she said to herself. "He successfully debugged it."

"You mean the room was bugged? By Void?"

"Ted, if the situation wasn't so serious, your naiveté would almost be cute."

Theodore's face felt hot. *The way she said that . . . could it be possible she doesn't totally hate my guts?*

"Drew's electronics wizardry, along with 'Howard's' help down at security, is going to ensure that no one suspects a thing. At least not until it's too late. They're not even going to know we're leaving the building by helicopter. All we have to do is wait for Drew to give the signal. That should occur in," she looked down at her watch, "about ten minutes. We'll wait it out till then."

She walked to the leather sofa and sat down. "How about offering me a beverage?"

Chapter Twenty-nine

A red-eyed Hattie Goodacre sat on a long beige couch in the waiting room of Peak County Hospital.

"They'll be okay, Mom," said Ben, sitting beside her. Hattie wished she could believe him. She could tell by his tight mouth, the obvious hurt in his eyes, that he wasn't convinced. The truth was, they just didn't know.

Cosmic Dan walked down the hall toward them, his expression serious, until Hattie caught his eye. He attempted to grin but failed. Hattie caught her breath.

She and Ben stood as Hattie dabbed her eyes with tissue. "You talked to the doctors?" she asked.

Dan nodded. "Since they were unable to get in touch with Theodore, they finally let me know a little bit about what's going on."

"What did you find out?"

"A few things."

Dan motioned for Ben and Hattie to sit back down and parked his long, lanky body next to Hattie's. His closeness gave her comfort. "You told me you knew the situation with Guinevere, Hat, and you said you told Ben this morning." He rubbed his jaw, visibly troubled. "The cardiologist, Dr. Ball, said she's in pretty bad shape, might not last the night."

Hattie burst into tears and Dan held her while she sobbed. Hattie blew her nose and made an effort to regain control of her emotions. "She was having problems even before Sally and Ewan died. And these last years, they've been a struggle. But Zera doesn't know, and Ted, well, he knows she's been sick, but he's never known just how serious her illness has been. That's what gets me. She swore me to secrecy, and I feel like I've been helping a stupid, stupid conspiracy because Guinevere wanted me to, and now it feels like a huge mistake."

"What about Zera?" Ben asked Dan. "Any change?"

"No." Dan's brow furrowed. "But she seems to be okay. It's strange. She won't wake up. It's not really a coma, there's no injury, and her brain patterns show a person who's experiencing deep sleep. It's all REM sleep, you know, rapid eye movement, like when people dream. It's unlike anything they've seen. No one can figure out what's going on and they want to wait until they get in touch with Theodore before they go further in trying to wake her."

"I told you what she said she saw up on Tava," Hattie said, her voice quavering. "Grandma Wren too. I'm sure it's got something to do with that." She dabbed her eyes again, tried to smile, then took a deep breath to compose herself. "I've got to pull myself together . . ."

Ben had put a hand on his mother's other shoulder and Hattie patted it. "I haven't been able to get in touch with Ted all day," she said. "Talked to that bimbo secretary in L.A. probably a half-dozen times. I finally got out of her that Ted left yesterday for some family emergency here in Colorado! I don't know what's going on." Hattie blew her nose again. "She said she's been unable to get in touch with Ted's boss. She did tell me Ted's president of their Biotechnology Division. Guinevere never mentioned that; I don't think she even knows."

"We'll find him," Dan said. "You just need to hang in there. Zera's going to wake up soon. And you're going to be right there with a beautiful smile for her."

Hattie tried to produce even a weak imitation of a smile, but found she couldn't. "Is Grandma Wren still with her?"

"Hasn't left her side."

Hard rock music came from the floor, the v-phone in Hattie's backpack.

"They call me Doctor (Doctor Love)
They call me Doctor Love (calling Doctor Love)"

Hattie looked at Ben and didn't know whether to laugh or cry. "Changed my ring tone again?" Ben jumped up as Hattie picked up her backpack from the floor. He looked ill. "That was . . . I did that yesterday after you all took off to Pikes Peak. I thought it'd be funny, to Zera. I'm going to get a drink of water," He took off down the hall.

Poor kid, Hattie thought. He had a crush on Zera, it was

written all over him, had been since he'd seen her at the house that first day back home. When he was out last night until 11:30 she suspected he might have gone over to see her. Could it have been just yesterday when they were all working in the garden so happily at Elsie Mayfield's? It seemed like a million years ago.

Hattie dug out her phone. "Maybe it's Ted, finally,"

She paused for a moment, staring. "Oh, all buttons! UGH!" She uttered a swear word as the tune of *Calling Dr. Love* continued, then stabbed at one of them. "Hello?"

An extremely handsome man appeared on the screen. "Hello. Is this Hattie Goodacre?"

"Yes." Even in her overwrought state of near-despair, Hattie couldn't help but think — *he looks like a movie star.*

"Ms. Goodacre, I'm Langston Void. I've been trying for hours to get in touch with Theodore Green. Is his niece okay? I heard she's had an appendectomy."

Chapter Thirty

Lily looked at her watch. "It's time, Ted. Let's go."

It had been one of the most uncomfortable ten minutes of his life.

The front desk was vacant, Meg gone. *Efficient,* Theodore said to himself, as he and Lily approached the elevator and got in. He thought again of the secretary's resemblance to Crystal, how eerie that was, and for a moment his mind touched on cloning. *No,* he thought, *that would be impossible, crazy.* His next thought mocked him — *as crazy as plants growing human organs?* He forced himself to think about what he and Lily were now doing. Lily had explained to him that Drew made sure digital imagery in the surveillance cameras were altered with "doctored" versions, to make it look as though he and Lily had left the building through the front doors. The security guard "Harvey," an expert forger, would take care of their signatures on the sign-out sheet, and make sure Fred was away from the desk when Lily and Theodore "left."

"Rooftop," said the female elevator-voice and the door opened. The landing-pad lights were the only ones on. The chopper's blades were revolving at a high speed. In the lighted interior of the helicopter, Theodore saw Drew, Bear, and Zera.

At the door Lily barked, “Next to Zera.”

The door opened and they climbed in, Theodore next to Bear and Zera, Lily up front with Drew.

In an instant they were whirring over the city, tens of thousands of lights twinkling below them.

“Is everything set for the lab?” Lily asked Bear.

Bear nodded. Lily glanced at the floor next to him to some gray metal cases and said, “Good.”

“How are you doing, Zera?” Lily asked.

“I’m okay,” Zera said.

Lily reached back and patted Zera’s knee. “You are an awesome young woman.”

With great difficulty, Theodore averted his gaze from Lily.

Chapter Thirty-one

Zera wasn't really okay, like she'd told Lily. She'd been on edge since their arrival at Void Corporation. For awhile she hadn't felt too worried, but as the night went on the calmness and well-being she felt after she materialized in the oak tree completely disappeared.

Everything was happening too fast. Bear and Drew, busy with preparations, hadn't told her any details about their plans. Now the helicopter moved silently through the nighttime sky, toward god-knows-what. Low and weaving almost noiselessly through the city, the craft reminded Zera of a dragonfly, specifically, the Blue-eyed Darner, or *Aeshna multicolor*.

My second flight today. A lump came to Zera's throat as she thought of Nonny, Hattie, and Grandma Wren. She'd had time to think since the ride from the country. *If I'm here, in California, did I disappear from Colorado? And if so, what's Nonny thinking — that I ran away?* Zera's stomach clenched and she fought hard to control her racing thoughts. *I thought Uncle Theodore was putting her through so much, and now look what I'm doing. Who I'm with. What the Green Guerillas are involved in is illegal and dangerous. If they're caught, and from what I sense from all of them, they expect to be, what happens then?*

Will they go to prison? Will I be taken away from both Uncle Theodore and Nonny for being a part of this?

She reminded herself to breathe deeply and saw her uncle looking at Lily again. It was clear that that he cared about her like he'd never cared about Tiffany or any other woman. Zera liked and trusted Lily. She had never felt that way about Tiffany. Yet, pangs of disloyalty troubled her. Tiffany had been in her life for several years; she had tried, in her own way, to connect with Zera. It was not easy to cast Tiffany aside after all.

She also thought about Ben. What was happening in Ute Springs? What was Ben doing now? *He said he wanted me to be his girlfriend. We kissed.* That thought made the others go away for a moment. She'd waited, forever it seemed, to have someone like him in her life. He really cared about her. Now what would happen?

Lost in her worries, Zera hardly registered the hour-long trip to the edge of the desert. The next thing she knew, Bear was pointing through the helicopter window to a structure in the distance. As they neared the huge building, a dim, ghastly-green glow became visible — the rooftop greenhouse she'd heard them mention. The light contrasted with the heavens visible through the helicopter's ceiling. Twinkling stars filled the clear desert sky. Zera thought of her mother and father and their appearance as the two stars at Tava. Her fears ebbed a little. What lay before her, no matter how fraught with danger, was important. This was where she was meant to be.

Theodore and Lily were also gazing up through the helicopter's clear plastic top at the stars. Zera sighed. Being in her uncle's nightmare, experiencing his fear and sadness, had given her a different perspective. For the first time since she'd known him, she saw him as someone whose life, like hers, operated on a crazy pattern of happiness and hurt, success and failure. She saw him now as not a guardian or uncle, but as a human being.

"I hope your invention works on the guards," Lily said to Bear.

Even in the darkened helicopter, Zera could see naughtiness dance in Bear's eyes. "Don't worry. My non-toxic knock-out gas will take care of them. They're set to get a small dose every 15 minutes for the next two hours."

Void Chemical Corporation's Research and Development building seemed deserted. The lighted guard towers were dimly lit but motionless. After a smooth landing on the helicopter pad at the side of the building, Drew cut the engine.

"Whatever happens," Lily said to Bear and Drew after they got out of the chopper, "we know we tried, that we gave it our all. You guys are the greatest." Lily hugged Bear, and then took Drew's hand and they walked a few steps away to be alone for a moment. Zera saw Lily kiss him and they held each other. Bear looked a little teary. Zera noticed her uncle stared at the ground. *So much guilt is coming from him — and a little jealousy.*

Bear handed equipment cases to Drew, Lily, and Theodore,

saying brusquely to her uncle — "You're helping too, Theo."

Lily walked over to Zera. "I hope we're doing the right thing, bringing you."

"You are," Zera said, although she felt unsure of herself.

As they walked toward the building, a young man headed toward them from the shadows. He behaved oddly, keeping his white lab coat secure over his head until the helicopter's engine completely stopped. Now, with the coat down, Zera saw what he covered. His skin and hair were stark white, same as the coat, and starting to blend in with the sandstone color of the building's walls. *Wow*, she thought, *if not for those dark pants, he'd be almost invisible!*

Theodore stared. "The kid from the lab," he said in a shaky voice. He was talking not to Zera, but to himself. His voice dropped to a whisper. "Oh, god."

They headed to the door leading to the clean room. As they came closer to James Dubson, Uncle Theodore gasped. Zera saw why. Even the irises on James' eyes were whitish-beige, the pupils an eerie blue. Zera nearly jumped out of her skin. *He looks like a ghost*!

"Hey, Mr. Green," James said. "I'm not lookin' too blue today with my blue lab cap, am I? Lookin' pretty white, huh? Lookin' like a *freak*." He moved closer to Theodore and from the fury she felt radiate off James, Zera thought he might try to attack her uncle. "Do the implications of anything you guys do ever cross your minds?"

Theodore stepped backwards. The case he carried slipped out of his hands. Bear, right behind him, grabbed it before it hit the ground. Theodore's knees buckled and Bear grabbed his arm, steadied him. "Easy, man."

Zera stared, her mind beginning to comprehend the magnitude of what lay ahead.

"What's wrong with you?" Bear said to Theodore. "Didn't you know?"

"I thought . . . Void said the cuttlefish cream was temporary. It's not? What happened?"

"What happened, Theodore," Bear said, bending over, breathing into Theodore's ear, "is that they messed with Mother Nature."

Cuttlefish? thought Zera. Immediately her mind brought a picture. *Cephalopods, related to squid and octopuses. They shoot out ink, change colors to camouflage, or attract, or hunt. Highly intelligent.*

"It's not temporary," James said. "I've been dealing with this, changing to match my surroundings any time I have a hint of anxiety, and not having control over it, since they sprayed me with that stuff six months ago. And let me tell you, it's been non-stop anxiety. There was no cream," he said hatefully. "They put me in a tanning booth thing, Mr. Green, covered every inch of me. I'm a freak now, thanks to scientists like *you.*"

"I didn't *know*," said Theodore. "And I wasn't responsible. How can I be responsible for this?"

James' face twisted. "There wouldn't be those things in the basement if you weren't showing the way, working on this stuff. Come on! Everyone who works on these projects, no matter what small job they do, is responsible in some way. Even me."

Lily shook her head.

In the clean room, Theodore shakily put down the case. "I feel sick."

A queasiness filled Zera as she watched him rush to the bathroom. Sounds of retching came from behind the door.

"This might not work out," said Drew. "He might not be able to keep up with you."

"He *will* do it," said Lily, heading for a dressing room. "I'll drag him around myself if I have to. I'll be back in a minute; I'm going to change."

After a couple of minutes, Bear, who now held a video camera in one immense hand, knocked on the bathroom door. "Gotta go, Theo." His deep voice echoed in the room.

Theodore came out looking like a badly beaten man going into the boxing ring for another round. He went to the sink and wiped his mouth, then his pasty, sweat-covered forehead, with a wet paper towel. He looked at all those in the room, including James. "I know it'll never be enough, but I'm sorry."

No one said anything. Zera found her sympathy was with James. *How is he supposed to live his life, like that?* She couldn't bring herself to give her uncle any words of comfort. *What can I possibly say to him,* she thought, *Hey, don't worry about it, it's all right?*

Lily came out of the dressing room. She now wore jeans and a green T-shirt with the white words *Green Guerrillas* across the chest. A bracelet of thickly engraved leaves and line symbols encircled one wrist. Theodore and Zera noticed it at the same time.

Lily saw Zera's reaction and smiled at her. "Your mother gave it to me, a long time ago. The writing on it's in the Ogham alphabet."

Theodore said, "Sally?"

"Yes. It was a birthday present. She gave it to me after you and I broke up. For my eighteenth birthday."

Drew interrupted. "This is where we part," he told the group. "I'll meet you at the helicopter in," he glanced at his watch, "exactly fifty-five minutes." He gave Zera a hard look and she felt his reluctance to leave her with the rest of them battling with his desire to complete the mission.

Bear and Lily checked their watches and nodded.

"Let's put these cases by the door to the lab," Lily instructed James. "We're going to the greenhouse first."

Chapter Thirty-two

Lily pressed the button next to the door in the clean room, and the entrance to the laboratory slid open. The huge room was bathed in a gray glow of dim lights. Rows and rows of white laboratory tables covered with microscopes stood empty.

"Down there," pointed Lily, "to the elevator."

In contrast to the lab, the light in the elevator shone bright white. Lily pushed the button for the roof and they stood, silent, while the elevator rose. A surveillance camera jutted out a few inches in one corner of the ceiling, but the power light was off. *James must have taken care of that,* Zera thought. She saw James' face, hair and hands had changed to a steel color matching the elevator walls. She looked away; he reminded her of the Tin Man in *The Wizard of Oz*.

The door opened and the voice chip in the elevator's computer announced in a masculine voice, "Greenhouse. Authorized personnel only."

Lily asked James, "No alarms are going to go off when we step out, are they?"

"No. Everything's cool."

The greenhouse was dim and glowing green. Plants surrounded them, all the way to the top of the multi-pyramidal ceiling. Zera saw James's head and hands were now green, but not only green. He, like the lights, was giving off a *glow*.

She flinched. James noticed and said, "Oh yeah, I get all bioluminescent, glow-in-the-dark too, just like the cuttlefish!"

Even the inside of his mouth.

Lily flipped on light switches and the greenhouse filled with noise, as if a thousand beasts had awakened. Odd barnyard sounds echoed from a corner; Zera heard something that sounded like snorting. *It's a jungle. More than plants . . . animals too.*

Lily looked around in disgust and nodded to Bear. Microphone in hand, she stood in front of the camera. Bear began filming. "We are in the greenhouse of Void Chemical Corporation's Research and Development Facility," Lily said, looking straight into the lens and gesturing with one arm. "We're here to show you some of the *products* Void Corporation is in the process of perfecting."

Theodore stood back, still, pale, and wordless while Zera took in the surroundings.

Here it is, she thought. *This is what they meant. All of THIS.* A wave of nausea went through her. She hoped she wouldn't become physically ill like her uncle.

Lily motioned to Bear and they strode to a table in the corner.

"Here we have milk-choco-cane prototypes," said Lily, "the combination cacao tree/sugar cane/*cow* plants that they're developing in hopes of making 'instant' chocolate and mountains of money."

The camera panned along rows of two-foot high, cane-like plants. Some of the plants' leaves and stems had white and black coloration, some looked almost furred, but most were just plain green. All were freaks. Interspersed on narrow stems, fat green pods, where the cocoa beans normally grew, hugged the cane. The pods were green, but — they *moved.* From some came a faint, bawling sound. Tiny green calves wiggled under the skin of green. The noises they made created a soft, lowing din, muffled cries of "Maw . . . maw . . . maw . . ."

"Now this batch is obviously rejects; after all, who wants a field of bawling plants? The little guys are still showing their mammalian genetic material, and we can't have that, can we, Void Corporation?" said Lily. "It can take years to get it all worked out. Meanwhile, there are thousands of failures like these. Failed experiments destined to be tossed into a landfill."

Zera wished she could cover her ears and her nose. The air stank from the soil, a chocolate-manure stench. She felt the calves' hunger and longing. *How could they do this? Create life, and then just kill them off? For chocolate?* Zera wondered if she'd ever be able to eat her favorite sweet again.

Lily continued, "You see, everything must be perfect before it goes out to the consumer, perfectly *hidden*, that is. All wrapped up in neat packaging and tied up with a pretty bow. Otherwise people might find these products morally questionable. Void can't have that, can they? They want our reality altered and sanitized.

"Now stop crying, babies," she said to the plants. "Even though there's no mother's milk for you, you'll soon be out of your misery. You're just a step in Void's *process*.

"But I digress." Lily faced the camera again. "This, my friends, is only the beginning of the freak-show here at Void Chemical Corporation's Research and Development facility. We'll take you on a short tour, here in the greenhouse, where the work is out in the open, at least to the employees — who are all, by the way, under contracts of secrecy. Then we'll descend into Void's top-secret research nursery, hidden in this building's underbelly. What you will see there will shock, sicken, and, hopefully, enlighten you."

Through her disgust and the growing sick feeling that came with her psychic connection with the plants around her, Zera admired the way Lily seemed so self-assured in front of the camera.

Lily walked to the next area. It contained a group of Christmas trees, a few dozen glowing, table-sized trees with hundreds of tiny yellow lights. The group followed her. *Pretty*, thought Zera. For a moment she was dazzled by the creations. *I wonder how they made these?*

Her arms spread wide, Lily indicated the trees. "These look nice, don't they? Might even be ready for next Christmas, but the 'Yule Fly' tree project has a few kinks in it as well." Bear adjusted the lens for a close-up, and Zera, standing next to him, saw through the flatscreen viewfinder the source of the lights — fireflies. On all of the branches were the glowing firefly tails, but the problem was that other parts of the insects' bodies were there too. Some lights had partial bodies attached; some even had heads with wiggling antennae. None had just the glowing tails of the insect. Zera looked at her uncle, standing next to James. His expression was blank.

Lily offered a grim smile. "Sometimes things look pretty and they seem cool — but when you look a little closer you get the whole story. This stuff can be cleaned up eventually, but the fact is that underneath, it is what it is. A *monstrosity*." She walked down rows of plants, to tall trees growing in immense water-nutrient tanks. The trees, some scrawny and some already more than ten feet tall, were struggling to grow, right before their eyes.

"They call these 'moaks.' Aren't they special?" Lily feigned appreciation for them, smiling into the camera lens. "A combination of mice and oak trees. A Void concoction for fast-growing trees to make fast-furniture, fast-homes, and other fast stuff. What they've discovered, though, is that supplying these trees with enough nutrients to match their fantastic growth rates is difficult. As you can see, they've been unable to feed this one successfully and the top is dying out."

Bear focused the camera on a tree. At the bottom, the bark wriggled with thousands of long gray tails. The tails twitched and moved like long worms. Farther up the tree the tails moved more slowly, and at the top, they hung motionless. The foliage was a deathly yellow and brown. The stench was horrible. Suddenly nauseated, Zera steadied herself by grabbing a table. No one noticed.

"Everything has a price," Lily said. "There are never easy solutions. And apparently it takes modern man too much time to find solutions to keep both our planet and our souls healthy. But I am relieved that they've 'finally gotten the squeaks out of this one.'" No one laughed. Lily shook her head. "That's one of the in-jokes at the lab here at Void. They have narrowed it down to just the *tails*!"

Lily headed to the far end of the greenhouse, and Bear, James, and Zera followed. Zera's stomach bothered her more every minute. Theodore lagged behind them all, paler than he was in the bathroom. Zera glanced at him periodically, but her uncle was in his own world, eyes downcast.

"Now for the walatoes. The walrus/tomato combination that Void is developing in attempt to grow tomatoes in the *Arctic*. We just can't get enough tomatoes, can we?" She stopped and turned to face the camera again. "Here they are. Lovely, aren't they?"

Table upon table was filled with what looked like tomato plants. Some of the red, super-large fruits sported walrus tusks, nostrils and whiskers.

"There are endless combinations possible. And look, some do not even have obvious walrus features. It looks like they're getting closer here."

The camera scanned a three-foot-tall plant, and Lily plucked a firm, ripe, normal-looking tomato hanging above one with walrus whiskers. As she picked it, the nostrils on a tomato next to it snorted, blowing tomato seeds on her. Another tomato, one closer to her with tiny tusks, lurched forward, feebly trying to jab her arm.

"Yum, nothing like a fresh, vine-ripened tomato," she said, wiping the seed-covered back of her hand on her jeans. "But I don't think I'll bite; what about you?" She held the tomato out to the camera and as the camera focused in, the tomato pulsated, as if it were going through its death throes. Lily set the tomato down and made her way toward the noisiest part of the greenhouse.

I'll never look at tomatoes the same way again either thought Zera angrily, the walatoes' rage carrying into her own emotions. While she had known about burg-fries, and other products, actually seeing these plants "in development" was a night and day difference. No one had said anything, but she was sure she was as flushed as Theodore was pale. She now felt hot, as if she had a fever. *The Green Man and Woman are right. It has gone too far.*

"Now I'd like to introduce a human experimentation, which is illegal, but, here at Void, they seem to be able to do what they want. James Dubson, a Green Guerilla who has been working undercover at Void Corporation."

Zera glanced at her uncle, who was grayer than the mouse tails on the dying moaks. *He knows*, she thought, her heart heavy. She remembered the nightmare, the nightmare they shared. *He finally understands*. The insight didn't make her feel any better, but she didn't feel like puking anymore. For the first time since they arrived she understood. She saw the entire picture, what it all meant. Zera heard the creations' voices and felt their longing to be what they were supposed to be. It was as if billions years of biology, adaptation, and struggle was a train derailed. At least now the world would know.

James moved to stand beside Lily, his face, hair, and eyes glowing a mottled green-white from trying to blend in with his surroundings and his lab coat.

"James," Lily said, "was in an illegal experiment, an attempt to create human skin coloration that serves as a camouflage. He participated in Void Corporation's JVS, Juvenile Volunteer Scientist program. This program is in partnership with, I hope unwittingly, state and local governments. Young people in trouble with the law, mostly kids in foster care, have the option of repaying their debt to society by volunteering for Void Corporation, participating in a 'work camp program,' doing clean-up work in the facilities and on the grounds, things like that. Well, James was in the program last year and after he completed the program and turned eighteen years old, he was contacted by Void Corporation. They asked if he'd be willing to participate in a secret experiment. James got a little more than he bargained for." She turned to James. "Did they give you any warning that this," Lily gestured to James' face and hands, "could happen?"

"No way," said James. "I was working at Burger Depot, and they called me, said I could be in this awesome experiment and they'd pay me some pretty good money. They said the effects would be temporary. That it'd be the coolest thing ever, that I'd be almost *invisible*.

"When it kept up," said James, pointing to his head, "they told me not to worry, that they'd come up with something to fix it."

"And have they, James?"

"The scientist who worked with me said that the genetic material has fused in a way they didn't expect." James looked down shyly, then back at the camera. He took off his lab coat and sat it on a table. He was wearing a black and white striped short-sleeved shirt underneath and as the coat came off his skin began to get mottled again, with darker spots — spots that changed to black and white stripes.

Zera's throat felt as if it were closing. *I can't believe this.*

"They used the genes of a cuttlefish," said James. "They're these tentacled creatures of the sea, related to octopus and squid that are experts in camouflage. I'm able to control it, somewhat, but if I get excited or anxious, I change. What's even worse is now, I've found I sometimes have these accidents . . ." James look embarrassed but his face retained the shimmering black and white stripes.

"Go on." Lily gave James a reassuring look.

"Octopus and squid, you know, if they get scared, well, they have this black ink they squirt. Now, if something really startles me . . . I squirt black ink out my . . ."

Zera stared in disbelief. *Poor James!* She glanced at her uncle and his face was now not only ashen, but had sweat beads all over it. *He looks like he might be sick again.*

"And we don't know how the skin spray they used on you, that you absorbed into your body, might have altered you in other ways?"

"It's been only six weeks, so, no, they don't know." James rubbed his arms. "Void's offering me a lot of money to go to a new lab in South America while they try to figure out how to fix it. They don't want this getting out."

"And you were the only one in the experiment?"

"The only one I know of. I think I was the first. That's what they told me anyway."

"I'm sorry, James." Lily addressed the camera. "James contacted us because he wanted people to *know*. He's been taking a big risk, joining the Green Guerrillas, going undercover. You're a good man, James." At this point, Lily's voice broke.

Bear paused the camera, moved his head away from the viewfinder. "Are you okay, Lil?"

Lily shook it off, cleared her throat. "Keep shooting."

James, black and white stripes now covering his exposed skin, looked directly into the camera. "I would give my life to stop what is being done here. This technology is just beyond stupid. It's evil."

"Well, there you have it," Lily said. She had regained control of her emotions, but the anger and sarcasm that had animated her earlier was gone. She now looked depleted. "A brief tour of the greenhouse, as I promised," she said softly. "Now we're going downstairs, where you'll see something even worse, if you can imagine, than what's going on here."

Bear turned off the camera. "On to the lab."

They headed for the elevator.

"We don't have much time," Lily said, looking at her watch. She sighed deeply. "This is so much harder than I thought it would be."

"Do you hear that?" asked Bear.

"Hear what? I can't even hear myself think, with the racket in here," Lily said.

Zera couldn't wait to leave. *It's a madhouse*.

James's head jerked skyward, towards the roof of the glass greenhouse. "It's a chopper!"

Zera's heart jumped. *Is it the police?* Her uncle was staring upward, his forehead creased in worry.

They hurried to the elevator. Lily pressed the button and turned off the greenhouse lights. The plant-animals quieted.

"Over there!" exclaimed James, pointing.

As the elevator door opened, a search light sliced through the sky and into the greenhouse. There were flashes of green, the momentary shimmer of the plants, and for a second, Zera's companions and herself, fully illuminated.

Lily stared into the light, defiant. "Let's get out of here! Move it, quick!"

They piled into the elevator. Zera watched the light, still slanted on the five of them as the helicopter hovered. The door closed. "Going down," said the elevator's masculine voice and a shiver traveled through Zera's spine. *Down . . . to what? Nothing good can come out of what is happening now.*

"When we get downstairs, we have to go *fast*. We have to finish," said Lily.

The doors opened and they ran, with Lily in the lead, through the lab, back to the clean room. As that door closed behind them, a flash of white light shone through a transom above the outside door. An exploding sound, another white flash, and a rumble came from the helicopter landing area.

"They must be attacking Drew!" Bear's voice boomed from next to the mirror-door leading to the underground laboratory.

Lily's jaw clenched. "We have to finish. Let's go!"

James pulled up the "Are You Clean?" sign next to the door to reveal the keypad. "Do it, Ted," directed Lily.

Theodore moved to the panel, his face gray and sweaty. "It's Demeter 911." He punched in letters and numbers, and then put his hand into the recessed opening. The door stayed shut.

Come on, Uncle Theodore, Zera pleaded silently, *Come on!*

"Damn," Lily said. "Maybe you punched it in wrong!"

An outside explosion shook the building. Lily looked as if

her knees were buckling and Theodore grabbed her arm. "Are you okay?"

"Let go of me!" Her face white, she punched in the code again. She grabbed Theodore's hand and pressed it again on the pad.

The door opened.

"What about the cases?" asked Theodore, gesturing to the cart piled with them.

"There's no time!" Lily said. "Go!"

The five of them sped down the long corridor lit by emergency lights, descending into the near darkness. There were no small, flying cameras following them this time. As Theodore ran, he gasped to Lily, "You're not taking any weapons to defend yourself? Isn't that what's in the cases?"

"No Theodore, it was something for the plants," Lily said, "to make them sleep — a permanent sleep." She nodded toward the camera Bear carried as they ran down the corridor. "This is the only weapon we have. The only one we've ever used. Everything we're doing is posting directly online. No matter what happens, they're not going to get away with what they're doing. Not anymore."

At the door, Theodore hurriedly punched in the password, correctly this time, and the door opened, revealing the bright-as-daylight interior of the laboratory.

Zera sucked in her breath. Hideous forms, grotesque combinations of man's organs and plant life, filled the room. The

Green Guerrillas had prepared, hardened themselves as best as they could for this moment, but she didn't have that luxury. Zera saw her uncle's guilt-stricken gaze. Zera found, to her amazement, that these sights didn't frighten her, but she was heartsick. The heart-tree, the lung-tree . . . the medical machines whirring, hearts beating, lungs breathing, the contradictory smells of rich, teeming-with-life dirt and sterile bleach, and the perfumed stench of these plants' blossoms. The plants spoke to her in soundless words, pleading, begging, for release.

"Come on, Bear," Lily said to her cameraman, who now looked as if he, too, were experiencing some serious queasiness.

Bear took a deep breath, and blew it out through pursed lips. "Ready," he said. He pointed the camera at Lily.

"We're in the laboratory," Lily's words came rapid-fire. "Void's trying to get into the building now. Here is where we show you the ultimate in god-playing."

Lily turned to the row of trellised vines next to the door, the human eye-vines. "Finally, all boundaries have been crossed. In our brave new world, body parts are commodities. 'Products' which will, no doubt, go to those with the deep pockets to pay for them. I shudder to think of where we go from here. We need to ask ourselves, is this really what we want? Is this human advancement?"

Dozens of eye-clusters stared blindly, un-activated by a human brain. There were no eyelids, just a thin, clear covering, like the skin on grapes. Brown, green, blue, hazel, and shades in-between stared immobile as Lily hurried down the row. Zera shuddered. She wondered — *where did the human genes come from to make these? Void employees? What would it be like, seeing your own eyes stare back at you, from a plant?*

As Lily moved toward the lung trees, Zera couldn't hear what she said anymore. Shrieks pierced her consciousness. Human fruit-hearts, veins pulsating with plant sap; lung trees, their fruits breathing in and out; trees with livers dangling pendulously. Silent to all except Zera. She heard the fast, thundering beating of the hearts, the shallow, quick, and terrified breathing, the psychic screams of protest, both human and vegetable. There was no doubt; they could *feel. They are in torment.* She longed to help them, to do something to ease their misery.

Lily rushed to another planting tank, gesticulating wildly, her mouth moving fast as Bear filmed. But Zera's ears were full . . . .

On trellises climbed vines with thick stems and giant leaves. Above them nets held fruit resembling bowling balls made of human hair. *What's next?* flashed through Zera's mind, *brains?* The medical machines' lights blinked wildly as paper printouts rolled out. *The printouts are showing their distress.*

The shrieks, the thunderous beats of the fruit-hearts, the eerie breaths faded, all at once. All sound faded, as if Zera had gone underwater. She saw Lily mouthing words, eyes darting towards the door.

The door slid open.

Chapter Thirty-three

Everything seemed to move in slow motion as a tall, handsome man, followed by a dozen other men in olive drab clothes and heavy boots, entered the room. *Soldiers?* Zera thought, standing half-hidden behind a heart-tree. The piercing cries stopped; she could hear again. Bear pivoted, camera in hand as the leader of the group yelled, "Stop what you're doing, now!"

Zera's focus went to the man behind the handsome and angry façade and she felt what he did: insecurity, desperation for control, and underneath it all, *pain*.

Still stronger than the man's emotions were those of the plants. The feelings were back again, full-out hysteria. The hairs on Zera's arms stood on end. Her consciousness shifted. She realized that she was somehow *one* with the plants. The boundaries that seemed to exist had never really had existed. *We made those boundaries.*

The men began shouting, "Stay where you are!" "Hands up!" Theodore moved protectively toward her, and one of the men yelled, "You, we said hands up!"

He lifted them, shaking his head.

Lily, her face twisted, confronted the leader. "It's him, Langston Void. God himself."

Zera's attention moved to the lung-tree, near Lily, and as she focused on it, she realized she could see and hear the room through *its* perspective. By moving her attention to the other human-plants in the room, she could see and hear the entire room. She no longer felt the plants' anguish. They had quieted and now she *was* the plants. Her spirit filled all of them, was the cause of their calmness. She could *be* them, one at a time or all at once. *How is this happening?*

You have opened yourself up, a voice answered her in her mind.

Sunny? Zera thought. *Is that you? Where are you?*

Yes, it's me. Whenever entities connect, they stay close.

Six of Void's dozen men carried laser rifles. They were spreading out to the perimeters of the room. The other six, wearing holsters with stun guns, flanked Void.

"Hands up!" a soldier yelled at her. "Move away from the tree!"

When she hesitated, Theodore said, "Do it, Zera."

Zera raised her hands and a couple of the tree's branches jerked. No one noticed.

"Zera?" said Langston, concern etching his features. "This can't be your niece. She's in Colorado. I spoke to Hattie Goodacre. She said Zera was in a coma."

"What?" Theodore shook his head. He, Lily, and Bear stared at Zera. Zera thought, *Oh my God, so that's what happened.*

Langston turned to Bear and commanded, "Turn off the

camera."

"Don't, Bear," Lily said. "Now the world can see who's behind all this."

"I'm not moving," said Bear.

Void nodded to the three men on his left. "Take it away."

The corporate soldiers moved toward Bear. When they came within distance, Bear kicked sideways, catching one of the men just below the chin, snapping his head back, causing him to fall. Before the others could pull their stun guns, Bear delivered a roundhouse kick into the mid-section of another, toppling him. The camera stayed in Bear's hands.

The first man lay on the floor to Bear's right, and he was starting to get back up. The other, to his left, gasped, fish-like, for air. Theodore moved closer to Zera, but he was watching Lily. They exchanged terrified looks. Fear ripped through Zera.

James moved in front of Lily and Theodore, hands up over his head. The black and white stripes on his arms and face, now glowing, began to revolve up his arms and face, swirling like a barber shop pole, moving up and up, faster and faster.

The third soldier drew his stun gun but then stood there, staring along with the others.

They're mesmerized. That's what cuttlefish do to their prey, they hypnotize them, confuse them with moving patterns.

Langston looked away. "Goggles," he said.

The men reached for goggles on their belts and slipped them over their eyes, breaking the spell. Void said, "We were ready for that, James."

Void motioned for the six rifle-carrying men to circle Bear. They pointed their weapons at him.

"Please, Bear, put it down," Lily said. "We have enough on them."

Bear laid the camera down on the floor and two men grabbed him, pulled his arms behind him, and slapped handcuffs on his wrists. Another picked up the camera, turned it off, and slid it violently toward the door. It skidded sideways and collided with the wall. The sound of shattering plastic caused Bear to grit his teeth.

Void's chiseled features warped into ugliness. His green eyes bored into Lily's brown ones. "Your plan didn't quite work the way you thought it would. Imagine, I've known Troy for years. All this time and never guessing . . ."

"Troy Sylvan has a conscience." Lily spat the words.

Langston Void smiled at Lily as if she were a naughty child. "Too bad he wasn't able to keep me from the office quite as long as you planned. Meg called some time ago, asking why Mr. Green was in the office when he was supposed to be in Colorado. It didn't take me long to figure out the rest. You underestimated me."

Lily walked up to Langston and he motioned for several men, who had begun to advance, to stay back. "We have a wondrous planet," she said. "We've found nothing like it in the universe. Many of us feel that it is *perfection*. How could you do these things? How could you tamper with billions of years of evolution?"

Void laughed. "Nature is *not* perfect, and all can be improved by the human hand. I think it's *you* who needs to evolve."

Lily moved closer, her small hands balled into fists. "The world is perfect in its imperfection!" She screamed. "Can't you see that?"

Zera wondered what she could do, and, more importantly, how. She tried to will the heart-tree to move and a few leaves stirred.

This time Void didn't call off his men. "The lady needs to be handcuffed as well. Give the handcuffs to Theodore Green," he pointed. "He's our president of biotechnology and was kidnapped by these fools."

Theodore moved to Lily's side. As the soldiers approached he stood in front of her and put his arms out protectively. "Leave her alone."

Void gestured for the men to wait. "Don't tell me that you're one of them too?"

"What you are doing is wrong, Langston," Theodore said. "And I've been wrong too, for a long time."

"Are you so sure about that, Theodore?" Langston's sculptured features were as cold as stone. "What if I told you that Hattie Goodacre said your mother was in the hospital right now? That she's needed a heart transplant for a long time? What would you say to that, Theodore? Would you still think it's all so wrong, if your work could save the life of your *own mother*?"

A chill swept through Zera as her uncle blanched. "You're lying."

"No. You see, your deception proved true. I spoke to Hattie not long ago. She's been at the hospital all day with someone with the ridiculous name of Cosmic Dan. Hattie cried when she told me how she's been trying to get in touch with you. She told me everything. And she said her own grandmother had spent the day at Zera's side. At *her* hospital bed. I checked it out; it's all true, Theodore."

"Zera? But she's here, Langston."

Langston glanced at Zera. "I don't know who this young lady is but I would guess she's another one of the Green Guerrillas' tricks. Your niece is in the hospital."

"You lying dog —" Theodore lunged for Void, but before he could reach him two of Void's men pulled him face down on the floor. A knee dug into his back, restraining him.

Zera watched her uncle struggle. Confusion and anguish shone in his eyes. She had nothing but contempt in her heart for Langston Void. She wanted to scream, but her heart was so heavy it rendered her mute. *Is Nonny in the hospital?* Zera felt her uncle's fear and torment over what might be true. The men handcuffed Lily and James, and they didn't put up a fight. Then they put cuffs on Zera.

"Leave them alone!" Theodore boomed, lifting his head off

the floor. Lily looked at him with surprise.

Langston stood over Theodore. "You could have had it all."

"What *you* don't understand, Langston," Theodore grunted out the words, as the soldier kept a boot in his back, "is that if you can't look at yourself in the mirror, then you have nothing."

"I have no problem with that."

"You're not even looking at your real face!"

Langston winced. "Handcuff him, too."

The men roughly secured Theodore. As the side of his face pressed into the cement floor, Zera realized with surprise that she could hear his thoughts. They were a jumble of fear and bargaining: *She's gotten worse? Oh, Mother! It can't be a lie; he said he spoke to Hattie. Maybe those hearts-plants can save her. All I have to do is tell Langston I can see I've been wrong. I could do it. I could save Mother.*

Then came another voice, it was the voice of the plants, in unison this time. *You ARE hearing him, like we hear him, the plants said. Like we can hear all of you, your thoughts, your feelings. We hear them through the chemistry of your body.*

Theodore's next thoughts, ones of despair that maybe Zera really *was* in a coma, tumbled toward her. *There's no logical explanation,* he thought, *why she's here.* Zera felt as if she were drowning in his confusion. *If something has happened to Zera . . . But she's here. There's no logical . . ."*

A soft, sweet voice, a voice she remembered from her dreams and, from Tava, entered Zera's consciousness. The

Green Woman whispered to Theodore; *Zera's in no danger.*

Zera felt a weight lift from her and she saw her uncle visibly relax, but only for a moment. The Green Woman's next words came with the impact of a sledgehammer. *Your mother is in danger — but you know she would not want help — not this way.*

Hopelessness weighed upon both Theodore and Zera. Zera knew the Green Woman's words were true. She felt her uncle, in his ocean of confusion, fighting to somehow accept this.

Zera searched her memory for clues to confirm what Langston and the Green Woman said. Nonny had looked older but Zera had thought nothing of it. *People get older, and Nonny's been through a lot these past few years.* Now Zera knew that was part of it, but not the whole story. *Why would he keep this from me? I had a right to know!* With a shock Zera realized *Hattie knew, too.* She remembered Hattie's reaction when they walked to her house that first day back, and when Grandma Wren didn't want Nonny to go to Tava. *I thought Hattie was being overprotective, but she KNEW.* Heartbreak settled in like a lead weight in her chest.

The soldiers dragged her uncle to his feet. Theodore's thought, *Mother's worse,* blocked out everything else.

She's been sick for a long time, Zera, even before your mother and father died. Your uncle has known. He wanted to protect you. Maybe that was wrong, but he did it out of love.

Zera heard another voice. *We must act,* it commanded. This voice was powerful, echoing, masculine. *The Green Man.* As the soldiers pulled her uncle to his feet, Zera's distress over Nonny became overshadowed by a more powerful emotion. Gone was the fear, the confusion, the hurt. The Green Man was right. She had to *act*. A power coursed through her. An all-encompassing surge of energy electrified the air — controlled by the Green Man, the Green Woman, and, now, by Zera. She began to move not one plant, but all of them. *I WILL free him. He has to get to Nonny.*

Vines slithered, first slowly, then rapidly, across the floor. Thin tendrils from eye-vines, thick ones from the melon-heads, curled, stretched, and curled again, creeping rapidly across the floor. The soldiers stared in disbelief as the vines reached their legs and coiled upward. The men tried to shake off the green shackles, but they were locked in place. Their eyes bulged in fright.

One of them screamed, staring at the fruit, "The . . . the eye vines grabbed me!"

The vines, growing and snaking on the floor, began to coil and wrap around themselves, in moments creating first the giant feet, then legs, then torso, then powerful arms, and, finally, the head of the Green Man. He towered to the top of the laboratory. His powerful voice boomed through the room, "If *you* do not like the look of something, you can choose to look the other way! Not so with us. We see. We feel. Everything!"

"Stop!" Void screamed, covering his ears.

Lily shrieked.

The soldiers struggled frantically to free their legs. Theodore, Bear, and James stared, mouths agape.

Vines traveled from the Green Man, clambering up Void's body, nearly covering him.

Recovering from their initial shock, the men with rifles began aiming and shooting at the Green Man. As lasers penetrated and cut, the vines separated and recoiled in pain, and tendrils of smoke rose to the ceiling. An eye-vine plant untwisted and raised its thick vines high, as if they were arms ready to grab and strangle. *I'm not controlling that plant*, thought Zera, *it's all them, now. The plants. The green energy has seized control.* As if in response, the face of the Green Woman, determined and angry, appeared in the foliage. The soldier cried out and delivered a long steady beam of wounding light from his laser gun into the vine's thick, woody base, blasting it. The air filled with the smell of burning plants. A torrent of energy vibrated in the air as the plant fell.

"Beeeeeeeeep!" went the medical monitor as a flat line appeared on the screen. A panicked soldier impulsively directed a laser beam at the sound. The monitor exploded.

The vines and leaves that made up the Green Man collapsed in a heap.

Zera felt it, a physically intense, but not painful, charge for one long moment, followed by calm. *This is death.* For a moment, time stood still and then she realized: *The energy is not gone. The Green Man is not gone. He just . . . went elsewhere.*

The vine's grip on the men loosened, and the men squirmed free. Langston ran toward the door.

We must show them. As this thought filled her, Zera sensed from Void the heart of a frightened child, much like her uncle's in his nightmare. But that did not matter; he would *not* win. Her strength returned. She focused. A new power flowed through her. She again became one with the plants.

Fruit sailed through the air. Inflated lungs dropped and exploded around the men. Yellow-gold pollen grains flew from flowers, whizzing like bottle rockets into the hot barrels of the men's rifles. The flammable pollen caused mini-explosions inside the lasers' barrels. *Boom! Boom! Boom!* The men threw down the weapons, grimacing.

Branches from the liver-trees bent down toward three men, and the livers twisted into the shapes of snapping, gumming jaws. One man screamed. The gumming jaws transfigured into giant, beautiful, dark sweet-smelling flowers that dropped from their branches onto three soldier's heads, covering their eyes and momentarily rendering them stupefied and sightless. Fist-sized hearts sailed through the air like grenades, thumping on their targets, and then falling before they, too, turned into fragrant flowers. A volley of melon-heads flew through the room. As they exploded in front of each soldier they turned into a shower of colorful petals, flower confetti.

Void, creeping towards the door, hid behind a piece of medical equipment. A melon banged into the machine before it, too, turned into flower confetti.

Tiny tendrils crept into the handcuffs of the prisoners, causing them to release and clang to the ground.

Void frantically placed his hand on the scanner and began pressing buttons, to no avail. The scanner and keys were covered in sap. Sap covered the floor where the flowers had landed. The soldiers had slipped in it, fallen to the floor, and were flailing, stuck firmly in the goo and petals.

Void turned around to see Theodore coming toward him. He pulled a stun gun and pointed it at Theodore. "Stay clear."

Zera's heart leapt. Another melon knocked the gun out of his hand. More confetti rained on the floor.

"You're not getting away," said Theodore.

Langston threw a punch at him. Theodore blocked it, but a kick made contact with Theodore's shin. Theodore winced in pain, bent to grab the injured limb, and Void jumped him. The two rolled on the floor. Void grabbed a piece of vine and wrapped it around Theodore's neck. Theodore's face reddened, his eyes bulged.

"Don't, Langston," he choked out the words.

"Stop it!" screamed Lily.

"You WILL stop!" The Green Man had materialized again from the damaged vines and leaves as the others had watched the struggle. The giant grabbed Void and Void immediately released Theodore. The Green Man lifted Void in the air with one hand and vines emerged from his fingers, whipping around Void's body, wrapping him completely in a tight cocoon. It happened so quickly and the vines were so tight that Void didn't have the air or time to scream. The green cocoon reminded Zera of what a spider does to its prey.

Zera felt Void losing consciousness. He would die if she didn't do something. "*No!*" she screamed at the Green Man, "*You can't do this!*"

The Green Man gave an angry sneer and the vines grew tighter.

"You'll kill him!" Zera looked around. She scrambled up the melon-head trellis near the door and jumped onto the Green Man. Both her arms clenched one leafy, rippling-with-vines arm. "Let him GO!"

"You defy me?" said the Green Man.

"Yes! You can't kill him! This is wrong!"

"There is only survival with us, Zera Green. Right and wrong is human!" The voice filled the room, thudding and reverberating.

The vines loosened, revealing an unconscious but alive Langston Void. The Green Man sat Zera down before transforming into a burst of ten thousand angry leaves that whipped around the room before pelting the floor.

Lily rushed over to Theodore as he sat up, rubbing his neck. "Are you all right?"

Zera heard a whisper, *We'll take it from here*, and her eyes met her uncle's.

The world around Zera grew dim, then black.

"I'm okay," said Theodore, rubbing his neck.

"Look!" Lily pointed at the video camera, hoisted up into the vines. It was on, pointing at Void, who was waking up.

"But . . . it was broken," Bear said.

"Where's Zera?" Lily spun around.

"Zera's not here," Theodore said.

"How can you say that?"

"It's hard to explain. I saw her disappear . . ." his voice trailed off.

Lily frowned. "You're not making any sense. That's impossible."

"More impossible than her appearing at the hide-out? In a lightning-struck tree? More impossible than all of this?"

Lily, Bear, and James searched the room, making their way around the twelve soldiers struggling in plant glue. "But I saw her," Lily protested.

"She's not here," Theodore said. "You have to trust me. I love Zera, I wouldn't leave her. I swear to you she's not here."

Bear grabbed the camera, which was now lying on the floor. Although the casing was broken, when he pressed the rewind button it worked. It took him only seconds to find exactly what Theodore had witnessed. "There it is, she's at the corner of the frame, then, she's gone. I don't know how, but it happened, just like he said."

"Then we need to get to Drew," said Lily. "If he's . . . if they haven't . . ."

"But what about the plants?" asked James.

"Leave them," said Theodore. The technology exists. People have to make their own decisions. You've done all you can for now."

"But what about their damage?" asked Lily. "They were damaged by lasers. We can't just leave them damaged like that." She looked around. "What?"

While they had been looking at the camera, the room had transformed. The plants looked full and lush. Branches and vines damaged by bullets had mended. The plants were glowing with health, except for one detail: All their human fruits had dropped off and become hard, shriveled, dried-out lumps on the floor.

The door to the lab slid open on its own. They ran up the hall, through the clean room, and out the door to the helicopter pad. Then they stopped. The area looked like a war zone. Helicopter pieces were strewn everywhere.

Lily fell to her knees and started to sob. "Drew! Nooooooo!"

The sound of a motorcycle made them look up. Drew rode up, yelling, "Bear, James, get the other bike. I've opened the gate; we've got to get out of here!"

The two men raced toward a second motorcycle.

Lily ran to Drew, who looked rough — torn clothes covered in grime, a big scratch on his forehead. Blood on his shirt.

"Are you okay?" said Lily.

"I'm a little banged up, I'll live. Where's the girl?"

Lily glanced at Theodore. "We don't really know."

"She's okay," said Theodore.

"There are only two bikes," said Drew. "They can't come with us."

By this time, Bear and James had pulled up on the second motorcycle. Without a word to Theodore, Lily hopped on the bike with Drew. The four of them sped off through the gate and out into the desert.

Chapter Thirty-four

Sunday, June 8

Zera opened her eyes to find her Uncle Theodore sitting beside her, staring toward a window. His clothes were crumpled, his face dark with whisker stubble, his hair a mess. She heard the voices of Hattie and Ben — turning her head she saw them standing and talking near the same window. She was in a bed, in a light-filled room. It took a few seconds to register . . . *I'm in a hospital.*

"Uncle Theodore?"

He started, turned toward her. Relief shone brightly on his features. "You're awake! Oh, Zera, thank God." He leaned over and gently folded her into his arms.

Everyone in the room rushed to her side: Hattie, Ben, Grandma Wren, and Cosmic Dan were there. They were smiling, but the smiles didn't hide the fact that something terrible had happened. Zera looked into her uncle's red-rimmed eyes, and knew. "Where's Nonny?"

Grandma Wren shook her head. Everyone but her uncle looked away. "Zera . . ." his voice cracked.

Zera burst into tears.

Theodore held her hand as she cried. A nurse entered the

room and barked, "You should have told me she's awake. I have to ask you all to leave."

Theodore stood up. "I'm not going anywhere. Not until I'm sure she's okay."

Zera saw that his warts were gone.

Many hours and a battery of medical tests later, Zera and Hattie found themselves alone in Zera's room, sitting on the edge of the bed. "I can't tell you how sorry I am," Hattie said. "But she was sick for a long time, sweetie."

Zera pulled her bathrobe tight around her hospital gown and pulled away from Hattie. "Yeah, I got that already, but thanks for letting me know — eventually."

"When did you find out?"

"Last night." Zera remembered it all; Void Corporation, the Green Man and Woman, Lily, Uncle Theodore, Langston Void. *I was one with the plants . . . somehow.* She remembered the fight, how they prevailed, and how everything when dark. *And then I woke up here*. "I was with them last night. Theodore and Lily."

Hattie gave her a look. Zera thought, *I can no longer feel or hear anyone's thoughts, but I can sure tell what she's thinking — 'the girl has lost it.'*

"Honey," said Hattie, "your uncle told me some things this morning, some amazing things, but I'm the one who found you. You collapsed yesterday morning in your room. You've been unconsciousness the whole time, asleep."

Zera shook her head. "That's what the doctor said. But I wasn't."

"We've been with you the whole time."

The door opened and Grandma Wren entered. She went to Zera, kissed her on the forehead. "Thank goodness you're okay." She took Zera's hand. "I was with your grandmother when she passed. She was at peace. The last thing she said was to tell her son and her granddaughter that she loves you both, more than anything."

Zera's tears came again. "Just when I thought I had a family again, and felt less alone. I understand now why Nonny didn't fight for me to come back to Ute Springs, but someone should have told me!"

Grandma Wren lightly squeezed her hand. "Everyone did what they thought was best. I am sorry, Zera, we all make mistakes. But please do not think you're alone. We are *all* your family: your uncle, Hattie, Ben, me, Cosmic Dan, all of us. And," her voice dropped lower, "you know your family extends much further than us. You are, have never been, and will never be, alone."

"We're not going to let you down again," said Hattie.

Zera looked into Grandma Wren's eyes. "I was there, with Uncle Theodore last night."

"That is what he told me," said Grandma Wren. "My walk in the spirit world foretold a death. I worried that it would be yours. It is hard that you lost your grandmother, but it was her time."

The women's relief that she was safe eclipsed Zera's grief, but for only a moment. She still felt raw. Over and over she kept thinking, *Nonny's gone. Now it's just me and Theodore*. She took her hand from Grandma Wren's. "Is everyone else okay? Where's Lily? Is Drew all right?"

"Everyone's fine." Hattie glanced at Grandma Wren, and Grandma Wren nodded. Hattie took a deep breath. "Now everything's going to be all right, don't get upset, but while the doctors were running tests, the police came. Ted's left for Los Angeles, but said he'd be back tonight. As for Lily, well, Ted told us that you'd be asking about her. He said to tell you that they all got away last night and he doesn't know where they are."

"But she's okay? They're okay?"

"He said they were."

"And Uncle Theodore . . . what if he doesn't come back?"

"Don't worry about your uncle. My phone's been ringing all day with offers of help. Dan's handling the calls."

"Offers of help?"

Hattie got up, strode to the second-floor window, and gazed down upon the street. "Ted arrived this morning at about 4 A. M. He seemed reassured that you were here and then, of course, he went straight to Nonny's side. She was already gone, Zera. He took it hard, but Grandma Wren comforted him. Not too much later, this man named Troy Sylvan showed up."

Zera remembered the name from last night. "From Void

Corporation?"

"Yes. He came to talk to your uncle. We heard about everything that happened last night, Zera, an incredible story. One I'm still having trouble believing."

Zera nodded. It all seemed fantastic to her, too.

"What about Tiffany?"

Hattie sighed. "She's okay. She's been on TV all day." She walked back to the table and poured some water from a pitcher into a glass. "Your doctor said you'll be released in the morning, but you have to stay here tonight. I'm staying with you — and Ben's staying too; he refuses to go home."

Hattie gave the glass to Zera and Zera took a sip. The knowledge that Ben was staying in the hospital, just for her, sent a thrill through her, and for a moment she forgot her sorrow. *He's been here the whole time. For me.* The thought of him at her bedside, worried about her, made her smile, and she felt a little awkward when Hattie noticed. She changed the subject. "Tiffany was on TV?"

"What happened last night has been all over the news, sweetie. Today has been an awakening. There are TV vans outside waiting for us to leave so reporters can question us." She gestured toward the window.

Grandma Wren, sitting in a chair near the window, nodded in agreement.

Zora went to the window and saw three vans in the parking lot.

"Void's spin people are trying to say the live footage from the laboratory was a hoax, but the public isn't buying it. There's been an energy in the air, like nothing I've felt before. An enthusiasm about opening our eyes to issues that have been ignored for too long. But some people aren't so enthusiastic. Especially Ms. Tiffany Taylor." She picked up the remote control and pressed a button.

"There she is again," Grandma Wren said. "The same interview we've seen three times today."

Zera, taking another drink of water, looked over and almost choked. Tiffany, nearly large as life. "Could you turn it up, please?" she asked, going back to sit on the bed. "I want to hear what she's saying."

Hattie groaned. "If you insist."

"Yes, I am planning to sue," Tiffany declared to the female interviewer. She looked great; clean clothes, hair and make-up done to perfection. She wore pink, of course. "I am in the process of preparing to sue the Void Chemical Corporation and these people called the Green Guerrillas. And also Theodore Green." Tiffany's hand moved up nervously towards her chin and then back down to her lap.

The two women, sitting in upholstered chairs, looked like they were chatting in a cozy living room. Before them on a glass coffee table was an enormous floral arrangement. Zera noticed immediately that most of the flowers in the arrangement were lilies.

"Mr. Green is your boyfriend?"

"*Ex*-boyfriend."

The reporter looked into the camera. "That would be Theodore Green, president of the Biotechnology Division at Void Corporation. He and Troy Sylvan, head of VCC's Research and Development, were picked up in Colorado and taken to L.A. this morning for questioning. Police are still looking for Lily Gibbons, leader of the Green Guerrillas, an environmental activism group, and other members of that group." The interviewer locked eyes with Tiffany. "I believe Theodore Green is being accused of being part of the Green Guerrillas. Did you have any knowledge of that?"

"There is no doubt in my mind that Theodore was involved in this all along."

"Why do you say that, Ms. Taylor?"

"He's known that woman, Lily, since high school. He had photos of her in his home."

"I see." The reporter leaned forward. "You claim you were kidnapped by the Green Guerrillas, is that right? And you escaped yesterday?"

"I was kidnapped and *tortured*." Tiffany's eyes glazed with tears, her voice in a whimper. "And then, I know you'll find this hard to believe, but when I escaped, they had plants there that, who, attacked me."

"Plants?" the reporter's eyes widened.

"Yes," Tiffany said, shifting in her chair, not so comfortable any longer. "When I got out of that horrible farmhouse, vines wrapped around my ankles before I could get to the road. They pulled me down. They held me down until after dark!"

"Then they released you?"

"Yes."

The reporter, eyebrows raised, nodded. "There have been similar reports from men who worked for VCC. They claim that they were attacked by plants at the Research and Development facility. But the satellite transmission showed nothing like that. What it did show was footage of some horrendous secret human organ experimentation. Footage that VCC claims to be fake. The live streaming showed Void's employees holding the Green Guerrillas at gunpoint. Then the footage stops. We're not even sure how the Green Guerrillas escaped."

"I don't care how they escaped." Tiffany sniffed. "As long as they find them and arrest them. And I'm telling you. It did happen. The plants are in on it!" She peered nervously into the floral arrangement. "That's not real, is it? Wait, are those *lilies*?"

The camera zoomed in on the interviewer. "So there we have it. Conflicting reports on what happened last night. Void Chemical Corporation claims it's a hoax, but is filing breaking and entering charges against the Green Guerrillas. And now we have Tiffany Taylor saying it was not a hoax, at least not what she experienced.

"To recap: Last night a satellite transmission went out all over the world, showing some horrific animal-plant, human-plant experimentation going on at Void Chemical Corporation. The transmissions are now being examined for authenticity. Members of an environmental group called the Green Guerrillas have claimed responsibility, and police are looking for them. Members include Lily Gibbons, Cornelius Curtis, Drew Bly, and James Dubson. Two prominent members of Void Chemical Corporation are also allegedly involved, Troy Sylvan, head of VCC Research and Development, and Theodore Green, who had just signed on as president of VCC's Biotechnology Division. Green was an employee of Biotech Multinational, the company that recently opened the highly successful Burger Depot franchises, and he is also the youngest son of Guinevere Green, former owner of the once world-renowned Green Seed Company.

"Other authorities, including the Food and Drug Administration, the Department of Agriculture, and the American Society for the Prevention of Cruelty to Animals, have announced investigations as well.

"The whole world is watching this story. As we speak, protests are being held at VCC Headquarters in Los Angeles and at all their offices around the world. You can be sure Channel 10 will be watching this story closely and reporting developments as they come to light. Thank you, Ms. Taylor."

The camera cut to Tiffany, who was still staring at the flower arrangement with a frightened intensity, as if it might attack. She had lost her tigery spirit; she now seemed more like a frightened pussycat ready to scat at a moment's notice.

A male reporter's face appeared. "That was footage from this morning's interview. On breaking news, we have learned that Guinevere Green died today. Ms. Green was Theodore Green's mother. She passed away early this morning at Peak County Hospital near Ute Springs, Colorado. Hospital sources say she had been ill with a heart condition for some time."

Zera hadn't noticed that Cosmic Dan and Ben had walked in. Hattie turned off the set.

"I'm sorry," Dan said to Zera, bending down to hug her.

"So am I, Zera," said Ben and put a hand on Zera's shoulder.

"Thanks." The air around her seemed dense with a suffocating sadness. She needed air. Zera turned to Hattie. "Is there any way I can get out of this room for a little while?"

Chapter Thirty-five

Theodore had not been formally charged, yet. Under the advice of his attorney, he had left the police station to go outside with Langston Void alone, to talk. They sat in the back of his limousine. Theodore couldn't remember when he had been more exhausted; it took all his willpower just to hold it together. *When will this nightmare end?* he thought. *I just want to get back; to Zera, to home.*

"I'm sorry about your mother," said Langston. "I really am."

The expression on Langston's face said he wasn't lying; in fact, Theodore was shocked to see how upset he looked.

Langston continued, "I'm sorry, but we've got to make some decisions about what's going to happen now. The media's all over this and they're going to want answers."

"We tell them the truth," said Theodore.

"I can't do that. There's too much at stake."

"Yes, I agree, there *is* too much at stake. That's why we're telling them the truth!"

"You don't get it," Langston said. "I can't let it end like this. I won't." Langston's voice grew quiet. "I do care about your future, regardless of what's happened, but I won't lose everything I've worked for. You have to come back to the company."

Theodore couldn't believe what he was hearing. "Are you insane? Did you not experience what I did last night? Those . . . those green *gods*, whatever they were? You don't know what you're messing with Langston. I know I don't either, but I have some idea now!"

Langston shrugged. "The Green Guerillas had some kind of knock-out gas. I'm pretty sure we were all under the influence of some kind of hallucinogenic substance last night — probably something they drugged you with when they kidnapped you."

Theodore shook his head. "You're crazy."

"Maybe. But I can't let this happen. You have to listen to me. If you come back, I'll make sure Lily doesn't go to jail, that none of them go to jail when they are caught, and I promise you they will be caught. But if you don't, if you go against me . . ." He swallowed hard. "You could lose custody of your niece and go to prison. Then what will happen to Zera?"

Theodore stared at him.

"You must decide now. I took you to your mother last night, and then I had to have you arrested. You see that, don't you? I have control here."

After all this? This is what it comes to? For an instant Theodore thought about what his mother would want, what she'd do, and he knew that she would certainly tell Langston Void to shove it right up his . . . But before that thought was complete, another came: *She made a mess out of things too, in her life. I can't make her mistakes. I can't leave Zera. I'm all she has now.*

Theodore stared into Langston's already-triumphant green eyes.

Chapter Thirty-six

"I heard they've been camping outside all night," Theodore said.

It was morning again, and he'd just returned from Los Angeles. They all stood at the hospital exit except for Zera, who sat in a wheelchair with a nurse at her side. They were waiting for Theodore to give the go-ahead to face the throng outside.

Hattie peered out the glass door over Theodore's shoulder. "It's going to be tough getting out of here. It's like piranha infested waters."

"It's fine," Zera said. "People should know the truth. We need to tell them."

"Listen, Zera," said Theodore, "let's not say anything today. There's a lot that's going on. I'll talk to you about it later."

Zera, a little surprised, looked up at her uncle. His mental state was reflected in his crumpled clothes, the dark circles under his eyes, the thick razor stubble. She'd never seen someone so exhausted.

"It'll be okay," said Dan. "It's just a crowd."

"That's an understatement," whispered Hattie. "I've never seen anything like this."

"We can handle it," added Ben, trying to be upbeat.

Grandma Wren's ancient face showed only curiosity.

The nurse moved into position behind Zera's wheelchair. "We can call Security for an escort, Mr. Green."

"It's not necessary." Theodore turned to Hattie, "Don't worry, Hat, it'll be fine." To Zera he said, "You ready?"

"It's weird to be in a wheelchair, but yeah, I guess so."

"Hospital rules, honey," said Hattie. "Once you get out the door, you can stand up and walk out of here."

Cosmic Dan grasped one of the door's metal bars. "I'd feel better if I spoke to them first. Be back in a sec."

As he stepped through the door they heard the hum of activity turn into a clamor. Dan faced the swarm: reporters, television crews, photographers, and behind them all, a mob of onlookers.

The ruckus died down as all eyes studied him. Murmurs traveled through the crowd as they took in Cosmic Dan's appearance: tall, thin, middle-aged, and good-looking. Cameras flashed. Then came shouting: "Where's Theodore Green?" "When is he coming out?"

Dan raised one large hand in an appeal for silence and waited. The crowd quieted. "Theodore's niece just came out of a *coma* yesterday," he said calmly. "Both of them have lost a loved one. You'll need to back off the sidewalk. *Please*."

They obliged. Dan disappeared behind the doors, and a moment later the group stepped into the sun.

The crowd waited as Zera rose from the chair, blinking from the brightness. Ben went to her side and took her hand protectively. Cameras flashed as Theodore put his hand on her other shoulder and whispered, "It'll be all right."

The crowd closed in as Dan led the way to the parking lot. Reporters shouted. "Mr. Green, Mr. Green!"

Theodore glanced in the direction of one of the voices and its owner bellowed, "Can you tell us anything about your arrest?"

"No comment."

"But what about the accusations, Mr. Green?" chirped a small woman with heavy makeup at Ben's side. She directed a microphone toward Theodore's face. "Was Void Corporation performing those horrible scientific experiments?"

"I've been advised not to make any statements."

Zera looked up at her uncle questioningly but he didn't meet her gaze. That comment was met with a dozen more questions as they worked their way through the crowd. Zera caught the smell of sweat from a few of the cameramen; they'd been out there for hours.

"What about Lily Gibbons? What is your relationship with her?" a woman asked.

"I'm not answering any questions," said Theodore, his face flushed. "Not today. There's been a death in our family—please, have some respect!"

As the group inched towards the parking lot, a reporter bulldozed his way toward them. He accidentally knocked into Cosmic Dan in an attempt to get closer to Zera, and Dan nearly fell. Behind Dan, a camerawoman trained her lens on the girl.

"For goodness sake, man!" said Dan. Ben's hand tightened on Zera's. She looked over to see that his other hand balled into a fist.

Hattie, behind them, whispered, "What a jerk!"

The young blond reporter ignored them both, directing his attention to Zera. "Miss Green," he said, "I've been doing some research into your family, and legend has it that the Greens can talk with plants. How about you? Can you communicate with plants? Do they talk back?"

Zera stopped and looked at her uncle. Theodore nodded, indicating that it was okay to say something. *But what?* How could she explain the connection that she had discovered, one that had been passed down through generations of her family, a gift that had seemed to cause nothing but trouble, but had become more, so much more than she had ever imagined? She was still trying to figure it out. The Green Man, the Green Woman, what was her role in all this? What would happen next in her life?

She blurted out the truth. "Yes, I can talk with plants. And yes, they do talk back."

The reporter's mouth dropped open, and then twisted into a sneer of amusement. Something *else* dawned on Zera, a bigger truth. The Greens had something special, but she knew it wasn't limited to them. She looked the reporter in the eye. "What I can do, everyone can do."

Cameras flashed all around her. Snickers rippled through the crowd. Ben squeezed her hand in support.

Zera took a breath, slowly, mindfully. She scanned the faces in the crowd — some, like the reporter, seemed amused, some concerned, some doubtful. Amazingly, she didn't feel self-conscious. Amid the feeding frenzy a peace filled her. Hattie and Grandma Wren were right. She was not alone. She had never been alone. No one was. She thought of those two twinkling stars in the night sky. Now they would be joined by the light and love of Nonny. They were with her, not out there, but close in her heart, always. The adventure of life would continue. As she took the next step toward the parking lot, she felt stronger than ever before.

Thank you for reading *Zera and the Green Man.* If you enjoyed my novel, please consider leaving a review at Amazon.com. You are also encouraged to share this story with a friend as I've enabled the lending feature on Amazon.

To keep updated on *Zera and the Green Man* news (including the upcoming second novel, special discounts for books, and contests to win free books and prizes), sign up for our newsletter at http://www.zeraandthegreenman.com.

Sandra Knauf

71744440R00226

Made in the USA
Columbia, SC
03 June 2017